THE DAN BRADY MYSTERIES

ENEMIES OF ALL

A NOVEL BY

EDWARD J. LEAHY

Black Rose Writing | Texas

©2023 by Edward J. Leahy
All rights reserved. No part of this book may be reproduced, stored in a retrieval system or transmitted in any form or by any means without the prior written permission of the publishers, except by a reviewer who may quote brief passages in a review to be printed in a newspaper, magazine or journal.

The author grants the final approval for this literary material.

First printing

This is a work of fiction. Names, characters, businesses, places, events, and incidents are either the products of the author's imagination or used in a fictitious manner. Any resemblance to actual persons, living or dead, or actual events is purely coincidental.

ISBN: 978-1-68513-197-5
PUBLISHED BY BLACK ROSE WRITING
www.blackrosewriting.com

Printed in the United States of America
Suggested Retail Price (SRP) $23.95

Enemies of All is printed in Baskerville

*As a planet-friendly publisher, Black Rose Writing does its best to eliminate unnecessary waste to reduce paper usage and energy costs, while never compromising the reading experience. As a result, the final word count vs. page count may not meet common expectations.

ALSO BY EDWARD J. LEAHY

THE KIM BRADY MYSTERY SERIES

Past Grief

Deceived By Ornament

Proving a Villain

"Tis known to you he is mine enemy;
Nay, more, an enemy unto you all…"
–**Cardinal Beaufort in**
King Henry VI, Part 2, Act I, Scene 1

ENEMIES OF ALL

CHAPTER ONE

Wednesday, September 24, 1941

"Mother of God, Danny, do you need a cigarette?"

Detective Daniel Patrick Brady stopped in his tracks on Sedgewick Avenue in the Bronx, just outside the 44th Precinct station house, and stared at his partner, Detective Frank Larkin. "You know full well I haven't smoked since we became partners."

"True enough," Frankie said, "but you look like you need a drink, and I know you'd never drink on duty. A smoke seemed like a reasonable alternative. Can't say I blame you, considering what they did to that kid, but you've seen worse, I'm sure."

It was after nine in the evening as they mounted the steps. Danny needed to clear his head and focus. The boy was only twelve. "Daylight Savings ends this weekend."

Frankie gripped the doorhandle but didn't open it. "When are you gonna learn not to let everything lock you down so tight? Why is that kid getting to you so much?"

Danny gestured toward the door. "Are we going in or not?"

His partner took one last drag and flicked the butt back toward the sidewalk. "Suit yourself."

Once inside, Danny made a beeline for his desk and began writing up his report. Victim: Josh Krantz, age twelve. Attacked on

East 178th Street and Grand Concourse shortly after leaving the Jewish temple on Grand Concourse between Burnside and East 180th Street by a group of boys, uncertain number, believed to range in age between sixteen and eighteen. Injuries: broken nose, two black eyes, cut lip, concussion. Treated by the family physician. Incident reported by Saul Krantz (father).

"Saul Krantz's boy, huh?" Lieutenant Paul Greco was reading over Danny's shoulder.

Danny jumped slightly. "Yeah."

"What's with him?" Greco asked Larkin.

"He's a wee bit on edge, but he ain't sayin' why."

Danny finished the report, pulled it out of the typewriter, and handed it to Greco.

"Thanks." Greco handed Danny a slip with an address on it. "Now, if it's not too much trouble, we've got a homicide to deal with in that new building that just went up on the Grand Concourse."

Larkin snorted. "Popular neighborhood tonight."

***

"What's been eating you?" Larkin had been his partner for five years. They read each other well.

"Nothing at all. Where's the place we're looking for?"

"Next block on the right. New building. And enough of the deflection routine. Spill it."

Okay, maybe he should tell him. Otherwise, Frankie would keep hammering at him all night. "It's just that it's the kind of thing the RIC used to do to people."

"Ah, yes. The Royal Irish Constabulary, back when you were running errands for the Sinn Fein. I don't suppose they ever did anything like that to you."

"No. They did worse to men I knew."

"So why the upset over this kid?"

"Because he's only twelve. Any one thug could have beaten him up, but they were in a group. He wasn't any kind of threat to them. You know I hate shite like that. And this isn't the first."

"You think it's that gang of toughs over by Yankee Stadium?"

"Possibly. Maybe Rossi can give us a line on someone to see." The two patrol cars parked in front of the building caught his eye. "This must be the place."

They got out of the car and were greeted by a sergeant. "Well, if it isn't Danny and Frankie. A fine evening for a homicide, ain't it? Follow me, lads, and I'll lead you to it. Third floor."

Danny got off the elevator first. "The husband found her?"

The sergeant nodded. "He did. Mr. Nicholas Panagos. He's still in there. Went to pieces, he did. Still a bit shaken. Place is a mess…"

"Your fellas didn't move anything, did they?" Danny preferred forming his own first impressions before asking questions.

"Ah, you know me better than that."

The apartment door was ajar, with two uniformed officers standing guard. Anxious neighbors tried to peer in.

"Thanks, fellas." Danny examined the door. No chips in the wood frame, and no scratches on the lock; nothing to suggest a forced entry. "You can close that door now." He introduced himself to a man in his mid-forties, sitting on the couch, badly shaken. "I'm so sorry for your loss, Mr. Panagos. If you don't mind, my partner and I will look around a wee bit and then we'll come back and ask a few questions."

Mr. Panagos nodded but said nothing.

Signs of a struggle were everywhere: a lamp on the floor next to an end table, its globe shattered; a wingback chair tipped over on its back; broken pieces of a vase on the still-damp carpet, the flowers scattered.

The dining room appeared undisturbed. Two cups and saucers with traces of tea, and cake plates with a scattering of crumbs; a half-full goblet of water and an open aspirin bottle. Whatever happened, it had started amicably.

Next came the bedroom.

Mrs. Panagos was sprawled on the bed. Her white blouse had been torn open and her skirt and slip were hiked up to her waist. One of her stockings was torn. A man's tie was knotted around her neck.

"Beautiful girl," Danny said, more to himself than to his partner.

"Bloomers torn but not pulled off," Larkin muttered. "It's obvious what the bastard was after."

"Mid-to-late twenties, I'd say." Danny checked more closely. "Scratches on her arms and face, and the beginnings of a bruise on her forearm and another on her left cheek. Looks like she put up a fight. Maybe she landed a blow or two."

"Guy from the coroner's office is here," Larkin said.

"See what they find. I'll have a chat with the husband."

He returned to the living room and sat next to Mr. Panagos. "I'm so sorry. Your wife…"

"Millie. That's what everyone called her. Her name was Melina, but we called her Millie. I waited so long…"

"Can you tell me what happened?"

"I… I don't know. I found her when I came home from work."

"And what time was that?"

"A little before nine."

"Long workday?"

"Yes. Eight to eight. She… wait. You don't think that I…"

"No, not at all. I just need to establish the timelines. Mrs. Panagos was a housewife?"

"Yes." He shook his head, unable to say more.

Dan placed a hand on the grieving widower's shoulder. "Take a moment, sir."

He nodded. "I met her on a trip back to Greece three years ago. Love at first sight. She's only part Greek. Part Persian."

"She's a beautiful woman." Danny kept his voice soft. "What happened when you arrived home a little before nine?"

"I called out to her. No answer. Then I saw…" He gestured to the mess. "I ran into our… Oh, God. The way she… I mean, how she…" He was crying now.

"Take your time."

Mr. Panagos took a deep breath. "Detective, I have to ask… Was she…? Did he…?

"We don't know, yet. The coroner will tell us for certain. But it doesn't look like it. Was anything taken?"

"Yes. Her wedding ring and everything in her jewelry box. A silver cigarette case with my initials engraved. And some money she kept in a jar in the kitchen cabinet—about fifty dollars, I think."

Danny made some notes. "Did she go out often?"

The question brought Mr. Panagos back to the present. "Mostly for church activities. She taught Sunday School. Our church is only three blocks away, and she's an active member." He shook his head. "Was active."

"I take it she was friendly and outgoing?"

"Only with people she knew. She was painfully shy. Didn't even like going out shopping very much. She often had things delivered. Why?"

"We found no sign of a break-in, which means she might have known her attacker. Is it possible that someone wanted to hurt you or your wife? Any enemies?"

"Hurt Millie? Why would anyone want to hurt Millie?"

"That's what I'm trying to find out. What kind of work do you do?"

"I manage the freight office of the Italian Steamship Line. What does that have to do with…"

"Just background, Mr. Panagos. Where is your office located?"

"Downtown. State Street."

"Any conflicts or problems at work? Any business dealings gone bad?"

"Detective, I tell you, Millie and I have… I mean, had… a nice, quiet life. No enemies that I can think of."

The next one was going to hurt. "Were you aware if she had any other… admirers?"

The husband flushed. "That's outrageous. Disgusting. Millie was as pure and virtuous a woman as I've ever known. We were devoted to each other, Detective."

"All right, Mr. Panagos. I'm sorry. We must ask."

Larkin emerged from the bedroom, caught Danny's eye, and mouthed the words, "No rape."

Mr. Panagos caught it. "What?"

"We found no sign that Millie was raped," Danny replied.

A sad smile. "She died fighting him off."

Danny nodded. "Looks that way. If we have any other questions, I'll come back. Please put together a list of the items that were taken. The fellas from the coroner's office are almost finished. The other officers are dusting for fingerprints and checking for any other evidence. They'll be finished as quickly as possible."

CHAPTER TWO

Danny sent Larkin to ask the priest about Millie Panagos while he checked with the neighbors. He started with the adjacent apartment. A heavyset, middle-aged woman answered the door. When Danny explained why he was there, she waved him inside the apartment.

"I heard she was murdered," the woman said. "I'm sick about it; she was such a sweet girl."

"Were you home this afternoon? Did you see her?"

"No, I was baking a cake."

"Did you hear anything during the afternoon?"

She thought for a moment. "I thought I heard glass breaking. I was taking my cake out of the oven. About three-thirty. It startled me, but then I didn't hear anything else, so I assumed someone had just dropped a dish or a glass."

"Did you hear anyone on the stairs?"

"No, I'm sorry. I wish I had. Oh, that poor girl."

"Did anyone have any reason to be angry with either Mr. or Mrs. Panagos?"

"No. They're the nicest people, wonderful neighbors. Poor Nicholas, to have to bury his young bride."

"Ever hear them argue?"

"Never."

He asked around the building, getting similar responses. Nicholas and Millie were the ideal couple, good neighbors, and everyone was horrified at her death.

On his way out, he asked the doorman, "Did you see any strangers entering or leaving the building that afternoon?"

"Yes sir, I did; a little before four, I seen this fella come out lookin' calm but walkin' fast. Know what I mean?"

Danny nodded. "What did he look like?"

"Kind of tall, maybe six feet with black hair, and what you'd call 'olive' skin. He had on a green jacket. Turned left once he was outside."

Larkin was waiting in the car. "Danny boy, if she'd been Irish, they'd already be callin' for her to be canonized. That Greek priest was almost sick to his stomach when I told him what had happened. And when I asked about the possibility of her doing a little canoodling, he almost took my head off. How about the neighbors?"

"The same. Not an enemy in the world. That's all until we hear from the coroner and the crime scene boys."

***

Lieutenant Paul Greco was waiting for them when they got back. "What's the scoop?"

Danny recapped what they'd found. "We'll check the husband's alibi tomorrow, but I believe him because if he was that good an actor, he'd be in Hollywood. She probably knew her attacker. Served him tea. And aspirin."

Greco was incredulous. "Aspirin?"

"There was an open bottle on the table, and a glass of water with a print. I called in the mobile fingerprint unit. Didn't match any of us, so it's got to be the killer." A sudden thought. "Wait a minute. He tried to rape her."

"He didn't succeed," Larkin said.

Danny turned to Greco. "I remember hearing about an odd connection between aspirin and rape. Or was it a robbery? I'm certain of it."

Greco brightened. "Yeah. Couple of months ago. Vince Rossi caught the case. He might still be downstairs."

Danny and Larkin found Rossi slipping into his coat. "Well, if it isn't the Irish Sherlock Holmes and Dr. Watson. Come down to talk a little treason?"

Rossi was one of the few detectives who knew of Danny's childhood adventures in Dublin working for Michael Collins, and the only one who teased him about it. "Actually, I thought I'd come down and try to probe that peanut-size guinea brain of yours."

Rossi guffawed. "Well, whaddaya know? Sherlock needs help."

"Only because my mind-reading powers aren't up to snuff this evening. It's about a rape case you had."

Rossi turned serious. "Which one?" He lit a cigarette.

"The victim was raped in her home with aspirin around?"

"Yeah. Over by the High Bridge Library, back in July. The victim's husband had picked up a guy hitchhiking, who said he came to thank him. Just happened to show up when hubby was at work. He complained of a headache and asked if she had any aspirin. She invited him in, and the next thing she knew, he was all over her."

"Did he steal anything?" Danny asked.

"No. But while investigating, I came across a case in Queens with the same fact pattern back in May, handled by Morris Klein at the 108th Precinct."

Danny's neighborhood. "Does she live in Sunnyside?"

"No, Woodside."

One neighborhood over. "What about the woman near the library?"

Irritation flickered across Rossi's expression. "You may have a problem with that one. I'll give you the complete file, but they're colored folks and her husband was angry and uncooperative. I couldn't tell if he blamed her or us for his wife getting raped, but shortly after we interviewed her, they moved out."

"Why would he blame her?"

Rossi blew out a stream of smoke. "You haven't worked many rape cases, have you?"

"None," Danny replied. "Why?"

"Most guys blow a head gasket when their wives have been raped. Who wouldn't? Some sewer rat getting what only the husband should? Sometimes, the guy can't help but wonder how she could have let it happen."

"You're forgetting," Larkin said, "our Danny is single, with no experience in the dealings of husbands and wives."

"Despite your wife's best efforts." Danny turned serious again. "You were saying, Vinnie?"

"Dorothy Clinton's husband was so steamed about it, they just pulled up stakes and moved. I'll see if I can track them down for you."

Not stopping there. "While you're at it, see if any other precincts have been favored by our aspirin addict's attentions."

CHAPTER THREE

Throughout the warmer months, the *Bier Garten*, a tavern on East 85th Street, turned its tiny yard into a reasonable facsimile of a real beer garden. Hermann Mueller was uninterested in atmosphere, but he craved privacy, and with the nights growing cooler, most patrons remained inside.

He grabbed his stein of Dinkelacker and ambled outside where his four comrades were waiting. They greeted Hermann with respectful nods and silence. He took the remaining empty seat at their table.

The oldest man, wearing a snap-billed cap, spoke at last. "What news?"

Hermann took a long, deliberate sip of beer. "What are you expecting, Hans?"

The others stared, but remained silent.

Hermann placed his stein on the table. "Roosevelt the Cripple now wants to arm merchant chips against our U-boats and send a billion dollars' worth of food to Britain. It is only a matter of time before America declares war on the Fatherland."

"We knew when they crushed the Bund that war would follow," Hans said. "Has Germany said anything since?"

"The Führer called an hour ago to say we should be of good cheer. The Luftwaffe and Wehrmacht stand ready."

Hans sank back in his seat.

Hermann continued in a more serious tone. "Direct contact with Berlin is nearly impossible, thanks to the FBI, and the dismal performances of our Bund leaders have left Germany with low expectations. Until we hear otherwise, we must prepare to support the Fatherland when the time comes. But we need to be careful, since Germany still worries about America breaking her neutrality."

"Does that mean you wish to act on your own initiative?" It was the youngest member of the group, his nephew.

"No, Dieter, I will be guided by Germany's last instructions and my judgment of the best way to follow them."

A man in soiled coveralls spoke. "Germany's last instructions were sent to Gerhard Kunze. I hope this doesn't mean you plan to challenge his leadership."

Hermann drained his stein. Christian worked at the Brooklyn Navy Yard. They could ill afford to lose such a man. "No, I do not. Fritz Kuhn failed because he exercised poor judgment. Gerhard Kunze is on the same track, and he will also fail, succumbing to the lure of personal aggrandizement rather than serving the Fatherland. I will not waste time and effort by opposing him. His most recent instructions to me were to stir up anti-Jewish sentiment and support the Reich when war comes."

"What is your plan?" the last member of the group asked.

"As I said last week, Paul, I see three goals. First, attack the hold the Jews have on America. This will be relatively easy, since Americans already harbor resentment of Jews that is not so different from Europe. The second is to locate and unite with other groups for possible joint action. The third is to be ready when war comes to attack America from within."

"That's an ambitious plan," Hans said.

Herman glared at him. “It isn’t a plan, merely a statement of goals. The English poet, Robert Browning, suggested one’s reach should exceed one’s grasp. To achieve our goals, there are several steps. The first is to encourage anti-Jewish activities among American youth. Dieter, I believe you have already begun that phase.”

“*Ja.* An old friend from my grammar school days is now something of a gang leader. He and his friends are more than happy to help. And, under your instructions, I never mention Germany.”

“How did you approach him, then?” Hans asked.

Before Hermann could respond, Dieter said, “At our last meeting, we spoke of disrupting Jewish businesses. I have worked out a plan for burglarizing them, but I’ll need a lookout. My school friend fits the bill, and I’ll pay him from the proceeds. His gang members don’t require compensation. They’re as effective as the old S. A.”

“We’ll need adults to inflict serious damage,” Hermann added, “so Paul and Hans will determine what can reasonably be done and how.”

Both men nodded, although Hans did not hide his resentment at being named second.

“Assessing the plausibility of hindering war production falls to Christian. Recall that hindering can take many forms, from sabotage to fomenting dissent and dissatisfaction among the workers. Start slowly.” Hermann lit a cigarette.

“The Führer would not approve,” Hans said, gesturing at the small cloud of smoke. “And what about you? Or does command excuse you from actual work?”

“Command excuses one from nothing.” He took a deep drag and exhaled. “Besides commanding, it will be my responsibility to connect with other groups and coordinate our activities if we share common goals. *Danke,* Gentlemen.”

CHAPTER FOUR

Thursday, September 25, 1941

He settled into the front seat of a 1939 model Dodge Luxury Liner with Pennsylvania plates. A getaway car with class.

"Where you headed?" the driver asked.

"Philly. Just returning from seeing my sister in the hospital up in Boston." He nodded toward the gleaming wood-finished dashboard. "Nice ride."

The driver, a guy in his thirties, had picked him up on U.S. 1 outside of Elizabeth, New Jersey, heading south. "Yeah, bought it right before the 1940 models came out, so I got a good price. Felt good to spring for a new car. My last one was an old Ford Coupe. Toward the end, I spent more time working on it than driving it."

"What went on it?"

"By then, everything." He laughed like someone who'd dug himself out of the hole by dint of hard work, the chump. "You know cars?"

Time for the story. "Yeah, learned a lot about them as a kid in my years at Boys Town."

"Boy's Town? Like in the Spencer Tracy movie?"

"Yeah. Fr. Flanagan is even nicer than in the movie." People loved it when he said it. "He taught me a lot about cars. This one sure is a doozy."

The driver checked his gauges. "Yep. Seats seven."

"Family man?" That might be a problem.

"Not yet. The wife's got one in the oven, though. Due in November. How'd you end up at Boys Town? If you don't mind me asking, that is."

Oh, no. He never minded at all. He responded with the usual story. Folks killed in a car wreck when he was five and his sister was nine; she got adopted, and he landed in Boys Town.

The driver glanced back at the gauges. "Getting low on gas." He pulled into the next gas station. "Fill 'er up." As gasoline fumes wafted through the interior, he pulled out his wallet and opened to a small photo. "That's the wife."

Dark neck-length hair parted in the middle, and lovely eyes. "She looks like Hedy Lamarr."

"You think so? Wow, she'd love that. Especially now. You know how women get when they're pregnant."

The attendant appeared at the open window. "That'll be a buck seventy, Mister."

The driver paid him and pulled back onto the road. "I'll take you into Philly. That's where I live."

"Gee, that's swell of you. Could you please give me your address? I'd like to send you a thank you note when I can." He pulled out a postcard from his coat pocket. "I write to Fr. Flanagan all the time. Tell him how I'm doing."

CHAPTER FIVE

Detective Morris Klein showed Danny into an interrogation room at the 108th Precinct in Hunters Point, Queens. A young couple stood at their places at the table. "Danny, meet Harold and Megan Corwyn. Folks, this is Detective Dan Brady, the guy I told you about. I apologize for meeting in here, but I thought you'd prefer privacy."

Mr. Corwyn was about five-eight, and the vest of his pin-striped suit looked a little tight, his complexion pasty.

In heels, Mrs. Corwyn, who couldn't have been a day over twenty-one, stood just a couple of inches shorter than her husband. She was slim, with large hazel eyes, a button nose sprinkled with a few freckles, and auburn hair pulled back from her face, a mass of soft curls framing her neck. Wearing an emerald shirt dress, she stirred a memory from long ago.

Danny removed his fedora and took her hand. It was ice cold and trembling. "Pleasure to meet you, Mrs. Corwyn, and I apologize it's not under more pleasant circumstances." Her husband's grip was firm, but he didn't look Danny in the eye.

"I've explained to the Corwyns that you have a case in the Bronx that could be related," Klein said.

Mr. Corwyn flopped back into his seat. “I don’t see how we can help.”

Megan Corwyn sat more slowly. “Let’s just see, Hal.”

“Detective Klein has shown me his file on your case,” Danny said. “I won’t ask you to tell it all again, but I have some questions. Is that okay?”

She gave a tight nod, making her curls shake.

“This occurred the second week in May, but you’d met your attacker before, correct?”

Her voice was soft. “Yes, we’d picked him up hitchhiking two weeks earlier.”

“Where was that?”

“On US Route One at the end of April,” Mr. Corwyn replied, “just before the Pulaski Skyway. We were returning from visiting my brother’s family in Princeton Junction.”

“He told us he was going to visit his sister in a Boston hospital,” Mrs. Corwyn said. “And he told us he’d been at Boys Town. He even mailed a postcard when he got out of the car.”

“How would you describe him?” Danny asked Mrs. Corwyn.

“Tall and lanky, with thick black hair combed almost straight back and parted over his left eye. Dark brown eyes that appeared to curve down by the nose, a longish nose.” She closed her eyes. “A kind of round face.”

Danny turned to Mr. Corwyn, who was glaring at his wife. “How tall would you say he was?”

Mr. Corwyn broke the glare. “A little under six feet, and he probably weighed between one-seventy and one-eighty. Does that match what your Bronx victim told you?”

Time to let this guy know others had worse troubles. “The victim in my Bronx case didn’t tell me anything. She’s dead.” He turned to Mrs. Corwyn. “You’ve provided a comprehensive description for us. Thank you. Now, you gave him aspirin, correct?”

"Yes, he complained of a headache. I showed the police the glass of water, but I had already washed it because I felt violated. I was desperate to cleanse everything."

Mr. Corwyn glared at her. "You said he tied you up."

She looked like she'd been slapped. "He did. He used your ties." She turned to Danny. "Our neighbor found me about an hour after he left. She untied me. Honest."

Danny patted her hand. "I understand." God, she was so young.

She was trying not to cry. "He tied my hands behind my back, stuffed a handkerchief in my mouth and told me if I moved or made a sound, he'd kill me. Then took my wedding ring and my engagement ring right off my finger and rummaged through my purse and took my money. He took his time. I thought that might be all there was to it, but then he unbuckled his belt and his trousers dropped to the floor, and he yanked my dress up…"

"Oh, for God's sake, Meg." Mr. Corwyn jumped out of his chair.

She burst into tears. "He raped me!"

Mr. Corwyn raised his voice. "Why in God's name did you ever let him in?"

Megan was sobbing. "You're the one who gave him our address."

Danny said to Stone, "Why don't you show Mr. Corwyn where the men's room is? Mr. Corwyn, you might want to splash some cold water on your face and take a few deep breaths."

"Right this way," Klein said. Corwyn followed him out.

"Thank you for coming in this morning," Danny said. "I am so sorry for your trouble. I was trying not to put you through anything like this."

She stared at the floor. "It's not your fault, Detective. I just can't get that horrible day out of my mind. I have nightmares." She dabbed at her eyes with a tissue. "The woman in your other case was lucky. She'll never have to relive the horror or face a husband who blames her."

"Her husband doesn't feel lucky at all, I can assure you. But this will pass, Mrs. Corwyn."

"I thought that, at first, but it was four months ago, and he's only grown colder. He never kisses me, never touches me, won't even look at me undressed. I disgust him. He'd prefer it if I'd fought the man and been killed."

Then he's a bloody fool. Danny bit his tongue rather than say it.

The door opened and Klein and the husband returned.

"Are you quite finished with us, Detective?" Mr. Corwyn asked.

"For now. I'll be in touch if there are any further developments. In the meantime, Mr. Corwyn, I wish you and your lovely wife a pleasant day." As he reached for his hat, he couldn't resist adding, "And thank you, Mrs. Corwyn. Your description will be extremely helpful."

"We can find our own way out," Mr. Corwyn said.

***

Larkin waved Danny into Lt. Greco's office as soon as he got back to the precinct. "Nick Paganos' alibi checked out. He was at work all day. Everyone there was real broken up about his wife."

"I never thought he was the guy," Danny replied. "What about other cases with the aspirin angle?"

"Rossi sent out a request to all precincts in the department for any cases matching our guy's methods. We got more than a dozen responses—cases here in the Bronx, also Manhattan and Queens."

"It's a fucking epidemic." Greco picked up a cigarette that he'd left burning down in the ash tray, as he often did. The long trail of ash flaked off, and he hastened to brush it from his trousers.

"No other homicides," Larkin said. "All rapes, some with robberies. Most of his victims' husbands picked him up hitchhiking, but some, he just knocked on doors."

"Cold calls, huh?" Danny pulled out a map of the city and the surrounding area. "Did the reports include the hitchhiking pickup points?"

Larkin rustled some pages of notes. "Yeah. They…"

"Start with the earliest assault we have on record."

Larkin put the sheets in order. "Okay, the first one was in May, the bird you saw this morning, Corwyn. About a week later, rape in Manhattan, Upper West Side, picked him up on the Boston Post Road, headed in. Two days later, rape and robbery in Greenwich Village, cold call. Another week, a victim in Queens Village, picked him up just outside of Philly. Wow, that was a long ride."

Danny waited until Larkin had finished. "This guy isn't just our problem. He travels in and out of the city. He's been picked up a few times coming in from the south, one of those close to Philadelphia, and several times from the north. All the same methods, same Boys Town sob story. Lieutenant, we've got to expand our search. I'd bet a month's pay he's had some victims in Philly. Since he was picked up on Boston Post Road, he's probably made some assaults in New England."

Greco held up a hand. "Wait a minute, Danny. We don't exactly have an army of investigators."

"Yes, we do." He picked up the receiver of Greco's phone. "This." He placed it back in its cradle. "If I'm right, there are dozens of police departments right now who are assuming they have a local pest and are scratching their heads over where he goes and how he does it, because that's what we've been doing."

"Okay," Greco said. "What do you suggest?"

"Let's get a description of our guy and his game out to every department from Philly to Boston and as far west as Pittsburgh. Up the Hudson Valley as far as Albany. Then, every time a department reports a case in which the attacker hitchhiked in from an area beyond our current search area—say, Philly reports a case where the guy was picked up in Maryland—we add the departments in that area, say, as far as DC."

“Sounds like a lot of overtime for teletype operators,” Larkin said.

Greco remained serious. “It’s like nothing we’ve ever tried before.”

Megan Corwyn flashed through his mind. “This guy is a menace.” He turned to Larkin. “Anything on those prints we lifted from the glass in the Panagos apartment?”

“Downtown is checking.”

“When they finish, we should try the FBI,” Greco said.

Excellent. The lieutenant was buying in. “Let’s get a large map of the east coast, and some colored push-pins to show where each assault occurred and what crime was committed.”

CHAPTER SIX

Meg trudged up the stairs in dread. Hal hadn't said a word since leaving the police station. The half-block walk to the subway, the seven-stop ride on the Flushing-Corona line, and the two-block walk to their apartment, all in stony silence.

He unlocked the door and stepped inside, letting the door hang open. At least he didn't slam it in her face. But then, he wouldn't.

She walked directly into the kitchen, as if to check something, waiting until he flopped into the easy chair before venturing back to the living room. He buried his head in the newspaper.

"A fine waste of a day off," he said at last.

"I said you didn't have to come. They wanted to talk to me."

The newspaper remained in front of his face. "How would it look you'd gone alone?"

"Is that all you care about?"

"It's all I have left."

No, this time, she refused to cry. She'd been crying for four months, and the nightmare continued, unabated. "Is that why you blamed me for letting him in?"

"I wasn't blaming you, Meg. I just can't understand how you could've shown such poor judgment."

"You're splitting hairs and you know it. How about your poor judgment? Maybe that's why you're so concerned about what the police might think."

He finally threw down the newspaper. "Will you lower your voice?"

"Oh, right, the neighbors might hear. Why don't you just go to the bank and say you didn't need the whole day? Turn the day into something productive."

Speechless, he stormed out.

***

"Jesus, another one." Rossi scribbled the information after he hung up the phone. "This one in Bay Ridge, Brooklyn. In January. Cold call, guy said her husband had lent him money, and he wanted to pay it back."

"Same aspirin angle?" Danny asked. "Same sob story?"

"Yep. Rape and robbery."

Greco stared at the map, now bristling with over two dozen push pins. "What's with the different colors?"

Danny pressed home an orange pin in Bay Ridge. "Each color signifies the specific crime committed. Orange is for rape and robbery; yellow is for rape only; green is for robbery only; the red one is for the murder."

"So," Greco said, "the Corwyn dame wasn't the first."

Danny stared at the orange pin in Woodside, Queens, just seven blocks from his own place in Sunnyside. "No, and I'm sure he was active between January and May. So far, his pattern is to change direction every week-to-ten-days, with an assault occurring every two or three days. Four months might equal over fifty assaults."

"Mother of God." Greco stared at the map.

Larkin entered carrying a thick sheaf of printouts from the teletype machine. "Gotta be thirty cases here." He started paging through. "Hartford, Albany, Stamford, Allentown, Hackensack, Providence, Yonkers, Perth Amboy… Jesus Christ, Baltimore."

"Okay," Danny said, "Rossi and I will get busy sorting them and pinning them. Frankie, widen the net. Send alerts as far south as Virginia and as far north as Maine. Anything from the FBI?"

"Not yet," Greco replied. "They're waiting to get the prints from the Panagos place so they can search their files. Downtown has found nothing, but they're continuing to check. What else do we have?"

Danny checked his notes. "He uses several aliases: Joe Dean, Mike Dean, Mike Taylor, John Kiley. One could be his real name, but I doubt it. The hitchhiking assures that he keeps moving, and so far, he's never hit the same neighborhood twice."

Greco studied the map a little longer. "All right, Danny. Anything you need, you ask. You're running the show. I want this bastard."

You and me both, Lieutenant.

CHAPTER SEVEN

Monday, September 29, 1941

"Jesus, Danny, didn't you go home at all over the weekend?" Larkin forced a laugh that didn't hide the concern.

"I did. Friday night, Saturday night, and Sunday night, and when the commissioner gets a gander at the phone bill, he'll have my head for sure. But there's no time off when critical work needs to be done."

"Did Michael Collins tell you that?"

Danny grinned at the mention of the Irish revolutionary who'd looked out for him and his ma. "As a matter of fact, he did." Back when Danny was not only running messages for the Sinn Fein, but warning Collins about the RIC's movements.

"No wonder you're a bachelor. No woman would put up with you."

Larkin's wife, Helen, was fond of reminding him of it whenever Danny was their guest for dinner.

Greco approached, a stranger wearing a gray suit following close behind. "Danny, this fellow is Bill Cogan."

Cogan shook Danny's hand. "I'm with the Manhattan office of the FBI. We've checked the fingerprints from the Panagos murder against our records. No matches. Sorry we couldn't help."

"You still might." Danny described the attacker's method. "We've already received many reports from police departments up and down the eastern seaboard. If you forward any reports you receive, it will help us track his movements."

"That's one of two reasons I came, rather than phoning." He handed a written report to Danny. "Your description jogged my memory, and I dug this out of my files."

Danny scanned the report from the police headquarters in Canton Ohio, describing an assault and robbery using a method identical to the attack on Megan Corwyn. "You mean he got as far west as Ohio? Jesus, Mary, and Joseph."

"Rape and robbery back in April." Cogan pointed to the map, which now had push pins running in a slash from Philadelphia to Hartford, and a scattering of pins away from the slash. "Fellow gets around. I'm surprised we haven't had more calls for help."

Danny placed a fresh orange pin at Canton, now the westernmost point. Another orange pin in Richmond, Virginia was the southernmost point. "Send alerts out to the Carolinas, Kentucky, Tennessee, West Virginia, Indiana and Michigan."

Cogan nodded. "I've also alerted our regional offices all over the east."

"This thing is getting massive," Greco said. "Rhode Island, Virginia, and Ohio? What if he never comes back to New York?"

"He always comes back," Danny replied. "I've listed each attack on paper in chronological order. The patterns show that no matter how far out he goes, he always returns here. After Richmond, he hit Baltimore, Edison in New Jersey, and then the Upper West Side. Then, up to New Rochelle, then back to the Bronx."

Greco considered it. "But we can never tell which way he's going to turn. When he was coming back from Richmond and he got to Baltimore, he could just as easily have caught a ride straight north and wound up in Harrisburg."

"But he didn't. He stayed on US-1, the same road where the Corwyns picked him up." Danny stared at the map with its cluster of push pins. "He likes New York because it's easy to get lost in a crowd, and no city has greater population density. But he knows if he remained here, we'd eventually nail him. So, he makes this his base of operations, probably stays in some fleabag hotel." He turned to Larkin. "Let's try to pull together a list of likely places, concentrating on Manhattan."

Larkin rolled his eyes. "Sure. In my spare time."

Danny ignored him and stared at the map. What was he missing?

"What's the significance of him staying on US-1?" Greco asked.

"He likes it for the same reason he likes New York. It's heavily traveled. Who's going to notice the occasional hitchhiker? Nobody. Happens all the time."

"So," Larkin put in, "how do you explain him hitting Canton?"

Danny checked the map. "US Route 30. Runs all the way from Atlantic City to Oregon." His eye snagged at Philadelphia. "And at Philly, it intersects with…"

Larkin got it. "US-1."

"Give the man a cigar."

"Detective Brady," Cogan said, "do you keep the telexes you receive from other departments?"

"Certainly. Why?"

"I want to track your progress and have our regional offices on alert." Cogan took the sheaf of pages.

Danny remained silent and studied the map.

"Where's he headed, Danny?" Larkin asked.

Danny fingered the red pin. "His last reported attack before Millie Panagos was in Westchester, which means he was southbound. Having killed Millie, he won't hang around, he'll continue southward."

"You don't think he'd double back?" Larkin asked.

"He doesn't vary his methods." Danny turned to Cogan. "You said you had two reasons for coming in person today."

"Yes. Have you seen an increase in anti-Semitic attacks recently?"

"Nothing out of the usual," Greco replied.

"The Krantz boy was certainly out of the usual." Danny repeated what had happened. "And Saul Krantz said something I haven't been able to shake. When I promised him we'd do our best to nail the guys who beat up his son, I added that this wasn't like Nazi Germany, and he said, 'Don't be so sure.' That's been bothering me ever since."

Cogan nodded. "I've been assigned to a project monitoring pro-Nazi activities in the Greater New York Area, such as activities by the German-American Bund."

A name Danny hadn't heard in months. "I thought New York eliminated them when they nailed Fritz Kuhn for tax evasion."

"Not quite," Cogan replied. "Gerhard Kunze has assumed the leadership, such as it is. We're investigating him and others for inducing draft-eligible German American boys not to register for the draft. If we can prove it, we'll lock him up and his friends."

Danny cast a side glance at Greco. "How does that involve us?"

"Since the passage of the Lend-Lease Act," Cogan replied, "pro-Nazi activities have been on the rise, although nothing like the old rallies at Madison Square Garden. We expect it will be more like the case you just described. My boss has been impressed with how we're working together on this case. He's approached your commissioner about similar cooperation on anti-Semitic crimes."

Greco's expression turned sour. "What do you have in mind?"

Cogan broke into a grin. "I'd appreciate it if you'd put the word out to the other precincts in the Bronx and Manhattan to advise you of any anti-Semitic criminal activity, since they're already in touch with you on this killer. It's important to focus on the most densely populated boroughs. We'll handle Brooklyn, since the Navy Yard is a federal facility, but we'll keep you informed."

Greco thought it over. "You'll track the incidents, Danny, just like you've been tracking this guy's movements. And you'll investigate crime scenes as needed."

"I don't think Frankie, Vinnie, and I can handle all that, Lieutenant." Greco should have been pushing back.

But he didn't. "Let's see how it goes."

"I'll check in with you daily," Cogan said. "In the meantime, I'll discuss this rapist case with my superiors to see if we can do more to help."

Danny shook his hand again. "Thanks, Bill, but it'll be easier if I check in with you."

***

This time, he didn't take anything. The woman was bleeding, and he needed to avoid getting any on him. The bed was a mess. He barely had time to wipe his fingerprints off the water glass before he slipped out of the apartment and started down the stairs. A woman coming out of the apartment a floor below looked at him funny.

Better avoid Philly for a while. Avoid New York, too, because that one in the Bronx croaked. Served her right for putting up a fight. At least he'd gotten a tidy sum from hocking some of the jewelry.

He walked to US-1, the southbound side. Yes, sunnier climes. That's what he needed.

He stuck out his thumb, and before long, he had a ride.

***

Dieter Mueller leaned against a brick wall in an alley off West 50th Street, a block from Pier 90, sharing a cigarette with Tommy McCardle.

They'd been classmates before Dieter's father made enough to move his family to Yorkville. Tommy had been in trouble early in school and had grown increasingly incorrigible with each passing year. They'd kept in touch after Dieter moved away. Dieter had graduated from high school with honors while Tommy had dropped out. Now, he was the toughest of the Hell's Kitchen toughs.

Dieter nodded toward the pier, where no ships were docked. "Have you stopped mugging wandering tourists as I suggested?"

"Yeah, but money's getting tight. You promised something better."

"I've spent the past two years working with my uncle, fixing locks, lots of times picking them for people who can't hold on to their keys but who look down on us. It's worse now because of the war in Europe."

Tommy laughed and took a drag. "Well, Dieter, you are a kraut."

He was pushing him, testing him. He still didn't realize Dieter was the one doing the testing. "Fuck you, Mick. You try working for fucking Jews."

"I don't work for nobody, especially Jews. Like I been telling you for years, working for people just don't pay."

"So, why don't we hit some of these fat Jew businesses?"

Tommy spat. "Holdups would get the cops on us for sure."

"No, we break in at night. Not real big places, with alarms and night watchmen, but small, fat businesses that keep their money in cash boxes instead of a safe or sell stuff we can fence."

Tommy broke into a grin. "Picking locks?"

"Yes, I've gotten quite skilled at it."

***

"I'm captain of a police precinct in North Philadelphia. Is this Detective Brady?"

"That's me, Captain. You have something for us?"

"We got a call this morning, shortly before ten. A rape, no robbery. Bad. Woman was seven months pregnant. Lost her baby. Guy told her that her husband had given him a lift late last week..."

Dan grabbed a notepad. "Just a second, Captain. Did he say what day?"

Muffled conversation on the other end. "Picked him up Thursday on US-1 someplace in New Jersey. Guy said he'd been at Boys Town. Like in the Spencer Tracy movie."

"He uses that a lot."

"The husband thought it was for real and even saw the guy mail a postcard to Fr. Flanagan."

Just as Meg Corwyn had said.

The captain continued. "We found an aspirin bottle and water glass on the table when we got there."

"Any prints from the glass?"

"No, we checked. Musta wiped it clean. Sound like your guy?"

"Spot on. Did the victim report anything he said?"

"She's not in any shape to talk, yet, but a neighbor saw him leaving and gave an excellent description."

It matched Megan Corwyn's. "Thanks, Captain. If your guys talk to her, I'd be interested in details. Did the husband say where in New Jersey he picked the bastard up?"

More muffled conversation. "Near Elizabeth, just south of the Pulaski Skyway, whatever that is. Listen, if you bag this fucker, we'd like a crack at him."

"We're after him for a string of rapes and robberies and one murder. When we get him, we're gonna stick him in the electric chair until he glows."

The captain snorted. "Can't argue with that. If we get anything else, I'll give you a call."

Greco was waiting as he hung up the phone. "Philly. You called it. Southbound."

Danny went to the map and stuck a yellow push pin in at North Philadelphia. "Hitched a ride on US-1 last Thursday, the day after he killed Millie Panagos."

"He raped a pregnant woman?" Larkin's face turned sour. "Jesus, this is one fucking sick bastard. Where's he going, Danny?"

"After another attack gone bad, I'd bet my last dollar he'll continue further south." He called Bill Cogan and relayed the latest. "Can you contact departments in the Philly area, see if they've had any complaints like this since Thursday?"

"Can do. What's your next step?"

"We know of two instances when this guy mailed postcards to Fr. Flanagan. I'll call him and ask if he got any, and how big his collection might be."

CHAPTER EIGHT

He sat back in the passenger's seat as the old Ford Model A that looked the worse for wear continued south. Amos, the driver, had been talking since Philly. They were now between Washington and Richmond, and he was still going strong.

"Where'd y'all say you was headed, again?" Amos asked.

"Augusta. Got an old friend there."

"I can take you as far as Raleigh. From there, you can get a ride further south." Amos glanced at him. "You look like you could use some shuteye, boy. Y'all grab some. I'll rouse you when we there."

The silence was a relief. Amos had mentioned a daughter, but that was too risky for now. First the bitch in the Bronx died, then the one in Philly bled like hell. Cops would look for him for sure. He needed to keep moving. Raleigh was a state capital. Surely, they had a bus station.

Other than having likely roused the cops out of their usual routines, the Bronx incident didn't really bother him. The bitch had it coming. He didn't mind some resistance. That was expected. Even fun. This one, though, kept resisting, denying what he wanted. No one told him what to do and got away with it.

Not that people didn't try. As far back as he could remember, he'd been fighting to do whatever the hell he wanted. Rules? Fuck the rules. Chores? Fuck chores. School? Who needed that?

A truant, they'd called him. Yeah? So what?

Stealing from his mother had been easy. Stealing from his father was harder unless the old fool was piss-ass drunk. By the time he was nine, his father was beating him regularly—when he wasn't busy beating his mother, that is. But he'd never given his father the satisfaction of even wincing. When he was ten, he even spat in the old bastard's face after a beating, and his father was too tired to continue.

"Hey, boy, wake up. We're here."

Instantly alert. "Thanks, Amos. Appreciate it. By the way, what's your address? I'll drop you a thank-you note."

***

"Good afternoon, this is Boys Town."

"This is Detective Daniel Brady of the New York City Police Department calling for Fr. Flanagan."

"Just a moment, please."

Rossi approached. "I finally located Dorothy Clinton and her husband."

Danny held up a finger. "I'm waiting to talk to the good Father."

"This is Fr. Flanagan."

"Good afternoon, Father." Danny described the attacker's methods, read Megan Corwyn's description, and recited the list of names used.

"The description doesn't sound like anyone I remember having here, but two names ring a bell."

"Some victims report him mailing postcards addressed to you after they've given him a ride."

"Just a moment." Danny waited while drawers opened and closed in the background. "Yes, I have a file, here. All in the same handwriting but using different names. He misspells my name. I kept them just in case."

"If you'd send me some by mail, special delivery, I'd be forever in your debt, Father." He gave the legendary priest the precinct's address. "And I'd be grateful if you'd keep the rest under lock and key. We may need them as evidence."

"I'll send them out today, Detective. I hope you catch this man."

Danny replaced the receiver.

Larkin joined them. "Was that himself?"

"It was, and in a few days, we'll have some postcards our roving aspirin man has sent. Which will give us another solid piece of evidence against him—his handwriting." He turned to Rossi. "Now, what about the Clinton family?"

"They live in an apartment on St. Nicholas Avenue, corner of 126th Street."

"Can you talk to them?" Danny asked. "I'd like to get their description of the guy."

Rossi looked doubtful. "I thought the Corwyn dame gave a good one."

"She did, but I want to make sure we have an air-tight case when we finally nail him."

Larkin put down the latest teletypes. "Kind of optimistic, aren't you, Danny? So far, we're just chasing his shadow."

It certainly felt like it. But he knew better. "We're building a house, Frankie, one brick at a time. No matter where he goes, the pattern remains consistent—out and back."

Larkin turned serious. "Yeah, but you don't know he's gonna stay that way."

"Yes, I do. His act never changes. He's clever, but I'm thinking he's not all that bright."

Rossi nodded. "If it's all the same to you, Danny, I'd rather not re-interview Mr. and Mrs. Clinton. I doubt I'd secure any cooperation from them and I'm not sure you will, either."

***

Hal was always home by six for dinner. Meg had been able to set her watch by him for as long as they'd been married. But it was after seven and still no sign of him. She tried his work phone number for the fourth time, but no answer. The dinner was cold.

She turned on the radio in case some awful incident was tying up the subways. But all she found was music and someone from America First ranting about President Roosevelt. She turned it off.

She called her mother-in-law. "Have you heard from Hal? He's late."

"No." The line went dead. Not surprising, as her in-laws had shunned her since the rape. Even her own parents were uncomfortable talking to her.

Steps on the stairs. A moment later, the door opened. Hal's tie was loose and his hair slightly mussed.

"What happened?" she asked.

He slammed the door shut. "Why?"

"You're late. I was worried."

He broke into a sneer. "Isn't that sweet?" His speech was slightly slurred, and he reeked of alcohol.

"Are you alright?"

"Yeah, fine." He laid his suit jacket over the back of a chair, but it slipped to the floor. He ignored it.

"Have you been drinking?" Very unusual. At social occasions, he often nursed a single cocktail or beer.

"I stopped for a cocktail. What's it to ya?"

"Nothing, it's just that I waited dinner for you and…"

"Already ate. Now leave me the hell alone."

She walked back to the kitchen and scraped both platefuls of food into the garbage. She hadn't thought things could get any worse.

By the time she returned to the living room, Hal was coming out of the bedroom, having changed his clothes. She sat down and picked up the latest *Look* magazine.

He stood over her. "So, what's your problem?"

"You asked me to leave you alone, so I am."

"I didn't ask you, I told you."

"Fine. You told me."

"And you don't approve."

Hal had never been belligerent the whole time she'd known him. Not with her, not with anyone. Maybe it was the alcohol talking. "Does that even matter?"

"As a matter of fact, no, it doesn't."

"So, there you go."

He grabbed her hair and pulled her out of her seat. She cried out but all he did was sneer again. "Shut up, Meg. Just keep your mouth shut."

***

The Clintons' apartment was on the second floor above a shoe repair shop. Danny arrived a little before eight, having come alone. Mrs. Clinton answered the door still wearing an apron.

"Good evening, I'm Detective Brady. I need to speak to you regarding the attack in April."

Her husband materialized behind her. "We already told them everything. You catch him, yet?"

"If I may come inside, I'll be glad to bring you up to date."

Mr. Clinton glared at him but didn't move.

Danny remained impassive. "I think you'll be interested in what I have to say."

"Honey, please," Mrs. Clinton said, her voice soft.

"Fine."

Danny stepped inside. "Thank you. I hope I haven't interrupted your dinner."

"No," Mrs. Clinton replied. "I was just doing the dishes." She gestured to the couch and Danny sat. "Can I offer you anything, Detective?"

"No, thank you. I..."

"So, what's this news you think we want to hear?" Mr. Clinton said as he threw himself into the easy chair. "I take it you ain't caught him. You always have this much trouble with rapists?"

"This is no longer a rape case. You may have read about the murder in the Bronx last Wednesday. That's my case, and it's connected."

Mrs. Clinton raised her hand to her mouth. "Oh, my Lord."

"We've also discovered a string of attacks committed by this man. We're interviewing as many people as possible to get a thorough description."

Mr. Clinton's eyes narrowed. "You're telling me this guy's attacked other women in this city the same way?"

"Not just in this city. We've uncovered a string of cases all along the east coast and as far west as Ohio. This morning, he attacked a woman in Philadelphia. We've alerted every police department from the Carolinas to Maine. When we get him, we'll need you to identify him and to testify against him."

"You mean if you get him," Mr. Clinton said with a growl.

"I mean what I say and say what I mean. I'm going to nail this animal if it's the last thing I do. Will you help me?"

"Any way I can," Mrs. Clinton said. She turned to her husband. "We have to, John." She gave Danny a description consistent with Meg Corwyn's but added nothing to it.

"Thank you." Danny left his card. "I'll contact you if I need anything else. In the meantime, if you need to talk to me, just call."

"Just one thing," Mr. Clinton said. "About her testifying, I hear rape trials are harder on the victims than the rapists. That ain't right."

"I completely agree. Let's bag this guy, first, then the DA can decide what he needs at trial."

CHAPTER NINE

Tuesday, September 30, 1941

"… with the new ten percent federal excise tax on luxury items taking effect tomorrow, New York has seen a major rush in the purchase of liquor, jewelry, furs, cosmetics, and other luxury items comparable to the week before Christmas…"

***

Hal had turned the radio on as soon as he emerged from the bathroom. Meg wished he had found something more soothing than the news. She finished making his eggs, sunny side up, toast not too dark. He came into the dining room just as she finished pouring his coffee.

After a brief hesitation, she sat down at her usual place with her toast and coffee.

He was almost finished when he finally said, "Meg, about last night…"

"Yes?"

"I guess I had a snootful."

"You certainly did." She waited for an apology. "I believe the next thing you're supposed to say is, 'I'm sorry'."

"Yeah."

At least he'd acknowledged his guilt. Sort of. "Will you be home in time for dinner tonight?"

He stood. "Yeah, maybe."

Hal left a few minutes later.

***

As he stepped off the bus in New Orleans, it was even hotter and more humid than he'd expected. The twelve-hour bus ride from Raleigh had left him stiff and hungry. He found a cheap hotel near the bus station. He still had enough money to stay awhile, but he'd need to replenish it if he wanted to take a bus back north. Best not to spend too much.

He took a streetcar to the edge of the French Quarter, then walked along North Rampart Street until he found a greasy spoon. He sat at the counter and stared at the signs while a woman in her forties took orders and chatted with the regulars.

Gumbo, creole, crawfish. A foreign language.

"You look lost." The counter woman. "You ain't from here, are you?" Her curly dark hair was flecked with gray, and her complexion was a little darker than his own.

He gave her his best shy smile. "No, ma'am."

She cocked her head. "Somewhere up north, I'll bet."

"Nebraska, originally." Too early to hit her with his story. Besides, a counter girl didn't figure to have much. "What's 'creole'?"

She turned around to glance at the posted menu. "If you mean our shrimp creole, it's a dish of tomatoes and shrimp, cooked with garlic and onions."

A burly workman took a stool at the opposite end of the counter. "*Bon jour,* Jeanette. Hear about the bank robbery yesterday?"

"*Oui.* I'm glad I never changed my mind."

The workman shook his head and laughed. “You’re one stubborn Cajun.”

She turned back to him. “I lost my late husband’s savings when our bank failed in ‘32. Haven’t trusted one since. The shoebox in my closet ain’t gonna fail.”

“What’s a ‘Cajun’?”

“Folks descended from French Canadian settlers.”

“I’ll have the shrimp creole.” He’d eat, then leave. But he’d return when she got off work. With any luck, she’d have some aspirin.

***

Meg stared at the priest, waiting for his reaction. A kindly man in his sixties, his face was creased with concern as he digested the entire story. His silence when she finished made her wonder if this had been wise. “This morning, he went off to work like nothing happened.”

The priest considered that. “This attack has damaged your husband as well as you, my child. Another man has… known you. That’s painful for a husband to accept.”

“You make me sound like an adulteress.”

“No, nothing of the sort. You’ve committed no sin of any kind. Neither has he.”

“But he’s done nothing to comfort me or show he still loves me. And he was brutal with me last night, pulling my hair. He’s never done that before.”

“That would almost certainly be the drink.”

“I’m not so sure. I don’t think he loves me anymore.”

The priest stared at her, stunned. “My dear, you each took an unbreakable vow to Our Lord to love and be true to each other as long as you both shall live. The bond of marriage is permanent.”

“But the church allows marriages to be annulled.”

The priest drew back. “Yes, if the vows were not valid when given because consent was not knowing, or one person wasn’t mentally capable of consent or was tricked into marriage, or one person was not free to marry. But, by your own admission, you both entered into marriage freely and happily. The marriage was consummated.”

Her admission, as if she were a criminal.

“Have you had any other problems before this incident?” he asked.

“No.”

“Then, I think you should give it more time. Time heals all wounds. Give him the help and support he needs, and he will come around. I’ll pray for you both.”

She left the rectory feeling she’d been dismissed. He’d made it sound as if Hal were the one who’d suffered, and that she was the one who should be understanding. Despair closed in on her as she made her way down 57th Street to Roosevelt Avenue. The clusters of shoppers under the el and the rumble of trains overhead did nothing for her blackening mood as she turned onto Skillman Avenue.

The only man who seemed to understand how she felt was that nice detective with the dark brown hair, brown eyes, firm chin and Irish brogue who’d patted her hand at the police station and tipped his hat when they left.

She stopped at the library, a large, stately building.

She needed something else to focus on—something to do in the evening when Hal didn’t talk. As she entered, the scent of all those books took her back to the part-time job she’d had in high school. The work had been a joy, the pay a pleasant bonus.

She approached the main desk where the librarian was stacking returned books on a cart for re-shelving. “I wonder if you could help me. I need an absorbing book to read, a story where I can lose myself.”

"Have you read *Rebecca*, by Daphne du Maurier?" The librarian smiled. "A young woman marries a wealthy widower, only to discover that he and his household are haunted by the memory of his late first wife, Rebecca." She snatched a volume from the cart and checked it out to Meg. "Enjoy it. See you soon."

"Yes, you will."

***

"Damn," Rossi said as he saw Danny pouring himself a cup of coffee from the precinct's Silex, "it's after seven. What are you still doing here?"

"I might ask you the same thing."

"Just got back from a complaint. Another Jewish kid, a student at Taft High School, got beaten up at the 170th Street subway station. How's the manhunt going?"

"Every time I turn around, we expand our search area, and we never know where he's going to pop up next. Please add the details of the latest beating to our anti-Semitic crime file."

"Where's Larkin?"

"Went home to his wife."

Rossi placed a hand on Danny's shoulder. "That's what you need, a wife."

"I'm doing fine on me own, Vinnie. Right now, I need to run this filthy bastard to ground and find who's behind these attacks."

Rossi chuckled. "You're relentless, another Michael Collins."

***

It was dark, and the French Quarter was coming to life. He'd spent most of the day on his feet, but the more he thought about the counter woman and her shoebox full of cash, the more energized he became. Each time he walked by the little greasy spoon he glimpsed her, keeping out of sight.

Here she came. "Well, this is a surprise. You coming back for dinner?"

"No, I was headed back to my hotel."

"The night life is getting started, if you like that sort of thing."

He shook his head. "No, I'm a small-town kind of guy."

"So, why'd you come to New Orleans?" She started walking.

"Can I walk you home? These streets must get treacherous at night."

She laughed. "Wild, yes, but not really treacherous."

"Wild sounds like it might get treacherous for a gracious lady like you."

"Aw, that's sweet. Sure, you can walk me home, just down Toulouse Street. Tell me about Nebraska."

"Not much to tell." He launched into the Boys Town story with the usual details.

She stopped outside a building with terraces on the upper floors with wrought-iron railings. "This is me, just one flight up. Thanks for walking me; that was so sweet of you."

He winced and shut his eyes, holding a hand to his forehead.

"Hey, you okay?" she asked.

"Yeah, in a minute. I got me a doozy of a headache. You wouldn't have any aspirin, would you?"

"Sure do. Come on up."

***

Danny arrived home at his apartment in Sunnyside shortly before eleven that evening. Rossi mentioning Collins had triggered a memory he usually kept buried, that awful evening in August 1922 when he'd learned that his hero, his ma's benefactor, was dead, killed by an assassin's bullet.

At twelve, Danny had seen more death and destruction than many people see in a lifetime. He'd also gotten to know Ireland's outstanding leader well enough to understand how much Collins loathed the violence at which he excelled, seeing it as his deal with the devil to bring Ireland freedom.

"You'll protect people when you're older," he'd said more than once, and Danny had taken those words to heart and carried them to his adopted country.

And he wouldn't sleep well until these hateful attacks were stopped and the rapist/murderer was brought to heel.

CHAPTER TEN

Wednesday, October 1, 1941

"President Roosevelt met with Secretary of State Cordell Hull for two hours yesterday to discuss the international situation. Included in those talks were plans to ask Congress to amend the Neutrality Act to allow for more effective Lend-Lease aid…"

***

"This is getting ridiculous," Greco said, "we're overloaded already. How can we keep expanding the search?"

Danny had gotten a report that morning from North Carolina, a case from early May. "Lieutenant, we have to keep expanding until we don't get any reports back."

Larkin approached with a package. "This just came for you, Danny, special delivery from Nebraska."

Danny snatched the package. Inside was a file folder bulging with postcards. "He sent the lot. May the good father be in heaven an hour before the devil knows he's dead. They're all postmarked, places and dates, another clue about his patterns of movement. We might anticipate his return to the city."

Greco nodded. "Anything new from Cogan?"

"Nothing yet from him or the other Philly departments." Danny scanned several postcards. "Frankie, get me another map of the Eastern US, the biggest you can find. I'll put these in chronological order and then mark the map with the dates sent. Then, we'll compare the postmarks and origins to the reported cases we have. For the ones with matching reports, we'll be able to tell us whether he sent the postcard before or after the attack. Any card without a matching case, we'll contact the local department and ask them to check its files."

"What are you thinking, Danny boy?" Larkin asked.

"He sent one when the Corwyns dropped him off, and he sent one when he got to Philly this last time. He's consistent in everything else except where he goes with each move. I suspect he sends a card upon arriving in a new location as a way of proving his Boys Town story. It could give us a better idea of the timing between arriving and his first attack."

Greco threw up his hands. "Even if Fr. Flanagan calls us when he gets a new postcard, it will be days after it was sent, and probably after the attack."

Danny only grinned. "But if he's on a long leg, each card will be a step in his current direction, and the most important direction to detect is when he's returning to New York."

"Is there anything concrete we can do?"

"Yes, Lieutenant. We need to predict where he's going to land when he returns, and with these postcards, we can compare his handwriting with signatures in registers. He probably stays at some flophouse, or the Salvation Army. Most of his attacks have been in Manhattan and the Bronx. Not too many places here, and he relies on getting lost in crowds, so Manhattan is our best bet."

"Could be anywhere from Chinatown to Harlem," Greco said in a growl. "How're you gonna narrow it down?"

"We're not. Larkin will take downtown, below 23rd Street. Rossi will take uptown above 59th. I'll take midtown. But let's do this analysis, first."

***

Danny finished marking up the new map in less than an hour. He'd need time to compare the postmarks on the cards to the attacks, but also needed to discover where he stayed when he was in the city.

Rossi handed him a note. "This came in last night. Mugging on the Upper West Side. Victim is an 81-year-old Jew."

Danny read the note: multiple attackers who came up from behind him, hit him hard on the head, knocked him down, beat and kicked him, then robbed him of his watch and wallet. "Appeared to be males in late teens, but the victim couldn't describe any of them. Well, he's an old guy, probably lucky to be alive."

"I think this is getting to be too much," Greco said.

"Let's bring up that portable blackboard we have in the basement so we can track this thing," Danny replied. "We can handle it."

Larkin approached, brandishing a sheet torn from the teletype machine. "Danny, you'd better look at this."

It was from the Atlantic City police department. An amateur artist had complained of a grifter who had claimed he'd gotten a lift the week before from her husband. But her husband had been dead for six years. The grifter fled, but she was so concerned that she'd drawn a portrait of him. "Sweet Jesus. A portrait."

Danny explained the search plan to Larkin. "You and Rossi get started. I'll drive down to Atlantic City, interview the woman, and get the portrait. I'll pick up the midtown piece of the search when I get back." He dialed Fr. Flanagan's number, which he'd already memorized, thanked him for the postcards and asked him to call when he received any others and give the location and date postmarked.

***

Danny held the unfolded portrait, sketched in charcoal. It fit Megan Corwyn's description and filled in some gaps. Definitely Hungarian or Romanian, something like that—dark, brooding eyes, thick brows, hair slicked almost straight back. It was hard to believe he was so successful in playing the innocent victim, but people often saw what they wanted to see. Too bad there wasn't a way to duplicate it and send it to all the police departments east of the Mississippi.

Still, the teletypes spewed reports from up and down the east coast. He called to see if Greco had anything new since their latest bulletin had gone out this morning.

"Glad you called," Greco said, "two rapes in North Carolina from last month and one from West Virginia a week before the Canton case. Where the hell does he get the energy?"

"Anything from Frankie or Vinnie, yet?"

"Nothing yet. You bit off one helluva lot this time, Danny. We need you back here."

"Should be back by this afternoon."

He thanked the sergeant for his help and sauntered out to the car.

It wouldn't start.

***

Hermann Mueller's little group was somber as they came together.

"The Cripple wants to weaken the Neutrality Act," Hans said. "War with the Reich is inevitable."

Hermann waved it away. "Therefore, we are preparing to assist." He turned to his nephew. "Anything new?"

"My old schoolmate has stepped up the attacks on Jewish students."

"Strange," Hans said, "I have seen nothing about that in the newspapers."

"And you won't," Hermann said, his patience wearing thin. "Do you think they would admit that their police force cannot protect the Jews?" He turned back to Dieter. "Your friend's activities are here in Manhattan?"

"Some, but more in the Bronx. I believe it's best to keep the police off-balance. I'm also about to launch the next phase of our campaign."

Christian rushed in. "They've asked me to work extra hours at the Navy Yard."

"The newspapers have reported increased production," Paul said.

"I'm afraid the only evenings I'll be free will be Thursdays," Christian added.

Hermann clapped him on the arm. "Very well. We will meet Thursday evenings starting next week."

***

It took a mechanic in the Atlantic City Police Department's garage an hour to determine Danny needed a new alternator, install it and get the car running. "Should get you back to the city okay, Detective."

They only charged him for the part. He hoped to come back one day and repay the kindness.

He'd called Greco while waiting. Neither Larkin nor Rossi had found anything on their first day. Danny cursed his car luck—he'd lost a whole day.

The latest reports were old, but they showed that Danny's hunch was correct. He'd said to Greco, "We need to go all the way to the Mississippi."

***

Meg had read several chapters and was already engrossed. For the first time since the attack, she was relaxed.

"Meg, I asked you what you're doing."

A sense of dread gripped her as Hal's question dragged her mind out of the story. "I'm reading."

"I can see that. Why?"

What a silly question. "Because I like to read."

"Since when?"

The dread grew stronger. "Since I was young. What difference does it make to you?"

"I don't know. It's just—it's the first time I've seen you reading a book since..." He stopped.

"You were about to say, 'since we were married', right?"

He turned away. "No."

She took a deep breath and reopened the book. "I realized how much I've missed it."

He snatched his newspaper back up and didn't say another word.

CHAPTER ELEVEN

Friday, October 3, 1941

So far, the canvass of cheap hotels had yielded no results. Danny had worked his way south from 59th Street to just below Times Square. He checked in at the precinct each morning, conferred with Greco, Larkin, and Rossi, and then headed out. There'd been nothing from any other police departments on the rapist since Tuesday.

This morning, Greco was waiting for him. "New Orleans."

Sometimes, Danny hated being right. "What are the details?"

Greco held up the torn sheet from the teletype. "He walked a waitress home, complained of a headache, then raped and robbed her."

"When?"

"Tuesday."

Danny reached for an orange push pin and placed it on the spot on the map for New Orleans. "Did Fr. Flanagan call?"

"Not yet."

It had only been three days. He could have attacked the day of his arrival, although Danny's analysis of postcards and the attacks that followed suggested that wasn't usually the case. "Any other details?"

"Just a number to call."

Danny called it and identified himself. "I need any details you can give me." He stared at the sketch as the officer on the other end read the description, confirming a match to everything they had, right down to the green coat. "Any other attacks like this?"

"No, sir. We don't think he stuck around long. This is one nice, well-liked lady. Forty-four, a widow, works in a little eatery in the French Quarter, everybody's favorite. And this animal cleaned her out. Folks are in an uproar about it."

"What do you mean? How much did he get?"

"Over three hundred dollars."

Larkin walked in.

Danny forced out the next words. "Did you check the bus station and the train station?"

"Yes, the station agent sold a train ticket to Washington, DC to a fella matching his description."

"Thanks, Officer." He dropped the receiver onto its cradle.

"Where?" Larkin asked.

Danny turned to stare at the map. "New Orleans. He scored big this time and took a train to DC. Jesus, Mary, and Joseph."

"We're fucked," Larkin said.

"No." Danny turned to face them. "He's bought himself some time. But he always comes back. We just don't know where from." He telephoned Cogan.

"I'm on my way," Cogan said.

***

Cogan studied the sketch the Atlantic City woman had made. "I can have this reproduced and get copies to our agents in the field and get it back to you tomorrow morning. Our Washington office will send some fellows over to Union Station," Cogan said. "You say our boy was wearing a green jacket?"

"Yes, but the train pulled in yesterday. You want to check the cheap hotels in DC?"

"Yes, and if he didn't stick around, a red cap might have seen what train he got on."

Worth a shot. "He scored big, but he won't be splashing out, much. Stick with the fleabag joints."

Danny turned to Greco. "We'll get back to canvassing Manhattan. I'll check in periodically during the day to see if you've heard anything. Frankie and Vinnie should do the same."

"Keep me posted," Cogan said. "On our other concern, where are we on the anti-Semitic crime front?"

"We're seeing attacks on school kids in Manhattan as well as the Bronx," Danny replied. "Unfortunately, the kids are always too shaken up to give us reliable descriptions."

"Are we only looking at assaults?" Larkin asked.

Cogan's interest was caught. "Why? What else have you had?"

"I understand we had a Jewish-owned business hit last night."

"Why didn't you say something?" Danny asked.

"Sorry, Danny, Rossi just told me on my way in here. He heard about it from some guy in the fifty-second precinct."

"I'll call the captain over there and find out the details," Greco said. "You guys get out there and nail this rapist."

***

As soon as she heard steps on the stairs, Meg closed the book and slipped it into the end table drawer. It was five after seven, and dinner once again sat, cold, on the dining room table.

The apartment door banged open, and Hal squinted at her, swaying, and mumbled a greeting.

"I don't suppose you want any dinner," she said.

"Nope, ate already." He staggered off to the bedroom.

She returned to the kitchen, scraped one dinner into the garbage and put the other into the oven to reheat. She pulled it out and ate half, standing at the kitchen counter, before throwing the rest out.

After an hour, she checked the bedroom. Hal was asleep on the bed, still dressed in his suit. She pulled off his shoes. No reaction. She shoved his shoulder as hard as she could.

"What…"

"Wake up, Hal."

But he was dead to the world.

She retrieved her book, but when she tried to read, she absorbed nothing. When she turned on the radio, the sound of dance music only depressed her more.

She returned to the bedroom and found Hal still sprawled across the bed. She changed into her nightgown and shoved him hard. He moaned and rolled over, leaving some space on her side of the bed.

CHAPTER TWELVE

Saturday, October 4, 1941

The moment he'd found the shoe box with the money, he'd known what his next move would be. Hanging around New Orleans hadn't appealed to him, nor did hitchhiking through the deep south. It had been tempting to head back to North Carolina and pay Amos' daughter a visit, but there wasn't likely to be any money in it. And he wanted the cash to last. In the end he treated himself, so he rode the train to DC in comfort.

Once here, he'd tried a few cold calls, but nothing had worked. Were DC women that much sharper than women in other places, or had he run into bad luck? After the Bronx and Philly, he'd started to feel like his luck was turning bad, but the New Orleans dame had sort of put that idea aside.

This place made even his usual dump in New York look good. The walls were cracked, the water ran rusty, the bathroom was filthy, he had one bentwood chair, there was no elevator, and the pay phone in the hall didn't work. Time to blow, maybe catch a bus or train back to New York.

Halfway down the stairs, he froze. Voices in the lobby.

"We're from the FBI. Do you have anyone staying here that fits this description?"

He recognized the voice of the desk clerk. “Yeah, he wears a green jacket, looks Greek or Hungarian or something…”

He doubled back up the stairs, keeping quiet. He slipped back into his room, opened the window, and stepped out onto the fire escape. It faced a back alley. Good, no prying eyes. He made his way down the steps, his stomach lurching every time they swayed with his weight.

Why the hell was the FBI looking for him? If they were checking hotels, they had to be watching the train and bus stations. His only choice was to take a local bus into Maryland and hitch a ride from there. Plenty of targets remained.

***

It was after eleven when Meg returned from her morning shopping, and Hal still was fast asleep, snoring like a lumberjack, the stink of alcohol hanging heavy in the darkened room.

Meg yanked the curtains back, letting in bright sunshine, and pulled open the window to allow the autumn breeze to penetrate.

Hal rolled over and moaned. “Jesus, Meg. What the hell?”

“Please go take a shower and put that suit in a bag for the dry cleaners. It stinks in here.”

He made a half-hearted attempt to pull off his jacket. “Can you give me a hand?”

“I’m not your mother, and you’re no child.” She stormed out.

When he emerged thirty minutes later, she had already washed out the coffee pot. He left without another word.

***

“Brings back memories, doesn’t it?”

The voice startled him, but Hermann Mueller didn’t jump. “Yes, my nephew, Dieter, marched on this parade ground. Camp Siegfried held such promise, then.”

His host gestured, and they started across the open field. "I remind you, Herman, this is not a parade ground, Camp Siegfried no longer exists, and I don't live on Adolph Hitler Street anymore. It's Park Street, now."

"It's a wonder they've allowed you to keep the name of German Gardens for the community, Friedrich."

"Fred."

"*Gott im Himmel.*" Hermann halted. "Have you changed your last name from Obermann to Smith?"

"We do not have the protection of large numbers of mongrel peoples surrounding us. The price we pay for being a beacon of Aryan sanity to the rest of the country is to be forced into hiding for the time being. We have no Stukas or panzer divisions to protect us. Those are currently driving at the heart of Soviet Bolshevism. Until they arrive here, it is safest for our families if we remain inconspicuous."

"You have no interest in supporting the Fatherland?"

"Interest, yes, but opportunities remain limited as long as the FBI still watches us."

Hermann considered it. "War will provide the opportunity."

Fred halted and stared. "Meaning what?"

But Hermann kept walking, forcing Fred to catch up to him. "In every country the Wehrmacht has conquered, underground movements harass our occupation forces."

"And they accomplish nothing, regardless of the propaganda served up in American cinemas."

"Correct, because Germany has the mightiest army on Earth. America's army is another matter, a ragtag collection of eager, untrained volunteers and less-than-eager draftees. As Germans, we will create a more effective underground than the Poles, Norwegians, Dutch, or French."

They lapsed into silence.

"May I assume," Fred said at last, "that you propose to command this underground?"

To be effective, they would need to act in concert, which meant that someone had to take command. But Herman's predecessors had failed because of the trappings of command. This effort would require a humble approach. "Not command. Coordinate. Each group must be independent, but they should cooperate. Based in the city, I could not possibly make intelligent decisions about a group operating out here in Suffolk County."

"A wise approach. Did Berlin suggest it?"

"I've had no communication from Berlin, and I don't expect any. Has your brother had any word? After all, he helped establish Camp Siegfried."

"No, none of his circle has remained in contact, and they are united in their desire to keep a low profile in the current environment."

"They'd have no interest in participating in underground activities?"

"My neighbors will not discard their love of the Fatherland if Congress declares war. But the known leaders of the community must avoid notice by the FBI, who already has dossiers on them, including my brother."

"Do they have a dossier on you?"

"If they do, there is nothing in it other than my residence here. Are you appointing me to head an underground group here?"

"I would, had I the authority. I only encourage." He wrote the number of the *Bier Garten's* pay phone on a scrap of paper. "Call me at this number from a pay phone at eight o'clock Thursday evening and advise me of your progress. Never call my home and never call from your home or business. On Thursday, we will arrange our next call. That is how we will operate."

Friedrich took the paper. "Heil Hitler."

***

After stopping at a Nedick's stand for a hot dog, Danny walked to the Foster Hotel on 35th Street and Eighth Avenue. The lobby was dingy, its chairs threadbare. He approached the desk and flashed his badge at the clerk. “Detective Dan Brady. I need to check your register book.”

“Um, I don’t know. I…”

“Please get the manager.” When the manager appeared, Danny repeated his request.

“May I ask what this is about?”

Danny pulled out a copy the sketch. “Ever see a fella looks like this?”

“Can’t say I have.”

The clerk’s eyes went wide.

“But you have,” Danny said to him.

“I think so.”

“The register, please.” Danny pulled out a postcard from Boys Town. Line by line, he compared each signature to the postcard’s scrawl. He turned back a page, then another, and when he reached August 11th, he found a match—Michael Taylor, an alias. He waved the clerk over. “This the guy?”

“Uh huh.”

He’d checked in two days before Millie Panagos was killed and checked out the day after.

Danny continued to page back, day after day, week after week, stopping to make a note of each date he came across the scrawl, more than a dozen in the past six months. Then he asked the manager if they could speak privately. “We believe this man will return, possibly soon. When he does, one of us will be behind the front desk as a clerk and the rest of us will be here in the lobby to apprehend him. We will do our best not to disturb your other guests. In the meantime, here’s my card. Call me immediately if he checks in.”

CHAPTER THIRTEEN

Sunday, October 5, 1941

The FBI had just missed the killer in Washington, and there'd been no sight of him at Union Station or the bus terminal. Nothing from any other department since the report from New Orleans.

Larkin signed in. "Ah, Danny boy, can there be anything sweeter than the four-to-twelve on a Sunday, followed by two days off for the shift change?"

Danny didn't break his gaze at the map in front of him.

"Sweet Jesus, boyo, have you been here long?" Larkin wasn't laughing.

"A few hours. I hate sitting around waiting for word that another woman's been raped."

"So why waste a Sunday morning doing exactly that? Don't tell me you've forsaken Sunday Mass to maintain your vigil."

"I did not. I came straight away following ten o'clock Mass at St. Sebastian's. Already heard from Cogan, and he's as fidgety as I am."

Larkin plopped down at his desk, which faced Danny's. "And will the good lieutenant be letting us set up shop at the Foster Hotel to await our man?"

"He will not. He doesn't want to commit several people for an indefinite period without a tipoff of when he's there. Can't say I blame him. Besides, the manager of that esteemed establishment has pledged to report to me the minute our man steps foot inside."

Greco arrived. "Brady and Larkin already settled in, and not yet noon. Does my heart good. What's today's good news, Danny?"

"He's headed back here, but he's taking his time. FBI agents in DC found the dump where he was staying, but he took off before they could apprehend him. Most likely, he hitchhiked out of DC, heading back here."

Greco's grin vanished. "You mind telling me how you came to this conclusion?"

Danny pointed to the map and pile of papers on his desk. "It's his pattern. A postcard to the esteemed Fr. Flanagan always signals his arrival at a new location. He usually waits anywhere from one to three days after arrival before he strikes. If it's a small town, he leaves after a single attack. If it's a city, he'll linger for more, depending on the size. Most of his attacks have occurred between Baltimore in the south and Boston in the north. Attacks beyond that range have always come following his most violent strikes or the largest clusters of attacks in one place. His latest in New Orleans fits perfectly, the longest distance he's traveled yet."

"Impressive," Greco said, "but it doesn't give us a clue about when he'll return to New York."

"No. And he doesn't send a postcard with every new arrival. It's more like every third or fourth. Fr. Flanagan got his last card from Philadelphia. I've asked him to call me whenever he gets one from now on. We can expect a call from him within the next day or so, and I'll bet we get a report around the same time."

"I might take that bet," Larkin said. "A sawbuck rich enough?"

Greco groaned. "I don't believe this."

Danny brightened. "A sawbuck it is. If you like, we'll make it double or nothing on whether he lands between Baltimore and Jersey City."

Larkin stuck out his hand. "Done."

Danny turned to Greco. "You want in on this, Lieutenant?"

He struck a match to light a cigarette. "No, thanks. It's against department policy to gamble with subordinates. And since you need something to keep you busy, here." He handed Danny the file on the burglary in the fifty-second precinct.

Danny scanned the file. "A break-in of a small department store on Bedford Park Boulevard, near Villa Avenue. Jewish owner. No sign of forced entry, no fingerprints. Sounds like a pro."

"Keep reading," Greco replied.

He saw it. "*Juden* painted in black on the front window?"

Larkin laughed without humor. "That don't sound like a pro to me."

"Could be both a Nazi and a pro." Danny kept reading. "All they took was the cash in the till. About fifty bucks."

"Why would a pro—even a Nazi one—knock over a small store for fifty bucks?" Larkin asked.

"The guy in the fifty-second said he wouldn't have bothered us with it if not for the paint job," Greco said. When Danny shot him a look, he added, "I somehow doubt he's as committed to this project as you are."

***

Hal had still been asleep when Meg returned home from ten o'clock Mass at St. Sebastian's. She'd bought a fresh ham for Sunday dinner but now hesitated to prepare it. With the king-sized hangover Hal was sure to be nursing, he wouldn't be in any condition to carve it, and probably wouldn't be up to eating much of it. But at least there'd be plenty left for sandwiches.

Facing the dry cleaners on Monday with the suit reeking of alcohol would be another matter.

CHAPTER FOURTEEN

Monday, October 6, 1941

"President Roosevelt returns to Washington tomorrow and will meet with leading senators from both parties to discuss changes to the Neutrality Act, spurred by recent sinkings of American vessels within the 'Neutrality Zone'. A recent Gallup poll shows that 70% of Americans now believe it is more important to defeat Hitler than to stay out of war…"

***

"Brady."

"Hello, Detective, this is Fr. Flanagan. I just picked up today's mail, and I received another postcard from our friend, postmarked Saturday from Bel Air, Maryland."

Danny checked the clock. 11:30. "What name did he use?"

"Joseph Dean. Should I forward this to you?"

"Not necessary, Father, but please hold on to it. If I need it, and any others you receive, I'll ask."

Danny was logging the call when Larkin walked in.

"I couldn't stand it, partner. If you're working on your day off, I'd better join you and keep you from jumping off any ledges." Larkin stared at the notes. "Don't tell me."

"Just heard from the esteemed father." He repeated the information and checked the map. "Bel Air is just off US-1, just below the Pennsylvania border."

"For the love of Mary." Larkin opened his wallet and extracted a ten-dollar bill and dropped it on Danny's desk.

Greco strode out of his office. "A double sawbuck, so our friend has surfaced."

"Northern Maryland," Larkin said, clearly irritated.

Danny called Cogan, who promised to notify all the police departments in Maryland, Delaware, and Pennsylvania, including their state troopers. "And don't forget New Jersey, Bill."

"Got it. You think he'll come right on?"

Danny checked the map again. "He'll hit once in Bel Air and take off. He'll make at least one more stop before he returns to New York, possibly two. Not Delaware, because US-1 just misses it, and he won't want to get too far off course. Figure one possible in Pennsylvania, between Philly and Trenton, and one definite in New Jersey between Trenton and Edison."

After the call, Larkin stared at him, amazed. "I have to ask, Danny boy, what makes you so positive about the locations?"

"Bel Air's tiny, so he'll want to get out fast and put plenty of distance between it and him in a hurry, just as he's done after every attack in a small town."

"As far as you know."

Danny wasn't fazed. "He'll keep moving north. It's unlikely he'd be inclined to stop much before Philly, or that any rides he catches would do so. Philly has the second largest number of attacks after New York, but it will still be too hot for him, so he won't want to stick around. If he strikes in Pennsylvania at all, it'll be just before he crosses into New Jersey."

Larkin nodded. "And why would he only strike between Trenton and Edison?"

"Because he's struck between Edison and Elizabeth four times that we know of—in Woodbridge, Plainfield, South Plainfield, and Perth Amboy. After the close shave with the FBI in DC, he knows something has changed, and he needs to be more careful."

With a bit of luck, Bel Air police would nab him, and they'd be done. Nothing to do but wait.

***

The woman at the dry cleaners wrinkled her nose as she opened the bag with Hal's suit. Meg looked away.

"Seventy cents, ma'am."

Meg laid a dollar bill on the counter and turned to leave.

"Ma'am, your receipt and change."

Meg took them without looking her in the eye and mumbled, "Thanks."

Hal had hardly said a word on Sunday and had hardly touched his dinner. And this morning, her "good morning" had been met with stony silence.

Her sense of dread was growing worse.

***

As he walked back to US-1, he swallowed his disappointment at the paltry sum he'd grabbed. Twenty-nine dollars and seventy-three cents. At least he still had most of the cash from New Orleans. Besides, he had other problems. Why was the FBI looking to pinch him in Washington?

He thought back on the snippet of conversation he'd caught. They'd given the clerk a description, the clerk thought he'd fit it. Of course, the big mouth had added the green jacket, so even if he wasn't the guy the FBI wanted—and he couldn't be, since he had broken no federal laws—the green jacket might be a problem. At least he had plenty left from New Orleans to buy a new one.

He stuck out his thumb as a 1937 Chevy Tudor Sedan approached.

The car pulled over and stopped. "Where you headed?"

"New York."

"I can take you as far as Princeton."

"You mean, like the university?"

The driver, a bespectacled gentleman in his fifties, laughed. "That's correct, son. I'm a professor there."

A college town, which meant lots of comfortable money. He slid into the passenger seat. "Thanks. I gotta get up to New York. My sister was in a terrible car accident up there. She's in the hospital."

***

"God damn it." Larkin's cry of disgust rattled the walls.

Danny didn't ask. He took the proffered telex from Larkin. Report from the Bel Air police department of a rape and robbery. "Seventeen-year-old girl just getting home from school. Attacker fits our guy's description. He got away with about thirty bucks." He called Cogan, who promised to alert state troopers in Pennsylvania and New Jersey to cruise US-1 and watch for hitchhikers. Somebody would nab him.

***

"How odd," the professor said. "That's the third state trooper I've seen since we crossed into Pennsylvania. They must be after someone."

He shifted in his seat. "Guess so." He'd been laying on his usual tale of woe and he hadn't noticed. Good thing the professor had.

"You're not a wanted man, are you?" the professor asked.

"Me? Nobody wants me." And that was the truth.

"Don't be so down on yourself. You can accomplish anything you wish if you set your mind to it."

He set his mind to avoiding state troopers. After several more minutes, they crossed the Schuylkill River into New Jersey. He forced an expression of nonchalance as he scanned the road for any sign of state troopers and found none. After another twenty minutes, he relaxed.

"You look somewhat pale," the professor said.

"I get headaches sometimes. This one's a real doozy. I sure could use an aspirin."

"If you're not in a hurry, why don't you come home with me? My wife will give you dinner as well as an aspirin, and if you like, you can stay the night."

He was debating with himself whether he should accept the professor's offer when a New Jersey state trooper whizzed by. "Thank you, sir. I'd like that."

***

Danny glanced up at the clock. It was almost six, and no word.

"You think he hopped on a bus?" Greco asked.

"No," Danny replied. "The Bel Air police checked the bus station, and no one there saw him. Pennsylvania state troopers reported seeing several hitchhikers, kids in their twenties but no one fitting our guy's description."

"He's one lucky son of a bitch," Larkin said.

"Luck runs out." Danny returned to the map. No new insights.

"Maybe we should stake out the Foster Hotel tonight," Larkin said.

"Didn't they promise to alert us if he checked in?" Greco asked.

"They did." And Danny didn't want to make his move too soon. "He's left Pennsylvania by now. I suggest if we hear of something in New Jersey, we move."

***

The professor's house was old, stately, and massive, reeking of comfort and well-being.

"Elaine," the professor said, "this young man is Joseph Dean, and he's down on his luck and traveling to visit his sister in a New York hospital."

He tried not to stare. He'd expected the wife to be a plump middle-aged woman with thick legs and graying hair. Elaine was in her early thirties, with rich honey blond hair and an hourglass figure accented by her high heels.

"I was his student," she said as she took his hand. "Isn't that scandalous?"

"Mr. Dean was complaining of a headache, my dear. Could we provide him with some aspirin before dinner?"

"My pleasure, and dinner is ready."

He took the two aspirin and sat down to a hearty pot roast dinner, repeating his Boys Town yarn. Elaine expressed genuine sympathy.

"I think we can allow Mr. Dean the use of our guest room tonight, don't you, my dear?"

"By all means," Elaine replied, with a wry grin. "Perhaps we can provide him with bus fare so that he needn't resort to hitchhiking."

"Very kind of you, Ma'am," he said. "I will return one day and repay your kindness."

CHAPTER FIFTEEN

Tuesday, October 7, 1941

The rattle of metal against metal downstairs in the kitchen woke him a little after nine. Sleep had been the only "good" in his night, and it had come in fits, as he'd been half expecting Elaine to slip into his room for dimly imagined pleasures. But after she'd shown him to the guest room, she'd never returned.

On his way to the bathroom, he paused in the hallway outside the master bedroom, its bed already made, and not a thing out of place. A large oak dresser with a framed photo of the happy couple on their wedding day. Against the far wall stood an oak chest of drawers. And there atop the chest sat a jewelry box.

After splashing cold water on his face and drying it on a pink face towel, he returned to the guest room and finished dressing. He checked the inner pocket of his green jacket, relieved to find the New Orleans money was still there. Not that they'd look, but the FBI and state troopers had put him on edge.

The aroma of sizzling bacon drew him downstairs.

"Good morning, Mr. Dean." Elaine was pleasant but showed no sign of flirting.

"Morning, ma'am."

She maneuvered around the eat-in kitchen in continuous motion, pouring coffee, placing bread in the toaster, tending to the bacon and eggs. “My husband teaches an early class on Tuesdays and Thursdays.”

“Early in and early out?” he asked.

“No, he teaches until three, except for an hour in the office from twelve to one. Milk with your coffee?”

“Yes, please, but no sugar, thanks.”

She leaned over to serve the breakfast. He breathed in her scent.

“The bus leaves for the city every hour on the half hour, and the bus station is five blocks from here. So, you have plenty of time for breakfast.”

The jewelry box was upstairs, but Elaine was downstairs. If he wanted the jewelry, he’d best forget about Elaine.

“Mr. Dean, you’re not eating. Are you feeling unwell?”

“I’m fine, ma’am. Just thinking.”

“Worried about your sister, no doubt. I hope she’s recovering.”

“Hope so. I’ll soon find out.”

He’d left his jacket in the guest room, which settled it. He’d grab the jewelry and scram. Damned shame to pass up on Elaine, though.

***

Cogan stared at Danny’s map. “New Jersey state troopers will scour US-1 for hitchhikers, and my guys are in touch with every police department between Trenton and Fort Lee.”

“Have the police focus on bus stations and train stations.” Danny checked the time, nine-forty-five. “Make sure they all have our guy’s description.”

“Consider it done.”

“Hedging your bets on the hitchhiking angle?” Greco asked.

“We need to cover all routes as best we can. I want to be lying in wait for him when he returns to the Foster Hotel.”

Greco pressed him. “What if he doesn’t?”

"He will, especially if he changes his mode of travel. He'll crave normalcy."

"But you're still betting on Jersey?" Greco asked.

"Without a doubt." Danny always had doubts, but his lieutenant needed reassurance.

***

Hermann Mueller took a deep breath as he sat on a bench facing the East River in Carl Schurz Park. Already, temperatures were dropping, and a chill breeze blew in off the water. But he forgot about the weather as his nephew approached. "What's wrong?"

Dieter broke into a grin. "Nothing at all, Uncle. Our brave troops are attacking, three million strong, and Moscow will soon fall."

"Things seem to be going well, despite Soviet claims to the contrary."

"And, my method works. I pick my targets with care, scout them out for a couple of nights, and then strike. If this continues to work, I should be able to contribute financially to our cause."

"And your assistant?"

Dieter shrugged. "He does what he's told, and I pay him from the proceeds. He doesn't take part in the assaults, so no victims can identify him."

"Have you given him a reason for them?"

"Yes, to distract the police from the burglaries."

He had to admit, Dieter had thought things through. "Very well, proceed."

***

He'd left Elaine downstairs, explaining he was fetching his jacket. Halfway up the stairs, he realized it had been a poor excuse. She wouldn't wait long before she wondered what was keeping him.

He slipped into the master bedroom and gasped when he opened the jewelry box. A necklace with a diamond pendant and matching diamond earrings stunned him. But time was pressing, and he slipped the items into his pocket.

"What do you think you're doing?" Elaine's voice, loud and demanding from the doorway, made him jump.

He kept his grip on the box and kept his back to her.

"Mr. Dean, I asked you a question." Her voice was like iron.

He had one choice.

"Mr. Dean?" Footsteps approached.

He swiveled and hurled the jewelry box at her.

She raised her arms in a reflex to ward off the blow. He rushed her before she could recover and wrapped his arm around her neck in a choke hold. As she flailed her arms, he dragged her to the closet and grabbed several of her husband's ties.

She kicked out her legs, trying to throw him off balance, sending a high-heeled shoe flying across the room. She lost her leverage, and he tightened his grip. He dragged her to the bed and shoved a tie into her mouth. "This will go easier if you don't fight it."

***

After two days of stony silence, Meg attempted a peace offering. Hal had arrived home the night before sober, a step in the right direction. She returned home from the butcher shop with chuck steak and lamb kidneys, which the butcher had trimmed for her. This afternoon, she would make Hal's favorite, her steak and kidney pie. When he arrived home, he'd be greeted by the savory aroma filling the apartment.

She feared he wouldn't come home until late, returning to drunkenness. Twice, she reached for the phone to tell him what she had in store for him, but both times she stopped. Perhaps calling would drive him back to the tavern.

She hated this. It felt dishonest.

A deep breath and she snatched the phone. She dialed Hal's office number and prayed. Please be there. Please be receptive.

"Hal Corwyn."

"It's me." Please, Hal.

"Hi, Meg." His tone was neutral, not hostile. "Everything okay?"

"Fine. Do you think you'll be home on time tonight? Because I have a pleasant surprise for dinner."

He didn't respond at first. Perhaps he was thinking about it. "Sure. Can you be more specific about the surprise?"

"Steak and kidney pie."

"I'll be there."

***

He sat back as the bus entered the Lincoln Tunnel, the first time he'd relaxed since he'd finished having his way with the professor's wife. He'd left her as he had the others, lying face down with a rolled tie stuffed in her mouth and her wrists tied behind her back.

It had all taken longer than expected, and he'd arrived at the bus station well after the 10:30 bus had left. The initial panic at taking the next bus faded as he realized he'd be safe in New York City before the professor arrived home and discovered his wife's risqué pose. Safety and anonymity awaited at the end of the tunnel.

As lights flashed by at regular intervals, he extracted the roll of bills from his inside jacket pocket, now augmented with fifty dollars he'd grabbed from his latest victim's purse, and he peeled off some singles to buy lunch. He fished the jewelry from his trouser pocket and slipped it into the jacket pocket before replacing the roll of bills. Tempted though he was to proceed directly to a hotel and collapse, he had to find a place to pawn the jewelry. He also remembered the desk clerk in Washington describing his green coat. He'd stop at Bond's in Times Square and buy a new jacket.

***

The Princeton Police Department called at five after three. Danny listened to the now familiar details: a kindly driver—in this case, a college professor—picked up a hitchhiker, invited him home for dinner. Danny could have written the rest himself. "Sergeant, please tell me what he stole, about what time he got away, and his likely avenues of escape."

"And the answer is…?" Greco asked when Danny hung up the phone.

"Fifty bucks, diamond earrings, a diamond pendant, and the victim is one Elaine Dugan. The window clerk at the Princeton Bus Station said a guy wearing a green jacket and fitting our guy's description left on the 11:30 bus for New York." He picked up the phone again and called the manager at the Foster Hotel. No sign of their guy. "We'll be there in half an hour. If he shows up in the meantime, call this number." He gave the manager Greco's number.

"Take Frankie and Vinnie with you," Greco said. "I'll have a couple of uniforms in an unmarked radio car follow you down. If anything breaks up here, I'll reach you by radio."

***

Meg took a bite. Yes, the steak and kidney pie had turned out perfect.

Hal tucked in. "This is fabulous, the best dish you've cooked in ages."

And he was behaving the best he had in ages. "How was work today?"

"The usual irritations. We have a new teller, and she can't balance to save her life."

"Maybe she's just nervous."

He laid down his fork. "You always give people the benefit of the doubt."

"I try. Sometimes people just need time."

He took up his fork again and smiled. "True, and I've been rather cross with her. Tomorrow I'll try more guidance and less criticism."

Sounded like a good omen for Meg.

CHAPTER SIXTEEN

Shortly before seven o'clock, Danny glanced up from the newspaper he hadn't been reading. He was seated across from the front desk while Larkin posed as the desk clerk and Rossi stood near the door like he was waiting for someone. Two uniformed officers waited in an unmarked car across the street from the hotel.

The lobby was musty, and the odor of stale cigar smoke hung heavy.

Their target had already been in the city for five hours, and this was his place in the city. He was coming tonight.

But there was no trace of him, yet.

***

After dinner, as Meg cleared away the dishes, Hal turned on the radio. When she finished in the kitchen, Harry James' orchestra was playing "You Made Me Love You". She paused in the doorway, swaying to the music with her eyes closed.

"Sounds like a perfect foxtrot," Hal said, taking her in his arms. "I'd almost forgotten how much you love to dance."

He hadn't been much of a dancer when they'd met, but she'd taught him.

It felt so good to be back in his arms, dancing around the living room.

Perhaps the nightmare was over.

***

Danny positioned the newspaper so that he could see the clock behind the front desk while appearing to read. At twenty past seven, Rossi cleared his throat and coughed.

A flash of green caught Danny's eye as a guy crossed the lobby carrying a shopping bag from Bond's, the Times Square clothier.

Frankie took his time, pretending to read something behind the counter.

"I'm looking for a room." Green Jacket had an edge in his voice.

Larkin didn't look up. "Be with ya in a minute."

Danny stepped up behind him but said nothing.

"Hey, what's the matter with you? I said I want a room."

Danny grabbed him and spun him around. "I think this is the fella we're lookin' fer, Frankie."

Green Jacket became indignant. "What are you talking about?"

Danny pulled out the copy of the sketch. "Remarkable likeness, don't you think, Mr. Taylor? Or is it Mr. Dean today?"

His face fell as Rossi sidled up to him.

"If you don't mind," Danny said, "please tell me your real name so I can use it when I place you under arrest for the murder of Melina Panagos."

He swallowed hard. "My name is George Babić."

Danny cuffed him. "Very well, Mr. Babić, you're under arrest. You'll be coming with us if you please." He opened the bag, which held a black jacket. "Vinnie, can you please take this?

Rossi took the bag.

"All right," Babić said, "but can I have some aspirin? I've got a doozy of a headache."

Danny guffawed. "You just said the magic words."

***

Bill Cogan was waiting back at the precinct. "I heard you bagged the son of a bitch. Congratulations."

Danny shook his hand. "Thanks, Bill. We couldn't have done it without you. Want to join me in the interrogation room?"

"A pleasure."

Babić sat at the small table, a blank expression on his face. On the table in front of him sat a diamond pendant and a pair of diamond earrings, already tagged as evidence.

"This is Agent Cogan of the FBI," Danny said.

Babić stared back. "What's the FBI doing here?"

"Same thing we were doing at the flophouse in Washington," Cogan replied. "Helping to track down an interstate fugitive from justice."

"That's you, Georgie," Danny said.

Cogan picked up an earring. "Mrs. Dugan will be happy to have these returned."

"Found them in his jacket pocket along with this." Larkin tossed a roll of bills on the table. "And this." He laid a silver cigarette case next to the roll of bills.

"Not a bad haul, Mr. Babić," Danny said. "By my calculation, you've been in New York since two o'clock this afternoon. Couldn't you..."

"I just got in an hour ago. Stopped at Bond's for the jacket and walked down to the Foster."

Danny leaned on the table, his face inches from Babić. "You got the 11:30 bus out of Princeton. The clerk at the bus station identified you. You went there straight from Professor Dugan's house, where you raped Mrs. Dugan and took this jewelry and fifty bucks. The 11:30 bus arrived at five minutes to two. Tomorrow, we will scour every pawn shop in midtown with these earrings, this pendant, and this cigarette case. We'll show them this sketch."

Babić blanched at the likeness.

"And we'll show them your ugly but memorable green jacket and ask if you tried to hock these items at their establishment. What do you suppose they'll say?"

Babić crossed his arms against his chest. "How should I know?"

Danny laughed. "Because, boyo, you spent several hours trying to fence these items." He picked up the cigarette case. "Let's talk about this. You didn't pick this up in New Orleans, or Washington, or Princeton."

"No."

Danny held the cigarette case in front of Babić's face. "Would you read the engraved initials, please?"

"Um, NP."

"Correct, so this can't be yours as neither your name nor any of your aliases have these initials. Whose are they?"

"I don't know."

"Bollocks. Where did you get it?"

"I, um, bought it at a pawn shop."

"Frankie," Danny said, "please be so kind as to fetch a pencil and paper so that Mr. Babić can give us the location of this pawn shop. We'll be wanting to verify it."

Babić was sweating. "I don't remember which one."

Larkin slid the pencil and paper in front of him. "You mean you didn't buy it where you fence your stolen property?"

"I don't…" Babić glanced from face to face.

"Let's try another way around," Danny said. "You've had this about two weeks, I'd say. True?"

Babić stared but said nothing.

"I'll be taking that as a yes. Now, a little over a week ago—ten days ago, to be accurate—a fella named Nicholas Panagos lost a case just like that one, complete with his own initials."

Recognition flickered across Babić's face.

"I think we scored a bingo there, Danny boy," Larkin said.

"Now," Danny continued, "this fella Panagos, he lost much more than a cigarette case that had been a gift from his lovely wife, Millie. He lost Millie, because the filthy gobshite who took this case killed Millie after trying to rape her. Like what you did to Mrs. Dugan and a bunch of others."

"I didn't kill anybody."

"Where were you the afternoon of September 24th?"

"I don't remember."

"You don't remember being in a building on the Grand Concourse in the Bronx that afternoon?" Larkin asked.

"The doorman to Millie Panagos' apartment building told us he saw someone matching your description leaving the building that afternoon," Danny said.

"Did you hock her rings?" Larkin asked.

Rossi joined in. "Sure, he did. And I'd bet that pawnbroker got some shock when he read what our boy had done to acquire them. And I'd further bet that's why he couldn't find any takers for these."

"That true, Georgie boy?" Danny asked. "Pawnbrokers want no part of you these days?"

"You ain't well-loved around here," Cogan said, "and folks in New Orleans are ready to host a lynching if we send you back."

Danny sighed. "That counter lady was so nice. But don't worry, Georgie. We won't send you back."

Babić gazed up with hope in his eyes.

Danny continued, "Nope, we'll fry you right here for poor Millie."

"I ain't saying nothing."

Danny gathered up the jewelry and cigarette case. "That's the beauty of it. We already have everything we need."

CHAPTER SEVENTEEN

Wednesday, October 8, 1941

Meg was bringing breakfast into the dining room when Hal turned on the radio. A commercial jingle ended, and the news came on. "New York City police last night apprehended George Babić, suspected in the murder of Bronx housewife and Sunday School teacher Millie Panagos. Mr. Babić has been the subject of an unprecedented dragnet investigation involving cooperation of many police departments along the east coast…"

Meg dropped a plate.

Hal looked up but didn't move. "You okay?"

She was shaking. Could it really be the man?

"… believe he was responsible for several robberies and assaults in the New York area…"

She tried not to cry. "They got him, Hal. Oh, my God, they got him."

"Well, I'm glad of that." He made no move to get up. And his expression turned stonelike.

She cleaned up the mess herself. It didn't matter. They had the rapist. It was almost over. Maybe now, they'd be able to get their lives back to normal.

The only part of her breakfast not on the floor was the toast, so she contented herself with that and coffee. She had just finished clearing away the dishes when the intercom buzzed. "Yes?"

"It's Detective Brady."

She buzzed him in, ignoring Hal's deep scowl. A moment later, she answered the knock at the door. "Good morning, Detective, please come in."

He removed his hat. "Thanks, I won't be staying long. I trust you've heard the news about…"

"Yes." Hal remained seated at the table. "Congratulations." His tone chilled her.

The detective studied him for a moment. "Thank you, but we still have a great deal to do. His fingerprints match what we took from Mrs. Panagos' water glass, so we have him cold on her murder. We're looking to get him on the assaults and robberies, too. Would you be willing to come in and identify him?"

"You already have him," Hal said. "Why do you need us?"

"We'll have him stand in line with several other men—police officers and detectives—of similar size, build, and coloring. I'll ask Mrs. Corwyn to point out which man assaulted her. We're asking all the victims we've identified here in New York to do the same thing."

"Why so many?" Hal pressed.

"We want absolutely no doubt that this is the guy, and we want to pile as many counts onto the indictment as possible."

She was going to confront him. "I'll do it."

Hal was stunned. "I think we should talk about…"

"No, I'll do it. You don't have to come." She turned to the detective. "When and where?"

Hal stood. "Meg, we need to talk about this."

"Tomorrow morning at ten o'clock at the 44th Precinct station house on Sedgewick Avenue in the Bronx. I can arrange for a car to pick you up and drive you home."

"I'm going, Hal." She was going to stare the animal down, a nail in his coffin.

"Thank you, Mrs. Corwyn. I appreciate that this will be difficult, but…"

Detective Brady was such a gentleman. "It may be easier for me than you expect."

"I hope so. Shall I send a car, then?"

Hal stiffened. "That won't be necessary. I will accompany my wife."

"That's fine." He gave her his card. "If there's any change, please call me. Otherwise, I'll see you tomorrow morning. Have a pleasant day." He tipped his hat.

"Thank you, Detective." She closed the door behind him and held her breath. She'd never defied Hal.

But when she turned around, he'd returned to his seat at the table and stuck his nose back into the newspaper. All the warmth from the previous evening had vanished without a trace. She returned to the kitchen to wash the breakfast dishes.

"Meg, come in here."

He'd rarely given her commands, and she'd usually deflected them with teasing. But this wouldn't be brushed aside with a humor she no longer felt. "I'm finishing the dishes. I'll be there in a couple of minutes." She took her time, placing each dish in the drain, just so. She wiped her hands on the dish towel and walked into the dining room. "What is it?"

Hal was red-faced. "I have to miss a day from work so we can go traipsing up to the Bronx to give them information they already have?"

She shrugged. "You don't have to go. You heard the detective. He'll send…"

"He has an eye for you."

She sat at the opposite end of the table. "Is that what this is about? You're jealous?"

"Stop it."

"True. How could you be jealous of someone showing an interest in me?"

His jaw dropped. "What the hell is that supposed to mean? I must say, Meg, it's getting impossible to understand you. You claim you want to put the assault…"

"The rape, Hal. It was rape."

"All right, the rape. You keep claiming you want to put it behind us, but now you want to go see this animal face-to-face."

"I want to see him caught in a trap he can't escape, to point my finger at him and say, 'He's the one who did it'. And to prove to myself they got him, so I can sleep at night, be assured he's going to prison, or better yet, the electric chair. Because then it might just be possible for *you* to put it behind *you*." She couldn't stop the tears. "Maybe then, you won't back away when I get too close. You'll brush my hair away from my face, show me kindness, even kiss me, hold me, treat me like your wife again."

He got up from the table. "Oh, for God's sake, Meg. It's nothing like that."

"Then, what is it?"

He grabbed his hat and left.

***

"Think they'll show?" Larkin asked as Danny drove onto the Queensborough Bridge.

"No question, she'll come even if he doesn't."

"Didn't think she had that kind of moxie."

Danny laughed. "Neither did she."

Larkin gave him a long, appraising look.

Danny knew what he was thinking. "No, Frankie, not in a month of Sundays. But I saw something in her this morning that I hadn't seen before. She reminded me of someone I knew years ago back in Dublin, a neighbor—pretty and sweet, kind of quiet, until you crossed her. Then, she'd come at ya like a banshee."

“And you were sweet on her.”

“Not a chance. She was six years older than me.”

“Bollocks. I’ll bet you even wrote her love notes and then ripped them up.”

No, he’d sent one, but he’d never admit it to Larkin. Nor would he ever tell of how she comforted him after Michael Collins’ death, or of how, two years later, when he was fourteen, she’d become his first lover before marrying someone else. “Bollocks yerself. Anyway, I’d appreciate you accompanying me on my visit to Mr. and Mrs. Clinton.”

“I take it the big colored fella scared the bejeezus out of you last time.”

“He did not, but I’m thinking it might be good if he sees more than one Irish cop on his wife’s side.”

“Danny, me boy, keep it up and you’ll one day be mayor of this fair city.”

***

Meg took her grocery basket and walked down to Queens Boulevard to do her food shopping. Keep everything normal, that was all she could do. Lord knew if Hal went to work or what else he might be doing or when he’d be home. She’d spoken her fears aloud for the first time this morning, the ones that had been building inside of her. And he’d walked out.

“Good morning, Mrs. Corwyn,” the butcher said. “I have some nice steaks today, New York strip.”

Hal loved steak. Mom always said that the way to a man’s heart was through his stomach. “Yes, I’ll take two, thank you, and a loin of pork.” That would make for a nice roast.

The butcher wrapped the steaks. “You okay, Mrs. Corwyn? You look a little pale.”

“I’m fine, thanks.”

"You sure? Because a lady as pretty as you oughta have roses in her cheeks."

She blushed. "Thank you."

"Did you make the steak and kidney pie?"

She struggled to hide the knifelike pain she felt in her stomach at the memory of dancing with Hal. "Yes, it was a success." Her voice caught. She covered it by adding, "It's my grandmother's recipe."

The butcher counted out her change. "You take care, Mrs. Corwyn."

***

"Let me get this straight," Mr. Clinton said. "You want my wife to come in and say whether this guy you got for the murder is the same one who attacked her?"

"Precisely." Danny repeated the explanation he'd given the Corwyns. "I want to make sure he never again sees the light of day."

"Fine. She'll do it. We'll be there."

But Dorothy Clinton wasn't as enthusiastic. "Will he be able to see me?"

"Yes," Larkin said, "but there will be several police officers there, and we'll leave ample space between you and him."

"Believe me," Danny added, "he won't be able to do anything to you."

"Unless he isn't convicted," Mrs. Clinton said.

Danny gave her his most reassuring smile. "The whole point of this is to prevent exactly that."

She turned to her husband and nodded. "All right."

At the door, Mr. Clinton took Danny's hand. "Thank you, Detective. Thanks very much."

"You're welcome. We'll see you tomorrow."

Back in the car, Larkin laughed. "Quite a difference between the Clintons and the Corwyns. He's rarin' to go and she ain't."

"We'll have to watch him. He was a little too eager for my taste."

"Indeed, he was. Might dispatch Babić to the nether regions before we can get him to the chair." Larkin checked their list. "Two more on the Upper West Side, then two downtown, and we can call it a day."

***

Hal didn't arrive until nearly seven o'clock, again reeking of alcohol. Meg served the steaks with onions, just the way he liked, and he wolfed it down. She ate only a small portion of hers and wrapped the rest. After dinner, Hal put the radio on and then promptly fell asleep in the easy chair. Tommy Dorsey was playing "I'm Getting Sentimental Over You", and Meg was almost finished *Rebecca*.

The music formed a pleasant background, but soon Hal was snoring, and concentration became more difficult. He'd be hung over in the morning.

She reached the end of a chapter and put the book down. She'd opened her heart for the first time since she'd been raped, and Hal's answer had been to get drunk after work. At least this time, he hadn't pulled her hair.

But they still had to get through facing her attacker.

CHAPTER EIGHTEEN

Thursday, October 9, 1941

Greco called Danny into his office as soon as he arrived. "You know Assistant District Attorney Dennis Monroe?"

A tall man in his mid-thirties wearing a navy-blue pinstripe three-piece suit stepped forward and shook Danny's hand. "Indeed, I do. Detective Brady is always an effective witness. I'm here to observe your lineup, as Lt. Greco calls it."

"We're looking forward to hitting this son of a bitch with the full truckload," Danny said.

Monroe turned away and said to Greco, "Let's see how this goes."

Not what Danny was expecting.

***

Hal didn't go to work, no doubt afraid of how it would look if he were the only husband who didn't go. Meg tried to force the malignant thought from her mind, but the sight of eight other women, all with husbands with the same look of discomfort on their faces, kept it front and center.

She turned to the closest woman to her, an attractive colored woman, and extended her hand. "Hi, I'm Meg." What made her do that? She was always shy around strangers, even at social gatherings.

"Dorothy." The woman was startled but took her hand. They held the clasp a little longer than Meg expected. The touch of another person had become so foreign to her, she'd almost forgotten how nice it could be.

Dorothy's small smile suggested that she might have been feeling the same way. "I'm a little bit scared. How about you?"

Meg relaxed a little. "I don't think there's much to worry about in a police station."

"You don't know my husband. He's liable to go crazy when he sees this guy."

If only Hal had that kind of devotion.

Detective Brady approached. "Thank you all for coming, ladies. Please follow me." So courteous and kind.

They climbed a flight of stairs, and the detective halted by an open door. "You've all met my partner, Detective Larkin. Please wait here, and he'll admit you, one couple at a time. When you enter you will see a line of six men. If you see the man who assaulted you among them, please point him out. In the meantime, please stand behind this line until your turn comes so that you can't see who the person ahead of you has named. We'll be changing the order in which they're standing for each couple. Mrs. Corwyn, let's start with you."

Hal stiffened, but Meg stepped forward, keeping pace with Detective Brady. This was it.

"Dennis Monroe from the District Attorney's office," the detective said, "is here to observe."

Monroe nodded. "Ma'am."

Hal lagged as she stepped toward the line. The first man was a little too short and heavy. So, not Number One.

Nor Number Two… Number Three…

Oh, God. Number Four. Meg raised her arm and pointed. "That's him. He's the one who raped me."

Number Four shrank back a little.

"Thank you, Mrs. Corwyn," the detective said.

But she couldn't move.

"Meg," Hal said in a whisper, "let's go."

It wasn't enough to accuse him. They could kill him, and it wouldn't be enough.

"Meg, come on." Hal tugged her arm.

She yanked her arm back, taking one step forward, glaring at her attacker.

And spat in his face.

Hal was aghast.

She pivoted and strode away.

***

Danny turned to Monroe, smirking. "I'd call that a positive identification."

Monroe chuckled. "Yeah, shift Babić to position number two for the next one. And have him wipe her spit off his face."

He waved to Larkin to send in the next couple, from the Upper West Side, an attractive young blonde wearing a hat and gloves. Her husband trailed three feet behind, just like Corwyn had. She stopped in front of Babić. "Him."

She walked past Monroe and joined Mrs. Corwyn. "That was easy."

Mrs. Corwyn broke into a smile. "Yes, I guess it was. I'm Meg."

"Clara. Nice to meet you." She glanced toward the two husbands. "Looking at them, you'd think they were the ones who were raped."

Danny turned to Monroe and shook his head. "Jesus, Mary and Joseph."

***

Meg watched as the couples kept coming, and no matter where they moved the animal, the women picked him out with no hesitation, the husband trailing behind, looking ashamed, then skulked off to join Hal and the other men. None of the men said a word.

"Here comes Dorothy," Meg said.

"You know her?" Clara sounded surprised.

"Only just met her coming in. She seems nice."

The animal had been shifted to the sixth position. Dorothy studied each man, but her husband was right behind her. Finally, she reached Number Six. "That's him."

Dorothy's husband barged past her and grabbed the animal by the throat. The five policemen in the line pulled them apart.

"Easy, there Mr. Clinton," Detective Brady said.

"I'll kill him."

"Please leave that to us," the detective said, which made Meg smile.

Clara glanced at the other husbands. "Pity more of them didn't take that kind of interest."

Dorothy joined them. "Well, I hope he got that out of his system."

"We were just wishing our husbands had shown that kind of fire," Clara said.

"He's big on defending me, sure, but he keeps his distance at home."

Meg glanced back over her shoulder. Uniformed police were leading the rapist-murderer away. "I don't care about the money and jewelry he took. But he stole my marriage."

Dorothy linked her arm through Meg's. "You said it, Sister. All of ours, too."

***

"Nine out of nine," Danny said as he joined Greco, Larkin, and Monroe in Greco's office. "Can't do better than that."

Monroe agreed. "Could've done without the big colored guy trying to kill him. Glad he was the only one."

"How about the dame who spit in his face?" Greco said. "Some dish."

"Megan Corwyn," Danny said before he could stop himself.

Larkin shot him a look. "Nice that you remember her name."

"I remember all their names." He turned to Monroe. "So, when do we go to the grand jury?"

"We'll be presenting on Monday, and we'll get an indictment with no problem."

"Monday?" The women had already left the precinct. "But don't we need the women to testify?"

Greco was shuffling papers on his desk.

Monroe lowered his voice. "Detective, my boss will prosecute the murder case, only. We're not going after the assaults and robberies."

"You mean the rapes and the robberies," Danny said. "That's unbelievable. We've logged eighteen cases here in the city, and over sixty more from New England to New Orleans, all with the same modus operandi. We owe it to those women to..."

Monroe held up a hand. "Detective Brady, you just said we had eighteen cases in New York City. How many of those victims participated this morning?"

"Nine."

"And how many did you ask?"

"All eighteen. I'm not saying indict him for them all, but let's at least get the nine."

"And suppose three women refuse to testify? Because I guarantee you all nine husbands will be against them doing so."

Danny glanced at Larkin, who was staring at the floor. "Then you still have six."

"Okay," Monroe said. "That leaves six women who must take the stand and be grilled about how old they were when they first had sex, how many times they had sex before they were married, how many times they've had sex with someone other than their husbands. Did they do anything to encourage Babić? Did he force his way into their apartments, or did they let him in? Were they wearing any makeup at the time? How much makeup? Do they always wear makeup during the day when their husbands aren't home? Why do they wear such makeup? What about perfume? Why didn't they put up more of a struggle?"

Danny felt sick. "I don't believe this."

Larkin spoke up. "It's like Vinnie said. Rape cases are the worst."

Monroe continued. "And if the woman even hesitates on a single question, it gets worse. The defense lawyer will attack her like a panzer division until she breaks down on the stand, which the jury will see as an admission that she asked for it. Reasonable doubt. Doubt for one leads to doubt for others because rape is something nobody wants to think about. Pretty soon, your alleged pattern of criminal activity goes out the window, and then we risk losing on the murder count."

"But we've got him cold on that," Danny said, "with his fingerprints and handwriting."

"That's right, and if we present that case, alone, it's as easy as pie, no doubts, effortless conviction. He gets the chair, and any guilty verdicts on the rapes make no difference. Dead is dead."

Danny turned to Greco. "Are we at least going to tell the women who came in this morning? We owe them that much."

Greco still didn't look up. "Nah, when we don't call, their husbands will be relieved. And when Babić is sentenced to death, they'll be satisfied."

It was too much. "I need some air."

***

They'd left the precinct before noon, and Meg assumed Hal would go into work. But he got off at the Lincoln Avenue stop on the Flushing Line and crossed Roosevelt Avenue with her.

"I took the whole day," he said. "Told them you had a doctor's appointment."

No surprise he'd been ashamed to say where they were going. "Why me?"

"Well, if I'd said it was me, they'd have asked what was wrong. So, I just told them you might be expecting."

She froze. "You *what*?"

But he remained unfazed. "I had to tell them something, and that seemed the easiest. When I say nothing more about it, they'll assume you weren't."

She strode away, her heels slamming the pavement with each step. He didn't catch up to her until she was inside, fumbling with her keys to the vestibule door.

He reached for her keys. "Here, let me…"

She yanked back. "Get away from me."

"I just wanted to help…"

"You help? That's a laugh." At last, she steadied her trembling hand enough to get the key in the lock and the door swung open. She stormed up the stairs. He slipped past her as they reached their floor and opened the apartment door.

"I don't get this," he said in his I'm-trying-so-hard-to-be-reasonable voice. "What do you care if I tell my boss a little white lie?"

"That was not a 'little white lie'. It was a whopper, the single most hurtful thing you could have said."

"Why would you care what I said?"

Her voice rose and grew shrill. "Do I look like the Virgin Mary to you? Because immaculate conception is the only way I could be pregnant."

"Meg, for Christ's sake, lower your voice."

She scanned the apartment for something to throw at him, her anger white hot. Nothing handy. Her mind turned to the events at the precinct. "You are such a coward. At least Dorothy's husband stood up for her, lashing out at that filthy beast. You did nothing. You skulked, crawled, and skittered away as soon as you could." She took off her hat and walked into the bedroom, desperate for distance.

But he followed her. "Meg, please…"

"No. You refuse to admit you can't accept what happened to me. I've become dirty, contaminated. You can barely stand to sleep in the same bed with me, but you invented the story that I was expecting, just so you didn't have to tell your coworkers the truth. Funny, I didn't even want you there. Didn't need you. You provided no support, no help. Dorothy's husband didn't make everything right for her by lashing out, but at least he was there for her. At least he showed some fire. I lashed out more than you did. You might as well have been in China."

"I wanted to help…"

"Then do the one thing you do well and leave me alone."

He left without another word.

CHAPTER NINETEEN

"Soviet sources confirmed that the German advance had forced them out of Orel, two hundred miles south of Moscow, and fighting remains heavy in and around Bryansk and Vyazma..."

***

The radio was on in the drug store on Ogden Avenue as Danny took a seat at the lunch counter. "Corned beef on rye with mustard and a coffee."

A few moments later, Larkin sauntered in and took the stool next to him. "I'll have what he's having." After the counterman walked away, he added, "I hear it's not healthy to eat when you're steamed."

"Bollocks."

Larkin sighed. "Vinnie tried to warn you. So did I."

"I heard you both." Danny dropped his voice. "And if you don't mind my saying so, it's all a load of shite."

Larkin waited until their sandwiches came. "I've known you a lot of years, Danny boy. You're a damned fine cop, you hunted Babić down like he was nothing more than a purse snatcher, and he's going to burn. You should be sipping some Jameson's and congratulating yourself. But you and I both know why you're not, why you're so steamed over the DA's decision, which makes perfect sense if you think about it."

Danny took a huge bite.

Larkin took a smaller bite and waited. "I can't say I blame you. She's a right sweet bird and her husband isn't worth the suits he wears."

"This has nothing to do with Megan Corwyn."

"I don't believe I was mentioning any names."

Danny ate the rest of his sandwich in silence.

"I gotta admit," Larkin said, "when she spit in Babić's face this morning, I was impressed. But this can't go anywhere. She's the type who'll gut it out and take what comes, no matter how miserable he makes her."

"You might very well be right, Frankie, but she's counting on having her moment in court to point the finger and say, 'he did it', and we're denying her that. She deserves to know why."

"I don't think the lieutenant will approve of you going over there."

"I don't plan on asking him."

***

She'd expected to break down and cry after Hal left, but she hadn't. Instead, she washed up, changed into a skirt and cable-knit sweater, and took her copy of *Rebecca* back to the library. "I loved it. It was a book I could lose myself in. Now, I need another."

The librarian grinned. "We have a display of recent best-sellers over on that table. Why not browse a little and see what appeals to you?"

"Thanks." Meg walked over and scanned the various titles, picking up the ones that caught her attention. *How Green Was My Valley* was the first volume she picked. The plight of Welsh coal miners wasn't what she was looking for. *The Grapes of Wrath*—looked too depressing.

Mrs. Miniver. She picked it up and read the inside of the book jacket. A woman and her family at the beginning of the war. She immediately carried it to the front desk.

"Excellent choice," the librarian said as she opened the book to the pocket in the back. "I love this book. I've read it twice. Enjoy."

Meg took the volume. "Thanks, I'm sure I will."

She stopped at the fish store on 43rd Avenue and bought some flounder fillets. It was only when she arrived back at the apartment that she remembered how Hal had left. He still wasn't back. But at least the fish could be fried quickly, so she'd wait until he came home to put them on. In the meantime, she'd settle in and read.

***

It was nearly seven when Danny reached the Corwyns' building. Good, dinner would certainly be over. He tried to force Larkin's comments from his mind. She'd shown such spirit, even while suffering her own pain. He recalled, just as he was pressing the buzzer to their apartment, the blowup she'd had with her husband that morning at the 108th Precinct. Maybe it wasn't a good idea to come when the husband was likely to be home.

"Yes?" Her voice.

"Mrs. Corwyn, it's Detective Brady."

The door buzzer sounded, and he made his way up the stairs. She was waiting at the apartment door, lovely, but something wasn't right.

He removed his hat. "I hope I haven't disturbed your dinner hour."

"Not at all. Please come in."

No sign of the husband and no aroma of food. The kitchen was dark.

"Would you care for anything?"

"No, thank you." Coming had been a mistake. "There's something I need to discuss with you."

"Please, sit down." She sat in the easy chair. "Did something go wrong today?"

He took a place on the couch. "No, you were excellent, even inspiring. The other women did well, too. But the District Attorney has decided…"

The apartment door opened with a loud bang and Mr. Corwyn entered. "What's he doing here?" He slurred his words.

"Detective Brady was just telling me something about the case."

Mr. Corwyn's gait was unsteady as he approached, and the odor of alcohol was unmistakable. "News? You got news?"

Dan stood and offered his hand. "Yes, I was just telling Mrs. Corwyn…"

Corwyn interrupted. "Dinner ready?"

She crossed her arms. "No. I was waiting for you." She turned to Danny. "Please go on."

Her husband was three sheets to the wind and in an ugly mood. "Perhaps I should come back another time."

Mr. Corwyn waved his arms. "No, no, no, Detective, we want to hear everything about the case. We're always interested in the case."

Danny hesitated.

She shrugged. "It's not likely to be any better tomorrow, Detective. Might as well tell us now."

He had no gracious way out. "Very well. After this morning's session, I learned the DA is only going to charge Babić with the murder of Mrs. Panagos. They won't charge him with any of the rapes or robberies."

"What?" Mr. Corwyn's cry was nearly a primal scream. "You mean we went through all that for nothing?"

She scoffed. "What do you mean, 'we'? You didn't go through anything."

"It wasn't for nothing," Danny said in the most soothing voice he could muster. "That you all agreed on the identification left no doubt in Assistant District Attorney Monroe's mind that we have the right man."

"So," Mr. Corwyn asked, "why not prosecute him for the…"

Danny cut him off. "I argued as vigorously as I could to do so, but the DA had some excellent reasons." He repeated what Monroe had said about simplicity, and about the death penalty making any additional sentence meaningless. The stunned look on Meg's face made him feel like a heel. "It also spares you the agony of being cross-examined on the rape charge."

Mr. Corwyn snorted. "What agony?"

Sweet Jesus, what an ass. But Danny's gut told him to tread lightly. "Defense attorneys in rape cases try to blame the woman. It's cruel and reprehensible on top of everything she's already endured, but that's the fact."

"You mean, making it look like she asked for it." Mr. Corwyn's mouth hadn't quite turned into a leer, but it was too close for comfort.

"Pretty much. Since we'll be seeking the death penalty, there's no benefit in terms of sentencing for leveling additional charges and there's no point in subjecting Mrs. Corwyn and the other women to all of that. And if for any reason he were to be acquitted on the murder charge, they could always indict him on the other charges later. But I can promise you, that won't happen. He's going to pay with his life." Danny stood to go.

"I see." Meg stood, too, and walked him to the door. "So, there's nothing else I need to do?"

"No, but thank you because your description was the key to running him down." He tipped his hat and left.

***

She waited at the closed door, listening to the detective's steps as he descended the stairs, and heard the vestibule door close as he left the building. It was so nice of him to come, and she'd forgotten to thank him. He knew every detail, and yet he always treated her with kindness, dignity, and respect. Such a nice man.

Hal's eyes were on her, leering as she turned around. "All that for nothing."

It felt that way to her, too.

He advanced on her. "They think you lied because you let him in and didn't resist."

"You know I couldn't fight him…"

"You heard him say it: the DA doesn't believe you can convince a jury."

This couldn't be happening. "That's not what he said. He said it wasn't worth putting me through it because…"

"Because the jury would think you asked for it, because you let him in."

"Hal…"

"You invited him in, and you didn't put up a fight."

"He was looking for you. You'd given him…"

"How long was he here?" He was almost on her. "You never even screamed. You might as well have dropped your pants for him."

She slapped his face with all the strength she could muster.

She never saw his punch coming.

CHAPTER TWENTY

Hermann Mueller checked his watch as the pay phone rang. Eight o'clock. He loved punctuality.

"Good evening, Friedrich." He'd be damned if he would use the Americanized version in a private conversation.

Obermann chuckled. "And good evening to you. I have identified several individuals whom I consider promising prospects for our little social group. Six have already accepted, encouraged by your leadership of the city group, and especially by your approach."

"That is excellent news, and I thank you. But I suggest you keep your group as small as it can be and remain efficient."

"Do you have a number in mind, *Herr Koordinator*?"

Hermann had thought using names without titles would be best, but Obermann's suggestion of "coordinator" struck him as both necessary to establish a hierarchy and appropriately humble. "You would be a better judge than I. Let caution be your guide. Anything else to report?"

"Just this. One of my recruits—my deputy if you will—is Marcus Schmidt. His cousin is Reinhold Barth, an official in the Abwehr."

Herman's breath caught. The Abwehr was Germany's intelligence agency. "I see. Are they in communication?"

"Direct communication has become difficult, so they correspond through a contact in Lisbon. If you like, I can ask Marcus to inform his cousin of our activities."

"With one club in Yorkville and another in German Gardens, mail may not be secure."

"Marcus and Barth employ secret writing, in which the actual message is revealed when immersed in water. Nothing would be revealed in the visible note."

Obermann was asking permission. Excellent. "Then I'd appreciate Germany knowing of us. Please thank Herr Schmidt for me. Call me at this number at nine o'clock one week from tonight and we'll confer on our mutual progress."

"I suggest four weeks, *Herr Koordinator,* as I'll be out of town, traveling to Chicago to see my cousins. Heil Hitler."

Hermann struggled to keep the excitement out of his voice. "Give them my warmest regards. Heil Hitler."

He returned to the others in the back room of the tavern. "Herr Obermann reports good progress."

***

Danny was numb as he walked the eight blocks to his garden apartment, nowhere near enough time to shake his anger. Or his guilt.

Tonight was supposed to give Meg Corwyn the satisfaction of having brought George Babić to justice, but he was haunted by the look of shock on her face and the ugly leer on her husband's.

"You mean, making it look like she asked for it," he'd said. And Danny recalled he'd hinted at the same thing when Danny had first interviewed them both two weeks ago. Blaming Meg.

Lovely Meg.

As he entered his apartment, he forced his mind to the assaults and burglaries still to be solved, the anti-Semitic crimes that were increasing in frequency. And before he'd left the precinct tonight, he'd studied the blackboard on which he charted each fresh attack. It was filling.

Four anti-Semitic incidents in the past two weeks: two near the Spanish and Portuguese Synagogue on West 70th Street, one a block away from Temple Emanuel on East 65th Street, and one a block from Central Synagogue on Lexington and East 55th Street. In every case, the attackers were males in their late teens or early twenties who robbed their Jewish victims of money and watches. In every case, the attackers beat their victims, kicked them in the genitals, and said, "Take that, kike."

The number of attackers varied, as did their descriptions, but the method was consistent. One attacker always approached from behind and grabbed the victim by the neck. Then other attackers joined in.

Assaults were now clustered in Manhattan, the burglaries in the Bronx.

CHAPTER TWENTY-ONE

Four Weeks Later, Thursday, November 6, 1941

"Japan yesterday dispatched seasoned diplomat Saboru Kurusu to the United States in what some describe as a last-ditch effort to resolve the issues that threaten war in the Pacific. The Pan American Clipper was held over an extra day in Hong Kong to allow Mr. Kurusu to catch the flight..."

***

The bruise left by the punch that first night had long since faded, but Meg had become adept at covering new ones with makeup. This week, Hal had been drunk every night when he came home.

She turned the radio off and left for the library, her only refuge aside from Mass on Sunday. The head librarian, Miss Soloway, greeted her, pretending not to notice the heavy makeup covering the week-old bruise next to her left eye, and thank God the eye hadn't been blackened. "Good afternoon, Mrs. Corwyn."

But Meg had another reason to be embarrassed. "Good afternoon. I'm afraid I've lost *The Grapes of Wrath.*" She'd decided the week before that reading about someone whose sufferings were worse than her own might help her spirits. And it had until

Hal tossed the book down the incinerator in one of his fits. "How much do I owe the library?"

Miss Soloway studied her. "You're one of our regulars, Mrs. Corwyn, and we have several copies. These things will happen. We can let it go this time."

But it wasn't the first time. Meg turned away. There was a sign on the desk: "Wanted—part time library assistant." What a treat that would be, but she couldn't even dream of it. Hal's hours were erratic these days. It was a wonder he could hold his position at all. "Thank you."

"Mrs. Corwyn, is there anything you'd care to talk about? Any help you need? I sense something is wrong."

Put on the mask. "I'm fine." Just like always. "Thank you for asking, though." She checked out another copy of the book.

When she returned to the apartment, Hal was sitting in the easy chair, his suit dingy and soiled, staring into space. Her first concern was what to do with the book. She couldn't afford to report a third copy lost. But something about him was different. "What happened?"

He didn't answer. He didn't even look at her, just that blank stare.

"Hal?"

He focused. "I lost my job."

Not exactly a shock. "What did they say?"

"My boss said my birthday was no excuse to show up drunk the next morning."

"That was a week and a half ago."

"That's when they fired me."

"You've been pretending to go to work after you got fired?"

"I couldn't face you. I couldn't admit that I'd failed."

"You failed me long before you got fired. Have you been looking for another job?"

"I'm not trained for anything but banking work, and I can't do that because I'd never get a reference from my old boss."

She picked up the phone. "You've outdone yourself this time."

"Who are you calling?"

"The library. They have an opening. I'm going to apply." Miss Soloway answered. Meg told her she was interested in the job.

"Do you have any experience working in a library?"

At last, she felt energized. "Three years at the Maspeth library when I was in high school."

"That's wonderful. Come in tomorrow morning and you can fill out the papers. It's half days, Monday through Friday, plus every other Saturday, and the pay is thirty cents an hour."

"Thank you. I'll see you in the morning." She hung up the phone. "Hired."

Hal was stricken. "This isn't necessary."

"You've been out of work ten days and done nothing. I can't wait for you to wake up."

"I found something, but it's not what you'd expect."

"What? Traveling salesman?"

"I joined the army and leave for Basic Training tomorrow morning. Being apart for a while is probably best for us, and we'll get back what we had when I come home. I'll send half my pay home to you."

She sat down, dumbfounded.

"So, there's no need for you to take that job. We'll be fine."

"Fine? Are you crazy? Do you think that when you come back from your enlistment—whenever that is, because it looks like we're going to be pulled into the war—everything will magically be swell? Will I become un-raped? Will the man who last month was convinced I 'dropped my pants' for another man suddenly rediscover his love for me?"

His face contorted. "Why do you always have to bring that up?"

"Because you refuse to acknowledge what happened, or its toll on me and on our marriage. You're a coward, and that won't change just because you put on a uniform."

***

Hermann Mueller hung up the phone and rejoined the four members of his group. Obermann had reported that most of the men he'd met in Chicago were deeply saddened by the prospect of war with Germany and hoped it could be avoided. None still dreamed of a glorious Reich, and they feared retribution by hordes of angry Americans who'd been turning increasingly against Germany since the fall of France the year before.

His four comrades were standing at their usual table, waiting. Almost at attention.

Hermann gestured toward the table. "*Bitte, meine Herren.*"

They all sat.

Paul spoke up. "We were just discussing the news that the American Congress appears ready to grant the Cripple Roosevelt's plea to arm American merchant ships. Another step toward war."

Hermann nodded. "So, we must continue to prepare. What news on explosives?"

"The simplest is gunpowder. The ingredients are readily available and cheap, and it is easy and safe to mix, but the drawback is the amount we would need to produce a blast sufficient for disrupting a rail line or a power station."

"Could we choose a smaller target, such as the waiting room of a train station?" Hermann asked.

"That would work but igniting it without alerting anyone would still pose a problem. Another potential solution is nitroglycerin. Again, the ingredients are easily obtainable."

Dieter spoke up. "Chemistry was my best subject in school. The mixing process can be dangerous. Nitroglycerin is highly unstable."

"How difficult would it be for any of us to do it?" Hermann asked.

Paul cast a sidelong glance at Dieter. "I do not believe that any of us should try. This needs a qualified chemist, or at least an advanced student of chemistry."

Hermann shook off his disappointment. "Suppose we could find such a person. Would we be able to develop enough to destroy a bridge like the Hell Gate?"

Dieter spoke up. "We might damage a track so that trains could not pass over it. But even transporting nitroglycerin to a target could cause an accidental explosion."

"What do you suggest?" Hermann asked.

Dieter pondered the question. "I have an idea that I need to analyze."

CHAPTER TWENTY-TWO

Eight Weeks Later, Wednesday, December 31, 1941

"Swiss sources report Soviet gains in the Crimea, while in the Pacific, Japanese forces continue to advance on Manila. Here in New York, Mayor LaGuardia asks for tonight's New Year celebrations to be muted, without horns or sirens, for fear of inciting panic…"

***

"Counselor," the judge asked, "do you have any other questions for this witness?"

The defense attorney was already walking back to his seat. "Not at this time, your honor."

The judge turned to Danny. "The witness is excused. We're in recess until two o'clock."

ADA Monroe followed him out of the courtroom. "Thank you, Detective. You were excellent up there. And on this entire case."

"My pleasure. Are you ready to wrap this up?"

"We'll get the testimony on the fingerprints this afternoon. Babić takes the stand tomorrow. Closing arguments follow and then the jury gets it."

Danny walked back to the precinct, despite the biting wind. As he walked past Yankee Stadium, he recalled how crowded it had been back in October when the Yankees had defeated the Brooklyn Dodgers in the World Series. Vinnie Rossi had crowed about the team and their biggest star, Joe DiMaggio, in a campaign to get Danny hooked on the game. If only DiMaggio were an Irishman.

As he walked up the Grand Concourse from the courthouse, his thoughts turned to Meg Corwyn. Yes, in the end she'd been spared the agony of cross-examination, but there was no way to know whether that was a beneficial outcome for her. Had her husband come around? How was she doing? For a moment, he considered calling on her or phoning, but he decided against it. Best to let sleeping dogs lie.

CHAPTER TWENTY-THREE

Friday, January 2, 1942

Meg was just finishing up the morning shift at the library. Working was the perfect tonic for her. She was her own woman, coming and going as she pleased, and she'd hardly given Hal a thought since he'd left.

Miss Soloway broke in on her reflections. "Meg, you know that Joan's expecting."

Joan handled the research desk, and she had recently spent almost as much time in the ladies' room as she had helping students. Meg had been filling in for her when needed. "Yes, I do."

"Her doctor wants her to stop working. I thought you'd like to take over the research desk."

"That's a full-time position."

Miss Soloway, who knew about Hal's enlistment, if not the reasons for it, lowered her voice. "Yes, but I've seen you working with the children. You're a natural, and we could help each other out. If you're willing to not only go full time but also work Saturdays, then I don't need to hire another part-timer and you get a nice income boost. The post of Research Librarian pays an additional ten cents an hour."

On impulse, she embraced Miss Soloway. "Thank you. This is marvelous."

"It sure is. Starting Monday?"

***

"You really going to join the army when you graduate?"

"Why not? Pay starts at thirty-one dollars a month, going to forty after four months. No room and board, and I ain't stuck in some factory down by the East River."

The snippet of conversation from two passing teenaged boys pulled Meg out of her reverie as she turned off Skillman Avenue on her way home. She'd been so pleased with her new pay scale that she'd forgotten that Hal was earning money wherever he was.

By now, he'd been out of basic training for two weeks. No letters from him, and no money. He was either throwing it away or sending it to someone else, and she had no doubt who that someone might be.

After checking her mail, she took the car and drove over to Kew Gardens, to the huge, tree-shaded center-hall colonial on Grenfell Street where Hal's parents still lived.

Hal's mother exhibited little warmth to anyone, and she'd been downright wintry toward Meg since the rape. She greeted Meg with a barely concealed scowl and a curt, "Yes?"

"Good afternoon, Mrs. Corwyn." The woman's scowl grew deeper at Meg's formal manner. Fine. "Your son has neither written to me nor sent me any of his pay, which he'd promised to do. Is he sending it to you?"

"Good Lord, I refuse to discuss this out here."

Meg followed Hal's mother into the living room. She took a seat on the aging davenport, facing a fieldstone fireplace, flanked on either side by book cabinets crammed with dusty volumes that hadn't been opened in years.

Hal's mother sat ramrod straight in a wingback chair next to the fireplace, no doubt to accentuate her posture. "Yes, he's been writing to me and sending part of his pay, which I deposit into a separate bank account in my name but earmarked for him. I keep a thorough accounting if you'd care to see it, although it's not much at present."

"Isn't it unseemly for a married man to send his money to his mother instead of his wife?"

Just the hint of an icy smile. "Odd, yes. Unseemly? Not under the circumstances." She held up a hand. "Harold has been accepted into Officer Candidate School and insisted I not divulge his present location. He does not wish to correspond with you at the present time."

"I could find out."

"No doubt you could but ignoring his wishes would only make matters worse. My son is using this interlude to take stock of himself and order his priorities. I suggest you do the same. He told me you practically threw him out of his own home."

Meg stood. "Did he tell you about his drinking or hitting me? Did he tell you he was fired from his job and ran off to enlist, like an old movie character joining the French Foreign Legion to get away from it all? No, he left those tidbits out?"

Hal's mother rose from her seat. "I think you'd better leave. And next time, do have the courtesy to call, first."

It was a little before two. An hour to make two stops.

***

Meg found Miss Soloway engrossed in several sheets of green columnar paper. "Can I talk to you for a minute?" She took a seat without waiting for an answer.

"I hope you haven't changed your mind about the position."

"No, but I need a huge favor, and I hope asking it won't change yours. I need to take a trip."

"How long a trip?"

"I'm not sure. What's the faster way to get to San Diego? Train or bus?"

Miss Soloway studied her for a few moments before answering. "They both take about three days, one way. The bus is cheaper, the train is more comfortable, especially if you can afford a sleeper. I hope you don't mind me asking, but is San Diego your final destination?"

Meg flushed. "No, it's Mexico."

Miss Soloway broke into a mischievous grin. "Yes, I've been there myself. El Paso is better—a half-day closer, so if you get a train from Grand Central tonight, you'll arrive in El Paso on Monday morning, Juarez on Tuesday. The process is faster in Juarez, but you can't just arrive unprepared. You'll need your birth certificate and your passport, translated into Spanish. You'll also need to hire someone there to represent your husband. It's not that costly, but will probably take a few days, as will the translation, so don't wait for one to be finished before you do the other. Keep me posted about your progress by telegram. I'll cover the reference desk until you get back."

Meg blinked back tears. "Thank you."

"When I said I'd been there myself, I didn't just mean the place. There's a reason I'm *Miss* Soloway. Good luck."

CHAPTER TWENTY-FOUR

"Mr. Monroe," the judge asked, "do you wish to cross-examine the witness?"

Danny knew nothing about reading jurors, but he couldn't believe that these men would believe anything Babić had just said.

"Let me understand this," Monroe began. "Your story is that Mrs. Panagos approached you on a bus in September, started a conversation with you, and subsequently invited you into her apartment?"

No answer.

"We've heard testimony from her husband, who knew her better than anyone, that Melina Panagos was a shy, reserved woman who avoided venturing out of the house for anything other than church activities. Do you expect us to believe she approached a stranger on a bus for no particular reason?"

No answer.

"Your honor," Monroe said, "please instruct the witness to answer."

"Mr. Babić," the judge replied, "you've told your story, now you must answer the prosecutor's questions."

Babić gave a tight nod.

"Thank you," Monroe said. "Now, you've admitted that you were in Mrs. Panagos' apartment on September 24th, that you pilfered a ring, and you grabbed her around the neck to keep her from screaming. You dragged her into the bedroom and bound her wrists together with a necktie and stuffed a handkerchief into her mouth."

"Told you, I don't remember that."

"But you also said that the testimony given by Detective Brady as to the condition in which she was found was true, did you not?"

"Yessir."

"So, you bound and gagged her and pushed her down onto her bed because she had seen you take the ring and screamed. Correct?"

"Um, yeah."

"Detective Brady also testified that he observed her on her bed with her skirt hiked up to her waist and her underthings disturbed. Did you leave her in such condition to stop her from screaming, too?"

Babić stared but said nothing.

"I mean," Monroe went on, as if having a casual conversation, "you had the ring and you'd silenced Mrs. Panagos. Why would you stick around?"

No answer.

Monroe dropped his voice to a growl. "And why did you take a second necktie and tie it around her throat, strangling her?"

No answer.

"Did you grab the two ties together, or did you go back for the second when Mrs. Panagos continued to struggle?"

No answer.

"Why, Mr. Babić? Why did you stick around? How did you conveniently forget the ties, the handkerchief, the indecent position in which you left her?"

No answer.

Monroe turned to the judge. "Your honor, this is like talking to a statue."

The judge leaned forward. "Please answer Mr. Monroe's questions."

Babić let out a sob, shaking his head.

Monroe waved in disgust. "No further questions, your honor."

"The witness is excused," the judge said. "Counselor, do you have any other witnesses?"

"No, your honor, the defense rests."

"In that case, I'll hear closing arguments on Monday. Court is adjourned until ten o'clock Monday morning."

***

It was twenty minutes to three when Meg got to Hal's old bank, where they still had their joint accounts. She strode into the office of the manager. "Good afternoon, I wish to close our account."

"Yes, Mrs. Corwyn. Is your husband here?"

"He's in the army."

"I'd feel more comfortable with him here, since…"

"These are joint accounts. We each have the power to close them, correct?"

"Yes, but…"

"Then, please do." She made a show of looking at her watch. "Almost three."

"Yes, of course." He dashed out, returning a few minutes later with two completed withdrawal slips. "The total balance is $773.82. Just sign."

***

Hal had taken the large suitcase with him, leaving her the smaller one she'd bought for their honeymoon nearly three years ago. He'd taken her to Bermuda. She'd only just turned eighteen.

The memories of that trip no longer warmed her, but only stirred her to action. She had a few hours to get to Grand Central.

One final checklist: she was packed, with her money and documents, including their marriage license, and three books she'd checked out from the library. The apartment was neat.

She had a train to catch.

***

Dieter entered the Bier Garten wearing a big grin. His method was working well, and he was about to step up his activities. He'd be bringing in more money to support the cause. Uncle Hermann would be pleased.

CHAPTER TWENTY-FIVE

Wednesday, January 7, 1942

Greco waved Danny into his office. "Monroe called to say the judge gave Babić the chair. The jury convicted the bastard yesterday after deliberating for twenty minutes."

Danny nodded. "Thanks, Lieutenant."

"That's not all. The DA wrote a glowing letter of commendation on you to the commissioner and the Chief of Detectives, as did Tom Donegan at the G." Slang for government agents like the FBI. "You'll get a promotion out of this, for sure. No telling what kind of command posts might come your way down the road."

"If you don't mind, Lieutenant, I'd just as soon stay where I am. I'm not the one for command."

"I beg to differ. You did a magnificent job, working with all those other departments and the FBI, tracking his movements around half the country, getting the postcards from Fr. Flanagan so we had his handwriting. I'd call you a dumb mick if you weren't so goddamned brilliant."

"All the same, I'm happy where I am."

Greco threw his hands in the air. "Okay, here's where you stay until they move you someplace else." He picked up a file.

"Meanwhile, this came in this morning. You can add it to your collection.

Larkin had heard some of it, and as soon as Danny sat at his desk, he gave him the eye. "Please tell me you were just having him on."

"I was not."

Larkin just shook his head. "Fecking jackeen."

Danny tried to immerse himself in the file Greco had given him, an assault on an Orthodox Jewish boy, but he couldn't focus.

"You know what I think, Danny boy? You're still thinking about that sweet bird who spat in Babić's eye. In Woodside, wasn't she? Ain't that just down the road a piece from you in Sunnyside?"

On any other day, he'd have taken Larkin in stride. But not today. "Frankie, do me a favor and shut your gob."

CHAPTER TWENTY-SIX

Three Weeks Later, Friday, January 30, 1942

"Despite heavy allied air attacks, Japanese forces landed in Western Borneo yesterday. In the Philippines, US forces continue to hold the line against Japanese forces advancing on Bataan…"

***

Larkin handed Danny a new file. "You ain't gonna be happy."

He hated when Larkin said that because it was always true. One glance at the report confirmed it. "Grand Concourse and 184th Street. A furniture store. No forced entry, no prints, register cleaned out—total cash loss of $72.50—and *Juden* painted on the window."

"How many is that, now?"

Danny pulled out the file on anti-Semitic burglaries, which he kept separate from anti-Semitic assaults. "That makes nine altogether, four within the past month, all the same method, all at night, all leaving the slur in black paint." He marked the latest site on his map of the Bronx. "And all within a short walk of the Jerome Avenue Line."

"Or the new Concourse Line."

Danny studied his map. Larkin was right, the new line was equally convenient to all but the first reported burglary. "Frankie, my boy, we have our first sign of a pattern. The Concourse is the key. The last three hits have all been in the Forty-Sixth precinct." He read more of the report. "Charlie Lavery caught this one." After a moment, he added, "I'll ask to have all such cases assigned to himself."

Larkin looked askance. "Are you having me on, or have you forgotten that our friend from County Down thinks ill of the sons of Abraham?"

"I have not. But in the current climate, I'm thinking he might make a suitable test case." He called Lavery and asked him to meet them to tour the three burglary sites.

***

Tommy McArdle lit a cigarette and stared out at the Central Park reservoir. "I'm not complaining. But so far, we've been strictly small potatoes. I mean, the money is okay, but this ain't gonna make us rich."

Dieter had been expecting this. "Since our first job, have any police been by to question you? Have you needed to avoid your usual hangouts? Have you hidden away for days on end so no one would see you?"

"No, but…"

"My method works. I pick a target, we observe police activity around it for several nights, and then we strike and leave no trace."

"Except your little love notes."

Dieter shrugged. "Which serves to frustrate the police. Frustration impairs logical thinking, which aids our cause."

Tommy flicked his cigarette into the water. "My cause is money, and I'm making less with this than I was rolling tourists."

"And taking far less risk. You need to balance the two. The most common reason for criminal failure is impatience fed by greed."

"Yeah, but…"

"We will soon expand our efforts. Either you're in or you're out."

"Expanding? Along the Grand Concourse? Won't that increase the risk?"

"No, we'll be finding new target areas. In or out?"

"Well, yeah, sure, I'm in."

As Dieter had expected. "Good, then we'll have no more discussion about it."

***

Meg parked the car in front of the house on Grenfell Street. Hal's mother scowled as she answered the door. "I thought I told you to call before…"

Meg pulled two identical documents from her purse. "Yes, I'm so thoughtless, but I won't take much of your time. I came to give you these."

Hal's mother stood and steadied herself, eyeing the documents with suspicion.

"Oh, don't be nervous. I've given your son what he wants and what I deserve. Freedom. I returned from Mexico last night." She shoved the documents into her former mother-in-law's hands. "Two copies of the divorce decree."

Hal's mother winced at the word divorce. "Oh, for heaven's sake, we need to discuss this in private."

Meg didn't budge. "There's nothing to discuss. I got a Mexican divorce. I could have filed in New York, where my documentation of your son's cruelty, drinking, beating of me and eventual desertion would likely have earned me a sizable alimony award against his future earnings. But I have no desire for any ongoing association with your son. So, I simply took the money from our joint bank accounts and opened a new account in my name in a different bank. Our landlord bought our furniture understanding that I'll leave it behind when I move into my new apartment."

"But…"

"I have a marvelous job—not saying where—and I'll be able to support myself. The car is in your son's name, so I'm leaving it here, with his belongings in two boxes in the back seat." She handed over the keys, waved with a gloved hand and turned to begin her walk to the subway. "Toodleloo."

Free at last.

***

"There he is, Frankie. The star of the County Down."

Detective Charles Lavery turned red. "The 'star of the County Down' was a woman, you fecking jackeen. Now, why has the commissioner's boy dragged me out for a tour of three minor crime scenes?"

"Because they're connected to others outside your precinct. My lieutenant is asking the commissioner to put all such related cases in the Bronx in your hands. That way, I only deal with one detective instead of the lot."

"There's a reason he's the commissioner's boy." Larkin turned to Danny. "Tell him about the G."

Lavery's expression changed from irritation to alarm. "What's the FBI got to do with this?"

Frankie, you should have kept your gob shut. Now, there's no choice. "They're looking at anything that could indicate a re-emergence of the Bund."

Lavery scowled. "Now that Roosevelt's gotten us into his war at last."

"In case you haven't noticed," Larkin replied, "the Japs attacked us, and Germany declared war on us four days later. It was in all the papers."

Time to bring this back on track. "Save the politics for another time, lads. We're dealing with a skilled burglar making a statement. He's confined himself to a narrow corridor of activity. Officers walking beats in the Forty-Sixth on the graveyard shift should be alerted to it. In our precinct, too."

"He hasn't hit our precinct," Larkin said.

"No, but he's going to extend himself, and we're a logical choice."

Lavery showed some interest. "Where was the first break-in?"

"Up near Bronx Science," Danny replied.

"So, you think the burglar is a Bronx guy?"

Danny shook his head. "His corridor of activity so far is along two subway lines to Manhattan. Also, the burglaries may be tied to a string of assaults, mostly in Manhattan. He may live there, but these cases aren't enough to draw a conclusion."

"And does your reach extend that far?" Lavery asked.

"Further," Larkin said. "Even Staten Island." They all laughed.

CHAPTER TWENTY-SEVEN

Six Weeks Later, Monday, March 16, 1942

"Despite Russian advances on Kharkov, Adolph Hitler predicts his panzers will destroy Russia's forces by the summer. Meanwhile, Tokyo broadcast a claim that fifty thousand men, including US forces, had been captured in Java..."

***

Several of Danny's colleagues had already enlisted, despite the exemption from military service afforded by their jobs. Since hearing the news of the Pearl Harbor attack, Danny had been agonizing over his own decision.

Larkin had noticed. "You're not still on about enlisting, I hope."

"It's the right thing to do. We can't be standing around waiting to catch purse snatchers and pickpockets with a war on. How many homicide cases have we caught since Millie Panagos?"

Frankie waved him away, muttering, "Fecking daft jackeen."

The answer was two, which was why Greco hadn't batted an eye as Danny spent more time investigating anti-Semitic crimes.

"One old man will not turn the tide of war," Larkin added.

"Thirty-one is not old."

"Almost thirty-two. Fancy taking orders from some twenty-three-year-old lieutenant fresh from West Point?"

As if on cue, Greco summoned Danny into his office, where Cogan was waiting. "What's the latest on our Nazi burglar?"

"Nothing since the break-in on Bronxdale Avenue a week ago Thursday. It was the third in as many weeks, all in that neighborhood, bringing the total to seven. Lavery figures he now comes and goes by the White Plains Road line, and he's requested the Forty-Third precinct alert all beat cops on the graveyard shift to keep a sharp eye out."

"That's four precincts alerted so far, including ours, and no results. Why these neighborhoods?"

"If you want to fish, you go where the fish are. Morris Park and the stretch along the Grand Concourse are heavily Jewish areas. The one that makes little sense is the one by Bedford Park Boulevard. Not heavily Jewish, and the store name isn't Jewish, yet this guy knew the owner was a Jew."

Cogan nodded. "That's why I suspect there's more in these burglaries than meets the eye. With Gerhard Kunze having fled to Mexico and the Bund dead at last, our entry into the war can only mean these activities take on sinister implications. Your role will become even more important."

Greco stood. "We're on it, Bill. Danny, here, will keep you posted."

"Thanks." Cogan left.

Danny closed the door and resumed his seat. "I need to talk to you about something else."

Greco stared at his desk. "Let me guess: you're off to fight the enemy."

"I've been giving it a great deal of thought, yes."

"Then please consider that in a country of a hundred and thirty million people, we'll have little trouble raising an army to fight the Japs and the Germans. But how will we fight the other enemy, the hidden one that worries Cogan? They won't be in uniform or arrive in tanks and planes, and they're the ones who could disrupt our war effort."

"Sounds like something the mayor should handle," Danny said.

"LaGuardia talks a lot about curbing anti-Semitic violence, but you and I both know that some cops just won't raise a finger, and LaGuardia can't do much about it. Irish cops are getting a bad name because a lot of the trouble comes from the Irish."

"So, you want me to stay because I'm Irish?" Enlistment was looking better with each passing moment.

"Come off it, Danny. I want you because you're a damned fine cop and have the brains to handle this assignment." Greco softened his voice. "I need you on this, but I need you fully committed to it. If you want to enlist, Lord knows I can't stop you and I wouldn't try. Take the week off to think it through and tell me your decision when you return."

CHAPTER TWENTY-EIGHT

Thursday, March 19, 1942

So far, Danny had resolved nothing. A long walk had taken him to the Woodside Public Library on Skillman Avenue.

That's what he needed, a good book. He'd had his library card for over two years and only used it once.

He stepped inside. Hardly a soul, except a white-haired woman sitting and reading. Near the front desk, a table displayed recently published books. He scanned the titles, but nothing appealed to him.

"Detective Brady?"

A soft, sweet voice that he recognized even before he turned to face her. "Mrs. Corwyn? This is a surprise." She was wearing a light coat, having entered the library behind him.

"Please call me Meg. I work here. Are you looking for something?"

"Yes, but I've not a clue what. Maybe you could help me. And please call me Dan."

"Be glad to, but..."

A young woman approached. "Miss O'Rourke, are you back from your lunch break, now?"

"Yes, Sheila," Meg replied. "Please tell Miss Soloway."

"Miss O'Rourke?" Danny asked.

Meg blushed. "It's a long story, and I'm afraid I have to get back to work."

"Does that mean you can help me find something?"

She slipped off her coat. "In here? I can find anything."

A sudden inspiration. "Do you have a copy of *The Informer* by Liam O'Flaherty?"

She hung up her coat and pointed to a cluster of stacked bookshelves. "That's the fiction section. Book are arranged by the author's last name, so…"

"Look for O." He found the correct row, and a couple of minutes later, he found the book. He returned to the Research desk. "Found it. Thank you."

"You're quite welcome. If you take it to the front desk, Sheila will check it out for you."

He hesitated. She'd given a firm hint that she didn't want to go into it, but he had to know. He bent down and lowered his voice, trying not to be distracted by her rich, dark curls. "Do you go by Miss O'Rourke for professional reasons?"

Her sweet smile vanished, and she lowered her voice. "No. I divorced Hal. O'Rourke is my maiden name."

"And a lovely one it is. I'm sorry, Meg. I didn't mean to pry."

"Perfectly all right. Enjoy the book."

There was a spring to his step as he walked back to his apartment. She'd cut herself loose from that pathetic gobshite.

CHAPTER TWENTY-NINE

Friday, March 20, 1942

Danny knew before he answered the ringing phone it would be Larkin.

"So, have you decided yet, Danny boy?"

"I have not." Although he had. "Things must be slow for you to be making personal phone calls at the department's expense."

"Ah, they are that. Are you at least nearing a decision?"

Danny picked up *The Informer* with his free hand. "Monday, Frankie."

***

Meg checked her watch. Five minutes to five, the last checkouts were done, and only Miss Soloway and Sheila remained in the library with her.

"Go ahead, Sheila," Meg said. "We'll close up."

"Thanks."

As Sheila walked out, Meg turned out all the lights except those over the front desk.

"Give me a minute," Miss Soloway said. "Just getting my coat."

Meg slipped into hers as the main door opened. "Sheila? You're back?"

"Dan Brady. Am I too late? It's not quite five." He held up *The Informer.* "Just wanted to return this."

"We can't check it in, now," Miss Soloway said. "We're closing."

But there was something about the detective's expression. "That's all right, Miss Soloway, I'll leave it here on the front desk and check it back in tomorrow morning."

Miss Soloway bit her lip. "How kind of you. You go ahead, Miss O'Rourke, and I'll lock up."

Wait. She hadn't meant…

He held the door for her, and they started walking along Skillman Avenue. "Sorry about that. I lost track of the time today."

"You finished it in a day. You must enjoy reading."

"I do when I have the time. I've taken a week off and found I had more time than I wanted. But I stayed up all night reading, and I finished it before the sun came up. You see, I've read it before. Do you walk to work?"

"Yes. I live on Skillman, between 47th and 48th Street."

"We're practically neighbors. I'm on 45th between Skillman and 39th Avenue."

"One of those courts with the private gardens? How lovely. Mine is a basement studio apartment, so I don't have access to the garden in the back, just the tiny square of green in front. But I love it all the same. What drew you back to *The Informer*?"

He thought a moment. "The story takes place in Dublin in the early twenties. I was just a lad back then, running messages for the Sinn Féin and the Volunteers. I knew Michael Collins and men like the characters in the book."

This was fascinating. "When did you come to this country?"

"After Collins, the first president of the Republic, was assassinated amid a civil war, I feared the violence would never end. When me ma died in 1927, I was seventeen. I scraped money together to emigrate. Once here, I wanted to help keep a strong and just peace."

He'd been ten in 1920, the year she was born. That made him 31 or 32 now. He looked younger but sounded older.

"Re-reading the book helped me with a tough decision." He explained his dilemma about enlisting. "I felt obligated to come to the country's defense, like so many others."

She stopped to let a car pass. "It's none of my business, but I hope you decide to defend the country at home."

His eyes locked on hers. "It is your business, Meg. I like you and I respect your judgment. And, yes, I've decided not to enlist." They resumed walking. "Greco—my lieutenant—suggested I apply for a command position, but I like what I do and a jackeen like myself has no business in administration."

"What's a jackeen?"

"An uncomplimentary term for someone from Dublin, usually used by culchies."

She couldn't help giggling. "An uncomplimentary term for…?"

"Country folk."

They arrived at the attached house with the separate entrance to her basement apartment under the main entrance. He turned serious again. "Could I perhaps have your phone number?"

For a moment, she couldn't breathe. It wasn't a casual request. She fumbled in her purse for a pencil and a scrap of paper and wrote her phone number, all the while seized by doubt.

He'd already taken it when she decided it was a mistake. "Dan, I'm sorry, but I'm not ready to see anyone. Thank you for walking me home." She made her way down the steps, trying to forget his stunned expression.

CHAPTER THIRTY

Monday, March 23, 1942
"General Jonathan Wainwright ignored a Japanese ultimatum of surrender of Bataan and Corregidor, while allied planes flew raids on several Japanese strongholds north of Australia, including Lae and Rabaul…"

***

Other than a terse, "Fine," Greco made no comment on Danny's decision to stay. Larkin was waiting for him.

Larkin grinned. "Back to the grindstone, Danny boy. Jimmy Fitzgibbon had a burglary Saturday night, pawn shop on Tenth Avenue and 43rd Street."

Manhattan. Danny had met Detective Jimmy Fitzgibbon at a St. Patrick's Day party several years earlier when a fight had broken out. Fitzgibbon, built like a tank with flaming red hair, had waded into the cluster of combatants and, single-handed, quelled the fight. When a captain demanded an explanation, Fitzgibbon had replied, "It's all a misunderstanding, Captain. Ya see, this fella from the Bronx bent down to pick up a dollar bill he'd dropped, and clunked heads with a fella from Manhattan, and everyone rushed to their aid to see if they were all right. Me and him…" He pointed to Danny.

Danny had immediately added, "We were just sorting it all out, and no injuries, saints be praised." Fitzgibbon and Danny had been fast friends ever since.

"Don't tell me," Danny said. "Jewish owner."

"Right you are, boyo," Larkin said, "another break-in with no break. Not a scratch."

"Sounds like our guy. But why would a pro knock over a pawn shop?"

Larkin clapped a hand on Danny's shoulder. "Exactly what Fitzgibbon said."

"I'm sure Jimmy said more than that." Fitzgibbon wasn't shy about his opinions.

Larkin chuckled. "Ask him yourself. Here he comes."

"Always glad to see a fellow former Dubliner," Jimmy said, his hand extended.

Danny took it. "And how's yourself?"

"Glad you're still with us. Word is you're the man to see about this stuff."

Larkin spoke up. "He is, indeed."

Danny turned serious. "Frankie tells me this one looks like someone who's been active in our neck of the woods."

Fitzgibbon nodded. "Broke in without a scratch, like the door had been left unlocked. The thief grabbed some watches and silverware and cleaned out what little cash was in the till. We dusted for fingerprints. Nothing."

Danny made some notes. "Sounds right. Anything else of note?" Jimmy would mention any painted slurs.

"Yeah. I said he broke in without a scratch. But he scratched this." He laid a photo on Danny's desk, a glass countertop with a swastika scratched into it. “Must have used a sharp instrument or a key.”

Danny studied the image. The symbol was composed of single lines neatly scratched within a block outline. “He took his time.”

“He did at that. The local precinct had a foot patrol officer in the neighborhood on the twelve-to-eight, and he passed the shop every ninety minutes. Never saw a thing. So, the burglar studied his moves before he made his. That’s a lot of trouble to knock over a pawn shop.”

Greco joined the discussion. “It’s a lot of trouble for the places he’s hit up here, too.”

“Since then,” Jimmy said, “my boys and I have been running down any pros we have on file. They all have alibis and claim they never heard of a job like this.”

“Sounds like our boy has expanded into other boroughs,” Greco said.

Danny recapped the eight incidents. “This is the shortest interval he’s gone, yet.”

“Yeah,” Larkin said, “but he didn’t paint the window this time.”

“Late night in Manhattan is busier than up here,” Danny replied. “The swastika inside is less risky than the painted slur outside.”

Greco agreed and turned to Fitzgibbon “What’s your territory these days?”

Fitzgibbon scowled. “Good question. Detectives and uniforms have been enlisting in droves, so I’m on call for anything on the west side from Hell’s Kitchen to Inwood.”

“Lieutenant,” Danny said, “we need a point man in Manhattan. I think Jimmy, here, would do just fine.” When he saw the horrified look on Fitzgibbon’s face, he added, “we have pull with the commissioner. Might get you off the other duties.”

“Not that much pull,” Greco replied, “but I’ll see what I can do.”

"Meanwhile," Danny said, "please call the precincts with Jewish-owned businesses in their neighborhoods and have them step up overnight foot patrols."

Fitzgibbon rolled his eyes. "Sure thing, Danny. Anything else? In me spare time, that is?"

"Yes. Have them make their passes at irregular intervals and keep me informed on the assaults.

CHAPTER THIRTY-ONE

Wednesday, March 25, 1942

Danny was staring at the board. No new entries since Monday.

"Still thinking the assaults and burglaries are connected, Danny boy?" But Larkin's voice had an edge.

He was worried. "The first of the assaults we've been tracking occurred in the Bronx. Now, they're all in Manhattan. All the burglaries have been in the Bronx until this last one, also in Manhattan."

"Meaning what?"

"Damned if I know, Frankie."

Greco joined them. "Ah, there's good news, though. The commissioner has approved making Fitzgibbon your Manhattan coordinator and relieving him of all non-homicide cases other than these."

***

It was nearly midnight when the beat cop passed Stoneman's jewelry shop on East 161st Street, half a block from Morris Avenue. This was the third night Dieter had watched him, and he now knew the cop always followed a brief interval with a long one. His previous interval had been a mere ten minutes, so this one would be much longer.

Tommy McArdle nudged him after the cop had passed. “We gonna move, or did you drag me up here just to watch cops all night?”

“I want to be sure.” He studied his watch.

“Well?”

Tommy had a point. Wait, and the cop would be back before they had time to break in and get out. “Okay, you stay here, and if the cop comes back, act drunk and get loud. That’ll be my alarm. If someone else comes along, ask for subway fare home or some other excuse, but keep their attention away from the shop. Either way, beat it, and we’ll meet up tomorrow at three in Central Park, Bethesda Fountain.”

Tommy pulled out a flask and splashed some whiskey on his face and clothes. “Sounds easy. My usual cut?”

Dieter nodded and slipped around to the back alley and the rear entrance to the shop. This was the third job on which he was using Tommy as a lookout. So far, he hadn’t needed him, but the cop’s irregular movements made Dieter uncomfortable.

One lock in the knob, and a deadlock above it. As he drew out his tools, he realized he’d forgotten his gloves. He’d need to wipe clean everything he touched.

The deadlock took three minutes. Twenty seconds after that, he was inside the shop. The register was empty, as was the cash box underneath. No quick cash from this one. Tommy wouldn’t be happy.

The glass display cases were undisturbed, the sliding doors locked. They were easy to pick, and he had the first one open in seconds. Gold necklaces, some with gold pendants, and gold bracelets, some with diamond insets. He pocketed them all.

On to the second case, which contained rings and watches. He cleaned it out and started to scratch a swastika before moving on to the third.

“My wild Irissshh rose…” Tommy. The cop must have come back. Shit.

He took a quick inventory, counting his tools. He had them all.

“A happy good evening, Officer. I was at a party, now I’m kinda lossht. Which way to the shubway?”

At least Tommy was walking him away from the store, but if the cop knew enough to double back to the shop early, he’d come right back after dropping Tommy off.

In the office behind the store, he found a bottle of carbon tetrachloride and a rag and wiped down the register, display cases, and the knob on the rear door.

CHAPTER THIRTY-TWO

Thursday, March 26, 1942

When Danny arrived just before eight, there was no coffee left in the station house. He was relegated to tea. He was still steeping his tea bag when the night desk sergeant entered the break room.

"I see they left you high and dry, Detective. Sorry about that. But one patrolman, McHugh, had a curious incident and came back late, stayed until three typing it up. He was walking his beat and noticed two lads, both in their late teens, strolling about but not actually going anywhere. He didn't like the look of it, and when he doubled back, he found only one, to all appearances drunk as a skunk."

"But he wasn't?"

"Quiet one minute, and a loud drunk ten minutes later. Didn't stagger much walking to the subway, and he sometimes forgot to slur. It's all in McHugh's report."

"Thanks." Danny returned to his desk and took up the report. McHugh had performed a close inspection of each of the shops. Something about Stoneman's jewelry store didn't look right. The front door was secure, so he walked around to the rear and found the rear door open, no forced entry. Inside, he found two of the three display cases were empty, but no evidence that they'd been forced open. Police presence was requested to watchdog the site. Fingerprint unit found no prints.

Danny checked the address of Stoneman's place. It was too far to walk. He dialed Jimmy Fitzgibbon's home number in Inwood. "Good morning, Jimmy. Pass a quiet evening last night?"

"I hope your call so early on my day off isn't a bad omen." It came out as a groan.

He must be hung over. "Ah, sure'n it's a friendly call on a lovely spring morning." Might as well have a bit of fun.

"You're an evil man, you are, Brady. Do me a favor and tell me, in as few words as possible, why you've interrupted my personal purgatory this morning."

Time to get serious. "I caught another burglary overnight. I haven't been at the scene, yet, but my gut tells me it's our friend. No forced entry, back door locks picked, display case locks picked, no prints."

"Yeah, could be the same guy."

"Except that guy didn't leave any prints. Our guys found no prints at all."

It took Jimmy a minute, but then he wasn't at his best. "None? In a jewelry store? That means…"

"That's right, Jimmy. The owner's prints should have been there, along with some customers' and any employees. But the whole place was wiped clean. Even the knobs on the back door, inside and outside. What's that suggest to you?"

A long silence. "He isn't a pro."

"My thoughts, exactly. A pro never would break in without gloves. I need a favor."

"Danny, it's my day off, for Christ's sake. We can meet at the shop tomorrow morning."

"I don't need you at the shop. The patrolman left me this description of the accomplice."

"Wait, let me get this down on paper."

"Okay, Irish kid in his late teens, five foot ten, about a hundred and fifty pounds but muscular, unruly dark brown hair, green eyes, nose bent slightly to the left like it was busted once."

"Sounds like a kid we've been watching, runs with a gang from Hell's Kitchen. Name is Tommy McArdle. We liked him for a string of muggings near the piers and started laying for him, but they stopped last September. What makes you think this kid was helping the burglar? Other than acting drunk when he wasn't?"

"The previous pass the patrolman had made, the shop was okay, but when he returned, the burglary had already occurred. I don't like coincidences. Can you run this McArdle character down and check his story?"

Jimmy's groan would have made the saints weep.

***

With Larkin and Charlie Lavery out and Rossi nowhere to be seen, Danny drove to Seth Stoneman's jewelry shop. The Crime Scene guys were already at work, including a photographer.

Mr. Stoneman was short, bald with just a fringe of gray hair, and inconsolable. "I had locks on the door, locks on the cases. What else could I do?"

"We'll talk about that later. He came in and left by the back door. Can you give me a list of the jewelry he took, and an estimate of what each was worth?"

Thinking over Danny's request had a calming effect, and the jeweler stopped sobbing. "Yes. I keep a listing back in my office of the contents of each section of the display. Will my asking price do as an estimate of value?"

"Absolutely. You mind if I look around in the meantime?"

"Sure, because if I can't trust a detective…" He wandered back to his office.

It wasn't a large shop, with six feet of space between the far wall and the display cases below the glass counter, behind which the proprietor could walk in a space four feet wide, and at the end of which stood the cash register. Behind the walk space stood another counter, with large glass display cases above it, none of which had been touched.

The burglar hadn't been there long.

"See anything you like, Detective?" The jeweler's voice startled him.

For a moment, Danny pictured a pearl necklace on Meg O'Rourke, but he shook it off. "Too rich for my blood."

The jeweler shrugged. "I can always work something out, especially for a police detective."

Maybe someday. "Thanks, but right now, I'd like to understand how this happened. Have you had any workmen in here recently?" It was too much to ask that Stoneman might have had a locksmith in, but no harm in asking.

The jeweler pondered it. "Just a glazier, about two weeks ago. Someone had thrown a rock at my front window and cracked it."

"An attempted break-in? Did you report it?"

A tired laugh. "No, it wasn't a break-in attempt, just another act of vandalism. And if I reported every one of those, neither you nor I would get any other work done." He sighed. "I suppose it goes with the times."

"How many have you had?"

Stoneman paused to think. "I'd say half a dozen since Pearl Harbor. The cracked window was the worst. Usually, they chalk swastikas on the sidewalk or smear dog dirt on the window. I put it down to kids." He laid a sheet of paper on the counter. "I've penciled in the prices next to each item. You can take it and copy it, but I'll need it back."

Danny placed the sheet on the counter and read, but his eye caught something else. "Mr. Stoneman, can you please look at this for me? Here, on the glass top, these scratches."

Stoneman examined them. "Odd, I don't remember that. I work hard to protect this counter, but perhaps I scratched it without realizing, placing something heavy on it."

Danny's gut told him something quite different. "Look closely, because that doesn't look like an accidental scratch." He waved a crime scene photographer over to get a close-up.

Stoneman chuckled. "You have a jeweler's eye, Detective, and you're correct, that couldn't be a casual scratch. The lines are equal in length and form a right angle." He grew serious. "What does it mean?"

"I couldn't say." Danny measured the lines. Both were exactly one inch long. "You asked me how to make this place more secure. I suggest new locks that are harder to pick and a burglar alarm." He handed his card to Stoneman. "In the meantime, please keep me informed of any acts of vandalism, no matter how trivial."

CHAPTER THIRTY-THREE

Dieter glanced around Riverside Park, as he didn't want his conversation with Tommy McArdle to be overheard. "Keep it down. There's a reason I wanted to meet you here."

"But a bracelet, a necklace and a ring?" Tommy was livid. "What about the cash? That flatfoot saw me real good. You realize I can't go home?"

Dieter started walking him along the path. "Yes, caution is advisable. There was no cash in the shop, but the bracelet is solid gold and those are diamonds embedded in it. The heart-shaped locket is solid gold, as is the diamond ring. Three valuable pieces, but don't pawn them for a while. Jews keep police well paid to protect them, and they'll be watching."

"Great. So, when's our next job, and how about one with cash?"

"We must be careful, but in the meantime, please have your friends keep up their activities with Jewish students."

"You said there'd be better money in this. Maybe I should go back to rolling tourists."

Dieter glared at him. "I expected better judgment from you."

Tommy blanched. Message received.

Dieter softened his tone and slipped Tommy five dollars. "In the meantime, stay out of sight. This should hold you for a few days. We'll meet at the Central Park boat house on Saturday at ten. If one of us can't be there, we'll try again next Tuesday afternoon at two."

"Dieter, is there something going on I should know about?"

"No."

***

When Danny returned to the precinct, he made two phone calls. The first was to the patrolman who'd discovered the burglary, Officer Sean McHugh, who confirmed he'd doubled back to the shop only fifteen minutes after his previous pass, and he'd heard nothing until he met up with the teenager, when the boy started with the drunk act.

The second call was to Bill Cogan. "A local jewelry shop was knocked over last night, and the method matches the others."

"He's getting ambitious, I see. Any paint or swastikas?"

Danny described the scratches on the counter. "They were the same size and at the same angle as part of the swastika in the pawn shop. Indications are a beat cop interrupted the proceedings, and the burglar got out of Dodge. If it is our guy, we've added to his profile: he works with an accomplice. Our Manhattan guy is now tracking down a suspect."

"So, the burglar is a pro after all."

"No, a pro would work alone. He wouldn't leave a calling card, and even if he did, he'd clean out the goods before he left it."

"What makes you think he didn't?"

"Because the most valuable stuff was in the undisturbed display cases. It was at least as important to him to leave the swastika as making off with the goods."

Cogan thought that over. "Sounds like another kid."

"Exactly. Now, you said the Bund was headquartered somewhere in Manhattan."

"Yes, Yorkville, in the East 80s and 90s, heavily German-American."

"I'm guessing our Nazi-sympathizing kid burglar is related to a locksmith. Any locksmiths from Yorkville or any other heavily German neighborhoods in your files who might be old enough to have a son or nephew in his late teens?" He'd leave for a later time the problem of how a German kid from the East 80s could have hooked up with an Irish kid from the West 50s.

"I'll get my guys started on it."

Danny glanced at the clock—only an hour until end-of-tour, and still nothing from Jimmy, which could only mean he hadn't found Tommy McArdle.

Not a good sign.

***

Hermann began the discussion. "Dieter has made progress on two fronts, *ja*?"

His nephew fought to suppress a grin. "*Ja.* My Irish friends are expanding their attacks beyond Jewish students to adults and businesses. One has been assisting me on the burglaries, from which you already have the proceeds. The most recent one was quite profitable."

"Many items of jewelry," Hermann replied.

Dieter continued. "I also leave a swastika in each shop we hit."

Hans scowled. "That's madness, telling the police we're behind it."

Dieter was unfazed. "The burglaries are not just to wrest ill-gotten gains from the Jews. They are also to terrorize them, and the swastikas tell them that Nazis will not let them escape unscathed. Yes, they understand Nazis did this, but they cannot know which Nazis. I break in without a scratch, leave no fingerprints, as quiet as the night, and my targets have been mostly in the Bronx, not Manhattan."

"Excellent." Hermann turned to Hans. "You and Paul dispose of the items Dieter's skill has procured for us and return the cash to me. Use multiple pawn shops, spread out around Manhattan."

"But none in Yorkville?" Paul asked.

"Correct."

Hans refused to back down. "You sound like you are giving commands."

"Someone must, because if we wait for you to stumble to a solution, the thousand-year Reich will be at an end. Christian, what have you got for us?"

"The navy yard is much better guarded now than when we began meeting last summer, and we are closely watched. I'll keep looking for opportunities, but we may do better to consider a power station or key transportation point."

CHAPTER THIRTY-FOUR

Friday, March 27, 1942

Meg locked her front door and climbed the steps into a frigid gust, making her crave spring.

"Hello, Meg."

She stopped in her tracks. She'd been trying to avoid thinking about Danny. Now, he was standing by his car on Skillman Avenue.

"Sorry to ambush you," he said. "Have you listened to the news this morning?"

She'd been sluggish dressing for work and so had left the radio off. "No. Why?"

"Please let me drive you to the library. I have something to tell you."

"Can't you just tell me here? It's only eight blocks."

"Please trust me, Meg." He held the passenger door open as she slid in, then got in the driver's side. "George Babić was executed last night up in Sing Sing."

Her attacker was finally dead.

"I didn't want you to hear it on the radio. I wanted to tell you in person." He started the engine.

Babić, the man who'd violated her, torn her marriage apart, and thrown her life into turmoil, was gone. Her eyes welled with tears.

Without a word, Danny offered a handkerchief, which made her smile.

"The record shows that Babić was executed for the murder of Millie Panagos," he said at last. "But you and I understand Babić paid for every woman he attacked, every life he sullied, and all the pain he inflicted. I realize it's not nearly enough, Meg, but it's something."

She pondered that as he drove. In losing her marriage, she'd learned that Hal had never been the husband she wanted and deserved. Now that Babić was dead, perhaps the shadow hanging over her would lift.

Neither said another word until he pulled over. "The library, Miss O'Rourke."

"Thank you, Danny, for everything." He'd been her best support. "And you're right, it is something."

"Time to get back to living."

***

The expression on Bill Cogan's face as he took the empty seat told Danny he'd drawn a blank.

"We didn't keep tabs on every Bund member, only the leaders and most active members, and none of them were locksmiths. Although they were headquartered in Yorkville, their membership was spread out all over the city. The clusters were in Yorkville, the East Side south of 14th Street, and Williamsburg over in Brooklyn, but they could have lived anywhere." He glanced at the blackboard. "Incidents are piling up."

And simply listing them, even with locations, wasn't providing any insights. "We should continue to list every incident, but not on the board. The board should be limited to repeat victims, repeat locations, and incidents of a more serious nature, such as the burglaries or anything involving serious injury or property damage."

"How does that help?" Larkin asked.

"Makes the damned board easier to read," Danny replied with a sigh, "which makes it easier to see patterns. But all we've got are the burglaries in two boroughs." He brightened as Fitzgibbon entered, but then he saw the look on his face. "Please tell me you've got something."

"Sorry, Danny, not a thing. I swear, my boys practically strip-searched the entire west side, and that kid is nowhere to be seen."

Danny wrote McArdle's name on the board. "He's gone underground, knows McHugh saw him up close, and realizes we're on his tail. Call off the manhunt."

Fitzgibbon was stunned. "What?"

Larkin almost spilled his coffee. "Are you having us on?"

"I am not. Our G-man, here, says the burglar could be anywhere in the city. I take it McArdle is crafty, capable at lying low?"

Fitzgibbon nodded. "He is."

"Then the best way to flush them both out is to ease off, let them think we've given up, moved on. Have a couple of undercovers monitor his neighborhood, but they're not to grab him if they see him, just monitor his movements."

"Doesn't that risk another business getting knocked over?" Larkin continued to regard him with caution.

"Probably, providing another opportunity to see a pattern or some clue as to the operation. In the meantime, Jimmy, here are several copies I made last night of the list of stolen goods from Stoneman's shop. Please have your guys check with the pawn shops around Manhattan for any items they've seen."

"Pawn shops in Manhattan." Fitzgibbon shook his head. "Care to narrow that down a little?"

"Start from midtown and work your way outward. Frankie and I will take the Bronx, and I'll get a detail on it in Brooklyn."

Vinnie Rossi walked by. "Morning, boys. A meeting of the Emerald Society?"

Danny grinned at him. "Vinnie, me boy, you've just been drafted." He handed a copy of the list to Rossi and nodded toward Larkin. "You'll be joining himself and me in a search of Bronx pawn shops for any of these stolen goods."

Rossi's face fell. "Thanks."

"Danny," Cogan said, "I'll have someone contact Brooklyn, and we'll get your list over to them, since you're already stretched pretty thin."

CHAPTER THIRTY-FIVE

Tuesday, March 31, 1942

Dieter watched as Tommy approached Bethesda Fountain as if he didn't have a care in the world. That boy had so much to learn. While his campaign against Jewish students was going well, Tommy was hopeless in more complex matters.

"Why the long face?" Tommy asked. "The heat's off."

Dieter started walking. "Who told you that?"

"Everyone who's had cops knocking on their doors for three days. They've stopped, and probably gave up. Any luck fencing the goods?"

"Waiting for the police to lose the scent." He cast a sidelong glance at Tommy. "I hope you haven't tried, either."

"No, I'm waiting for the word from you."

"Good. Don't believe for a moment the police have lost interest. They're hoping we'll drop our guard, and we must remain vigilant."

"You mean I have to keep lying low?"

"Exactly." Dieter slipped him another five dollars. "I wouldn't want you to starve."

"What the hell am I supposed to do with five bucks?"

“Spend it wisely and inconspicuously, and don’t be insulted because my next job will be solo.”

Tommy stopped and glared at him. “You just said we have to lie low.”

“No, I said we must remain vigilant. You lie low because they know what you look like. They have no clue who I am or where I’m likely to strike. Striking now will frustrate them.”

“What about carrying the goods?”

“I’ll worry about that. Meet me under the clock at Grand Central Friday morning at 8:30.”

CHAPTER THIRTY-SIX

Wednesday, April 1, 1942

Greco's ash tray was already full of butts when Danny walked in at eight in the morning, and he just gave him the bare facts: 90th Precinct, Brooklyn, a shoe store on Division Avenue, Williamsburg, large Jewish concentration, mixed with second generation German-Americans.

"Now, there's a lovely combination," Larkin said as they drove off.

Danny parked a block away from the store. "The subway might have been quicker." The Brooklyn crime scene guys had already established a perimeter, but a nervous crowd kept vigil.

A lieutenant greeted Danny as they approached. "Brady, right? Glad you're here. Brace yourself, it's ugly."

Before Danny could ask how ugly a shoe store burglary could be, they were inside and nearly overcome by the stench. "What in God's name is that?"

The lieutenant, now holding a handkerchief over his face, pointed to an enormous pile of shoes in the center of the store. "All the display shoes and some of the stock. He made a pile and then dumped a bottle of acid on it."

Danny continued to the glass top counter. The register drawer was open and empty, and an empty cash box lay open on the floor. "How much did he get?"

"The owner and his son arrived around 6:30 this morning," the lieutenant replied. "The old man was overcome by the fumes the minute he walked in. No forced entry. The son says there was about sixty bucks in the cash box."

"Anyone touch this counter?"

"Just the fingerprint guys dusting for prints."

Danny peered at the glass top. "Son of a bitch." There was the scratched-out swastika, exactly as it had been in the Times Square pawn shop. "Is there a phone, here?"

For the first time, the owner's son spoke. "In the stock room."

The stock room was a mess, with fallen boxes and shoes scattered on the floor. A pay phone hung just inside the door. Danny called Cogan and told him the latest.

"Three boroughs," Cogan said. "Makes little sense."

"That's what he wants us to think."

Cogan remained silent.

Danny elaborated. "He's methodical. After starting in the Bronx, he hits Manhattan, then back to the Bronx, followed by a thrust in the opposite direction to Brooklyn."

"So, you think he lives in the Bronx?"

"No, more likely Manhattan, like his sidekick. These outward thrusts are to convince us he can hit anywhere, which suggests his next target will be in Queens."

"Isn't Queens mostly farmland?"

Danny laughed at the common misconception. "Lots of building in the past twenty years, but I expect he'll hit older sections like Kew Gardens or Forest Hills."

Larkin was waiting for him. "No one saw anything. This area gets real quiet at night. You sure it's our guy?"

"He left his signature on the counter." Danny went back to the pay phone and called Greco with the update.

"Glad you called. We heard from a pawn shop on the Lower East Side, north side of Delancey between Norfolk and Essex. A guy pawned a gold necklace and a couple of watches this morning. I was about to call Fitzgibbon."

"Thanks. Please have him meet us there. We're leaving now."

***

Meg hung up her coat after returning from lunch and froze as she turned to sit at her desk. A single rose had been placed on the seat.

She strolled to the front desk, peering around the library. The sole visitor, an elderly woman, sat in a chair by the window, reading. "Sheila, was anyone else here while I was out?"

Sheila nodded toward the woman. "She's been sitting there the whole time. And a boy from St. Sebastian stopped in. Why?"

Meg held up the rose.

Sheila giggled. "You have a secret admirer."

"What did he look like?"

"An older boy, seventh or eighth grade." She giggled again. "He's in love."

"Did he go near my desk?"

"Sorry, Meg, I was shelving books and didn't notice." Sheila retrieved a small vase.

Meg waved her away. "I'm not going to keep it."

"Oh, you must. If he comes back and doesn't see it, he'll be crushed."

Meg studied Sheila's face. "Why are you so interested?"

But Sheila laughed. "Ease up, Meg. He's at that age and it's spring."

"Okay." She grinned, filled the vase with water, and placed it on her desk with the rose.

***

"What do you mean, he wasn't a kid?" Danny fought to remain calm.

"He looked about forty," the pawn shop owner said, "stocky, brown hair, brown eyes. spoke with a slight German accent. I could tell he didn't know anything about jewelry. He took what I offered."

"How much was that?" Danny asked.

"Seventy-five for the lot. Here's the bill of sale. I had a feeling I might need it."

There had to be more to it. "Was anyone with him?"

"Nope, didn't give a name, either."

And if he had, it wouldn't have been his real one. "Okay, we'll take these to see if they're the ones that were stolen. If they're not, we'll get them right back to you. Thanks."

"Think it's the burglar's dad, helping the lad out of a tight spot?" Larkin laughed as if he'd made a joke.

Danny wasn't laughing. "Could be, but if it isn't, this thing gets even more sinister."

Larkin turned serious. "How so?"

"It's not just a couple of kids, adults are involved, which suggests a bigger agenda." As he crossed the Macombs Dam Bridge, Danny added, "For once, I wouldn't mind if a lead didn't pan out."

But the moment Mr. Stoneman saw the necklace and watches, his face lit up.

***

By four in the afternoon, they'd heard from three more pawn shops.

One near Union Square reported a man matching the description of the Delancey Street customer had pawned three gold neck chains with pendants and two rings, saying his wife was sick, and they needed to pawn her jewelry to pay her medical bills. Rossi had been dispatched to collect the items and Stoneman had identified them as among the stolen items.

The second, around the corner from the Foster Hotel, where they'd arrested George Babić, reported a tall thin man in his thirties, with blond hair and blue eyes pawning two diamond rings, two watches, and a gold pendant. Jimmy Fitzgibbon had retrieved the items, and Stoneman had verified they were his.

The last, near Times Square, had reported a short, stocky man with olive skin and black hair pawning a gold brooch, but Danny didn't bother since no brooch appeared on the list of stolen items.

Danny noted that half the stolen items had been recovered. He entered the information on the blackboard while Greco watched. "We now have the makings of a ring: two kids, two adults. I'd give my right arm to bag that Irish kid because he ain't a true believer."

"What makes you say that?"

"Most American kids wouldn't know a Nazi from a taxidermist. An Irish tough from Hell's Kitchen is hired help for sure, easy to squeeze."

"Where does that leave us until we can find him?"

Danny pointed to the upper right-hand corner of the blackboard. "A pro-Nazi ring, mostly adults but with one kid with lock-picking skills, either the son of a locksmith or works for one. At least some members are veterans of the Bund."

Cogan strolled in and checked the board. "I'm impressed. I've also alerted some of our boys out on Long Island to keep their ears to the ground."

"You think someone from out there might be involved with this?" Greco asked.

"Could be. There's a neighborhood out there, German Gardens, used to have streets named after Adolph Hitler and Hermann Goering. They changed the names after the Bund collapsed, but that kind of fanaticism doesn't vanish overnight."

"Danny," Greco said, "you mentioned Queens as the next place our burglar will hit, but any idea when?"

Greco's tone suggested he was slagging him, but Danny played it straight. "It was three days between the pawn shop and the jewelry store, then five days until the shoe store. An odd target for a burglary, probably chosen more for its location than what the burglar hoped to gain. After all, he thought to bring a bottle of acid with him. I'd look for him to hit his Queens target around the end of the month."

"What kind of pattern is that?"

No doubt now, Greco was slagging him. "He's left his signature at three crime scenes, so he's telling us it's him. But he's intelligent and wants to evade capture, and he knows we know what his sidekick looks like. I expect him to give us a few weeks to lower our guard."

Greco raised his hands in surrender. "Okay, okay."

Danny pointed at the board. "Three pawn shops, Lower East Side, Union Square, and Garment District, and two German guys doing the pawning."

"What's your point?" Greco asked.

"So, how did the Irish kid get paid? Stoneman had no cash in the store, so the only payoff could come after they hocked the jewelry."

"Maybe he was paid in advance." But Greco's tone suggested he didn't believe it.

"Not a chance. I'm guessing he got paid off with some of the items. I'll call Fitzgibbon and have him visit the Hell's Kitchen pawn shops."

"Wouldn't they have called, as the others did?"

"Someone might not want to squeal on a neighborhood kid."

CHAPTER THIRTY-SEVEN

Thursday, April 2, 1942

"We will begin with Hans," Hermann said. "How much jewelry have you and Paul pawned?"

"More than half the items, at three different pawn shops, for one hundred sixty dollars."

"Excellent, and there were no questions?"

Hans cast a nervous glance at Paul. "None. We offered the explanation of a seriously ill family member. My two transactions went smoothly."

"They asked me no questions," Paul said, "but the clerk glared at me for a few moments before he made me an offer. I believe my accent and my appearance may have aroused suspicion, and we thought it best I avoid any further transactions."

Hermann nodded. "I agree. Dieter, your activities have also provided additional cash?"

"*Ja*, sixty dollars from the Jewish shoe store. I also soaked a pile of their shoes in acid. If our brave men on the Russian front cannot have proper boots, it is offensive that Jews should have the luxury of shoes."

Hermann clapped a hand on his nephew's shoulder. "Indeed." Hans was the only man frowning. "You object to proper treatment of the Jews, Hans?"

"No, but I wonder if such, er, flamboyant acts will cause the police to intensify their efforts against us."

Dieter spoke up before Hermann could fire off a rebuke. "They can intensify all they like, but they will not find me. The city is too large, and they cannot predict where I will strike next. I leave nothing that could identify me because I am cautious and thorough. The only signs I leave are tributes to German defiance and the indomitable spirit of the Reich."

CHAPTER THIRTY-EIGHT

Friday, April 3, 1942

"What happened to you?"

Tommy looked disheveled. "I hocked the stuff at a place near me and celebrated at a friend's place with a bottle of hooch."

Dieter took a moment to control his anger. Tommy was a foot soldier who needed to believe he was a partner. "That was risky."

"Relax, the owner was a friend of my dad's. He didn't ask questions, and he said the cops are asking all pawn shop owners to report any jewelry being pawned in the last week. He promised he wouldn't but told me to be careful."

"So, you got drunk."

"At an old friend's place, where I stayed the night. Look, I don't tell you how to get your thrills in life, so don't tell me. I just did you a favor with the information about the cops."

Proving he was valuable in his own way. "Fine, there are no hard feelings. Maybe you should leave the city for a while. Until the end of April."

"And go where?"

"Queens."

"That's still the city."

"There are still some farms around. You'll manage, especially if you haven't spent all your money on drink."

"Nope, I still have plenty left."

"Good. Meet me three weeks from tomorrow at noon in front of the Queens Borough Hall. We'll discuss our next move then."

***

Fitzgibbon stopped in just before four. "No pawn shop owners in the Hell's Kitchen area received any jewelry of any kind since before Christmas. But there's this one fella, has a shop on Ninth and 46th Street, who wouldn't quite look me in the eye. He didn't have much jewelry on display, and what he had looked like it had seen better days. I mentioned McArdle, and he said he knew a kid by that name, but he hadn't seen him since New Year's Eve."

"That's convenient."

"That's what I thought. He might know something, but not everything. I thought about pressing him but decided it was better to let him believe he'd fobbed me off."

Danny agreed. "Let's drop in on him together on Monday or Tuesday, give him a few days to relax." He checked his watch. "End-of-tour. Think I'll call it a day."

CHAPTER THIRTY-NINE

Tuesday, April 7, 1942

As he walked along Jerome Avenue on his way to the station house, Danny noted that there had been no further vandalism against any of the stores. He considered stopping at the coffee shop next to Gold's Department Store but decided against it. He began the long climb up Shakespeare Avenue, and the coffee would be tepid when he got to the station.

Halfway up, he was regretting his choice of route. It was bitter cold, and he was walking into the teeth of a stiff wind.

A short way past the intersection with Anderson Avenue, he passed a few single-family houses nestled among the apartment buildings. In the narrow passage between two of the houses, a young couple clung to each other in a passionate kiss. They parted as he passed, and he recognized Sean McHugh, the patrolman who'd discovered the Stoneman burglary. The girl, with long, thick black curls, looked familiar, but as Danny hurried past, he wasn't sure who she was.

By the time he made the turn onto West 168th Street, he was panting. Escaping the wind and turning downhill gave relief. At Ogden Avenue, he stopped at the coffee shop.

The woman behind the counter greeted him with a grin. "Cold one, eh, Detective?"

"That climb up Shakespeare into the wind." He chuckled. "Bacon sandwich with that coffee, please."

"Coming up." She gestured toward a newspaper lying on the counter. "Looks like things are getting worse on Bataan. My son is over there. I pray every day for him."

"I'll say a prayer for him, myself." He paid her and left.

At the corner, he couldn't avoid McHugh. "Morning." He hoped McHugh hadn't seen him.

McHugh gave him a curt nod. So much for that.

After walking a short distance in tortured silence, Danny made the best of it. "Hope I didn't cramp your style too much back there."

McHugh relaxed. "It's just a little awkward."

"Who's the girl? I did my best not to look."

"Rebecca Stoneman."

Danny tried not to appear surprised. "The jeweler's daughter. No wonder she looked familiar. I'm guessing she wasn't just thanking you for your work on the burglary."

McHugh blushed. "No, I met her last month while on the four-to-twelve. It was after seven, and she was closing the shop since her dad had gone home early. I insisted on walking her home because who knew what might happen to her with all these incidents going on."

"Hell of a long walk."

"Yeah, it pulled me off my beat for a long spell. We talked the whole time. Lucky for me, it was a quiet evening. When we got to the house, I didn't want to leave, but she insisted. She didn't want to get me in trouble, and she knew her dad would worry if he saw her with a cop."

They made the half right turn onto West 167th Street.

"At end-of-tour, I went home but couldn't sleep. I got to the store early the next morning. When Rebecca showed up an hour later to open the store, she couldn't believe I'd dragged myself out."

"And you played it cool and said it was no bother?"

McHugh's blush returned. "No, I said I'd hoped she'd be opening and wanted to be there."

"Seems like things have moved along rather quickly."

"I guess that's what happens when you fall for someone you can't have. Whenever I'm with her, I convince myself that the obstacles don't matter. Love conquers all and the like. Which works until reality crashes down on me. I'm Catholic and Rebecca's Jewish. It's just her and her dad, so she's responsible for keeping kosher. She couldn't convert even if she wanted to."

They turned onto Sedgewick Avenue. Danny said nothing. McHugh had to talk this out.

"And it's not just that I'm Catholic, it's my family. Some of them think we're fighting on the wrong side, that Hitler's not such a bad guy. Holidays are awful because I'm forced to listen to their crap, and if I argue, my mom gets upset. Imagine me bringing home a Jewish girl."

"I guess you're not converting soon." It wasn't difficult to see what McHugh liked so much about her. "Not sure I can give you any advice, or if you even want any."

"An objective view would be helpful. I really love that girl."

"Yes, well, sometimes, obstacles really can't be surmounted." Danny had to step carefully or else reveal more than he wanted. "If she lived in Berlin, that would be an insurmountable obstacle. What you've mentioned are obstacles only if you allow them to be."

"You make it sound easy, but it isn't."

"What I glimpsed back there was no casual kiss. Have you two discussed any of this?"

"No, I think she's as afraid to discuss it as I am. When we're together, it's usually like what you saw back there."

"That's an indicator. All I can tell you is the sooner you both face those tough questions, the sooner you'll get on to a solution."

As they approached the precinct building, a fierce wind blew off the Harlem River.

"Thanks for the advice. On a different matter, what's the best way to get one of those gold badges?"

Danny welcomed the change of subject. "Look for a chance to transfer to a uniform position in a detective unit."

"Any chance for one in yours?"

"I'll keep an eye out for you."

As they entered the building, Danny wondered if he'd been talking about McHugh or himself but shook it off. He was meeting Fitzgibbon on Ninth and 46th Street at ten.

***

It was downright grubby, even for a pawn shop. Fitzgibbon, who was late, had gotten it right, as everything in it looked shabby. How did this guy stay in business?

"Help you out?" the owner asked.

He made a snap decision to fly solo until Fitzgibbon arrived. "I'm looking for a quality piece of jewelry for my girlfriend, something that'll knock her out."

"I don't get a lot of jewelry in here these days. Ever since war production picked up a couple of years ago, fewer people face tough times." He gave Danny's best suit, which he almost never wore on the job but had made an exception today, the once over. "What kind of piece?"

"Not sure. I was thinking of a bracelet or necklace, something sharp."

"Whaddaya looking to spend?"

"Maybe fifty. Maybe a little more."

The owner hesitated.

Danny would bet his pension the sonofabitch had the goods.

"I recently got a couple of pieces in that might interest you, and I could let you have one in your price range. Give me a second." He disappeared into the back office. A moment later he returned with two items wrapped in tissue paper. He pulled the tissue apart on the first bundle, revealing a diamond-studded gold bracelet. "I can let you have it for sixty."

Danny picked it up, wondering if Meg would like it. "She'd really go for this." The fictional "she", not Meg. "What about the other one?"

The owner grinned as he unwrapped a heart-shaped gold locket on a fine gold chain.

Danny took his time studying it. "How much?"

"Normally, I'd ask seventy-five, but you seem like a nice guy. You can have it for fifty, flat."

"Seems like a good price to me."

The owner's eyes lit up. "So, deal?"

"Sure, got a box?"

"Let me hunt one up." He searched some small drawers behind the counter.

Slow him down. "I'm curious why didn't you have those items out front. They'd look better than your other stock."

"Yeah. Thing is, you put two quality pieces in with the crap, it turns off buyers who can only afford the crap."

"Guess pieces like that locket don't hang around long." A cool draft alerted him the door from the street had been opened.

"No. Quality moves fast." The owner's manner grew guarded.

Keep it friendly. "How long have you had this one?" Don't look back.

The owner was still searching for the box and growing agitated. "Um… not too long."

"About a week?"

"More or less."

"Now, that's odd," Fitzgibbon said from just inside the entrance. "On Friday you told me you hadn't acquired any jewelry since before Thanksgiving."

The owner froze. "Please tell me you guys aren't together."

"I won't lie," Danny said as he displayed his badge, "and it's in your best interest not to, either. Those two items are hot. I'm going to take a wild guess that you got them from a local tough named Tommy McArdle. I'll take another guess that you have one or more additional items from the same source. You can save us all time and trouble by producing them now."

No response.

Danny never tired of this part. "Your choices are limited. You can produce the items. You can give me permission to search for the items. Or we can all stand around and do nothing while my colleagues request and are granted a search warrant; while we wait, I can call an officer from my precinct and ask him to bring the daughter of the owner of the jewelry store from which these were stolen, and she will so identify them, which will give me probable cause to conduct a warrantless search. If you cooperate, we'll file no charges against you. If you don't and any of these items prove to be stolen, you will be charged with trafficking in stolen goods."

"Okay, okay. McArdle came in last Thursday. He's not a bad kid. I knew his dad before he was killed trying to hold up a gas station."

"Apple didn't fall far from the tree," Danny said.

"It wasn't like that. The guy was desperate. The mother's a drunk and Christ knows what else. I've looked after Tommy ever since. He's not a violent criminal."

Fitzgibbon walked up to the counter. "You mean he says 'please' and 'thank you' when he mugs tourists coming off ocean liners?"

"I told him to keep away from that shit."

"Well," Danny said, "this kid who's 'not so bad' is mixed up with a Nazi who's masterminded several burglaries. So, put away the violins, bring out whatever else he sold you, and tell us where we can find him."

The owner ducked into the back. returning with a diamond ring. "That's the only other piece he sold me." He turned to

Fitzgibbon. "You've already checked every place I could give you. He told me he was lying low for a while."

"Did he give you any clue about where he might go?" Danny asked.

"No. He said he didn't want to put me on the spot."

Danny pulled one of his cards out of his jacket. "You know what I'm going to say next. And I know you're going to nod and say yes, you will contact me if you see him, and tell yourself, 'No way in hell'. But if you let him slip away again, I will hunt you down."

CHAPTER FORTY

While Greco was still absorbing the latest news, Danny called ADA Dennis Monroe to arrange for the arrest warrant on McArdle. "Officer McHugh's statement, as confirmed by Detective Fitzgibbon, places McArdle at the crime scene, and the pawn shop owner's statement establishes him as a participant in the crime and a trafficker in stolen goods."

"Not a problem. I'll drop it off in an hour."

"Now, you need to find him." Greco lit another cigarette. "How you going to manage it?"

"Working on it. In the meantime, we could use more manpower."

Greco grew exasperated. "Jesus, Danny, I already commandeered Rossi for you and the Chief of Detectives has put Fitzgibbon and Lavery at your disposal. We don't have enough detectives to go around."

"We're working with the G on this, Lieutenant. No time to get cheap. How about drafting a uniform for temporary duty?"

Greco took a deep drag. "Let me take a wild guess—you have someone in mind."

"I was thinking McHugh might be a good fit."

"Isn't he the guy who sniffed out the Stoneman burglary? Word is the captain is hoping he'll make sergeant."

"Then he shouldn't mind giving him an assignment that could get him noticed for advancement." When Greco scowled, Danny added, "You want these burglaries solved or not?"

"You can't tell me that drafting McHugh solves the case. And as much as you want to believe there's a sinister Nazi plot behind it, there's a good chance it's just a burglar being a wise ass."

Danny rarely showed genuine anger to his superior, and he realized it wouldn't help him here. So, he swallowed it, counted to three, and forced a smile. "Okay, then explain to me why a wise ass burglar would carry a bottle of acid all the way to Williamsburg to dump on a pile of shoes."

"Angry that there wasn't more cash? And what if he lived in Brooklyn?"

"Then explain the robberies in Manhattan and the Bronx or how anyone would expect cash in a shoe store at night." But Danny wouldn't win this one, yet.

CHAPTER FORTY-ONE

Wednesday, April 8, 1942

Another single rose awaited Meg as she returned from lunch, the third in six days.

Sheila was intrigued. "It's getting to be quite a mystery. I stayed at the front desk, watching who came and went, and I got a thorough look. An eighth grader, but not the same boy as before."

Miss Soloway joined them. "Are we discussing Meg's mystery admirer?"

A second boy? "Are you certain it was a different boy?"

"Positive. The boy on Monday was a skinny kid with pimples."

Miss Soloway grinned. "Puberty."

"But this boy looked like a football player, must be the biggest boy in his class. Either you have two admirers, or the one boy is getting his friends to help."

Miss Soloway stifled a chuckle. "Perhaps the real admirer is using schoolboys to deliver the flowers."

"Afternoon, ladies." A familiar man's voice.

Meg wheeled around and saw Danny. "It's you."

He chuckled. "Apparently."

Sheila and Miss Soloway exchanged knowing glances and withdrew.

"No, I mean you've been…" She stared at the rose in her hand.

"Oh, that. Guilty as charged, your honor. I stand in violation of the child labor law, having employed boys under the age of fourteen in a dangerous occupation during school hours."

"Dangerous?"

"Never cross a librarian when she's working." He steered her back to the reference desk. "How are you?"

"Fine, now that I don't have a crazed adolescent stalking me." She softened. "How about you?"

"Sure, and I thought you'd never ask. Been busy."

She gestured with the rose before adding it to the vase. "Thank you."

"My pleasure."

She turned serious. "I mean for everything."

"Does that mean you're ready to see me socially?"

She bit her lip. "What did you have in mind?"

"I hadn't given it much thought. How about a movie tonight? I'll take you anywhere you want to go. I can meet you here at five and we can have dinner at the little café down the street, then the movie."

She tried to look severe. "Not that you've given it much thought."

"I have not." But his grin said otherwise.

It was infectious. "Okay, how about 'The Fleet's In', with Dorothy Lamour, William Holden and Eddie Bracken? It's playing at the Forest Hills Theater."

"Your wish is my command."

***

He didn't care much for the movie and sensed that Meg hadn't. either. When it ended, he suggested dessert and coffee, not wanting the evening to end. Meg suggested Jahn's, an ice cream parlor in Richmond Hill, and she directed him there.

He laughed when he parked the car. "We have one in the Bronx, over in Mott Haven. Been there since the 1890s."

"My dad used to bring my sister and me here. There's a surprise inside." She led him past the ornate soda fountain with red Tiffany lamps emblazoned with "Coca-Cola" overhead to a back room with tables and chairs and a player piano.

He ordered two coffees and a large sundae that they shared. "So, you grew up around here?"

"No, in Maspeth. We were lucky during the Depression. My dad's work hours were cut, but we managed. I got a part-time job in the library when I was fourteen, and I turned part of my pay over to the house and started buying some of my own things. But I was shy and got a reputation as a bookworm. So, I saved my money and the following summer I took ballroom dance lessons. I love dancing."

"That doesn't sound so shy to me."

"I was shy everywhere but on the dance floor. There I learned the Waltz, Foxtrot, Lindy Hop, Balboa, and the Tango. I was still a bookworm in school. But I love dancing and l always try to see movies with a lot of music and dancing. Tonight's wasn't what I expected. The songs were pleasant, but not much dancing."

He knew he should wait, but he couldn't. "Then I suggest dinner Friday night, followed by some dancing?"

Her momentary stunned expression gave way to a grin. "I'd love it."

He drove her home and walked her down the steep steps to her door.

"Thank you for tonight, Danny. I haven't had so much fun since…" She hesitated; a cloud passed over her face. She shook it off. "Well, in a long time." She unlocked her door before turning back to give him a quick kiss on the cheek. "Goodnight."

CHAPTER FORTY-TWO

Friday, April 10, 1942

"The War Department confirmed last night that the American and Filipino forces defending the Bataan Peninsula had finally surrendered to the Japanese onslaught, a force of 200,000. No sooner had the fighting on Bataan ceased when the Japanese turned on the island fortress of Corregidor…"

***

Greco snapped off the radio in his office. "Shouldn't our boy have struck by now?"

"I told you," Danny replied, "he's going to keep quiet for a while. When he strikes again, it figures to be Queens."

"Anything new from Fitzgibbons?"

"Nope. All quiet on the Manhattan front. Fitz says it figures. If McArdle's gone quiet, so have the rest of his boys."

"So, you've got a lull. Larkin's going home early. You should, too."

Excellent idea. But first, he had a stop to make.

***

Meg stared into her drawer of stockings and sighed. Only five pairs remained. Silk stockings were a distant memory, and the disappearance of silk had forced up the price of nylon stockings to over ten dollars a pair. Now, her supply of those was dwindling as the country's stockpile of nylon was going for tires and parachutes. She hoarded her remaining pairs like diamonds, saving them for the most special occasions.

Like tonight.

She selected a pair. On her bed lay her best dress, midnight blue with sheer sleeves, cinched at the waist and a flared skirt, with her most comfortable dress pumps nearby.

Danny was taking her dining and dancing.

***

The light was on over her door. Excellent, he wouldn't stumble down those dark steps. He rang the bell.

The door opened. "Hi."

He stood riveted to the spot. She was lovelier than he'd ever seen her. He followed her inside, admiring the sway of her skirt, the swish of her stockings. He held her coat for her.

"Thank you, sir." When he said nothing, she added, "Are you okay?"

He reached for something witty, but blurted, "My God, you're beautiful."

***

Hal had never complimented her like that. She remembered her first meeting with Danny, thinking he cared more than Hal about her. But she'd never guessed how much more. This wonderful, caring man.

"Can't believe the traffic, considering there's a war on," Danny said. "And all the bright lights. No wonder the army is pushing for a blackout."

"Leaving the streets dark at night?" She shuddered, thinking about walking home from the library during winter.

"The Germans are sinking lots of ships at night because light from the city shows their silhouettes."

The maître d' at Gallagher's Steakhouse greeted Danny. "Good evening, Detective." He bowed to Meg. "And good evening to you, Miss."

"Our reservation is for eight," Danny said. "We're a wee bit early."

He searched the crowded dining room. "Step this way, please, Detective. I have a nice table for you."

"That was fast," Meg said as they sat. Danny was grinning. "What?"

"I dropped in this afternoon and gave him a generous gratuity to reserve a special table."

***

Hermann Mueller sat on a bench in Carl Schurz Park facing the river. Paul sat next to him. Next to Dieter, whom he loved like a son, Paul was the member of the group he trusted most.

"A victory for our yellow allies," Paul said. "But the war on the Russian front goes badly. Our recent attacks have done nothing to break up their offensive."

"You mustn't place too much stock in American news reports. They are hardly objective."

"I believe we will be needed by the Reich more than Berlin realizes," Paul said. "Roosevelt, the Cripple, has said their aim is to defeat Germany first."

Hermann allowed himself a brief smile. "Of course. But America is not in this war because of us, they are in it because of the Japanese and their dastardly sneak attack. I doubt they will delay their vengeance while Roosevelt pursues his Bolshevik ambitions. My friend in German Gardens has connections to the Reich's command structure. We will hear when we are needed."

***

He took her to Roseland after dinner. "You said you love dancing, and this is the place for it." Or so Larkin always said. After being seated at a table far from the dance floor, they ordered drinks.

"They don't know you here, huh?" Meg was grinning.

He stared for a moment. "A side of you I've never seen, slagging me—giving me the business."

"You give it to me, why shouldn't I give some back?"

"I'm not complaining, Meg. The more I learn about you, the more I like."

The orchestra played the introduction to Glenn Miller's "In the Mood". Meg's eyes bore into him as couples raced onto the dance floor and began doing the Lindy.

But he watched the frenetic dancing and swallowed hard. "Sorry, but I can't do that."

"It's okay." She sipped her drink, watching the dancers with obvious longing.

He felt like a heel and tried to will the band to keep it short.

The orchestra swung into Benny Goodman's "Let's Dance", and Meg's eyes sparkled with hope. A fast Foxtrot. He'd been hoping for something slower, easier, but he couldn't disappoint her twice.

She was already half out of her chair. "Ready?"

"Sure." He prayed she couldn't see his nerves. His first steps were stiff and felt awkward, but she followed, remaining smooth, and he recovered. Soon, they were gliding around the dance floor.

When the song ended, Meg was radiant. "You were superb."

They followed with "Tuxedo Junction", an easier tempo, and he shed the last of his misgivings. He held her a little closer.

The orchestra slowed it down even more with "Stardust". He pulled her closer still. She held his hand a little tighter, her hand on his shoulder a little more secure. The steps were the same, but the mood was changed. He imbibed her scent, thrilled to her softness.

***

"So, what are you saying?" Hermann asked.

"I don't like to sew discord," Paul replied, "but I don't believe Hans can be trusted. He says nothing positive, and in our research work on explosives, he's done almost nothing. I don't believe he is committed."

Hermann considered it. "Hans fought in France in the war and was maimed. He was left with one leg shorter than the other."

"Yes, we all suffered. But perhaps he suffered so much he can no longer fight. There's no shame in that, but you need to consider it when you entrust him with anything."

Hermann clapped the younger man on the shoulder. "I shall bear that in mind."

If he could afford to.

***

"You really are an excellent dancer," Danny said as he drove along Queens Boulevard.

"So are you once you get going." She grinned to keep the mood light.

"Not really. Sorry about the Lindy."

Wonderful. He'd brought it up. "It's not a hard dance to learn. I think it's easier than the Foxtrot."

"Think you could teach me?"

"Sure." Too fast? She hoped not. When he didn't respond, she added, "Just tell me when."

He made the turn onto 47th Street and waited for the light under the viaduct. A train rumbled overhead. "I'm on the eight-to-four this week, so any evening is fine. How about Tuesday?"

She'd stop at the butcher on her way home from the library on Monday and she'd take Tuesday off. "We can have dinner and then the Lindy lesson."

"Is that an invitation you're giving me?"

"It is." She froze.

"You have enough space?"

Her studio apartment was too cramped for dancing. "Not really."

"I have a good size living room. Why don't I meet you at your place and we'll walk to mine together?" He parked in front of her apartment.

"And I'll bring dinner."

He walked her to the door. She edged down the concrete steps, holding his arm.

She put her key in the lock. "Thank you, Danny, for a magical evening."

"Then we must do it again. I promise to be an attentive student."

The brush of his lips against hers was brief, and as she entered the apartment, she wished it had been longer.

CHAPTER FORTY-THREE

Tuesday, April 14, 1942

"In an editorial yesterday, Pravda, the official Russian newspaper, warned Japan not to violate their year-old neutrality agreement by attempting to annex Soviet Siberia. The piece cited Japanese acts of aggression up to and including Pearl Harbor and stated that Russia currently has hundreds of bombers and submarines less than 700 miles from Tokyo…"

***

"Nearly three weeks," Larkin said, "and not a single anti-Semitic crime."

Danny was staring at the board with him. "Meaning Tommy McArdle is behind the assaults, as well as the burglar's sidekick. Where is the little bollocks?"

"At least," Greco said, "the crime spree has stopped."

Danny glared at him. "Paused. These burglaries and assaults have been a statement, and the guy behind them won't stop."

Greco pointed at the board. "You've been saying that for three weeks."

"He's got to strike soon," Danny replied. "And we need to be ready when he does, otherwise we're never going to catch up to him."

"You still think it's going to be Queens?" Larkin asked.

"Yes." But a nagging doubt pulled at him.

***

Meg opened the door wearing a robin's egg blue shirtdress, saddle shoes and bobby socks. "I just took dinner out of the oven a short while ago." She pointed to a large box tied with string.

"And will you not be telling me in advance the contents of our feast?" Danny asked.

She replied in her best imitation of his brogue. "I will not."

"Do you not trust me, then?"

"I do not."

"I'll say this for you. If you're not pure Irish, you do a fine imitation."

She put her hands on her hips. "Are you quite ready?" She picked up her purse and the record she'd selected, and he took the box. It was four blocks to his second-floor apartment.

Once inside, she said, "Very nice."

He laid the box on the kitchen table, which he'd set that morning. "You see, I'm no slob." He led her into the living room.

"Immaculate, in your own way."

"Meaning what?"

"You don't mind a little dust, so long as it stands at attention." She laid the record on the table.

"What's that?"

"Glenn Miller playing 'Little Brown Jug'. That way, we'll have actual music for our dancing."

His expression turned to discomfort.

"It's an excellent song to learn the Lindy," she added. "The right mood but an easy tempo. I promise I'll handle your record player with care."

He stared at the floor. "I haven't got a record player."

"What did you think we were going to use for music?"

"I'm sorry, Meg, it never occurred to me. I was only thinking about the space. It seemed like such a good idea."

She met his eyes. "You just wanted to entice me here." But when he gasped in horror, she couldn't contain herself and burst into giggles. "We'll be fine. Here, let me show you."

She took him by the hand, leading him to the center of the room. "Dancing is counting, and the Lindy is an eight count. Quickly. As we come together in the usual pose, it's five, six, seven, eight. Then we swing clockwise, counting one to eight, then reverse, counting one to eight, release and swing back, still holding hands, then return and repeat. That's the basic dance."

"What about the bit where I stand, and you twirl?"

"Later. Right now, we just want the basic steps. Ready?"

"What about dinner?"

"Dinner is lukewarm by now. Let's put it in the oven to warm it up, and we can start dancing."

In the kitchen, she opened the box while he lit the oven.

He stared at the pie. "Is that…?"

"Steak and kidney pie, my gram's recipe, from back in the old sod." Back in the living room, she counted from five to eight and they came together. She continued counting, singing the numbers to the tune of "Little Brown Jug".

"Hey," he said after a few minutes, "you're right, this isn't difficult."

She stopped, slightly out of breath. "But singing while dancing is."

After dinner and a little more dancing, he walked her home. "I think I'm ready for a field test. How about Saturday night? We can go to that club in Elmhurst, The Boulevard."

"I've passed it many times. Two shows nightly. I'd love it."

When he kissed her, she wrapped her arms around his neck and lost herself in it.

***

Hermann greeted his nephew with warmth at his favorite meeting place. "Paul and Hans continue to struggle with a solution to our explosives problem. I'd like your thoughts."

Dieter stared out at the river. "Let them focus on something else. I'm working on other ideas. I'll let you know."

CHAPTER FORTY-FOUR

Wednesday, April 29, 1942

Unable to stand doing nothing, Danny finally convinced Greco to put them on the midnight-to-eight shift. "Frankie and I will cruise Queens tonight and the next several nights. I've arranged for a car with a radio, and for the Queens precincts to send an alert in the event of a burglary of a business."

"It's not like you to chase a hunch."

"This isn't a hunch. It's a calculation based on the facts, and if I'm right, and he hits Queens this week, I expect to get McHugh."

***

Larkin gestured to the Queensboro Arena on their left as the roadway from the 59th Street Bridge reached ground level. "Seen any good fights there, lately? One stop away on the Flushing line, right?"

Danny kept his eye on the road, making certain he didn't wind up on Northern Boulevard by mistake. "Three stops, and, no, I haven't."

"So, where we headed, Danny boy? Perhaps stopping at your place to play a little pinochle?"

"No, there aren't a lot of Jewish businesses in Sunnyside."

"What's after Sunnyside?"

"Woodside, and there aren't many there, either."

"Just Mrs. What's-her-name." Larkin let that hang for a moment. "Still carrying a torch for her?"

For once, Larkin wasn't slagging him. More like concern.

"Mighty big torch, judging by your mood these days."

He considered telling him about his recent nights out with Meg. "Leave it, Frankie. I asked Greco if we could get McHugh on temporary assignment."

Larkin stared at him. Debating whether to press the issue? "We could use the extra pair of hands, that's for sure, but why McHugh?"

"Greco can't get another detective, and McHugh's familiar with our burglar's MO."

"Granted. And we could call ourselves the lovelorn unit. Rumor has it he's got eyes for the jewelry store owner's daughter. I understand she's not bad looking for a Jewish girl."

"What's the basis for the rumor, and how widespread is it?" Danny already could guess the answer to the second question—the whole precinct. Rumors spread like wildfires.

"Not sure about the basis. Could be somebody saw them together. Are they canoodling?"

"How should I know?"

"Because you know the rumor's true. Did he tell you or did you see something?"

He had to laugh. "You're not a bad detective when you put your mind to it, Frankie. How about focusing on the case?"

"Yes, Father Brady, right after I say an Act of Contrition and my penance. So, where are we headed?"

"I thought we'd cruise Queens Boulevard between Forest Hills and Kew Gardens, since they're the most likely bets."

"Some boulevard. It's like the Grand Concourse, minus the buildings and people."

***

The sun was already peaking over the horizon down Union Turnpike when Danny turned onto the Grand Central Parkway and headed for the Triboro Bridge.

"One shift down, nine to go," Larkin said with a groan as he slumped down in his seat. "Think I'll catch some shut-eye. I'll need me rest for the rest of this wild goose chase."

"I never said we'd nab him on our first night out."

Larkin chuckled. "Come to that, boyo, you never even said we'd nab him at all."

***

Greco was waiting as they entered the station house, a bad sign. A worse sign was his expression. Danny hated when Greco got dramatic. "What?"

Greco gestured toward his office. "I take it you lads didn't catch your burglar last night."

"We did not."

"Well, I received a call from the captain of the Fiftieth. Between the flu and enlistments, he's fresh out of detectives and he was wondering if I could spare a couple. Since you two haven't been overly stressed, I thought you might lend a hand on a break-in last night."

"Where?" Danny was back on full alert.

"Bronx High School of Science. Take McHugh with you. At least he'll stay awake."

***

Danny recognized the guy from the Fingerprint Unit as the one who'd been at the scene of Millie Panagos' murder. "What do you have for me?"

"Sorry, Detective, no prints, no sign of forced entry."

"Sounds like they're playing your song, Danny boy." But there was no teasing in Larkin's voice.

The Fingerprint Unit guy continued. "The janitor comes in by a side entrance. This morning, the door was unlocked, but he swears he locked it last night, as he always does."

"Show me." Danny followed him to the door with Larkin, McHugh, and the janitor close behind. Danny knelt, staring at the cylinder. "Frankie, look."

Larkin stared at it. "What am I looking for?"

"Just look and tell me if you see anything that shouldn't be there."

"Just a minor scratch."

Danny knelt next to him. "It's right on the edge of the key slot."

"Proves nothing," Larkin replied. "That could have happened by someone putting the key in wrong."

McHugh knelt to study it. "I'm not so sure. The metal inside the gouge is bright, like it's recent, and it's too small to be from a key."

"My thinking, exactly," Danny said. He gestured to the janitor. "Ever see that before?"

"No."

"Any other locked doors penetrated?" Danny asked.

"The chemistry lab and the lab's storage room. Both were locked last night. I checked 'em myself."

Danny examined the locks to both rooms. Both had similar gouges. "Frankie, make sure the crime scene guys get photos of these. I'll want to check the ones from the previous burglaries." He entered the storeroom and glanced around. A forest of bottles with a slight unpleasant odor. "What did he take?"

"I don't know," the janitor said. "You'd have to ask Mr. Quill, the chemistry teacher."

A voice from the classroom. "What is this? What's going on?"

"That's Mr. Quill," the janitor said.

Danny explained what they knew of the burglary.

"Why would anyone break in here?" Quill asked.

"That's what we're trying to discover. Could you please examine the storeroom and tell me if anything is missing?" Danny led the others out, relieved to be in fresher air. He waved the janitor over. "Can you think of any reason a burglar would choose that door for the break-in?"

The janitor stared, dumbfounded.

"I can think of a few," McHugh said. "It's far from the street, and probably not well lit at night. When leaving the burglar could slip out in several directions…"

Danny grinned. "Thanks, Sean, but right now I'm interested in the janitor's thoughts."

"Well, that young fella's right. But if you mean, is there anything special about the door, yeah, we've had some trouble with the lock over the years. It don't always lock right. That's why I always leave by that door and double check it every night before I go. And I'm tellin' ya, it was locked last night."

Danny patted him on the shoulder. "I never doubted it."

Quill returned from the storeroom. "I haven't taken a detailed inventory, Detective, but five one-liter bottles of nitric acid that were there yesterday are now missing."

"Did you notice anything defaced, any markings that weren't in the classroom yesterday?"

Quill frowned. "What kind of markings?"

"Anything."

"No. Why?"

"Just asking. One other thing. What are the most common uses for nitric acid?"

For the first time, Quill relaxed. "If you mean household uses, none. We use it here as a laboratory reagent. Industrial uses include producing nitrate salts, fertilizers, explosives…"

"Wait," Danny said. "What types of explosives?"

Quill shrugged. "You name it. TNT, dynamite, gun cotton, nitroglycerin, fulminate of mercury. I could go on."

CHAPTER FORTY-FIVE

Thursday, May 7, 1942

It was twilight, and Hermann Mueller, as usual, was early for the group's weekly meeting. His internal alarm sounded when he saw his nephew approaching a block before he reached the *Bier Garten*. "What's wrong?"

"Nothing, but I won't be at the meeting because of other plans. Is your friend, the furrier, still in business?"

An interesting question. "He is."

"And is he loyal to the Fatherland?"

An even more interesting question. "Undeniably."

Dieter nodded with satisfaction. "I may have some items for him."

***

"I don't know about you," Larkin said as they cruised their now-familiar route along Queens Boulevard, having started an hour early. "But I'm getting kind of tired of this. With each passing night, I'm more convinced we're barking up the wrong tree. Ever stop to think that while we're wasting time here, the trail on our burglar is going cold?"

"It isn't. We're on his trail now."

"The progression was supposed to be Bronx-Manhattan-Brooklyn-Queens, but you think he did the Bronx Science break-in, which broke the progression. He didn't leave his signature, and the motive was stealing a specific chemical. The principal is conducting his own investigation of the student body with Lavery's help."

Danny sighed. "The first burglary was on Bedford Park Boulevard. He knew the neighborhood, knew the location of a Jewish-owned business. Right near Bronx Science, where he knew the best way to break in. That's where he went to school."

***

Dieter climbed the stairs to the street from the subway station at Continental Avenue in Forest Hills twelve days after giving Tommy his instructions.

A forlorn Tommy McArdle leaned against the railing. "About time. I've been going nuts the past month."

Dieter led him down 71st Avenue toward Austin Street in Forest Hills. "Don't tell me you ran through all the money."

"Not quite. What's in the bottle?"

"Pig's blood."

"What the hell for?"

"To express my dissatisfaction if there's no cash. Now, quiet." They were at the rear of a furrier on Austin Street. Uncle Hermann's friend could fence a fur coat, but Dieter was less concerned about the money than he was about lashing out at rich Jews who flaunted their furs while good men were freezing on the Russian front.

The place was alarmed. He'd known all along he'd eventually have to pass this test. "Stay at the entrance to the alley. Warn me if you see any police or hear any sirens, and this time, don't get caught."

He waited until Tommy took up his position. Magnetic sensors were visible on both the main door and the back door. The back window had been painted over, but he was certain it, too, was alarmed. One thing that wouldn't set off an alarm was a window that wasn't opened.

The painted over window showed no sign of foil, but to be sure, he scratched away the paint in several places. He found an old towel on the ground, placed it over the glass, and broke through the window. The towel muffled the shattering of the glass. He climbed through with the bottle.

And no alarm. Perfect.

CHAPTER FORTY-SIX

Friday, May 8, 1942

Danny was about to parry another Larkin thrust about Meg when the radio run came through: "Cohen's Furs, active alarm, Austin Street between 71st Road and 72nd Avenue, Forest Hills, no sirens."

Larkin jotted the information and noted the time. "12:04AM. The gobshite set off an alarm? Might not be our guy."

Danny floored it. "I'll bet money it's a central alarm, and he missed something."

***

"Cops!"

Dieter dropped the coat with the $188.00 price tag and rushed to the back window. "Wait for me at Grant's Tomb." How did they know? Already out the door, he remembered the empty bottle, but had to leave it. Tommy was already gone, and a car screeched to a halt nearby. He hopped the fence into an adjoining yard. The house was dark. Either no one was home, or everyone was asleep.

"This is the place," a voice called.

No time to run. The house had a screened-in porch. He tried the door. Locked. He forced the latch back with a small screwdriver.

It opened.

He locked it behind him and cowered next to a chaise lounge.

"Frankie, you check the neighboring yards, I'll check inside."

A beam of light pierced the darkness of the porch. Dieter flattened himself on the floor as the beam of light probed for several seconds until Frankie, whoever he was, moved on.

***

Danny was already inside when the uniforms climbed in. He flashed his badge.

"Okay, Detective," the sergeant said, "but don't touch nothing until the crime scene guys get here."

He studied the broken glass on the floor and a towel next to the window. Shining his light on it, he caught the reflection from broken glass. "Please hit the lights."

A moment later, the store was bathed in light, but the storage area in the back, where he was standing, remained mostly dark until the light fixture overhead flickered on. That's when he saw a thin wire hanging loose. "So, that's what got him."

"Simple but effective," the sergeant replied. "They never think about the trip wire across the window. The alarm signal went to the phone company, and they notified us."

"Sarge," a uniformed officer said, "what the hell is this?" He held up a small bottle.

"Shit, that looks like blood. Where was it?"

"On the floor. Looks like he splattered it on the furs before he took off."

The sarge looked troubled. "How did he know when to run?"

Danny explained the situation. "He has a sidekick, an Irish kid named Tommy McArdle who functions as his lookout."

"If he's your guy," the sarge said.

Larkin returned. "No sign of him, Danny. But the first uniforms on the scene saw a kid running up the street who fits Tommy McArdle's description."

"He's our guy, all right." Danny turned to Larkin. "Did the officers see which way he ran?"

"Looked like he was headed for Queens Boulevard, probably the subway."

Danny turned back to the sarge. "Can you have your guys check the station for him? We have a warrant for his arrest."

The sarge detailed two officers to check the subway station.

Danny thanked him. "If you nab him, please have your dispatcher put it out on the radio and we'll come get him. And please contact me at the 44th Precinct if you get any prints."

"Danny," Larkin said, "he don't leave prints, remember?"

"True, but tonight he left in a hurry. Sarge, please have them dust that bottle and have them take prints of the officer who picked it up without gloves so we can identify them."

The sarge shot the offending officer a glare. "Sure thing, detective, but aren't you sticking around?"

"No. I want to cruise Queens Boulevard and see if we can run down McArdle. Just because he ran toward the subway, that doesn't mean he's going to take it."

"He ain't gonna double back," Larkin said.

"But he might head for the next station in either direction."

***

Two hours after the police departed, Dieter was still hiding by the chaise lounge. Two cops remained to guard the scene, one of them in the alley. The other had to be on Austin Street. The sky was lightening, and he had little time remaining to leave undetected.

A light appeared in a second-floor window of a neighboring house.

The alley cop walked to the end and back at a steady pace. Dieter waited for him to begin another cycle, counted to ten, and then slipped out the screen door. He walked between the houses to the side street, crossed the street, and strode at a normal pace toward the subway.

The detective had mentioned a warrant for Tommy's arrest. American police weren't as ruthless as the Gestapo, but it wouldn't take Gestapo methods to crack Tommy. He wasn't nearly as tough as he pretended.

He also wasn't nearly as helpful as Dieter had hoped. Twice, he'd bungled his assignment as a lookout.

***

"US naval forces delivered a devastating blow to the Japanese navy in a battle off the Solomon Islands, sinking at least seven naval vessels and damaging two more…"

***

"Okay, Danny, you sold me. You get McHugh. I'll square it with the captain."

Danny loved it when Greco capitulated. He also expected there would be a cost because there always was.

Greco didn't disappoint him. "So, you're hot on this Nazi's tail, now. What's his next move?"

"Fitzgibbon has a detail watching McArdle's place and his usual haunts. If we can bring him in, he'll give up the burglar. Jimmy's also watching the pawn shop owner, the one guy McArdle might turn to. Since I put the fear of God into him, he'll call us if he finds out where the kid is."

Greco sat back. "Fine, but I didn't hear a prediction on the burglar's next move."

Best to play it straight. "The near miss last night complicates things. If we'd missed him completely, I'd have said look for him to hit another place in Manhattan, and soon, but the close call is likely to scare him, making him less predictable."

Back at his desk, he pondered what that might mean. It was after eight in the morning, but he couldn't go home. Not now.

Larkin brought him back to the present. "What's the matter, Danny boy? Not enough sleep last night?"

"I blew it last night. McArdle had to be the lookout, like he was at Stoneman's. He warned the burglar." He closed his eyes, picturing the scene in his mind. "McArdle's at the window, yelling a warning. What does he do, next?"

"Gets the hell out of Dodge."

"And our guy?"

"The same. What's your point?"

Danny flipped open his notebook. "The uniforms saw McArdle running up 71st Road, but no one else."

"So, the burglar ran out the far end of the alley."

"That would have put him on 72nd Avenue, and he would have run smack into us. The front door to the shop was undisturbed, so he didn't slip out onto Austin."

Larkin took a moment to digest it. "So, he was hiding somewhere in the neighboring yards? You saying I screwed up?"

"No, Frankie, I did. It was stupid to chase after McArdle when he had that big a lead. We should have hung around. This kid's got balls."

McHugh rushed over. "Thanks, Detective, I just got the word."

"What word?" Larkin asked.

"McHugh, here, has been attached to our unit on temporary assignment," Danny replied.

Larkin barely suppressed a grin and shook McHugh's hand. "Welcome aboard, kid."

"First things first," Danny said. "We're not 'detective' to other members of the team. He's Frankie, I'm Danny."

"And you're…?" Larkin asked.

"Sean," McHugh replied.

"Jesus Christ," Russo said with a moan as he joined them, "it's the fucking Sinn Féin."

Danny laughed. "He's Vinnie, the token wop."

Greco came out of his office. "I just got off the phone with the Fingerprint Unit. They got a print from the bottle besides the cop who picked it up. They're checking their records for a match, but it'll take a few days."

Danny took that in. "Maybe last night wasn't a total loss." His phone rang.

It was Fitzgibbon. "I've caught a homicide and you need to be on it. The body was found at the entrance to the New York Central's tunnels next to Riverside Park, near Grant's Tomb."

"Please tell me it's not Tommy McArdle."

"You wouldn't want me to lie."

***

Danny stood with Larkin and McHugh on the side of the tracks away from the river as Fitzgibbon gave them the rundown. "We're damned lucky his body is still in one piece. A track maintenance worker was doing a routine check around 5:30 this morning and spotted what looked like a drunk passed out on the tracks. Body was still warm, so the maintenance guy didn't realize at first McArdle was dead."

"The time of death couldn't have been earlier than five and was probably a bit later." Danny turned to Larkin. "He waited until about four in a yard near the store, then high-tailed it back to the city to meet McArdle."

Larkin stared down at the inert body. "Hell of a way to get fired."

"But for that maintenance worker, our boy here would be shredded cabbage by now."

Larkin winced. "Jesus, Danny, that's cold."

"So is our killer." He saw someone from the coroner's office studying the body. "Any opinions?"

"No signs of gunshots or stab wounds. His head is at a funny angle, so that suggests a broken neck, possibly coupled with a blow to the head as I see some traces of blood in the right ear. The autopsy will tell the tale."

Danny turned toward the wooded section separating them from the roadway at the top of the hill. "He wasn't killed down here, and there's no path down. Frankie, Sean, let's spread out and slowly climb this hill following a zig-zag course, Frankie on my right, Sean on my left."

"What are we looking for?" Larkin asked.

"Any kind of path someone might have made, so look for snapped stems, crushed grass or weeds, or broken branches." Danny started his own climb.

Halfway up the hill, he was breathing harder. He couldn't imagine dragging an inert body down in predawn light.

"Got something." It was McHugh.

Danny made his way over. Weeds, stalks of wildflowers, and grass were matted down in a straight, wide path down the hill. "They didn't walk down. There would have been two narrow paths and not so smooth. McArdle was killed up on the roadway and rolled down afterward. You two examine this path, take your time, and tell me if you find any traces of blood, bits of clothing, anything that looks like it doesn't belong here."

He was panting after reaching to the top. A low wrought-iron fence separated the strip of park land from the roadway, which police already had blocked off. The crime scene guys were hard at work.

Danny flashed his badge. "Don't worry, lads, I'll be careful."

From the point where the crushed path began, he surveyed every direction, attempting to discern how the crime had occurred—a spatter of blood, a piece of torn clothing. But there was nothing. He walked toward the Grant memorial, keeping near the low railing, scanning the ground.

Nothing.

He reached the front of the memorial, crossed the roadway, and started back. As he approached his starting point, a small round object in the roadway caught his eye.

A button. Too large for a shirt, round and deep. Almost certainly from a coat.

A man's coat. Upon examination, he discovered several threads hanging from the holes at the back.

He located the top of the path they'd found and crossed over to it.

"Find anything?" It was Larkin.

Danny didn't answer. Instead, he climbed over the railing, pausing when he saw fibers stuck to the rim. He plucked them away and compared them to those attached to the button.

"Hey, Danny!" Larkin again.

Not yet. He started down the slope.

"Danny, they're packing him up."

"Have them wait." Danny hated being rushed at a crime scene, but he couldn't take the chance they'd leave, so he skittered down. "Frankie, please walk slowly back up the path and make sure we haven't missed anything."

"You mean you haven't missed anything, don't you?"

Danny ignored him. They were about to slam the doors shut on the meat wagon. "Hold it, I need to check something." He ignored the technician rolling his eyes. "He still wearing a coat?"

"Yeah, why?"

"Let me see it."

The technician pulled the body out and stepped back as the odor of decay wafted over them.

Danny waved McHugh over and showed him the button and the fibers "Both obviously torn from a coat, so the only remaining question is whether it was his coat."

Ignoring the odor, he pulled at McArdle's coat. The top button was missing, and the remaining buttons matched the one from the roadway. He laid the fibers next to the coat. "Look close. Does that look like a match to you?"

McHugh bent lower to check, wrinkling his nose. "Looks like it."

"Not good enough. You're on the witness stand, and the prosecutor has just asked you if the fibers match. With that answer, the defense attorney would be all over you. Come on." Danny nodded to the technicians that they could take the body.

He led McHugh back up the hill to where technicians were examining the crime scene and turned the button and the fibers over to them. "Please check them for a match to the victim's coat."

Larkin caught up to them. "Danny, I found this halfway up the hill, half buried in the undergrowth, like someone tossed it aside."

Danny rifled through the decrepit wallet. "McArdle's Social Security card. That's amusing. No money. A slip of paper with a phone number on it." He stared at the number, TR-2-8677. Tremont 2 was a Bronx exchange. "The lieutenant will have to make certain the press stories include nothing about the condition of the body."

CHAPTER FORTY-SEVEN

Saturday, May 9, 1942

Sitting on a bench facing the river in Carl Schurz Park, Hermann remained completely still as he listened to Dieter. His nephew epitomized the best of the youth who'd attended Camp Siegfried. He sometimes forgot Dieter was still quite young. And, having been born in America, a trace of naivete remained.

Dieter finished his narrative. "I don't know what else I could have done."

Hermann stood and gestured for Dieter to follow him through the deserted park on this unseasonably cool, dreary day. "I thought you recruited the Irish boy merely to harass Jews."

"Initially, yes."

"It was a mistake to involve him in anything further."

"I understand that now, but he was engaged in petty crime, robbing wealthy tourists by the piers. He was certain to be apprehended. I thought enticing him with booty from the burglaries would be a good way to keep his interest and his loyalty."

"Bribed loyalty is only effective until something more lucrative is offered. The Irish can only be useful to a degree."

"I mentioned nothing to him about our work."

That was something. "How did you explain your carved swastikas?"

"I told him it was to further annoy the Jew owners. He thought it was funny."

One more detail. "The newspaper said he was found in a train tunnel. Was that the best choice?"

"I left him on the track fifteen minutes before the first train was due to come through. I saw no one else around. The train should have crushed him beyond recognition."

"Very well, you must remain inconspicuous for a while. Avoid our meetings on Thursday. Halt the burglaries until we can develop a more effective plan for them."

***

Larkin hadn't been pleased when Danny left him behind to await word from the crime lab and the coroner, but no one else could ask the right follow-up questions. Besides, McHugh had tracked down the address for the phone number in record time. Danny liked this kid more each day.

"I know this neighborhood," McHugh said as Danny made the turn off Jerome onto East 177th Street. "I have cousins who live near here. The address we want is up here on the right, just across from the playground."

The neat, semi-attached two-family house was one of a handful tucked between two apartment buildings. Danny rang the lower of two doorbells.

A woman in a worn, green housecoat answered. "Yeah?"

Danny flashed his badge. "I'm looking for someone at this address who might know a boy named Tommy McArdle."

"Never heard of him. My husband ain't here, he's at work. Gets home around seven if you want to ask him."

"Are you by any chance the landlady?"

"Yeah, what's it to ya?"

"Are your tenants at home?"

"Upstairs, no. She's a widow, works for the telephone company. Downstairs, a divorced woman, works for a trucking company and whatever else she does, if you get my drift."

Danny couldn't help but grin. "I get it."

The landlady sighed. "No wonder her lout of a kid ain't no good."

"How old is he?"

She brightened. "Oh, yeah, he might be who you want. He's eighteen, can't hold a job to save his life."

"Is he home now?"

"Who knows? He comes, he goes. Name is Eddie Connors. They have a separate entrance under the stoop."

Danny thanked her and walked down to the lower entrance. He pressed the button twice before leaning on the button and held it.

"Awright, awright, gimme a minute."

"The lout lives," McHugh said.

The door opened, and the boy glared at them, unsteady on his feet. Danny flashed his badge. "Eddie Connors? I'm Detective Brady, this is Officer McHugh. Do you know a Tommy McArdle?"

"No."

Danny showed him the paper with the phone number. "This your number?"

Connors squinted. "Yeah, why?"

"Because I got this from Tommy. He called it. So, cut the crap. Why did he call?"

McHugh took a step closer, and Connors drew back. Message received.

"Yeah, he called about one thirty this morning. Good thing my ma wasn't here."

"What did Tommy want at such an hour?" Danny asked.

"A date with your mom?" McHugh added.

The kid flushed. "Fuck you."

"Easy," Danny said, trying not to make eye contact with McHugh. "Just tell me about the call."

"He was in trouble, said he needed to hide here. Sounded like he was having a fit. I told him to call me in the morning. Why, what's he done?"

"He's dead," Danny replied.

All Connors' bravado evaporated. "Shit."

"May we come in?" Danny closed in, and Connors retreated. The apartment was a mess. "Before the phone call, when was the last time you spoke with him?"

"About a week ago. Came here during the day. He had cash on him but said he had to keep a low profile. Wouldn't say what he was up to. And before that, I hadn't seen him since my mom and me moved up here."

"When was that? Danny asked.

"Right after she dumped my father five years ago. We lived in Hell's Kitchen before that. That's how I knew Tommy. We went to school together. He was always the schoolyard tough."

"You mean bully, don't you?" McHugh asked.

"I mean he did what he needed to do to hold his standing. It was a tough neighborhood, not your typical schoolyard."

"Mostly Irish kids?" Danny asked, and Connors nodded. "What about the rest?"

"A few wops and Jews. We kept them in line…"

"In other words," McHugh said, "you beat them up."

"Sometimes things got rough."

Danny loved how McHugh was keeping Connors off balance. "Any others?"

"A few German kids. They kept to themselves, mostly."

"Ever have any German kids from Yorkville or the Lower East Side?" It was time to get some answers.

"Hell, no. Why would they? The German kids in our classes moved out as soon as their families could afford it."

"Any who might have been friendly with Tommy?" Danny hoped he sounded more nonchalant than he felt.

"Never saw him chummy with any of them. But there was one…"

Danny shot McHugh a look to keep quiet. "Yes?"

"Back in sixth grade, Tommy had been ragging this one kid who fought back. Tommy roughed him up after school, and the kid squealed on him. The next day, Tommy was suspended, but a German kid in our class went to the teacher and said Tommy had spent the afternoon with him and his uncle, and the uncle would confirm it. Suspension over."

"The kid Tommy beat up, was he German, too?"

"No. Jewish."

It was thin, but it was something. "You remember the German kid's name?"

"I think it was Peter. He moved away soon after."

"Thanks." Danny gave Connors his card. "Call me if you think of any other details."

As they drove back to the precinct, Danny said, "Check out the school on Monday. It's on West 44th Street. Sixth grade for McArdle would have been the 1933-34 school year. Check the class lists starting in '31-32. Make a note of any male classmate with a German surname."

"And a first name of Peter?"

"No, all German surnames. We'll narrow it down from there."

***

He was making a note of the school on the board when Larkin, smirking, interrupted him. "You got a visitor, Danny boy."

A lovely woman with brown-black hair in thick, tight curls and warm brown eyes extended her hand. "Detective Brady? I'm Rebecca Stoneman. I understand you've recovered some additional items from the burglary. Is it possible to have them back?"

He gestured for her to sit. "Ordinarily, I'd have already returned them, but these were pawned by one of the participants in the burglary, and he was murdered early this morning. I'm sorry, but we need them as evidence. I promise I'll return them as soon as I can."

"Can you at least tell me which items they were?"

"Yes, a gold diamond-studded bracelet, a diamond ring, and a gold heart-shaped locket on a gold chain." He hoped she didn't hear the catch in his voice when he mentioned the locket.

The corners of her mouth turned up in the hint of a grin. She'd heard it, all right. "I'll explain it to my father."

"He can call me if he has questions, unless you'd rather ask Officer McHugh."

She blushed. "Thank you, Detective."

Larkin returned as Rebecca left and gave a low wolf whistle. "I see what interests our junior associate." He turned serious. "Coroner's office called about McArdle. Cause of death was a head injury and the internal bleeding that resulted. In addition, there was some bruising of the lower back. Time of death was between five and five-thirty. Congratulations, Sherlock Brady, you've done it again."

"The killer hit him over the head by the roadway, grabbed him by the coat, slammed him into the railing and sent him rolling down the hill. Anything from the lab?"

"Yeah, the fibers on the button and the ones you pulled from the fence were from McArdle's coat, and they found prints on the wallet. McArdle's palm print and some partials, also McArdle's. No others. So, either the killer was wearing gloves or McArdle threw his own wallet away."

Danny scowled. "Or it fell from his coat pocket and the killer never saw it. Which makes sense, because it bothers me that the killer would go to all the trouble of luring him there to kill him and then toss aside a piece of evidence where it could be easily found."

"Well," Larkin replied, "you said yourself this guy's an amateur."

"He's an amateur burglar, but a cold-blooded killer."

"In other news, the bottle from the burglary contained pig's blood. Downtown is already going through their records, looking for a match on the prints."

"They won't find one. He's McArdle's age." Danny left it at that. He was taking Meg out for dinner and dancing again the following night.

CHAPTER FORTY-EIGHT

Monday, May 11, 1942

When Danny arrived a little before eight in the morning, his head was still swimming from the weekend. But a note McHugh had left on his desk on Saturday snapped him back to the here-and-now. *The chemistry teacher from Bronx Science, Mr. Quill, called after you left. He finished taking inventory and thinks the burglar also took two bottles of mercury and a bottle of alcohol.*

He called Cogan but couldn't reach him.

***

Miss Soloway broke into a wide grin when Meg walked in. "Do I… detect… somebody had a good weekend?"

"Yes, I did."

"Well?"

"Another dinner at Gallagher's Saturday night, followed by dancing at Roseland." No need to mention the surprising necking session that followed. "Then, I saw him at Mass yesterday morning, so he took me out to breakfast." No need to mention the necking session that followed in her apartment, either.

Miss Soloway's grin grew wider. "I won't ask about whatever bits you've left out." She broke into uproarious laughter when Meg blushed.

***

Dieter's uncle was waiting for him at the park in the usual spot, overlooking the East River, his face impossible to read.

"Sit down, Dieter. Have you seen the newspapers this morning? The police say they have leads."

A chill ran down Dieter's back. "I apologize."

"We've no time for recriminations. Our mission requires us to take precautions." He placed two sealed envelopes in Dieter's hand, one with his own name, the other bearing the name Fred Obermann and a Long Island address. "You will read the letter addressed to you when you're alone."

Dieter willed himself not to shiver as a gust of wind swept across the park. Low angry clouds suggested an early thunderstorm was on the way. There wasn't another soul in the park. "*Ja.*"

"In my letter, you will find specific instructions. Follow them without variation. Do not go home or contact your parents. They cannot learn where you've gone. I will explain things to your mother. You will find sufficient funds to maintain you. You will present the second letter to Herr Obermann. I spoke with him last night. He will tell you when you may return. Questions?"

Dieter knew better. "*Nein.* But in my bedroom are eight bottles of chemicals for making fulminate of mercury, a powerful explosive."

His uncle stood. "Very well, I will pick them up. Heil Hitler."

***

McHugh returned just after lunch and laid a list of names on Danny's desk. "I've listed names by school year, starting at '33-34 and working backward for three years. Five names appear on all three years. One is Dieter Mueller."

Danny chuckled. "Dieter, sounds like Peter." He tried Cogan again and this time got him. "Please check your Bund records for any mention of a kid named Dieter Mueller, or anyone with that surname."

"Geez, Danny, any idea how many Muellers there are in New York?"

"But I'm sure most of them weren't Bund members. Also, if you find him, please check for any locksmiths in the family."

"In my spare time, sure."

"You want this guy or not?"

"Just kidding, Danny, sorry. I guess this case is getting to you."

"No, not at all. Sounds like you're jammed up. Anything serious?"

Cogan sighed. "Agency crap. The director's fretting about saboteurs among our German, Italian, and Japanese populations. No one's thinking about external threats."

"Are there any?"

"No idea, that's why I'm so interested in our project. I'll see what we can find, but it'll take time to go through those old files."

Danny mentioned the other items that the burglar had taken from Bronx Science.

"Holy shit," Cogan replied. "Maybe the director is right to be worried."

CHAPTER FORTY-NINE

Tuesday, May 12, 1942

Cogan had come up empty on Dieter Mueller. McHugh had searched Manhattan phone books from 1930 to 1937 for anyone named Mueller living in Hell's Kitchen. He'd found two in the '30 and '31 books, but they disappeared in '32.

Meanwhile, they'd interviewed everyone from storekeepers on Austin Street in Forest Hills to beat cops near Grant's Tomb to see if they'd noticed anyone loitering in the days before the murder. No one had seen anything unusual.

And no match had been found for the fingerprints left on the bottle of pig's blood. Danny told Greco he'd send the prints over to the FBI.

"You'll forgive me if I don't hold my breath," Greco said. "It sounds like a dead end."

Danny refused to concede it. "Cogan's still checking their files on the Bund."

"It's been four years since the Bund was holding rallies at the Garden. He would only have been fourteen or fifteen." Greco's glare warned against arguing.

Danny often ignored warning glares. "But he'd have been the perfect age to attend Camp Siegfried."

"What the hell was that?"

McHugh jumped in. "Sort of a Nazi summer camp, where Bund members sent their kids to become like the Hitler Youth."

"Cogan says the FBI kept eyes on it, but never got lists of attendees," Danny added. McHugh had guts.

"Okay." Greco's tone grew more reasonable. "Let's consider—just humor me, here—that this guy isn't a trained Nazi, and maybe he's a lone wolf sympathizer."

"He's not a lone wolf," Danny replied. "He has at least two adult collaborators who pawned some of the jewelry. We know when, where, and how the murder happened. We have a reasonable motive, and a profile of the killer. All that's left is to find him."

"Is that all?" Greco asked.

"Cogan wants me to meet with him. I'll tell you how it goes. Frankie, let's go."

***

Cogan's door was closed when Danny and Larkin arrived at the FBI office on East 69th Street, which was unusual. Cogan was notified they were there, but kept them waiting more than half an hour, which was more unusual. Danny was ready to give up and leave when Cogan's door opened. "Sorry to keep you waiting."

There was another man inside.

"Sir," Cogan said, "meet Dan Brady and Frank Larkin, the two detectives I told you about. Danny, Frank, this is Tom Donegan, who heads our New York Office."

Donegan's handshake was firm but quick. "Thanks for coming."

"I've been briefing Tom on your work, particularly the burglaries and the murder." Cogan broke into a grin. "He's been concerned with the man-hours we've spent on this case."

"Don't worry, Detective," Donegan put in. "I'm not cutting you off. This case disturbs me to the extreme. Most Bund members never showed the cunning and tenacity of your killer. Left to his own devices, he might not threaten national security. But with the right outside help, it's another matter."

"We've taken some unusual steps," Cogan went on. "But first, the bad news. We couldn't find a match for the fingerprints you provided in our records."

"Not a surprise," Danny said. "There's good news?"

"According to the city's birth records, Dieter Mueller was born on May 23rd, 1923, in an apartment on West 47th Street to Leopold and Frieda Mueller, whose maiden name was Osterkamp."

"And is Leopold a locksmith?" Larkin asked.

"No, according to his tax returns, he's a machinist for a tool manufacturer. Frieda is a cook for a family on Sutton Place. The Mueller family moved from West 47th Street to East 93rd Street in 1934."

"Yorkville," Danny said.

Cogan grinned. "Yes, and while there's no evidence of anyone in the family among those we kept tabs on in the Bund, there is a locksmith on Second Avenue near East 87th Street named Paul Osterkamp."

"The grandfather?" Larkin asked.

"More likely an uncle," Danny said.

Cogan nodded agreement. "There's also a Hermann Mueller, a plumber, on East 86th Street. Here are the names and addresses."

They all stood.

Donegan shook Danny's hand. "I can't stress enough the importance of keeping Bill informed of any connections you find to larger organizations."

***

It was a tidy little shop, not a thing out of place. A young woman in her late teens or early twenties sat on a stool behind the counter. "Can I help you?"

Danny showed his badge. "Is Mr. Osterkamp here?"

"Is something wrong?"

"We just have a few questions. Is he here?"

She pulled back a curtain leading to the rear. "Poppa? Police."

Paul Osterkamp appeared. "Yes?"

Danny introduced himself and Larkin. "Do you know anyone named Dieter Mueller?"

The girl frowned, but Osterkamp remained impassive. "Yes, he's my nephew, my sister's boy. Why?"

"Does he work for you?"

"He did for about two years, in the summer and after school, until his last year in school."

"I imagine he did pretty much what she does?" Danny nodded toward the girl.

"No, he worked with me, in the back and going out on jobs."

"Why did he leave?"

A momentary hesitation. "He lacked patience with customers and was sometimes rude to them. It's a pity. He's quite skilled."

"What bothered him about customers?" Larkin asked.

Another hesitation. "They often treat us like we work only for them. Dieter is a proud young man. He couldn't accept such treatment."

"Any group of customers in particular?" Danny didn't hide his expectation of a group to be named.

"No."

Too fast. "Have you seen your nephew recently?"

"Not since Christmas. When he stopped working for me, it was with some rancor on his part. I never understood why."

Danny turned to the girl. "What about you?"

She wouldn't meet his gaze. "No, Dieter and I were never close."

He was certain she had much more to tell, but not in front of her father. They'd have to follow up. Back to the locksmith. "What hours do Dieter's parents work?"

"My sister rarely gets in until after seven, later if her employer is giving a dinner. My brother-in-law's regular workday is eight to five, but he often works extra hours, what with wartime demands."

"Okay, thanks. We'll be back if we need anything else." Halfway to the door, Danny stopped. "Oh, I almost forgot. To your knowledge, has Dieter or anyone in your family ever been involved with the German-American Bund?"

The girl gasped.

"I wouldn't know," Osterkamp replied in a low growl.

Danny remained pleasant. "Just asking. Thanks." Back outside, they started up Second Avenue.

"Was that smart? They'll just all keep their heads down, now."

"Frankie, their heads were down before we walked in. The girl's face told way more than her father's answers."

"At least we've confirmed Dieter's our guy."

"He is that. Now, to find the little bollocks."

***

On a whim, Meg called Danny at home, but she got no answer. For a moment, she considered calling him at the precinct, but decided against it. If someone took a message, he might worry that something was wrong, and she didn't want to upset him.

But it was after seven. Why wasn't he home?

***

Dieter's parents made quite a pair. Leopold was short and wiry, as compact a man as Danny had seen. By contrast, Frieda was nearly as tall as her husband, broad-shouldered and full-bosomed, the archetypal middle-aged German housewife. She, not her husband, would answer their questions, if she chose to answer them.

"We're looking for your son," Danny said. "Do you expect him, soon?"

"Our son is not here."

"As I see. Where is he?"

She considered the question, as if calculating which course to take. "Why do you want to see him?"

"We're investigating a murder, Mrs. Mueller. Please just answer my questions honestly."

She crossed her arms. "I am no liar."

"I didn't say you were. Where is Dieter?"

Another pause. More calculating. "He went to visit an old school friend."

"Who, when, and where?" Enough of pulling teeth.

"He didn't say who or where. But he left two weeks ago."

"Your son's been gone for two weeks without a word? Doesn't that concern you?"

She lost a little defiance. "Dieter is a very willful boy."

"How does he feel about the war?"

Her defiance returned. "We are all loyal Americans."

"Did Dieter register for the draft when he turned eighteen?"

"Of course, he did."

Danny made a mental note to verify that with Cogan. "Did he ever attend Camp Siegfried?"

She jumped from her seat. "I've had quite enough of your insinuations, Detective. We are loyal American citizens who left Germany after the war and made this country our home. We've watched the rise of Hitler with disgust. I must ask you to leave, now."

Danny tipped his hat. "Sorry to have disturbed you, ma'am. Enjoy the rest of your evening."

Out on the street, they walked toward the 89th Street stop on the Third Avenue El.

"That sure was one waste of time. That kraut battle axe wasn't giving anything up."

"Frankie, listen to what they don't say as carefully as what they say."

"And just what does that brilliant statement mean?"

"She didn't say, 'My good little boy never attended Camp Siegfried', or even 'What's Camp Siegfried?'"

"Doesn't prove anything, Danny boy."

"True, it does not. But I don't need proof, yet, I need a scent, a direction. And she gave me one. So did her pretty little niece."

CHAPTER FIFTY

Thursday, May 14, 1942

Danny and Larkin camped in the coffee shop across the street from Osterkamp's shop, waiting for him to leave on a call. "There goes our friend." Danny paid the bill for their coffee.

The girl grew nervous as soon as they walked in. "My father isn't here."

"That's all right," Danny replied. "It's you I wanted to talk to. What's your name?"

"Annelise."

"A lovely name. It suits you. When we were here the other day, you said you and your cousin Dieter weren't close. Why?"

"We just aren't."

"I'm surprised. After all, you're about the same age…"

"I'm a year older."

"And I'll bet you're a popular girl," Danny said.

"Not really. Aside from my work here, I'm a homebody."

"Mostly socialize with family?"

"Yes, and…" She froze.

Danny softened his tone. "Annelise, you need not be afraid. I understand how immigrant families are. I'm an immigrant myself, came over from Ireland when I was young. Keeping close to my cousins was important to me." He ignored Larkin's arched eyebrows.

She relaxed. "We were close when we were young. He was very shy and quiet like Uncle Leopold. Aunt Frieda ruled with an iron fist, always grumbling about how Uncle Leopold should toughen Dieter up."

"Did he?" Danny asked.

"No. The summer after Dieter turned thirteen, he went away for several weeks. I never knew where. I didn't see him till Octoberfest that autumn. He'd changed."

"How so?"

"It's hard to explain. Even though I'm older, he was almost talking down at me. And that autumn, I was, um…"

"Blossoming?" Larkin asked.

Annelise giggled. "Yes." The smile vanished. "And he made some suggestive remarks to me about how his friends would like to… well, you can guess. We were never close again."

"How did Aunt Frieda react?" Danny asked.

"That was the worst part of it. It didn't bother her. Uncle Leopold made sour faces but said nothing."

There had to be something else. "So, after that, your father employed him?"

"Poppa thought working would ground Dieter, help him past whatever phase he was going through. I never knew what they talked about while on calls, but Poppa always had a sour expression when they returned. He said that Dieter had extraordinary skills, and a great capacity to learn."

Which they already knew. "Is your father close to your Aunt Frieda?"

Annelise shook her head. "He was, once, but no longer. I don't think she's close to anyone other than her brother-in-law."

Larkin appeared ready to say something, but Danny pre-empted him. "Who?"

"Uncle Leopold's brother, Hermann. They talk in whispers."

One more question. "Where did Dieter attend high school?"

"Bronx Science. He graduated with honors."

Danny gave her his card. "If Dieter contacts your poppa, or anyone in your family, or if you see him, please call me. I need to talk to him. Will you do that for me?"

She nodded. Danny and Larkin had already turned to leave when she blurted, "This is something to do with Nazis, isn't it?"

"Please just call me if you hear from him," Danny replied.

Outside, Larkin grinned at him. "What cousins?"

***

The knock at the door startled Hermann. No one had called.

Another knock.

He decided not to answer.

"Mr. Mueller?" Not a voice he recognized. "Police, Mr. Mueller. We saw your truck parked out front."

A slight brogue. Observant for an Irishman. Hermann mussed his hair and tried to look like he'd just awoken. "Just a minute."

He pulled the door open, facing two men in jackets, ties, and fedoras. One held out a badge. "Mr. Mueller, I'm Detective Brady, this is Detective Larkin. We have a few questions for you. May we come in?"

Whatever it was, he'd rather it be discussed behind closed doors. He nodded his assent, and they followed him inside.

"Do you know a young man named Dieter Mueller?" Brady asked.

"What's this about?"

"If you don't mind, we'll ask the questions. Do you?"

"Yes. He's my nephew. Is he in trouble?"

"We just need to ask him some questions," Brady replied.

Discovering what they already knew without giving anything away was the challenge. Stonewalling them would only make them more persistent. “What about? If he’s done something, my sister would want to be told.”

“We spoke to your sister. She didn’t know where Dieter was. That struck us as odd.”

“Did she tell you to ask me?” If he said she had, it would show the detective was lying and was looking to spring a trap. And if he admitted she hadn’t, he could ask who had.

“No. I saw the name on the van out front and took a chance. So, Dieter’s whereabouts?”

This Irishman was cagey. He wasn’t giving anything away. “I’m sorry, I don’t know. My sister said something about him going to visit a friend someplace upstate.”

“Thanks for your time, Mr. Mueller.”

“I’m concerned about what kind of trouble he’s in. I’d like to prepare my sister.”

The detective’s face was impassive. “Possibly none. The sooner we question him, the sooner we can move on.”

Hermann sat when they’d gone.

They know.

***

“He sure was anxious to find out why we were looking for Dieter,” Larkin said as they walked toward the Third Avenue El.

“He wanted to learn what we know. I didn’t tell him, so he’ll assume we know things we don’t.” When they reached Third Avenue, he crossed the street.

“Danny, that’s the downtown side.”

“We’re briefing Cogan, and then I’m taking the afternoon off. I’ll see you back on our scheduled four-to-twelve tomorrow.”

***

Hermann called each member of the group, spacing the calls out across the entire afternoon. He made certain he had an unrelated reason to call each one, so that the cancellation of their weekly meeting would be an inconsequential addition. With Christian, he asked about a minor injury he'd suffered a week earlier. With Paul, he mentioned a fishing trip in the late spring. He asked Hans about his sister's recent surgery.

Hans turned contentious. "Eventually, you'll explain what has happened to Dieter, what trouble he's in."

If the police or the FBI were tapping his phone, this could be fatal, but it was impossible to convey that without being obvious. "To the best of my knowledge, Dieter is visiting a friend. The subject is closed."

***

As Hermann walked to the tavern, he prepared for his conversation with Obermann. He had to convey caution but not panic, proceeding with care.

The pay phone rang at nine on the button.

"Good evening, *Herr Koordinator*," Obermann said. "Our visitor has settled in nicely. Marcus is happy to have him as a house guest, so long as he does not return their daughter's interest."

Hermann couldn't decide whether Obermann was speaking plainly or in some strange code. "I take it he knows better?"

"Yes. The girl is only fifteen. The lad is more concerned with other family members, distant relatives. They've begun corresponding. How's work going?"

Marcus had put Dieter in touch with his cousin, Reinhold Barth, providing a direct connection to the Abwehr. Frieda would be proud if she knew, but that was impossible. "I've had a problem on my most recent job and I had to turn off all the water. Naturally, the tenants are unhappy."

"They'll be grateful when the water is turned back on. Talk to you next week."

Their efforts would shortly come to Germany's attention, perhaps to the Führer himself. After the war, Hermann might have his choice of returning to the Fatherland or remaining in America as a minister of the Reich.

He quickly pushed such grandiose thoughts from his mind, the thinking that had brought down the Bund's leaders. He refused to succumb.

At the door to the street, he was stopped by Hans.

"Good evening, Mueller. You were able to come, after all."

Not here, not now. Hermann pushed past him and left the tavern.

Hans caught up to him on the street. "Was that your Long Island friend on the phone just now?"

A quick glance confirmed they were not being followed. No one was within earshot. "You are a damned fool. I canceled tonight's meeting because the police have been sniffing around."

"Looking for Dieter?"

Hermann made a quick calculation. "It occurs to me that, from the beginning, you have contributed the least to our efforts while criticizing the most. Perhaps it's time you withdrew from our group."

It pulled Hans up short. "You'd never allow me to walk away."

"Naturally, there would be security concerns. You'd be expected to do the honorable thing. Can you be honorable, Hans? Is it in you?"

"I served the Fatherland on the battlefield in the Great War, from the Somme to Mons, where I was wounded and left for dead. Don't you dare lecture me on honor, Hermann."

"And I was wounded at Amiens after serving in the Spring Offensive that pushed the Allies back. I had no part in the army's ultimate defeat."

Hans sneered. "Shell shock."

So, that's where this was going. Time to settle it. "What are you saying? You claim your honor from having served in a defeated army but show none for the Fatherland today. You repeatedly moan about my decisions but offer no suggestions. Shall we consult the group?"

Hans took a moment to absorb that. "I apologize, Herr Mueller. We all did what we could, and we do what we can now. There is no need to involve the group, I will endeavor to be more helpful."

Hermann walked the rest of the way alone, having only postponed the inevitable.

CHAPTER FIFTY-ONE

Friday, May 15, 1942

As Dieter turned the corner of the field that had once been the Camp Siegfried Parade Ground on his customary long early morning walk, he allowed his mind to wander to the one he'd tried to ignore, young Hedy Schmidt.

She'd flirted with him shamelessly since his arrival, despite her father's obvious disapproval. Since her father was providing both shelter from the probing eyes of the police and contact with a Reich official, Dieter did his best to rebuff her. When Herr Schmidt rebuked her, Dieter assumed his difficulties were behind him.

But she'd found more subtle ways. Frau Schmidt had not helped matters, seating Dieter across from Hedy at meals, next to Hedy's younger brother. Dieter did his best to avoid eye contact with the girl, but she had an uncanny talent for meeting his eyes with hers anytime he glanced her way.

Those eyes, bright blue, and her dark brown hair and porcelain skin. One glance, and it took all his willpower to resist. Dieter wasn't sure how long he could continue.

She emerged from behind a tree and stood in his path, grinning. "Good morning, Dieter."

He sidestepped her and continued walking.

She fell in beside him. “I’ve gone to the trouble to rise at this ungodly hour just to talk with you. At least be civil.”

Stoic silence was the best response. He kept walking.

She kept pace. “Wonderful days, weren’t they?”

“What days?” The words were out before he could stop them.

“Here, all of you marching and drilling on this field, ringed by beaming parents. And the one they all said would make a great leader one day stood out.”

He halted. “Who?”

“You, Dieter. They all said so—my father, Herr Obermann, everyone, and your uncle beamed with pride. I was only nine, but I was entranced. You were my soldier hero.”

He had to chuckle, and they resumed walking.

She linked her arm through his. “I’m sure you saw me as a bratty little girl in long braids with too much to say, if you even noticed me.”

“I noticed you.”

“Really? What did you notice?”

“A bratty girl in braids with too much to say.”

When they reached a cluster of trees at the far end of the field, she stopped and took his hands in hers. “You weren’t so shy back then.”

“You weren’t old enough to make me shy.” Another unintended slip.

Her eyes held him. Those enchanting eyes. “Dieter, have you ever kissed a girl?”

He couldn’t stop the blush. “No.”

“I want to be your first.”

***

“So, tell me,” Larkin said as he sat at his desk across from Danny’s at the start of their shift and stirred four lumps of sugar into his coffee. "What next? Other than the description, nobody gave us anything useful yesterday."

Danny stared as Larkin took a gulp. "How can you drink the swill we brew here? I wouldn't use it to clear a drain."

"If rationing comes in, like they say, you'll wish you had this nectar."

McHugh walked in with a faintly visible smudge of red next to his mouth.

"Cut yourself shaving, boyo?" Larkin touched his own cheek.

"Shit." McHugh grabbed one of Danny's napkins and wiped his mouth.

Danny tried not to laugh. "Cogan confirms that Dieter Mueller registered for the draft last May. His cousin's account suggests he may have attended Camp Siegfried in 1936."

"All of which means nothing," Larkin said.

"It convinces me Dieter Mueller is our burglar/killer and a potential saboteur. Sean, how'd you make out at Bronx Science yesterday?"

"Talked to the chemistry teacher again," McHugh said. "Dieter was an excellent student with a quick mind. But Quill's had no contact with him since graduation and doubts he's the burglar. I also picked up this."

"Bronx Science 1941 yearbook." Danny found Dieter's portrait. "Thanks, Sean."

"His mama said he went to visit a friend in Yonkers," Larkin said. "You buying that?"

Danny checked his notes. "And his uncle said he went 'somewhere upstate'. Sounds to me like someone doesn't want us to look east."

McHugh spoke up. "Or maybe they want us to look east and assumed we would if they emphasized Yonkers."

Larkin laughed. "Watch it, boyo. You'll wind up chasing your tail with logic like that."

"Perhaps," Danny replied. "But let's see if there's anything to that Yonkers story. Sean, you still have that list of classmates from

Mueller's school in Hell's Kitchen and this yearbook. Check the Yonkers phone book for any last names that match. Ask Cogan to check with the Motor Vehicles Department. They'll have driver's licenses. Check their current addresses. Ask Cogan to check the birth records for parents' names that match.

"Just the German names?" McHugh didn't hide the note of hope.

"All names. Mueller might have had friends among the other kids. Listen, me buckos, before we rule out Yonkers, I want to make certain we're not missing anything. In the meantime, I'll run this down to Cogan, so they can reproduce the photo and get it out to the field."

***

Meg's bell rang shortly after 9:00 in the evening. It was Danny, holding the note she'd left on his door an hour earlier. "What's the matter, Meg?"

She flew into his arms. "I've tried three times this week to call you, just to say hi. I thought you were working eight to four this week."

He held her, then kissed her. "I'm sorry. These days the hours of my shift are more of a guideline than anything else. I'm on a case, now, that's… well, it's complicated."

She looked him in the eye, keeping her arms around him. "Complicated how?"

"Nothing that should worry you. I'm fine."

"Are you in danger?"

He laughed. "Not even remotely. It's just that these days, I'm often out of the Bronx because of this case. How about another night of dinner and dancing tomorrow?"

She relaxed. "Okay." He pulled her back into a deep kiss.

Only a trace of doubt and worry remained.

CHAPTER FIFTY-TWO

Tuesday, May 19, 1942

Danny arrived at the precinct early. Larkin wasn't in, yet, but McHugh was. "There were two last names in the phone book that matched names on the school list. Cogan got back to me this morning. One has a driver's license and is now living in Brooklyn. The other doesn't, but his father's name differs from the name in the Yonkers phone book. Think it could be a cousin?"

Danny flopped into his chair. "Dieter Mueller's on the lam, so he goes see a cousin of an old school friend? Don't think so." He stewed about it as Larkin walked in. "Screw it, give me the boy's name and address."

"What's the plan?" Larkin asked.

Danny gave McHugh Hermann Mueller's address. "He's a plumber, and his truck is usually parked in front. Camp there until you can identify him."

"Want me to tail him if he goes out?"

"No, stay in the car. Don't let him see you."

"And what are we to be doing this fine spring day?" Larkin asked.

"I'll be going to Yonkers."

***

The moment Herr Schmidt called him into his workshop, Dieter was worried. Had Hedy said something she shouldn't?

"Please close the door, Dieter. I guess you must be getting eager for action."

"Yes, sir."

"I appreciate you resisting my daughter's temptations. Hedwig is a singularly willful girl, and Frau Schmidt and I have failed to curb her flirtatious ways. Your determination to remain focused on your duty to the Fatherland is admirable. You will make a fine soldier for the Reich."

"Thank you, sir." He tried not to think of Hedy's eyes, or of the sensation of holding her in his arms.

"I've had a letter from my cousin in Berlin, through Lisbon. He and his superior officer have proposed an operation to the Führer."

"A military operation?" Might they be planning to send him to Germany to train with the Wehrmacht?

"No, a covert operation. Sabotage. He has asked if I might recommend anyone qualified to join in such an operation."

Dieter kept still, not even blinking. Showing enthusiasm would eliminate him from consideration.

Herr Schmidt only stared. Dieter stared back.

After an eternity, Herr Schmidt continued as if the pause had only been a few seconds. "I will tell him I have total confidence that you will succeed, whatever they plan."

***

Danny returned from Yonkers after eight. The listing McHugh had found was a dead end.

Larkin met him at the door. "So, we can rule out Yonkers."

"Barring unforeseen developments. But something is eating at me. Dieter Mueller isn't working alone, and whoever else is involved is older. It isn't Osterkamp, and it isn't Leopold Mueller. Not sure about Hermann. I don't want to tail him because he might sniff it out. But there's a tavern on 85th Street that'd make a convenient gathering spot for potential troublemakers."

"You want the FBI to send someone in there?"

"No, I want to send in someone who can pass for one of their own, a quiet observer who can watch and listen without appearing to watch and listen. It can't be you or I, and Vinnie would stick out like a sore thumb in that neighborhood."

McHugh approached. "Got a good long look at him and he never saw me."

Danny clapped him on the shoulder. "Great. Interested in doing a little undercover work at the *Bier Garten*? Nothing confrontational, just watch and listen."

"Think I can pass as a Nazi?" McHugh broke into a grin.

"No, just a German-American. Think you can handle hearing offensive stuff?"

"Sure, I can…" McHugh froze. Rebecca Stoneman was approaching.

"Go ahead, Sean, I'll clear it with Greco tomorrow. Your secret is safe with us."

Rebecca's face was creased with worry. "I closed the shop over an hour ago. Where were you? I thought…" She noticed Danny and Larkin. "Hello."

Danny tipped his hat. "Good evening, Miss Stoneman. Please don't mind us. See you tomorrow, Sean."

Rebecca linked her arm through McHugh's and leaned against him as they walked back up the 167th Street hill.

Larkin watched them go. "You sure about this, Danny boy?"

CHAPTER FIFTY-THREE

Wednesday, May 20, 1942

Danny walked into Greco's office and, without preamble, explained his plan to send McHugh into the *Bier Garten*.

"I don't like it," Greco said. "McHugh's a good kid, but he's not even a detective, let alone trained for undercover work. Not to mention his, ahem, outside interests."

Good, it was on the table. "McHugh's a good man—smart, perceptive, cool in tough spots. As far as his interest in Stoneman's daughter goes…"

"I hear it's gone way beyond mere interest."

He made a mental note to remind McHugh to meet Rebecca elsewhere. "Probably not too far. She's a nice girl. I've already told him he'd have to be ready for stuff that will piss him off. He can handle it. As for the undercover work, he'll just watch and listen. He may be the strongest guy on the team."

"That's a hell of an endorsement. How do you want to proceed?"

"I want to know if Hermann Mueller shows up, and if it's a meeting place for troublemakers."

"How will he recognize Mueller?" Greco asked.

"I had him stake him out yesterday."

"Take the rest of today and all day tomorrow. If you're right, the ring—whoever is in it—will watch for strangers to invade. Give them some time to drop their guard."

"You're allowing me to send McHugh in undercover?"

"If I refuse, you might do it behind my back."

CHAPTER FIFTY-FOUR

Friday, May 22, 1942

When Hermann Mueller saw the envelope with the Yaphank postmark, he retreated to his apartment. It was from Obermann. Strange, they had spoken by telephone the evening before.

Dear Hermann,

Just a quick note since we rarely get to speak. We had talked about a fishing trip this summer. I am looking for a boat to charter. I will have a better idea when everything is in the water.

Regards,
Fred

They'd never discussed fishing.

This must be something that couldn't be discussed on the phone. He reread the letter.

"... in the water." That was the key. Friedrich had described secret writing methods in their last conversation.

He filled a bowl with water and immersed the letter. Impressions that had been made on the paper when Friedrich had wet it now stood out, discernible against the note he'd written on top of it when the paper had dried. "Abwehr planning a mission to land saboteurs on Eastern Long Island once a proper team is assembled. Dieter will be their guide once they land. Marcus and I will send him to stay out east once we learn the details. Dieter will bring them to the city for their mission. Your team's help will be appreciated. Details to follow."

After letting it dry, he burned the letter, dropping the flaming paper into an ash tray. Then he dialed Paul's office number. "Meet me in the usual place this evening at six, please."

***

Hermann paced in front of the usual bench at Carl Schurz Park. It wasn't like Paul to be late. Several disastrous scenarios ran through his mind while he paced. The FBI might have picked up Paul or Christian. Hans could have turned traitor and informed on them.

He shoved such poisonous thoughts away, refusing to crumble at the first sign of difficulty. Paul was reliable. He would arrive as soon as possible.

Paul approached along the path. "Sorry I'm late, but I was detained."

"Who by?" Hermann tried to ignore the clutching sensation in his stomach.

"Hans. He's concerned that Dieter has brought suspicion on all of us, and that we are all at heightened risk.

A gust blew in off the river, and they both turned their backs on it. It gave Hermann an opportunity to survey the park for unwanted listeners. He found none.

"Hans has stood in opposition to you from the beginning," Paul said. "Yet he contributes nothing positive and has speculated more than once about Dieter's whereabouts."

"Is he seeking information to sell?"

"I would not make such an accusation without evidence."

"But it's possible?"

"I cannot rule it out."

Hermann stiffened his back against another blast of wind. "Do you have any suggestions?"

"For now, I suggest we not discuss certain matters in front of him."

It was a relief to hear him say it. Hermann briefed him on the Obermann letter.

Paul said, "Then that settles it. We must proceed with you in formal command. I will support you. Christian will, too."

"We will meet Monday evening in my apartment for a friendly game of cards."

CHAPTER FIFTY-FIVE

Monday, May 25, 1942

Mueller didn't show up at the *Bier Garten* all weekend, and McHugh described his conversations with the bartender: "As thrilling as cold sauerbraten." Cogan had suggested neither the *Bier Garten* nor Hermann Mueller was worth watching.

"Face it, Danny," Greco said, "the trail's going cold. You've given Cogan the kid's picture and they've circulated it out east. You checked out Yonkers, and I even got the Yonkers, Nassau County, and Suffolk County police departments on it. Fitzgibbon camped on the pawn shop owner's tail. And after all of that, you've got nothing."

"Not quite nothing." Danny hated being pushed into corners, especially now, when he was sure the next words out of Greco's mouth would be, "Focus on something else." But Greco had waited until Larkin was involved elsewhere before calling Danny into his office, knowing Danny would fight him.

"Okay." Greco sat back. "What have you got?"

Danny had looked for Meg at Mass on Sunday but hadn't seen her. He needed to focus. "No burglaries since the fur shop, so Dieter Mueller's our guy. He's not here in the city, and wherever he is, he's lying low. Probably out east."

"So, what's your plan?"

"I want to take Larkin and re-interview his parents. Who knows? Squeeze his pa and something useful might spill out."

"What about his uncle?" Greco asked.

"No, the mother was sullen, but Hermann fenced with me. And I'm not ready to give up on the *Bier Garten*. Let's back off a few days and then send McHugh back in."

"Cogan said…"

Danny cut him off, which he rarely did. "Cogan isn't running the murder investigation, I am. I've never allowed anyone else to control my investigations and I'm not starting today."

Greco sat back and lit another cigarette. "Then, what?"

"Let's put a tap on Hermann Mueller's phone. His nephew's a fugitive and Hermann knows where he is."

Greco gestured surrender. "Okay, stick with it and keep me informed. But do yourself a favor and take your scheduled two days off tomorrow and Wednesday, will ya?"

***

It was after six when Hermann remembered he was out of schnapps. He stopped in at the *Bier Garten*, which was much closer than the liquor store. As usual, the owner, Emile, was behind the bar.

"Anything new?" Hermann asked as Emile made change.

Emile glanced around the empty bar. "*Nein*, things have been quiet. The stranger who was here over the weekend hasn't been in."

"German?"

"Could be, but definitely Northern European. I talked to him a bit, but he had little to say, and that's odd. Most Americans can't hold their tongues when they drink. Then again, he doesn't drink much. A couple of beers, and that seems to be his limit."

"Could be police or FBI. Watch yourself."

"I always do. If he's ever here when you come in, I'll ring up the cash register as a signal."

Hermann tipped his cap and left. Christian, Paul, and Hans all arrived at his apartment separately, all within a few minutes of each other. Hans arrived last. Hermann poured a little schnapps for each of them.

"From the beginning, I have treated this group as a society of colleagues, tolerating dissent, soliciting advice, weighing alternative suggestions. But now, for our mutual safety and the sake of efficiency, we'll be better served if we operate with military discipline." Hans snorted. With calculated calm, Hermann asked, "You regard this as amusing?"

Hans didn't back down. "Not at all, but I've been expecting this."

"Expecting what?"

"You assuming command of the group."

Hermann took a sip of schnapps. "I am not assuming anything. You're here to vote: should we adopt such a structure, and if so, who should command?"

Hans sneered. "And who might the candidates be?"

"That is entirely up to the three of you."

"Herr Mueller," Paul said, "I move we adopt a command structure with you in command."

"I second the motion," Christian said.

"All in favor?" Hermann asked.

Paul and Christian raised their hands, and Hans followed with an expression of resignation.

"Thank you," Hermann said. "I will continue to seek your advice, but I must ask for each of you to swear that you will reveal nothing of what we do or discuss to anyone outside the group for any reason, under pain of death."

"I do so swear," Paul said.

"My allegiance is total," Christian said, "and I so solemnly swear."

Hans paled and muttered, “I swear.”

“As do I,” Hermann said. “And now, gentlemen, let us finish our schnapps.”

They all drank.

***

Frieda Mueller glared at Danny and Larkin as she opened the door. “I have nothing more to say to you.”

Danny adopted an expression of mild surprise. “We wondered if you’d heard from your son. Is he back?”

“No.”

“And where did he go?”

“To see a friend in Yonkers.”

“Have you recalled the name of that friend?”

“No, I trust my son.”

“What’s he doing for money?”

“I imagine he gets by. What do you want with him?”

Danny gave a slight smirk. “You mean, if I tell you, you’ll tell me where he is?”

“I don’t know where he is.”

“Wow,” Larkin said. “Some mom. Son’s gone for weeks, but you don’t know where and don’t care. If my son were missing, my wife would move heaven and Earth to find him.”

Frau Mueller’s eyes flared. “How dare you!”

Danny stepped in. “It’s the appearance you give. For what it’s worth, I’m certain you know where he is, why he fled, and why we want to talk to him, but I’ll play along. We suspect he killed an old classmate named Tommy McCardle. If he turns himself in, he can explain what happened and the DA will go easier on him than if we track him down.”

“My son didn’t kill anyone.”

"In that case," Danny replied, "he can tell us where he was at the time and who he was with, and that will clear his name. Think about it, Mrs. Mueller, before he gets in any deeper."

As they returned to the car, Danny turned to Larkin. "What son? You have a daughter."

Larkin shrugged. "You have your cousins. I have my son."

CHAPTER FIFTY-SIX

Wednesday, May 27, 1942

Hermann was taken aback when Frieda rang his bell. “You shouldn’t be here.”

“The police came back. They’re trying to discover where Dieter is, but they know he killed that Irish boy, and probably more than they’re letting on.”

“The police often pretend to know more than they do.”

“They want to talk to him,” she said. “I thought perhaps we could give him an alibi for the night of the…”

“No, because that would mean bringing Dieter back here, which would lead to his arrest. We can’t afford that. Germany has plans for Dieter.”

“Is he returning to the Fatherland?”

“*Nein.* His work is here. Now please remain calm.”

After she left, he walked over to the *Bier Garten*, bracing himself for the telltale ring of the cash register when he walked in, but Emile was busy filling steins and didn’t see him. The place was crowded and loud. No one would hear the call he placed, and the mere placing of an unscheduled call would signal a new alert status to Friedrich.

CHAPTER FIFTY-SEVEN

Thursday, May 28, 1942

"I got something." McHugh didn't even have his coat off. Danny grinned and gestured for him to continue. "Mueller came into the *Bier Garten* last night around eight."

"Did he talk to anyone?"

"No, he went straight to the phone and called some guy named Friedrich. It was a quick conversation, only a minute. He hardly said anything, just 'How's the wife and family' and 'talk to you soon'. In between, after a long silence, he also said, 'Yes, I've been considering that myself'."

Interesting. "Mueller lives alone, so why would he make a phone call from the tavern? Did the bartender ever talk to him?"

"No, I don't think he even saw him."

"Did the bartender engage you in conversation?"

"No, but he looked me over."

Something to probe. "Return tonight. See if he gets friendly. Also, see if Hermann has any buddies show up. In the meantime, check with the phone company and see if they can tell us what number he called and where it is."

***

Dieter jumped at the knock on the door to the guest room. He laid aside his copy of *Mein Kampf* and answered the door. "Herr Schmidt, Herr Obermann." There had been a development.

"May we come in?" Herr Schmidt asked.

"Please." Dieter closed the door behind them.

"Thank you." Herr Schmidt sat on the bed while Herr Obermann took the one chair, at the desk, as Dieter remained standing.

"I received two letters today from my cousin." Herr Schmidt handed a sealed envelope to Dieter. "This one is for you. Ignore the written greeting and immerse the letter in water."

He did so, and another message appeared.

Herr Mueller,

Marcus has reported to me on your activities on behalf of the Reich, and has attested to both your skills and your character. The Führer has approved an operation to land a team of saboteurs on the eastern end of Long Island near Amagansett by U-boat in early June. Your assignment is to meet the team on the beach at night and guide them into New York City. More details will be provided by the team leader upon arrival. Heil Hitler.

Reinhold Barth

"You uncle advises me the police have been looking for you and have questioned your family," Herr Obermann said. "We think the FBI may already be sniffing around here because of our past, and it would be prudent for you to leave."

Hedy. How could he leave her?

“Don’t worry,” Herr Schmidt said. “We’re not throwing you out. I have a friend who lives in Amagansett who has agreed to put you up until late June. He is the head groundskeeper at the Beach Hills Country Club and will find work for you there.”

Herr Obermann took over. “This will allow you to blend in. We won’t have to construct a fiction to get you there when the time comes. Also, there is a Coast Guard station at Amagansett. You will have time to study it, see how thoroughly they patrol the beaches, and develop a plan to get our team off the beach undetected.”

“When do I leave?” Thoughts of Hedy were almost overwhelming.

“Tomorrow morning,” Herr Schmidt replied. “I’ll drive you out.”

***

Minutes to midnight, and still Dieter couldn’t sleep. The house had gone quiet two hours earlier. He tossed and turned again, trying to sleep.

The door opened, creating a slight draft, and closed again. A rustling of fabric.

A moment later, the covers were pulled back, and someone slipped into bed with him.

“Relax, it’s me.” Hedy’s soft voice.

He turned to face her, a sliver of moonlight falling across her cheek. He reached to embrace and kiss her. She pulled him in, wrapping her legs around him.

She’d shed her nightgown.

CHAPTER FIFTY-EIGHT

Friday, May 29, 1942

It wasn't the breaking of dawn that awoke Dieter, it was Hedy slipping out of bed. She was already pulling on her nightgown when it registered. "Where are you going?"

She snickered. "I'm saving your life by returning to my bedroom." When he sprang from the bed, she giggled at his nudity and embraced him. "I am yours, and yours alone. I'll wait however long it takes. And for your sake, I won't be around when you leave. But I will be here when you return. Until then, you must be strong."

With one last kiss, she was gone.

He dressed and packed his small valise, leaving *Mein Kampf* out to read until the family awoke. But try as he might, he could not focus on the Führer*'s* stirring words and galvanizing ideas. Only lovely Hedy filled his thoughts.

Finally, at seven, Herr Schmidt knocked on his door. "Up, dressed, and packed already? I admire your enthusiasm. Come, my wife has a lovely spread of bread rolls, gouda cheese, and ham waiting for us."

After breakfast, Herr Schmidt drove him east. "You'll be working during the day and free to roam in the evening. Karl—Mr. Griswold to you—is not sympathetic to the Reich, so he is ignorant of your mission and must remain so. When you leave to rendezvous with the team, you will say nothing to him or his family about leaving."

"Should I then return here? And should I tell Herr Griswold anything?"

"First, it's Mr. Griswold. He is very Americanized. Do not use German words or phrases at all while you are in Amagansett. Act as American as you can." He broke into a sly grin. "I'm sure Hedwig gave you some pointers on that."

Had he learned of their morning walks? Last night? Dieter had to acknowledge the comment, but how?

Herr Schmidt rescued him. "I realize you could not comply with my request about Hedwig, who is as clever as she is willful. But having watched her in the time you've spent with us, I—or rather, Frau Schmidt—formed the opinion that she is in love with you. I strongly suspect her feelings are returned."

"Yes, sir." It felt so good to say it, he ignored the possibility of a rebuke or worse.

"Keep a note in your room addressed to Mr. Griswold saying that you've had to return home and will call him when you can. Make sure it's well hidden before you leave for work each morning."

"Yes, sir." But having admitted his feelings for Hedy, he needed to say something about her. "If I may, regarding…"

"Rent a post office box and check it frequently. Drop me a postcard with the address." He drove the rest of the way in silence. He finally pulled up to a bungalow near the beach. "When this is over, you have my permission to pursue Hedwig."

***

Hermann was walking in Carl Schurz Park when he saw Hans sitting on a bench, alone.

"Ah, *Herr Koordinator*." It was impossible to ignore the sneer.

"Good afternoon, Hans." A quick glance around showed no one else nearby.

Hans caught it. "Oh, yes, always be careful, be prudent. Is that characteristic of a good *Koordinator*?"

Hermann sat next to him on the bench, sniffing for the telltale odor of alcohol. "Get into the schnapps a little early today?"

"I'm much too good a soldier for that."

"You were a good soldier, but you've forgotten what that means."

Hans laughed without humor. "No, I haven't. Soldiers look out for one another, and one of ours is missing. The youngest and the brightest, but you placed too much responsibility on his shoulders too soon. You can't deny the police are looking for him."

"They are, which is why I discontinued our meetings at the *Bier Garten*."

"You might have mentioned that the other night."

Hermann struggled to hold his temper in check. "I mentioned it when I told each of you about the meeting."

"Not to me, you didn't." Hans waved it away. "Regardless, where is Dieter? As an accomplice, I have a right to know."

"You have no right to information that endangers him. Why would you think otherwise? Are you looking for information to sell?"

Hans rose from his seat. "That's contemptible. You'd better hope that I'm not."

Hermann watched him go. They had reached the crisis point. Time for his first hard decision.

***

Danny was just getting ready to leave at the end-of-tour when Cogan walked in. "Glad I caught you. The phone company provided a list of calls made from the pay phone in the *Bier Garten* the night

McHugh overheard Hermann Mueller, including one made to a number in Yaphank."

"German Gardens?"

"Likely. Our agents on Long Island will cruise the streets of German Gardens for Dieter Mueller armed with his photo. Sorry it took so long to get the photos to them, but chemicals for developing are growing scarce, what with the war effort."

CHAPTER FIFTY-NINE

Saturday, May 30, 1942

As Danny walked into Roseland with Meg on his arm, the maître d' asked them to wait a moment.

"Why, if it isn't me old mate, Danny boy."

Oh, no, it couldn't be. The odds against it were too great. But there was no mistaking the voice, and when he glanced up, his worst fears were realized. "Hello, Frankie, is Helen with you?"

"She is, at our table." Larkin turned to Meg. "Mrs. Corwyn, I believe?"

Danny resisted the urge to punch his partner.

Meg extended her hand. "Not anymore, Detective. Miss O'Rourke."

At least Larkin had the good grace to blush. "My apologies. Detective Brady can be most Sphinx-like when he chooses."

Danny couldn't resist. "A lesson for some."

She broke into a grin. "Just call me Meg, and we'll get along fine."

The maître d' returned. "I have your table, sir."

"That's all right," Larkin replied. "They're joining us."

The maître d' noted the surge of incoming patrons and sighed with relief. "As you wish, sir." Relief became a grin when Danny slipped him a sawbuck. "Thank you, sir."

***

The orchestra took a break and Meg clung to Danny as they made their way back to the table. She couldn't believe their luck. After she'd been introduced to Frank's wife, Helen, and they'd enjoyed a drink and some conversation, the orchestra had played "Little Brown Jug". Meg had popped up and led Danny by the hand to the dance floor, calling back over her shoulder, "I taught him to Lindy to this."

Helen's stunned expression had been impossible to miss. And, once on the dance floor, Danny had danced like a pro. Frank and Helen had joined them, and they'd danced the entire set.

As they returned to the table, Danny stopped in his tracks. "It's McHugh."

Meg recognized the name. She glanced at Helen.

Helen's smile vanished, and she whispered in Meg's ear, "Our evening out is about to be cut short."

Danny introduced Officer Sean McHugh to the ladies, but, leaving no time for pleasantries, said. "What's happened?"

"Got a call from Detective Fitzgibbon to meet him at Grant's Tomb immediately if not sooner. I came as fast as I could." He turned to Danny. "Sorry, Fitzgibbon said you'd be here."

Helen looped her arm through Meg's. "You boys take Danny's car, I'll drive Meg home."

While Helen kissed her husband, Danny kissed Meg's forehead. "I'm sorry…"

"I understand, duty calls. Please call me when you get in." Danny nodded and turned away, but she pulled him back. "No matter the time."

***

By the time Danny and Larkin arrived at Grant's Tomb, the coroner's office had taken the body and gone, and the scene was quiet.

"Sorry to drag you boys from your Saturday night festivities." Fitzgibbon was leaning against the rail near the spot where they'd found the fibers from the first victim's coat, smoking a cigarette. "Everything was the same as McCardle's murder. Head injury, followed by a roll down the hill from here. Body next to the tracks was reported by a train conductor who spotted it on the way into Penn Station. Train arrived at 8:18, which means it probably passed this spot around ten after."

"Estimate on time of death?" Danny asked.

"Guy from the coroner's office thinks between seven and eight this evening."

A train emerged from the tunnel. Danny waited for it to pass. "Couldn't have been earlier than eight, because there would have been more train traffic at that hour. What did the victim look like?"

Fitzgibbon checked his notes. "About five-eight, looked about one-sixty, mid-to-late forties, light brown hair with a little gray at the temples, heavy mustache. I'd say northern European of some sort. I tell ya, Danny, I could do with a dram about now."

The description rang a bell, but Danny was still annoyed about leaving Meg and couldn't place it. "Tough day?"

"Saturday night, I promised to be home on time." Fitzgibbon pointed toward the hill. "Looks the same as last time."

"Not everything," Danny said after a moment. "Evening rather than dawn, body rolled down the hill but not left on the tracks. Different spot from where the first body was rolled down. Was the victim's wallet on him?"

"No."

"Did you find it?"

Fitzgibbon snorted. “Come on, Danny, it’s pitch dark on that hill.”

“Got a flashlight?”

***

Helen Larkin had talked nonstop from the moment they’d climbed into the car. She talked about the time she’d tried to teach Danny to Lindy, and he’d hurt his ankle. She’d fixed him up with friends and cousins. They’d found him nice, but nothing ever developed. “You, however, are another story. I watched him dancing with you, Meg, and there was a light in his eye. I’ve known him almost as long as Frankie has, and I’ve never seen that before.”

Meg tried to answer but could only blush.

Helen burst into laughter. “That’s what I thought. That big lug is like a brother to me, and I’m thrilled, wishing you the best.”

Must slow this down. “We’ve only just started going together.” She recounted Danny’s first attempts, and then the flowers.

Helen was undeterred. “The clock’s been running since you first met him, you just didn’t realize it.”

No use arguing. “I guess so.”

After a brief silence, Helen turned thoughtful. “So, ask me.”

“What?”

“The one question I suspect is burning away at you, but you’re too polite to ask.”

Meg could only think of one. “Do you worry about Frankie?”

Helen broke into a momentary grin. “That’s the question. I worry every time he goes out that door with that pistol in his shoulder holster. It’s why I wanted to scream when I saw that guy walk into Roseland. I didn’t know he was McHugh, but I realized by the look in his eye why he was there. We develop a sixth sense about that kind of thing.”

“We?”

“Police wives. We stick together, tell each other whatever we find out, because our husbands don’t tell us half of what they’re doing.”

"I'm sure Danny would." Only after she said it did she realize what she was admitting.

"He won't, Meg. He'll want to protect you, like they all do, and he'll be more tight-lipped than most."

***

As with the McCardle murder, Danny patrolled both sides of the roadway, searching for anything that might have been dropped, like the button from McCardle's coat. Despite an hour of painstaking search, he found nothing.

He scanned the underbrush on the hill for another forty-five minutes until the batteries in the flashlight ran down. No sign of anything.

"Forget it, Danny," Larkin said. "Even the crime scene guys have packed it in for the night."

"Then we'll return in the morning and look."

"I'll drive you home, Frank," McHugh said

After driving several blocks, Danny stopped in a bar and found the phone booth. It was eleven-thirty—late to call Meg, but she'd insisted.

She answered on the first ring. "You okay?"

"Sure. I…"

"Are you home? I hear other people."

No sense in fibbing. "I'm still in Manhattan. I was concerned because it's so late."

"Please stop here on your way home." Her voice softened. "I need to see you."

***

Meg was already in her nightgown, so she donned a floor-length wraparound robe and waited. It was after midnight when Danny knocked twice on her door.

As soon as he was inside with the door closed, she threw her arms around him.

He didn't break the embrace until she was ready. "I'm sorry about this evening, Meg. We'll do it again, soon."

She kissed him. "I just needed to see you're safe."

"It was just a crime scene investigation. The criminal was long gone when we arrived." He looked her in the eye. "I expect Helen Larkin filled you with a lot of…"

"Helen and I had a pleasant talk. We'll be good friends."

"Yes, but…"

"She explained cops don't tell their wives much, so they won't worry. But wives do worry. And I worried tonight, just as I'll worry every time you go off to work."

His manner turned sour. "Helen shouldn't have spooked you like that. I know about wives gossiping, and there's no point in it. The less said the better."

"No, Danny. I was worried sick about you tonight."

He scoffed. "It was nothing. Just a crime scene." He leaned forward to kiss her on the forehead.

She pulled back. "What crime? Tell me." He said nothing. "Murder?"

"Nothing for you to worry about."

"I can't live like that, Danny. I can't."

CHAPTER SIXTY

Monday, June 1, 1942

"Let me get this straight," Greco said in a growl. "A John Doe in his borough, and Fitzgibbon calls you in? What was he, drunk?"

"Similarities to the McArdle murder. Same place, same cause, same method."

"So, your burglar-killer is back in town?"

Danny hadn't slept pondering that very question and trying to keep his mind off his talk with Meg. "There are more differences than similarities. McArdle had been observed fleeing the scene of a burglary committed by our guy. The killer chose Riverside Park hoping the body would be obliterated by a train. Fitzgibbon and I returned to the site this morning, and we found nothing else, no wallet, no other evidentiary matter." They'd combed the entire damned hill.

His mind drifted back to Meg. They hadn't seen or called each other on Sunday.

"Danny?" Greco broke in on his thoughts. "You with us? You don't think Mueller's back?"

Greco should be smarter than that. "The known facts don't support a conclusion either way. Who is this guy? Fitz and I checked him out at the morgue yesterday." He dropped a photo on Greco's desk.

"The moustache tells me he's a kraut," Greco said.

"And without it, he'd look like any of a half dozen other nationalities. But the coroner found one interesting feature." He dropped a second photo on the desk. "Look at the scarring on his legs. This area, here, that's from a severe burn. These impressions, on his left leg, look like deep puncture wounds from irregularly shaped objects, and the smaller scars on the opposite side of the leg are probably exit wounds."

Greco's interest was caught. "Shrapnel? So, this guy was a veteran?"

"That's the likely explanation."

"Yeah, but what war and what army?"

Exactly what Danny had been asking himself. "Given his age, I'd say the last war. What army is another question. The coroner says the left leg is shorter than the right. The heel on his left shoe was an inch-and-a-half thicker."

Greco studied the two photos. "Fitzgibbon mention anything about the shoes?"

"No, but it was dark. Now, if you'll excuse me, Lieutenant, I'll review my notes and for anything ringing a bell with this guy. Because if our burglar-killer didn't do this, someone else went to great lengths to make it appear he did, someone who knew the details of McCardle's murder."

***

It was almost one, time for Meg to take her lunch break. She walked along Roosevelt Avenue to the drug store where she often ate at the lunch counter. But she stopped at the phone booth first and dialed the number she'd memorized over a year ago.

"Detective squad, Brady."

"Hi, it's me. Just wanted to see how you're doing."

His voice brightened. "Oh, hi, Meg. I'm okay. Just busy."

"Would you like to come to my place for dinner tonight?"

"I'd really like that. But when I'm on a case like this, my hours go all haywire. My library never closes."

"I can manage. It's not about the meal; I need to talk to you."

A moment's hesitation. "Thanks. I'd like that. I'll call you when I figure out what time I can make it, okay?"

"Sure. Bye."

***

As Danny hung up, Larkin's eyes were on him. He refused to look up, focusing instead on the notes of the burglary cases. He'd been in the middle of something with potential before the phone rang.

Larkin cleared his throat.

Danny kept reading. It was the description given by the pawnbroker on Delancey street of the guy who'd pawned some of Stoneman's jewelry.

Larkin couldn't wait any longer. "Meg? About Saturday night?"

Danny still didn't look up. "Good partners don't listen in on each other's phone conversations." He had mentioned nothing about their argument.

"Couldn't be helped."

Danny thrust the photo of the John Doe and his page of notes at Larkin. "If you want to help, tell me what you think of that."

Larkin turned serious. "Could be a match."

"But that description could also fit a thousand other guys."

McHugh spoke up. "Danny, how much longer do you want me going to the *Bier Garten*? There isn't anything interesting going on there."

Danny showed him the photo. "Ever see this guy around there?"

McHugh studied it. "This the guy from Saturday night?"

"Yeah. Frankie, let's show this photo to the pawnbroker who gave us this description."

***

They were almost at Delancey Street. Larkin hadn't said a word the whole ride. But Danny knew it was coming.

"So, you two are finally an item. Good."

"I thought you didn't approve."

"I didn't approve of you torturing yourself over a married woman. Helen thinks it's serious."

Danny pulled into a parking space on Norfolk Street. "Do me a favor, Frankie, just focus on this case."

They entered the pawn shop, only to find a young man behind the counter, no older than his mid-twenties.

"You the owner's son?" Danny asked as they flashed their badges.

"Yeah, why?"

"Can we speak to your dad?"

"Be kinda hard. He's home in bed. Had a stroke, blind in one eye, his good eye, and he ain't quite right in the head."

"Could we speak to him?" Larkin asked before Danny could stop him.

"Geez, guys, you gotta be kidding. He's waiting to die. Just leave him, can't ya?"

Danny inserted himself. "We meant no disrespect. We only want to ask him if he recognized the man in this photo. He might have pawned some items of jewelry here a couple of months ago."

The son gestured to see the photo. "This guy's dead? You want to show my dad a picture of a stiff?"

"We didn't know your dad was ill," Danny replied. "Have you ever seen him?"

"No." He shoved the photo away.

"Please take another look," Danny said, his voice soft. "We're trying to catch his killer, and any information you can provide would help."

"I told you, I ain't never seen him before, okay?"

Danny glanced at Larkin and nodded toward the door. "Okay, thanks. Hope your dad gets well."

As they returned to the car, Larkin asked, "Is it my imagination, or are we having a run of real bad luck on this case?"

***

Dieter had followed Herr Schmidt's instructions to the letter. He'd allowed Griswold to introduce him around as a friend of the family, and he'd taken on every job Griswold assigned him with good cheer, from groundskeeping to busing tables in the country club restaurant.

He'd also rented the post office box.

Mealtime conversation soon confirmed that the Griswolds had no desire to be enemies of their adopted country. He assured them he, too, loved America, and his habit of taking nighttime walks along the beach, listening to the pounding of the surf, and taking in the panoply of stars in the sky over the beach, allowed him to feel serene.

***

The pawn shop on Fourth Avenue between 16th Street and 17th Street was Danny's last hope. He brightened when he saw the same man behind the counter whom they'd seen the last time. Even better, he remembered them. "Not another heist, I hope."

"No, but I need you to examine a photo and tell me if this man looks familiar." Danny prayed Larkin wouldn't say anything. As much as he needed a lead on this case, he needed it to be accurate.

The owner took his time studying the photo. "Definitely looks familiar. I recognize the moustache and the gray hair around the temples. I think he's the guy who pawned the jewelry I gave you."

"Do you remember anything else about him? Did he speak with an accent? Anything you noted that's not in the picture?"

"He walked slowly. Not limping but being careful. I remember that because most guys hocking hot goods can't get out of the shop fast enough."

Danny thanked him, and they left the shop.

"Okay," Larkin said. "What, now?"

"Time for another visit to the G-man."

CHAPTER SIXTY-ONE

"Wait," Cogan said. "The guy who hocked some of the Stoneman jewelry was killed by the guy who had him hock it?"

Danny took a deep breath. "Dieter Mueller didn't kill the John Doe. He doubtless knows by now that leaving McArdle on the tracks didn't work, and he wouldn't leave the body where it was certain to be found within minutes. So, the killer wants us to think the kid did it, that he's back in town, and whoever is running the group knows we're looking for the kid and wants to throw us off. They likely have plans for him."

"Okay," Cogan said, "you sold me. What do you suggest?"

"Anything from your Long Island office on German Gardens?"

"Not yet. They're proceeding low key. I'm hoping that since they now have the kid's picture, it might shake something loose."

Danny exchanged glances with Larkin. "Any way to make it high key?"

Cogan lowered his voice. "Tough sell right now. The Director's busy trying to round up German and Italian immigrants like he's done with the Japs, but we're running into resistance because, let's face it, the Krauts and Wops didn't bomb Pearl Harbor. Going low key is as much to avoid Mr. Hoover's notice as it is to avoid tipping off any Nazis lying in the weeds."

"So, you've got nothing?"

"Not quite. Our national office came up with one Reinhold Barth, former resident of Long Island, returned to Germany in 1939 and now holds a position with the Abwehr. I've asked the Long Island Office if he left any relatives behind."

***

Hermann wasn't surprised when the two detectives rang his bell, looking for Dieter. That was the plan.

"We have some questions for you," the lead detective said, the one named Brady. "May we come in?"

"Yes, of course." He would appear to be the very soul of cooperation.

"Have you ever seen this man?"

The sight of Hans, dead, unsettled him. He stared at the photo for a few moments, as if studying it. "No, I've never seen him before. Why?"

"He was murdered Saturday evening," Brady replied.

"How awful. I'm sorry to hear it. Why do you think I'd know him?"

"Because we suspect your nephew may have been involved in his death. The means and location were the same as the murder about which we wish to question him. Have you seen or heard from your nephew since our last visit?"

This was the key part. He averted his eyes, as if afraid to meet the detective's glare, and hesitated. "No, I haven't."

"Something wrong, Mr. Mueller?" It was the other detective, Larkin. "You had to think about it?"

"No, it's just that I miss him, and his mother is so worried."

"Really." Brady looked incredulous. "Because we just came from talking to her, and she seemed remarkably composed."

"She's a strong woman. But I assure you, I have not seen or heard from Dieter."

"Okay, thank you, we'll be in touch." He and his partner were already out the door when Brady turned back. "You're a veteran of the Great War, correct?"

The question was so unexpected, Hermann had no time to dissemble. "Yes, the Kaiser Wilhelm Regiment. Why?"

Brady shrugged. "Just curious."

He waited while the detectives made their way downstairs, then watched from the window, standing back so he would not be seen. They crossed to their car without looking up and drove away.

After another half hour, he ventured out, because he had to determine if the police were still watching the *Bier Garten*. The short walk relaxed him.

There wouldn't be too many customers, and he could talk with Emile.

But as soon as he walked in, he heard the shrill ring of the cash register, and Emile was staring down, giving tiny shakes of the head. A tall young man sat at the bar with his back to Hermann, but he was staring at him in the mirror.

Hermann turned and walked out.

***

After leaving Mueller's apartment, Danny had driven two blocks and parked on 88th Street.

"No question, Danny boy, you shook that Kraut up. I can't believe he just blurted it out."

In an exaggerated German accent, Danny replied, "He vuss proud uff his service to der Fatherland." Then in a normal voice, "And it caught him off guard." He glanced at his watch. "I told McHugh we'd meet him here at six, but if he's on to something, we might have to wait."

"There's a pay phone over there," Larkin said. "You should call her if she's expecting you tonight. Don't let her think you're standing her up."

"Can't risk Mueller seeing me. I told her I might be late." Another glance at his watch. Ten after six. Come on, Sean, get along lively.

"The four of us should go out again sometime. Helen likes her."

A knock on the window, McHugh at last. He slid into the back seat. "Sorry I'm late, but I finally got something. A guy came in an hour ago, real chatty, and mentioned some guy named Hans, like he hasn't been around. But the bartender shook his head, and the guy shut up. Then, about fifteen minutes ago, Mueller walked into the place, and the bartender rang up zero on the cash register. Mueller walked out without a word."

"So," Danny said, "the bartender realizes you're a cop."

"You think Hans is our stiff?" Larkin asked.

"Only one way to find out." Danny drove to 85th Street. They all showed their badges, and the bartender blanched.

"May I introduce Officer McHugh," Danny said, "who speaks highly of your Dinkelacker. Please tell me if you recognize his man." He displayed the photo of the murder victim.

The bartender froze.

"His name is Hans, isn't it?" Danny asked, his voice soft. "A World War I veteran?"

The bartender's eyes grew wide. "How did you know that?"

Danny ignored the question. "What is his full name?"

"And before you answer," McHugh said, "remember that I was here when you shushed a customer who asked about him. You don't want us to assume you're involved in his death."

"He's dead?" the bartender asked in a croaking voice.

Larkin pointed at the photo. "That ain't his graduation portrait."

"He was murdered last night," Danny explained.

"*Gott im Himmel.* I had no idea…"

Danny turned severe. “His name?”

“Hans Brach. A decent man.”

“Any family?” Danny asked.

“No, he lived alone on 92nd Street. I don’t have the exact address.”

McHugh was already flipping through the pages of the tattered directory that hung on hinges beneath the pay phone. “Got it.”

Danny leaned across the bar, his face inches from the distressed bartender. “Did you ever see Hans Brach and Hermann Mueller together?”

“Well, yes, they would sometimes be here at the same time, as well as several other customers.”

“Don’t get my Irish up. Were they friends, acquaintances, what?”

“I-I don’t know.”

McHugh joined them. “Why did you shut that guy up this afternoon when he asked about Hans? What was Hans involved in?”

The bartender swallowed hard. “I thought you might be from the FBI. I don’t know that Hans was involved with anything, but he hadn’t been around, and I didn’t want any suspicion cast upon my business. It’s an honest business.”

“Were you a member of the German-American Bund?” Larkin asked.

“We can find out,” Danny said, “so just tell us the truth.”

Now, he was sweating. “Yes, I was. It was a way to show a sense of community around here. But I never went to any meetings or rallies, and I’m a loyal American citizen.”

“Then tell us about Hermann Mueller’s group, the one with his nephew, Dieter,” Danny said.

“I know nothing about any group, and Dieter hasn’t been here in several weeks.”

“What about Hermann Mueller?” Danny asked. “Is he as loyal as you?”

"I can think of nothing to suggest he wouldn't be."

Danny thanked him and they left. Outside, he said, "Let's visit Herr Brach's abode."

Larkin stopped. "Hold it, Danny boy, that doesn't require three of us. Junior, here, and I can easily handle it. You've been on this case nonstop since Saturday night, and we both understand you have good reason to be elsewhere. Drop us at Brach's place and take yourself off, and I'll have a full report for you in the morning."

***

He'd said he'd be there by six, and he'd call if he'd be late. But it was now seven-thirty and there was no sign of him.

She checked herself in the mirror and touched up her makeup and hair. The blue day dress with the white collar was okay. She'd decided against stockings and heels because they weren't going out and she was trying hard to preserve her stockings. Besides, he liked the saddle shoes and bobby socks.

The door buzzer sounded, making her jump.

"I'm so sorry," he said when she opened the door. "I was all over today and came straight from Manhattan."

"It's okay, I'll reheat dinner." She took his coat. When she turned back, he held out his arms.

"Danny, please. We've talked a lot about the future and made some beautiful plans. We both deserve a happy life, and the first ingredient is complete honesty between us."

"I'd never lie to you, Meg."

"I know. But we both know that omission is as wrong as commission. I can live with known threats, but not with unknown ones. Officer McHugh wouldn't have chased you down at Roseland unless it was serious. I also recall that when we first met, you were working on a homicide. And that's what this was, true?"

"True. You'd make a pretty good detective yourself."

She took his hands in hers. "I'm strong. You know that."

"You did spit in that beast's face." He chuckled. "If I hadn't fallen for you before, that sealed it."

She pulled him closer. "Then respect that. Don't make me imagine the worst. Let me face it with you." Her voice caught. "Because that's the only kind of marriage I want."

He looked her in the eye and held the gaze as a tear spilled down her cheek.

"Please, Danny." She could see the internal struggle playing out in his eyes.

"Okay," he said at last.

"Everything?"

"Everything. Nothing left out."

She threw her arms around him and held on tight. Then she let him kiss her. "If I don't put dinner in the oven, we might never eat." She kissed his cheek to soften the blow. "I bought some Burke's stout."

"You are an angel of mercy." He turned serious. "And beautiful." He reached for her again.

She pirouetted away. "Do you want to eat tonight or don't you?" She lit the oven. "Let's give that five minutes, then I can heat the leftovers." She poured two glasses of stout and sat at the table, gesturing for him to sit across from her. Time to get serious. "So, what happened?"

He told her everything about the burglaries and the murders.

"Looks like you're in the war after all."

He agreed. "It's liable to get worse, Meg. Steel yourself."

CHAPTER SIXTY-TWO

Tuesday, June 2, 1942

Larkin and McHugh had been through Hans Brach's apartment with a fine-toothed comb and, aside from a dog-eared English-language copy of *Mein Kampf,* there was nothing remotely related to Germany.

"Other than that, Mrs. Lincoln," Danny said, "how was the play?"

Larkin turned sheepish. "Well, yeah, but what would you suggest, now?"

Danny turned to Cogan, visiting the Bronx yet again. "Could you get a listing of who served in specific regiments of the German Army during the war? Mueller served in the Kaiser Wilhelm Regiment, and Brach was wounded in the war."

"Yeah," Larkin said, "but Mueller denied knowing Brach."

"Which I don't believe for a second and neither do you. Leopold Mueller is no Nazi, but I wouldn't put it past Frieda, and it looks like Dieter attended Camp Siegfried."

"All of which means what?" Cogan asked.

"Brach had a copy of *Mein Kampf.* That's not exactly light reading, especially for a veteran. If Dieter's father didn't take him to Camp Siegfried, might it not have been his Uncle Hermann?"

Cogan's interest was caught. "Keep going."

"If Hermann and Brach were in the same unit together and remained pals here," Danny continued, "someone else who served in the same division might be part of their group. Neither Hermann nor Brach fit the description of the second guy who hocked the goods from Stoneman's."

"That's right, he was a fellow in his mid-to-late thirties." Larkin considered it. "But the war ended twenty-four years ago, so he'd have been a kid."

"The German army was taking 15-year-olds near the end," Danny said. "If our man is thirty-eight or thirty-nine now, he'd have been fifteen then. It's worth a shot."

Larkin threw up his hands. "Great, call Meg at the library and ask for a listing of German soldiers by unit."

"I have a friend in our Washington office who has contacts in the War Department," Cogan said, "but don't get your hopes up. American forces mostly occupied the Rhineland. It's not like we took over running the country."

***

Hermann started when, upon returning home from a job and checking his mail, he saw the envelope. It was addressed to him, and the return address was Mrs. Greta Helverson, 59 Carmen Blvd, Brookhaven, NY. It showed no signs of having been opened. He waited until he was safely inside his apartment to open it.

Dearest Hermann,

Thank you so much for the book of poetry. I shall treasure it always.

With deepest affection,

Greta

But he recognized the handwriting as Obermann's and immersed the letter in a dish of water. *Our guest has gone to greet some of his cousins, who hope to gain from the booming economy. They will try to pay you a visit.*

The T in visit was crossed with a tiny swastika, an amusing touch. Hermann burned the note and the envelope before he allowed himself to dwell on its meaning: saboteurs from the Fatherland, and Dieter was to guide them.

He had to talk to Paul.

***

Cogan summoned Danny and Larkin that afternoon. "I have some news. Our Long Island group informed me of a resident of German Gardens who reports having seen a young man fitting Dieter Mueller's description walking with a young lady on the grounds of the old Camp Siegfried. However, after having deployed undercover agents for ten days, we couldn't locate him."

"So, he's moved on?" Danny asked.

Cogan nodded. "That would be my conclusion. The question is, where?"

"Back here?" Larkin asked. "Thinking the coast is clear?"

Danny shook his head. "I'm damned sure Uncle Hermann would signal when it was clear, and he knows we're watching him, so he won't do that. Especially if he's involved with this murder of Hans Brach, which was made to look like Dieter could have done it. No, I'm thinking he may have pushed further east."

"Only so far he can push before he runs out of island," Larkin said.

Danny turned to Cogan. "How obvious were your guys?"

"Not at all. No ties, no fedoras. Besides, the witness who reported this told our agent that he'd last seen the kid a week earlier."

"So, the agents didn't scare him off." Danny thought for several moments. "Something's up." A pause before he added, "And it's going to start somewhere on Eastern Long Island."

Larkin's expression changed to one of alarm. "Aw, shit, Danny, tell me you're not thinking enemy agents."

"Christ, I hope not," Cogan said. "It's the Coast Guard's responsibility to guard the coastline and the Army's job to defend the beaches."

"Can we tell them to be on the alert?" Danny asked.

"For what?" Larkin asked. "A Kraut teenager who's a helluva lock picker?"

Danny struggled to keep his temper. "And who recently stole ingredients for several types of explosives."

"Sorry, Danny," Cogan said, "it's not enough. Besides, they'd need more to go on than just 'someplace on Eastern Long Island'. We're talking about hundreds of miles of coastline, what with all the bays, islands, and inlets."

The phone on Cogan's desk rang. He answered it and listened. "Shit. Okay, thanks." He replaced the receiver. "That was the agent we have watching Hermann Mueller. He was tailing him on the subway but lost him in the crowd at the Union Square station."

"So, he knew he was being followed?" Danny asked.

"Could be, although the agent doesn't believe he's been made. Mueller probably assumes it. He's no babe in the woods."

***

Hermann climbed the stairs from the subway station at Eighth Avenue and 14th Street and walked down into the heart of the Meatpacking District, careful not to lose his footing on Belgian Block streets slick with meat sludge.

"Interesting meeting place," Paul said as he approached.

"I needed to slip away from my constant companions." He handed over a sheet of paper. "These are the instructions Dieter left for making fulminate of mercury. Can you follow them?"

Paul read, then reread, the instructions. "Yes, but he warns this could be dangerous."

"You are the most careful and knowledgeable member of our group, and you have the maturity that Dieter lacks, for all his brilliance." He glanced around. No one was within earshot, but he started walking toward the river. "Help is coming. I can't say when or how many, but Dieter will guide them once they land. Common sense suggests that they cannot bring too much in the way of explosives ashore, so Dieter may need us to provide him with some."

"You expect him to return?"

"On a mission, yes."

Paul glanced around, uneasy. "Then it's possible he expects to produce the materials himself. After all, he's the chemistry genius, not I."

"But you received some training in demolition during the war."

"Only very rudimentary before I was rushed into active duty when things turned dire in 1918." They walked in silence until they came to the river. "I will do some further reading at the library. Then, if you need me, I can help."

"I have a better idea. I'm sure Dieter kept notebooks, which may contain more extensive notes. Meet me at noon tomorrow in front of St. Patrick's Cathedral carrying a notebook, something innocuous. I'll approach from the south; you approach from the north."

***

Dieter had finished work at the country club, having worked from eight to eight, first as a caddy, then busing tables in the dining room. He preferred the latter, as busboys were virtually invisible.

Mrs. Griswold had dinner waiting when he and Mr. Griswold arrived home. He parried questions about how he liked it here with assurances that it was perfect for him.

"Do you have a girl?" Mrs. Griswold asked after her husband had excused himself.

Hedy. He missed her so. "Er, no, I don't."

Mrs. Griswold broke into a grin. "You hesitated, Dieter. Perhaps there is a young lady you like, but you're too shy to pursue her." She patted his hand. "Your secret is safe with me."

He thanked her for her hospitality and excused himself. By the time he reached the beach, it was dark, and a navigation beacon was flashing down the beach to his right. Off to his left lay a Coast Guard station. The surf rolled in at regular intervals. He walked down from the scrub covered dunes toward the water, then toward the beacon—a long stretch of beach.

He veered back toward the dunes when he saw the silhouette of a man against the flash of the beacon, and he pulled his snap-billed cap down. "Evening," he muttered as he passed the man, a Coast Guard patrolman walking the other way.

"Nice one," the patrolman replied, and kept walking.

Dieter checked his watch, waiting until the coastguardsman was further down the beach before finding a spot behind an extensive collection of scrub on the dunes. He watched the beach to the east and checked his watch at regular intervals. By the time the coastguardsman passed in the opposite direction, nearly two hours had passed.

Hardly a rigorous patrol. Excellent.

CHAPTER SIXTY-THREE

Thursday, June 4, 1942

Dieter was up at six, and Mrs. Griswold had a hearty breakfast waiting for him and Mr. Griswold. The children weren't up, yet.

"You really think Dieter will be needed to caddy on a Thursday?" she asked her husband.

"With all the war work," Mr. Griswold replied, "some members can't get out to play on Saturday." He turned to Dieter. "We haven't yet seen what the new pattern will be, so you might be needed. Otherwise, you'll have a calm morning and just work the dining room this afternoon and evening."

A pot of fresh coffee sat on a small mat in the middle of the table. Mrs. Griswold poured a cup for Dieter, then resting her hand on his shoulder, said, "Don't let them work you too hard."

"I don't mind hard work, ma'am."

"You're an industrious young man." She gave his shoulder a gentle squeeze and smiled. For a mother of two in her mid-thirties, she was rather attractive.

Mr. Griswold, having been left to pour his own coffee, remained silent and scowled.

***

"I'm surprised you would come here," Frieda Mueller said. "Aren't the police watching us?"

Hermann laughed. "They are, but the most they will do is ask if you or I have heard from Dieter, and we haven't. Did Dieter keep his high school chemistry notebook?"

"In his room."

"I need it. A friend of mine has been doing some research, and I thought Dieter's notes might help."

Frieda stared at him. "If the police catch you with it, things could be bad for you."

He picked up the notebook from a bookshelf. "I won't get caught."

He walked down Madison Avenue to 50th Street, then one block over to Fifth Avenue. When he turned onto Fifth, he was pleased to see the sidewalk crowded with the usual midday rush. When Paul entered the crowd from the other side, Hermann entered from his. They bumped, each dropping his notebook, bending down, and picking up the other's.

"Beg pardon," Paul said.

"Perfectly all right," Hermann replied. He continued north while Paul continued south. No one stopped either of them.

CHAPTER SIXTY-FOUR

Friday, June 5, 1942

Danny snatched up the phone on the first ring. "Brady."

He'd just emerged from Greco's office after a ten-minute harangue about "two unsolved murders" and "this isn't up to your usual standard."

It was Cogan. "I may soon have something for you. My friend's contact in the War Department has casualty lists that were found in the records of some German field hospitals. One of them is from the Spring Offensive in 1918. It lists names and units involved, and one unit is the Kaiser Wilhelm regiment. He's hand-copying the list for me with whatever information is on it. I'll call you if it has the names you're looking for."

***

Paul was keeping Hermann informed. He'd had no difficulty obtaining the materials Dieter had not already supplied. "I've reviewed all of Dieter's notes and I'm proceeding with caution. I've produced a cluster of crystals and I'm looking for a place to test them."

"Lots of open land in Eastern Queens," Hermann said.

"Anyplace in particular?"

"No, just choose with care."

***

It was a short walk from the country club to the post office, and Dieter made the trip every other day on his lunch break. Someone would send information, soon. Otherwise, he wouldn't be able to accomplish his mission. Each day that he checked and found nothing, it was a slight letdown.

But now he opened the box and caught his breath. An envelope postmarked Lisbon. This was it.

He stuffed the envelope down his pants, not trusting the security of his pockets and desperate to keep it hidden. That evening he retired to his room above the garage after dinner, taking the letter out and opening it. He soaked it in his wash basin before holding it up to the light to read.

Four visitors to depart on 28 May. Estimated arrival night of 12-13 June.

They were already en route.

His gaze dropped to the note. It had to be destroyed. Slowly, methodically, he tore it into narrow strips, then tore the strips into tiny pieces, dropped the fragments into the toilet, and flushed.

Shortly after eleven, he slipped out for his evening walk. A light fog had moved in, making it easier for him to remain hidden from the patrolling coastguardsman.

How would he get them off the beach? Where to go afterward?

He followed a rough path away from the dunes and toward a row of bungalows. Beyond that, he knew, was the East Hampton-Montauk Highway. The fog was getting thicker, so he decided not to scout out his route tonight. As he turned over his plan in his mind, he took a direct route back to the Griswold house rather than double back to the beach.

"Hello, Dieter." Mrs. Griswold was standing by the stairs to his garage loft. She took a puff from her cigarette. "Not an enjoyable night for a walk on the beach."

Did she suspect him? "No, too much fog."

She pointed in the direction from which he'd come. "You found that way more interesting?"

"I started out at the beach but thought the fog wouldn't be so thick if I went further inland." He shrugged. "I was wrong."

She tossed the cigarette away. "Fog can be heavy here. See anything interesting?"

He broke into a grin. "Hardly saw anything at all." He started toward the garage. "Well, good night."

She didn't move. "I saw you coming out of the post office today."

He remained calm while he searched his memory. As always, he'd been careful, and he hadn't seen her.

She smiled. "I was in the coffee shop next door." Her smile faded. "You have a post office box?"

He had to admit it, otherwise there would be no logical explanation for him being there. "Yes, ma'am."

She crossed over to him. "Please don't call me 'ma'am' when it's just you and me. Call me by my name, Lurline."

"Pretty name."

She bathed him in a warm smile. "Why, thank you. You're such a nice young man."

"Thank you… Lurline."

She touched his cheek. "It sounds nicer when you say it. Curious that you'd rent a post office box. Your mail could come here, care of us. I bet you have a girl."

"Yes, I do."

She patted his cheek again. "I'm glad. I'll say no more about it, and I'll try not to be jealous."

CHAPTER SIXTY-FIVE

Saturday, June 6, 1942

"A great naval and air battle continues to rage as Japanese forces retire from Midway Island in the Pacific. Japanese losses include aircraft carriers and other classes of vessels…"

***

"Thanks for bringing this in," Danny said to Cogan as he looked over the list of names and units, grateful that Greco had turned off the radio.

Cogan had underlined Hermann Mueller's name and Hans Brach's. "Brach and Mueller did not serve in the same regiment, but Brach's date of admission is February 1918, while Mueller's is late July, and neither shows a discharge date. They were still there when the Allies arrived. Plenty of time to get acquainted with one another."

"So, we have a link," Larkin said.

Danny spoke up before Greco could react. "Hospital buddies during the war, both emigrated after the war, settled in the same city. But that doesn't prove they knew each other or were friends."

"But both in Yorkville?" Larkin asked. "That's an awful lot of coincidence, Danny boy."

"We need someone to put them together. And I know just who to ask."

***

Hermann was still staring at the headline heralding the news of Midway on the front page of *The New York Times* when Paul sat beside him on the park bench by the river.

"Sorry," Paul said, "I didn't mean to startle you. I've succeeded in testing my crystals of fulminate of mercury."

Hermann's interest was caught. "And are they effective for our purpose?"

"Placed in small cloth packets, they can be detonated with a lit fuse or by hard contact. I conducted tests yesterday in Queens in a wooded area by an old rail line just off North Hempstead Turnpike. The blast from one packet brought down a small tree."

"So, larger packets would produce a more intense blast?"

Paul scowled. "Yes, but we must be careful, because increasing the amount of the compound also increases its instability, to where mere jostling could set off an explosion. Our best course would be to produce many small packets and cluster them for effect. Igniting one packet with a fuse or electric charge would ignite the other packets."

Hermann forgot the unfortunate American victory for a moment. "So, we could damage a bridge, or a ship under construction?"

Paul heaved a sigh. "Theoretically, it's possible, but transporting sufficient amounts of the compound to the target would risk an accidental explosion."

"Begin making the packets and store them in a safe place. When Dieter returns, we will supply him. In the meantime, Christian will seek potential targets for a small cluster of packets.

***

When Danny and Larkin entered Paul Osterkamp's shop, young Annelise turned away.

The locksmith was immediately irritated. "What is it, now? I already told you everything I can about my nephew."

Danny leaned on the counter. "I'm not sure I believe that, but I'm not here about him. The Osterkamps and the Muellers emigrated about the same time, correct?"

"Yes, not long after the war."

"Along with other German families?"

"Yes, but…"

Danny laid Hans Brach's photo on the counter. "Do you know this man?"

The locksmith gasped but said nothing.

Just the reaction he'd been hoping for. "I'll take that as a yes."

"Hans is dead?" Osterkamp asked.

"Murdered."

"And you suspect Dieter?"

Danny picked up the photo. "No, I'm certain Dieter did not kill Mr. Brach, but someone made it appear that he did. Now, I'm going to ask you several questions, and I expect completely truthful answers. Should I later find you've lied to me, I'll arrest you as an accessory to Hans Brach's murder."

Osterkamp looked stunned.

"I rarely threaten people up front," Danny said in his most reasonable voice, "but you must understand how high the stakes are."

"I haven't lied to you, and I won't."

"Don't withhold anything, either. First, to your knowledge, were Hans and Hermann Mueller acquainted?"

"Yes, they were in the war together."

"In the same regiment?" Best to test Osterkamp's veracity at the outset.

Osterkamp frowned. "I'm not sure. But they knew each other from their war experience. They might have been in hospital together. Hans was wounded in the leg, and Hermann was hospitalized for shell shock near the end of the war."

Danny exchanged glances with Larkin. "So, you would say they were friends?"

"Yes."

"Were they members of the Bund?"

Osterkamp cast a rueful glance at Annelise, who was watching him with interest. "Yes."

Annelise gave the slightest of nods, as if confirming a suspicion.

"Active members?" Danny asked.

"Yes."

"What about your sister and brother-in-law?"

"Not as far as I know."

An interesting response. "But…?"

"Frieda expressed sympathy for the Nazis. It's what drove us apart."

"Did Dieter attend Camp Siegfried?"

"I believe he did, in the summer of 1936."

Annelise gasped. "That's when he changed."

Danny asked the next question before the locksmith could react. "Mr. Osterkamp, are you aware of any other friends of Mueller's from his war years or from the Bund?"

"No, after he became active in the Bund, I ceased to have anything to do with him."

Danny turned to Annelise. "Did Dieter ever express an interest in chemistry?"

She nodded. "He was always interested in science of any kind."

"Did he ever evince an interest in explosives?"

Osterkamp gasped. "You don't think…"

"I don't know," Danny replied. "Annelise, did he?"

"He enjoyed shooting off fireworks when we were kids, but that was all."

He'd only gotten some of what he wanted. "Thank you, both. If you see or hear from Dieter, or learn anything of his whereabouts, please alert me."

Back in their car, Larkin asked, "So, where does that leave us?"

"If Mueller didn't kill Brach, he gave the order to whoever did." Danny smirked. "He wants us to think Dieter's back in town, so we won't find out where he is."

CHAPTER SIXTY-SIX

Monday, June 8, 1942

It was after two in the morning when Dieter followed the familiar trail up from the beach. By now he had chronicled the comings and goings of the men who patrolled the beaches at night. Like the beat cops of New York City, they followed regular patterns but, unlike beat cops, when they grew irregular it always resulted in less frequent patrolling. As he approached the Griswolds' garage, he decided he'd destroy the sheets on which he'd been recording the observations he'd committed to memory.

"Another late night, I see." Lurline Griswold was sitting on the wooden stairs leading up to his apartment, wearing a skirt and a blouse unbuttoned at the neck. She took a deep drag on her cigarette and tossed it away. The hem of her skirt was pulled up over her knees.

Keep calm, steely calm. "Yes, I couldn't sleep."

She broke into a grin. "Well, I knew you couldn't be stargazing."

He allowed himself a chuckle. "No, too much fog."

"I'm surprised you didn't wander into the surf."

"I kept close to the dunes."

"Summer nights, kids sneak down there at night for sex." She licked her lips. "Maybe someday you'll meet your girl there."

"She doesn't live near here."

"Aww," she said with a pout, "you must get so lonely." She stood and strolled over to him, brushing a lock of hair off his forehead. "I like you, Dieter."

"I… I like you, too… Lurline."

"You remembered." She kissed his cheek. "But then, I'm not surprised. You have a sharp mind and an excellent memory. And such wonderful powers of observation."

Oh, no. That wasn't a casual remark.

She kissed his cheek again, a little softer and longer this time. "I wanted to do something nice for you, so I cleaned your room this afternoon."

His notes. Don't react. "Thank you."

"Don't mention it." She draped her arms around his neck. "It was the least I could do, and I felt closer to you." She began stroking the back of his neck. "Don't worry, I left everything just as I found it. Your notes—whatever they are—remain exactly where you left them."

"Thank you." Her stroking of his neck aroused him, as Hedy's had.

"I bet you haven't been kissed in a long time," she said. "Neither have I. I'll be sad if you don't kiss me, Dieter. You don't want me to be sad, do you?"

A threat. She'd seen his notes, and she could report him, destroying his mission. "Of course not."

After a frantic kiss, she led him upstairs to his room, closed the door, and unbuttoned her blouse. "I've wanted this since you arrived."

***

"Early for you, isn't it?" Danny asked as he entered the precinct and found Cogan waiting for him.

"Yesterday, a foreman at the Brooklyn Navy Yard called. He'd noticed a worker wandering around someplace he shouldn't have been. When questioned, he said he'd been looking for a coworker."

"So?" But Danny was used to Cogan's methods. Something didn't smell right. The in-person visit underlined his concern.

"Except that he'd been 'looking' someplace the coworker didn't need to be, either."

"Let me guess. The wandering worker was German?"

"Yep, and everyone's been jumpy about saboteurs, lately."

Danny took a sip of coffee. "And they called you?"

Cogan snorted. "I call them regularly, given Hoover's obsession with fifth columnists. This was the first time they've had anything to tell me. Probably nothing."

"If you thought that, you wouldn't be here. What's got your hackles up?"

"The worker's name is Christian Jenner, lives in Yorkville, Ninety-fourth Street, between First and Second Avenue, over a tailor shop. Emigrated as a twelve-year-old. He's only 32, so too young to have served in the war. However, there was a Martin Jenner on that hospital list."

"And did Martin emigrate after the war?"

"No, Martin died in the hospital in August 1918. So, there is nothing at present to connect him with young Christian."

Now, Danny was chuckling. "Except the fact that he lives in the same neighborhood as two of his late brother's former hospital mates, which is way too much coincidence for either of us. I don't suppose you've got…"

Cogan laid a photo on the table. "Courtesy of the Brooklyn Navy Yard."

***

"Looks like there won't be any golf played today," Lurline said, gesturing at the steady downpour outside the kitchen window. "Karl took one look, groaned, and went back to sleep."

Dieter had been on tenterhook, waiting for his boss to come to the breakfast table. "Wasn't he feeling well?"

"Off to school," she said to the children, scooting them away from the table. She waited until they were gone, then sat in Dieter's lap and pulled him to her breast. "You were wonderful last night." She giggled. "I mean, this morning."

"But your husband…"

She kissed him again. "He'll be sleeping it off for at least two more hours. He can't hold all that beer he drinks at dinner, which is why he's always so quiet in the morning, and why he didn't hear me come in last night." Another long kiss. "What do you really do when you go for those long walks at night?"

She'd seen his notes. Only one way to handle this. "I can tell you, but you must promise never to tell anyone, not even your husband or your best friends."

She turned serious. "You can trust me, Dieter, just as I trust you never to tell anyone about our little secret." She giggled. "A girl needs to feel she's loved."

So, keeping her happy would keep her quiet. "I actually work for the War Department, traveling all along the east coast inspecting our shoreline defenses and the quality of the patrols. That's why I made all those notes, they're for my report."

She pouted again. "You mean you won't be here much longer?"

"I'll stay as long as I can, but probably not much more than another month."

Her hand slid down to tease him. "Then we'd better make the most of our time together. I'll come to your room in ten minutes."

***

Osterkamp scowled when Danny entered his shop. “If my neighbors see police coming and going, they’ll suspect I’m up to something.”

“I’ll have you make a key for me, if that’ll help.”

Annelise laughed, which helped ease the tension.

Danny laid the photo of Christian Jenner on the counter. “Ever see this fella before?”

Osterkamp studied it. “Not that I can recall.”

“I have,” Annelise said, taking it. “I think he lives near here.”

Now for the key question. “Ever see him with anyone? Say, Hermann Mueller?”

“No.”

“Where have you seen him? On the street? Coming out of shops?”

“I’ve seen him a few times going into the *Bier Garten*.”

At last. “Any times or days in particular?”

“Always evenings. I pass there on my way home. I can’t remember specific days, though.” She thought a moment. “No, wait. Thursdays. I remember because one evening I saw him was the Thursday after the *New York Times* carried a story about a German bomber that could fly across the Atlantic, and everyone was still talking about it.” She thought a little longer. “And I recall seeing Dieter inside, because I realized he was no longer underage.”

“Was Dieter at the bar when you saw him?” Danny asked.

“No, he was standing by a table toward the back. I couldn’t see who with.”

CHAPTER SIXTY-SEVEN

Tuesday, June 9, 1942

"Ensign George Gay, a rescued navy torpedo-plane pilot, reported he saw three burning Japanese aircraft carriers during the Battle of Midway with planes circling and no place to land."

***

Danny turned the radio off as he parked outside the FBI building. "Sounds as if Midway might have been a complete rout."

"I'm still confused why you wanted the G to pick Jenner up," Larkin said.

"Because the Brooklyn Navy Yard, a federal facility, alerted the FBI as to his suspicious behavior, giving the FBI probable cause, which we don't have. And I want him on the defensive when we question him."

"Considering they've had him for a few hours, now, I'd guess you have nothing to worry about on that score."

Once inside, they were led down a long corridor past Cogan's office to an interrogation room. Jenner was seated at a table smoking a cigarette. The collection of butts suggested he'd been chain smoking.

Cogan made the introductions. "Mr. Jenner denies all allegations of espionage or sabotage."

Danny and Larkin took seats directly across from Jenner.

"That so?" Danny asked.

"Yes." Jenner added a curt nod.

Danny opened the file folder Cogan had handed him. "You emigrated from Germany in 1922 with your mother and father and older brother, Martin, correct?"

Jenner's head snapped up. "No, just my mother and father. My brother was killed in 1918 in the war. Are you holding that against me?"

"Not at all." Danny flashed a warm smile. "I just want to understand all the facts. My sympathies on the loss of your brother. Was he killed in action?"

"No, he was wounded and died later in hospital."

Danny turned serious. "I'm so sorry. Losing Martin when you were so young must have been painful."

"Yes."

"And how long have you known Hermann Mueller and Hans Brach?" He'd asked Cogan not to mention either name.

"Ever since…" Jenner froze. "Wait, how did you…?"

Danny looked him in the eye. "I'll answer your question once you've answered mine."

Jenner stared but did not answer.

Danny glanced down at the folder. "Martin Jenner was in the same hospital as Brach and Mueller in 1918. You've already confirmed to our satisfaction that he was your brother. You've been seen patronizing the *Bier Garten* on East 85th Street in the company of Mueller's nephew, Dieter Mueller, currently a fugitive from justice. Now, how long?"

Jenner froze.

Time to press his advantage. "Dieter Mueller is wanted for two murders and a series of burglaries, including one at his old high school, from which he stole materials useful for making explosives.

If you do not cooperate with us, we will charge you as an accessory to his crimes and obstruction of justice. And Agent Cogan here will consider charges related to your suspicious activities in that light. But if you cooperate, things will go much better for you."

"I've done nothing," Jenner said.

"We'll be the judge of that," Larkin said.

Danny leaned forward. "Did you belong to the Bund, along with Mueller and Brach?"

"Yes, and that wasn't a crime."

"Not then," Danny replied. "But we have to view your current activities in light of your membership. So, about Mueller and Brach?"

"I've known them since we first came to this country. They were part of our community. They helped with our homesickness."

"Did Dieter Mueller attend Camp Siegfried?" Larkin asked.

"Yes, Herman said he was destined to be a leader."

Cogan stepped back in. "What were you doing wandering around the Navy Yard? The truth this time." He paused for a moment. "Nothing you say here will be held against you if you give us the whole truth. Hans Brach is dead, and Mueller can't help you."

"I know about Hans."

"Who killed him?" Danny asked.

Jenner hesitated.

He knew. Danny leaned forward. "Who killed him?"

"Paul… Wolfe. He was the fifth member of our group—Paul, Hermann, Hans, Dieter, and me. Hermann formed us into the group to carry on the cause when the Bund collapsed. After Pearl Harbor, he wanted us to support Germany in any way we could. That's what Dieter's burglaries were all about. But Hans argued with Hermann on his decisions and Paul agreed with Hermann that he was a threat, and he killed him."

"And the Navy Yard?"

Jenner was close to tears. "I was assigned locating suitable targets for sabotage, but that's not what I was doing. I was looking for examples of why sabotage wouldn't be effective so I could tell Hermann to drop the idea."

"And where were you going to get the necessary explosives?" Cogan asked.

"Paul was researching explosives, but he never said what he found."

"Where's Dieter and what is he doing?" Danny asked.

Jenner blanched. "No one knows."

Not possible. "Doesn't Hermann?"

"He swears he doesn't."

Larkin rolled his eyes. "Yeah, that convinces me."

Danny waved to Larkin and Cogan to step outside. "I don't think we're going to get anything else out of him, Bill. He's more scared of Mueller than of us."

"The only thing we can prove," Cogan replied, "is that he was someplace in the Navy Yard he didn't need to be. That's not a crime."

"How about conspiracy to commit sabotage?" Larkin asked. "I think I heard him confess to that in there."

Cogan shook his head. "No, just that he sat in on meetings where it was discussed. And his alibi that he was looking for reasons to not target the Navy Yard is believable, even if I hadn't given him immunity, which I did."

"I believe him on that score," Danny said. "He's obviously afraid of Mueller and would look for an excuse rather than defy him."

Cogan gestured to the closed door. "At all events, we have no basis for holding him. The best I can do is put a shadow on him and a tap on his phone. You already have one on Mueller's."

"Who expected that and apparently takes his important calls at the *Bier Garten*," Danny said. "Good idea for the shadow and tap, though."

Larkin spoke up. "Doesn't Jenner's statement give us probable cause to pick up Mueller?"

Danny exchanged a glance with Cogan. “It does, and we might squeeze him on Dieter’s whereabouts.”

Cogan thought about it. “Wouldn’t he just claim he didn’t know? We can’t prove that he does. If Dieter contacts his uncle, we have a better chance of tracking him down. I’d leave him for now.”

Danny nodded. “Okay, Frankie and I will head over to the address Jenner gave us for Wolfe and pick him up. Can you hold him here for an hour so he can’t stop at a pay phone and warn Wolfe?”

Cogan laughed. “Sure thing, Danny. You can appreciate how long all that paperwork takes.”

***

As soon as the phone rang, Meg knew it was Danny and that he was canceling for the third night in a row. She was big about it. “Are you at least close to solving the case?”

His hesitation told her everything. “I’m sorry, Meg, some cases are just that way.”

“Hey, are you okay?”

A humorless laugh. “I will be when we finally nail these guys.”

These guys, not this guy. No wonder he sounded so forlorn. “It’s okay, darling, I love you.”

“I love you, too, and I’ll make it up to you, I promise.”

***

Danny hung up the pay phone feeling like a heel and got back in the car.

“We’d better step on it,” Larkin said. “Cogan will have to spring Jenner. Wolfe’s address is another few blocks up Second Avenue. On the east side of the street. Is she okay?”

Danny hadn't said who he was calling, but Larkin knew. "Yeah, and she didn't even give me a hard time about it."

"Nice girl. Next block is... Jesus, Mary and Joseph."

Danny pulled up at the address Jenner had provided, a large white structure with an awning that proclaimed, "Wolfe Funeral Home." He slammed the car door as he got out, and his gut warned him they were now wasting valuable time.

An usher met him at the door. "Which family, sir?" Two parlors were jammed with mourners.

Danny flashed his badge. "I need to speak with Mr. Paul Wolfe."

The usher frowned. "Paul Wolfe? There's no Paul Wolfe here."

"Who owns this place?"

"That would be Mr. Geoffrey Wolfe."

"May we speak with him? It's urgent."

A moment later, Danny was facing the owner. "We're looking for a Paul Wolfe and were given this address. Do you have a son or other relative named Paul?"

"I'm afraid not. Not a single Paul in the family, at least as far as I know. It seems someone has played a joke on you fellows."

Danny scowled. "I assure you, sir, that murder is no joke. Do you know anyone named Christian Jenner, Hermann Mueller, or Hans Brach?"

The undertaker turned serious. "Those are all German names. My family is English."

"You don't have German acquaintances or German customers?"

"I have very few German acquaintances, and none by those names. And I don't recall ever having any clients with those names. However, I will have my secretary search our records tomorrow in case my memory has failed me."

Danny pulled out a card. "Call me if she finds anything. Sorry to have disturbed you."

"What now?" Larkin asked as they walked back to the car.

"Over to Jenner's place to arrest him, if he's still there."

"Why not call Cogan?"

"Because whoever he's got tailing Jenner probably doesn't carry a two-way radio."

CHAPTER SIXTY-EIGHT

Danny was certain that the man in the fedora sitting in the car parked across the street from the dilapidated brownstone Christian Jenner called home was the agent assigned to tail him, but he didn't stop to chat before he and Larkin entered.

The vestibule door was unlocked, so they proceeded to Jenner's apartment on the second floor. Danny rang the bell three times, but there was no answer and no sound from within. He tried the knob even though he knew it was a waste of time,

The door opened.

He turned to Larkin. "Not good."

They both drew their weapons and entered the apartment. No lights, and it was twilight outside. Danny felt for a light switch and found it just inside the foyer. The living room was straight ahead, the tiny kitchen to the right.

Larkin flipped on the overhead light in the kitchen. "Not here."

Danny turned on a living room lamp. "Nope."

"Think he skipped out on us?"

Danny checked the living room window. "Locked, and no fire escape on this one." He checked the bedroom window. "Locked."

"So, he didn't sneak out. I'll check the bath—sweet Jesus."

Danny smelled the blood before he even entered the bathroom. Jenner's body was in the bathtub. "The gobshite slit his own throat."

"He must've figured we'd come looking after striking out at Wolfe's."

"Deeper than that, Frankie, he was protecting the ring."

***

"I know what my wife is doing," Mr. Griswold said as he drove out of the country club parking lot.

Dieter kept silent. No matter what he said, it would make his situation worse.

"She pretends to be a good wife and mother, but I see how she is with you. The little touches, the puckered lips. She's a shameless flirt."

He had to say something. "I try to be polite. She's been so kind to me."

"So, you admit she's flirting with you."

"I hope you've noticed I do not invite it, nor do I return it." At least not in your presence.

"Yes, and I appreciate your decency, but I need you to be forceful in your rejection of her advances."

Gott im Himmel. He wanted Dieter to tell her to go back to her husband. The only thing more craven than a cuckold was a coward. "Mrs. Griswold has extended hospitality to me, and I can't be rude to her. I can only continue to resist her advances."

When his host said nothing, Dieter added, "If my continued presence here is causing a problem, perhaps I should leave." With only three days until the German team arrived, that would be disastrous, but Mr. Griswold didn't know that. And despite his bluster, he had to realize that forcing Dieter to leave would enrage his wife.

"That won't be necessary."

CHAPTER SIXTY-NINE

Wednesday, June 10, 1942

It was after midnight, and Danny was no closer to calling it a day. The news since they'd discovered Christian Jenner's body had been uniformly bad. He listed what they knew on the blackboard.

There hadn't been enough time to place the wiretap on Jenner's phone. But at 7:05 PM, a little over an hour before he and Larkin discovered Jenner's body, the tap on Mueller's phone had recorded a call comprising one whispered phrase: "Valhalla." Which, according to one of Cogan's agents, was the hall of slain warriors in Norse mythology. The call had been too short to be traced and the whispered voice was impossible to identify.

Larkin laid a cup of coffee on Danny's desk. "It was suicide, Danny, he was still holding the bloody knife."

Danny peered at the cup. "Where did you get that?"

"The Silex in the back."

Danny reached for it. "You made a fresh pot?" Very un-Frankie-like.

"You kidding? I just heated what was there."

Danny jerked his hand away. "Jesus, Mary and Joseph, it's probably been there since Old God's time." He turned back to the blackboard.

Larkin shrugged. "Suit yourself. Now, you mind explaining why you're wasting valuable board space on a suicide?"

"He wasn't holding the knife; he was dead and it was lying against his hand in the bathtub."

Larkin threw up his hands. "So, you don't think it was suicide? No prints but Jenner's on the knife, no sign of a break-in, no signs of a struggle. Also, no one reported hearing any voices in the apartment, and there was no sign anyone else was there at all."

Danny laid down the chalk. "You're right. Had to be suicide."

"Good. Now, can we for the love of Mary go home?"

Danny stared at the board. "Why did he admit he'd been told to look for targets in the Navy Yard?"

Larkin stared at him. "Trying to get out from under."

"Yes, but why not stick to his original story about looking for a coworker? Why didn't he say he was lost in his own thoughts and wandered off? Or thought he heard someone call him? Frankie, he could have given any of those excuses or a half dozen more, and we'd have been stumped."

"Maybe he just panicked and blurted it without thinking."

That was possible. "Jenner had been rattled, so it makes sense he'd blurt something he'd later regret."

"Exactly." Larkin took a sip of coffee and winced. "God, that's awful."

Danny turned back to his notes on their interrogation of Jenner. "He fingered Mueller, admitted he knew about Dieter's burglaries, but sent us on a false trail for Paul Wolfe."

"He might have been more afraid of Wolfe—or whatever his name is—than Mueller. But then neither could have known what took place in that interrogation room."

"But either could have known he'd been picked up by the G."

CHAPTER SEVENTY

Dieter peered at the radium-lit dial of the clock. 3:30. Lurline's arm was draped across his chest. He gave her shoulder a gentle shake.

"Mmmm…"

"It's getting on toward four. Shouldn't you be getting back to your room?"

Her eyes flew open. "Are you throwing me out?"

"I told you, he suspects us. If he wakes up and you're not there, he'll know for certain. I have to work with him."

She giggled and kissed his neck. "No, you don't, you have your job at the War Department."

Not the reaction he'd expected.

"Dieter, darling, you are simply the best thing that's happened to me in years. I understand this won't last, so I'm enjoying every moment while it does. That cold fish of a husband of mine could make things uncomfortable for you, but I'll always protect your secret."

"Sleeping together is our secret, not just mine."

She nestled closer to him, laying one leg over his. "I don't mean that. Personally, I don't care that he knows. I prefer it that way. I mean your secret." She laughed. "If you worked for the War

Department, you wouldn't need free room and board with us and you wouldn't need a job at the country club. And walking on the beach in the early hours of the morning is a strange habit, especially when the fog is heavy, as it often is. Then again, you don't walk much these days; you just sit among the dunes."

He was afraid to breathe.

"But," she went on, "I live a limited life, and my only concern is my pleasure. No one has given me more than you have. I appreciate that, so I don't ask what you're doing, why you sit among the dunes for hours. I'm content to come and wait for you and make love. You keep your side of the bargain, and I'll keep mine."

***

Cogan welcomed Danny into his office. "We've been tailing Hermann Mueller since yesterday morning."

"It might have been nice if you'd let us in on his whereabouts. We've been looking for him."

Cogan shrugged. "Sorry, Danny, he's a slippery bastard. But it's probably better you didn't find him." He slid a photograph across his desk. "One of our guys took that in Carl Schurz Park yesterday afternoon. Any idea who that is sitting on the bench with Mueller?"

"Never saw him before. But..." Danny studied the man.

"Yes?"

Danny pulled out his pocket notepad and flipped several pages. "That the only shot your guy got?"

Cogan laughed. "No, but he had to be discreet, looking like a tourist."

"Did he get a clear one of the guy standing?"

Cogan pulled another photo out of the file. "Right here."

Danny found the page he wanted. "Hold on to it and describe him to me."

"Okay, a guy in his late thirties, about six feet tall, thin, straight blond hair, fair skin, can't tell the eye color. Long face, straight, narrow nose, prominent chin."

"Okay, now, listen to this." He read the description the pawn shop owner had given of the unknown man who'd fenced the Stoneman jewelry.

"Sounds like it could be the same guy." Cogan gestured toward the notepad. "The mysterious Paul whatever-his-name-is?"

Danny recounted the interrogation. "Jenner probably realized he had to change the surname. How long did this encounter last?"

"About three minutes," Cogan said. "And, to answer your next question, they exchanged nothing other than words."

"The knife Jenner was holding when we found him is a bayonet, standard issue in the German army during First World War." Danny chuckled. "Another veteran, how about that?" Sudden thought. "Have a copy of that hospital list?" He took it and began scanning. "Five soldiers named Paul, none with the surname of Wolfe."

"Too bad they didn't list their ages. He'd have been rather young."

It was enough that there were only five. "Hand me the Manhattan phone book." One by one, he searched for a match to each of the names. "This is a possibility, Paul Gunther, lives on East 87th Street."

"I'll put a detail on him. Don't make any moves on either. Let me check with immigration to see what they have on his file. I'll get back to you as quickly as I can."

CHAPTER SEVENTY-ONE

Thursday, June 11, 1942

As the calendar crept closer to the designated day, Dieter was growing more anxious. Every night when he returned from his reconnaissance, Lurline was waiting for him, ready to teach him new pleasures. And each morning, she left later to return to her husband. Hedy had faded to a distant memory.

Mr. Griswold only spoke to him when necessary but took no other action against him. Coward.

It was nearly three in the morning when he climbed the wooden stairs to his room over the garage. Lurline was sitting on his bed, smoking a cigarette, wearing a negligee. "You're late."

He calculated the timing of the tides and gleaned from the comments of passing coastguardsmen that a sizable sand bar lay offshore. He hoped the U-boat captain bringing the team knew of it as well. "Sorry, but I told you it would be like this for the next week or two."

"You didn't say why, though."

He glared at her. "You claimed you didn't want to know, that you cared only for pleasure and love giving me pleasure. Were those lies?" If he killed her, it would need to appear to be an accident, otherwise he would endanger the mission.

Her eyes reflected something new. Fear. "Of course, they weren't. I'm sorry, Dieter, it's just that I love our times together. Don't you?"

Good, message received. "Yes, but we each have a role to play, and you must let me play mine, even if you don't understand."

She rushed to him. "All right." She kissed his cheek. "Let's make love."

He could break her neck and throw her down the outside stairs and snap one of her heels to make it look like the cause. He'd report it to the police himself, claiming he heard the noise in the middle of the night, but when he investigated, it was too late. Yes, he'd say, she had been flirting with him shamelessly, but he'd resisted her advances. Mr. Griswold wouldn't believe him, but he'd back up his story for the sake of pride.

"Dieter? Please? I promise I won't bother you about your work or interfere with you. But please don't push me away."

He cupped her chin, as he often did, but this time he squeezed hard.

She whimpered. "Please, Dieter, don't hurt me."

He maintained his grip. "You may stay one hour, but when I say to go, you go."

"Anything you say, darling. Anything."

He still didn't release her. "After tonight, do not come here again until I comment on the weather over dinner. Is that clear?"

"Of course, darling."

"And do not, under any circumstances, attempt to follow me when I walk to the beach in the evening. Never!"

Now, she was shaking. "No, I won't. I thought you would find it amusing."

"I don't." He finally released her. "Good." He kicked off his shoes and pulled down his trousers. He turned a dazzling smile on her. "Now, for pleasure."

***

Danny was waiting when Larkin arrived to begin their eight-to-four. "I finally got the information from Cogan on Gunther's immigration file."

"Anything worth waiting for?"

Danny read from his notes. "Gunther was born on March 15, 1903, in Cologne, Germany. He enlisted in the German army in 1918 and was wounded in battle. He arrived in the United States in 1922, the same year Christian Jenner's family arrived, and became a citizen in 1927. Married in 1928, divorced in 1933."

"Who gets him, us or the G?"

"They've been tailing him since Monday. He works for a book publisher, an editor of some kind, mostly in the sciences. Long hours."

Larkin was baffled. "This is our secret Nazi?" But then he saw Danny glaring at him. "What?"

"Works long hours for a publisher of science books, not Mickey Spillane novels. Sounds to me like he would have lots of time to do his own research on scientific matters."

Larkin nodded. "Like how to make explosives."

"Let's go talk to his neighbors."

***

Paul Gunther's neighbors had little to say about him other than he was quiet and kept to himself.

"The worst kind," Larkin said.

"One neighbor left," Danny replied. "Across the hall." He rang the bell.

A woman in her thirties answered wearing a green duster and her hair tied back. "Yes?"

Danny and Larkin flashed their badges.

"I didn't call the police."

"No, ma'am," Danny replied, "we want to ask about your neighbor, Mr. Gunther."

"Don't see him much."

But something in her expression—a sense of distaste—caught Danny's eye. "Anything you don't like about him?"

"No, he keeps to himself."

"But…?"

"I don't know what kind of hobby he has, but lately there's an awful stench at night."

"What kind of stench?" Danny asked.

"I can't describe it. Chemicals, I guess. Sometimes it's so bad, I feel sick to my stomach."

"When did you first notice it?" Danny had his notepad out.

"A few weeks ago. At first, it was just annoying, but it's gotten much worse in the past two weeks, until a couple of nights ago, when it stopped. Maybe he couldn't take it anymore."

Danny gave her his card. "Please call me if you smell it again."

"So, what now?" Larkin asked once they were outside. "Try to get a search warrant?"

"Based on foul smells? I doubt we've got much of a shot, but let's see what we can do."

CHAPTER SEVENTY-TWO

Friday, June 12, 1942

"The White House announced an understanding between the United States and Russia on the tasks needed to create a second front in Europe this year. The two nations have signed a master lend-lease agreement providing reciprocal defense aid and designed to create a new and better world after victory is won."

***

Danny focused on the note from ADA Dennis Monroe.

"What's the trouble, Danny boy?" Larkin asked.

"My favorite ADA."

Larkin snorted. "You were damned relieved Meg never had to take the stand. What's our legal beagle have to say today?"

"He couldn't get a search warrant without a more specific complaint about the odor, linking it to potential explosives."

"And all that dame could say was that it stunk. Any other bright ideas?"

"We know who our guy is, Frankie. We just can't prove it, yet. Maybe it's time we shake his tree and see what falls out."

Larkin lost his grin. “Didn’t Cogan ask us to back off while they tailed him?”

“He did, and we have for nearly a week. But he won’t lead us to a stockpile of explosives or to Dieter Mueller’s hideout. Besides, we’re working with the FBI, but it’s our investigation.”

***

Hermann Mueller stared at his sister-in-law. “You should appreciate I can’t tell you that. I thought you were the strong one.”

Freida crossed her arms. “I am strong, but you’ve told me nothing since he left, and the police have been probing. I deserve to be told. It’s not like I’m a security risk.”

He had to grant her that. “He is assisting the Fatherland.”

“Where? How? Doing what?”

She wouldn’t stop until he told her at least some details. “He is out east…”

“Still at German Gardens?”

“No, further, and he’s preparing to assist a secret mission approved by the Führer himself. I can’t tell you more because that is the extent of my knowledge.”

“And the rest of your group?”

He froze. He had never told Freida about the group.

She broke into a sad grin. “You underestimate how close I am to Dieter, and how much he trusts me. Hans Brach is dead. I suspect you had good reason for wanting him dead. He was an idealist, a weakling. But then I read in the newspaper that Christian Jenner is also dead.”

“By his own hand, I believe.”

“No, you don’t, and neither do I. You’d better take advice from your genuine friends, Hermann, because your judgment is faltering.”

Time to change the subject. “Be careful who you call. Your telephone is likely tapped.”

“Certainly, it’s tapped. My son is wanted for burglary and murder. Yours is tapped as well. As a loyal German, you have only two choices: fight or do the honorable thing.”

***

They saw Paul Gunther approaching the publisher’s building.

“Good,” Danny said. “No eavesdroppers.”

Larkin slipped off to the side while Denny positioned himself to intercept Gunther as he made it to the sidewalk.

“Paul Gunther?” Danny flashed his badge as Larkin closed in from behind their prey, arms out, ready to grab him if he bolted. “Detective Brady, New York City Police. I need to ask you a few questions.”

“What’s this about?” Gunther asked.

“We’ll ask the questions,” Larkin said from behind, making Gunther jump.

Danny took an apologetic tone. “Sorry, this is my partner, Detective Larkin.” He recited Gunther’s address.

“Yes, that’s where I live. Is there some problem?”

“Do you know someone named Christian Jenner?” Danny asked.

“His brother and I were friends in Germany.”

“In fact,” Danny said, “you and Martin Jenner were hospitalized together toward the end of the war, correct?”

A little of Gunther’s calm slipped. “Er, yes.”

Danny added an edge to his voice. “Where you also knew two other men, Hans Brach and Hermann Mueller.”

“No, I don’t recall that.”

Too fast. “But you’ve known them since.”

“I didn’t say that.”

Danny broke into an icy grin. “You didn’t have to.”

"See here," Gunther said in a huff. "I don't know what you think I may have done, but I've never heard of anyone named Brach or Mueller, and Christian Jenner was only a minor acquaintance."

Larkin jumped on it. "Was? So, you know he's dead?"

"No, how did it happen?"

"Someone cut his throat," Danny replied. "With a German bayonet from the last war. You see our interest, now."

Gunther drew himself up. "Detectives, I only knew Christian slightly, and I haven't seen him in several months. I do not know the other men you mentioned. Now, if you have anything else you'd like to ask me..."

Danny resumed a conversational tone. "What are your hobbies, Mr. Gunther?"

"I like to write."

"Novels?" Larkin asked.

"No, books on science. I'm hoping to interest my company in publishing a book I'm working on right now. It's about the potential for manufactured fertilizers."

"Manufactured horse shit?" Larkin asked, laughing.

"No, chemical fertilizers. I anticipate a great need for food production when the war is over. I've done some experimentation of my own in how it can be done."

"We'd like to see that," Danny said. "How about you show us your setup?"

"I'm sorry, Detective, but the chemicals I work with can be dangerous if not handled properly. I couldn't risk one of you getting hurt."

Danny took a step closer. "Chemicals like nitric acid?"

A momentary flicker of the eyes. "I mean many chemicals. Now, if you'll excuse me, I must get to work."

***

Griswold had Dieter caddying, and it was a relief to be outside despite the drudgery. The strenuous work carrying clubs helped him work off his anxiety over the coming operation, although his fatigue was compounded by his lack of sleep.

When the golfer finished eighteen holes, Dieter returned to the caddy's shed. Griswold was waiting for him. It was nearly five o'clock.

"They won't need you in the dining room tonight." As usual, he was pouting.

The news didn't surprise Dieter. He hadn't been working in the dining room much in recent weeks, and he was convinced Griswold was doing it to reduce the money he could make from additional hours and tips. That the reduced working hours meant more time Dieter could be with Lurline did not occur to his host.

"How much longer do you think you'll be staying with us?" Griswold asked on the way home. "Mrs. Griswold has been more moody than usual this week, and I fear that the extra work of having a guest in the house may be too much for her."

Dieter maintained a somber expression, although he wanted to laugh out loud. Lurline had been very snappy since their last encounter, taking it out mostly on her husband while hardly speaking to Dieter at all. Whether she missed the sex or being in control, he couldn't say. But denying himself physical pleasure was necessary to discipline himself for what lay ahead and having seized control of their relationship made it all the easier. "Are you asking me to leave?"

"No, not at all." As always, the coward's first instinct was retreat. "I wanted to know what to expect."

"I'm waiting to hear from some relatives of mine about a situation. That should be sometime soon. I assure you I will be as little trouble as possible until then."

CHAPTER SEVENTY-THREE

"Goddamn it, Danny," Greco snapped the moment Cogan left, "you're supposed to be cooperating with the G, not upstaging them. What the hell were you thinking?"

Larkin and McHugh sat with Danny in a semi-circle in front of Greco's desk. McHugh looked scared while Larkin stared at the floor.

Not a time to flinch. "Sorry, Lieutenant, but we have to get this thing off the dime."

"All you did was let him know we're on to him," Greco replied. "Explain to me how that helps."

"Gunther is part of the circle that included Hermann Mueller, Dieter, Hans Brach and Christian Jenner. The burglaries and the two murders are all linked, and Gunther is cooking something up in his apartment using the nitric acid Dieter stole."

"And we can't prove any of that," Greco said.

Larkin waved a slip of paper in the air. "I'm not so sure, Lieutenant. This message was on my desk. I saw it just before you called us in." He handed it to Danny. "Must have been left there by mistake."

Danny read it twice to make sure. "The lab says there was a partial print at the base of the blade of the bayonet that killed Jenner, and it's not his."

Larkin shook his head. "I wondered why a guy would get into a bathtub to kill himself. What next, Danny?"

"Let's give him the weekend to think he's thrown us off and let Cogan calm down. In the meantime, have the Fingerprint Unit look through their records for a match. If nothing shakes from that, we can pick him up for questioning and while he's here, offer him a nice glass of water."

Larkin broke into a grin. "And dust the glass for prints when he leaves."

Danny feigned stunned surprise. "Why, Frankie, what a brilliant idea."

Greco tried to keep from laughing but failed. "Get the hell out and go party. Take the weekend off."

Back outside, before Danny could thank him, Larkin said, "He's right, and for once you're going to do what I say. Call Meg now, tell her to put on her best dress, and meet Helen and me at 7:30 at Gallagher's—no, wait, it's Friday, so make that Le Pavillon. Introduce her to their filet of sole bonne femme. After dinner, to Roseland. Do it." He turned to McHugh before Danny could react. "Why don't you call your secret love and join us?"

***

Griswold drank far more than he ate at dinner, while Lurline slammed down dishes and pouted. The children ate in a rush and left the table.

Dieter took his time, finished his meal, and patted his mouth with his napkin. He helped clear away the dishes once Griswold finished his beer and staggered inside.

When Lurline spoke, it was in a whisper. "Karl says you will leave soon."

"And this upsets you?"

"What do you think?"

"Your husband is jealous and growing hostile, so I told him that to placate him. I'm uncertain when I will leave."

She sniffled. "Why are you punishing me?"

"Stop being so dramatic. You invited me to bed, and I accepted. You wanted a vigorous man to love, and I am doing my best to comply. I am more than happy to stay while I am welcome, but there are other concerns which I can't share with you. Just as you wanted me to trust your judgment, you must now trust mine. My bed will be open to you again, soon."

***

Meg had nearly shrieked with delight when Danny called, and only the concern about messing up her makeup and making them late had kept her from losing herself in his greeting kiss.

"I hope you don't mind going out with Frankie and Helen."

"No, I like them very much. This will be great fun."

"Sean McHugh is bringing his Jewish girlfriend. They'll meet us later at Roseland."

"An Irish lad dating a Jewish girl? Sounds like a brave soul."

"He's a good kid. So is she."

Frankie and Helen were already seated when they got to Le Pavillon. Meg and Helen exchanged air kisses.

"Frankie likes to come here to pretend he has class," Helen said. "Have a martini."

"As opposed to Meg," Danny replied, "who clearly has class."

Meg blushed. "I'll stick to wine, thanks."

***

McHugh and Rebecca met them at Roseland. Helen was reserved toward Rebecca until Meg greeted her with genuine warmth.

Meg was just coming off the dance floor with Danny, having concluded a set of several songs by dancing cheek-to-cheek to "It's Been a Long, Long Time" and finishing with a kiss. She felt a tap on her shoulder.

"Hello, Meg." Hal stood before her in a crisply pressed second lieutenant's uniform. "You look terrific."

"Thank you. I'm sure you remember Danny Brady."

Hal gave a curt nod. "Detective."

Danny's nod was just as curt. "Home on leave?"

"No, I'm in the city on official business. I'm stationed in Washington, assigned to the Quartermaster Corps, and there are supply issues at Fort Hamilton." He turned to Meg. "I always knew there was something between you two."

Frank Larkin, who'd been about to sit, remained standing until Helen yanked him down into his seat.

"There always was mutual respect," Meg said, "now, there's much more. I hope you find whatever you're seeking, Hal." She turned her back and took Danny's hand as they returned to their table.

"Well," Frankie said after he'd gone, "it's good to know Fort Hamilton will be sufficiently stocked with canned peaches."

***

Dieter had been at his position among the dunes since shortly after eleven. The letter had named tonight as the night. They were more likely to be late than early, but relying on classic German efficiency, Dieter was certain they wouldn't be too late.

He checked his watch. Five minutes to midnight. The fog was the thickest he'd seen, and visibility was almost zero. The tide was out, which meant his outpost was a good hundred meters from the water's edge. He strained to hear anything other than the pounding of the surf.

CHAPTER SEVENTY-FOUR

Saturday, June 13, 1942

Voices.

Dieter struggled to hear, unsure whether he'd caught a snippet of German or his ears were deceiving him.

One voice, clearer this time. "… trying to get to Montauk, our boat ran aground, and I don't know where we are."

"This is Amagansett." That voice he knew, one of the coastguardsmen who patrolled the beach. "Why don't you come up to the station and stay for the night?"

The breaking surf drowned out the next snippet until he heard the stranger say, "We've been clamming."

Then a third voice, German, though Dieter couldn't quite catch what he'd said.

"Shut up and get back to the other guys," the stranger said.

The team of saboteurs, and they'd walked right into a coast guard patrol. For a moment, he considered walking down to meet them and letting the coastguardsman walk away, but there wasn't anything he could add. He wasn't even armed, and if more coastguardsmen arrived, the mission would be defeated.

More talking he couldn't hear, then silence.

A shadow passed in front of him, moving from right to left toward the Coast Guard station. That also meant the other men were somewhere to the right.

He left his hiding place and crept along the line of dunes to the right, near the gully at the end of the path he'd first followed to the beach. He stopped when he heard what sounded like digging.

"I can't believe he let him go. The orders were specific—if we encountered anyone, we were to overpower them and send them back to the U-boat."

"Forget it for now. We must get these crates buried so they won't find them."

"All right." The voice he'd heard talking to the coastguardsman. "Finish changing out of those fatigues and into civilian clothes."

"They're all wet. Keeping them in a seabag was stupid."

"Quiet, Hoffstadt, they'll dry. Bury that seabag in the dunes, and the shovels, too." A few minutes later, the familiar voice said, "How is this Mueller fellow supposed to find us in this fog?"

Dieter emerged from behind the dune. "I'm Dieter Mueller." He was taken aback when the leader was a short man wearing a red sweater, a gray coat, dungarees, and a fedora, all wet.

"How do I know that's true?" the fedora man replied.

No time to fence with him. "Reinhold Barth."

"I think it's him," another said.

"He's just a lad," a third added.

The leader took over. "Shut your mouths, all of you. Dieter, I'm Gerhard Dröge."

Dieter saluted. "Heil Hitler."

Dröge raised his hand in a half-hearted salute and peered out at the surf. The rumble of a diesel engine was audible, and the odor of fumes hung on the edge of the breeze. "Our sub ran aground. Hope he gets away before daylight."

Unimpressive. "Did you bring any supplies with you?"

"*Ja*." One of the other men sidled up to Dröge.

The leader wheeled on him. “How many times do I have to tell you? No German, idiot.” He turned back to Dieter and continued in a calm voice. “Allow me to introduce the rest of the team.” He pointed to the man he’d just called an idiot, six feet tall and wearing a soaked navy-blue coat. “Josef Hoffstadt.”

He gave a crisp salute. “Heil Hitler.”

The man standing behind Hoffstadt was shorter but stocky. “Rudolf Kircher.” He wore a green zippered jacket that was likewise soaked. When he saluted, Dieter noticed the jacket was torn under the right armpit.

A fourth man, only slightly taller than Dröge and thinner, slogged toward them.

“This is my second-in-command, Eugen Bakhaus.” The man nodded but did not salute.

They had all the dignity of Bowery bums. Perhaps it was a façade, and underneath they were skilled saboteurs. “We must get off the beach before that coastguardsman returns.”

Dröge chuckled. “Nah, he’s okay. I slipped him three hundred bucks.”

Hoffstadt grumbled. “And you call me an idiot.”

Uncle Hermann had always said he was a leader. Time to lead. “Never mind, my orders are to get you into New York City. For that purpose, you will follow my orders.” He turned to Dröge. “That coastguardsman will be back soon, probably with others. What supplies did you bring besides those?” He gestured with disdain at their attire.

Dröge said nothing, miffed at his loss of authority.

“Two waterproof crates of explosives and detonators,” Bakhaus replied. “Our orders were to bury them, procure a car once we get to New York, and return to retrieve them. We buried them under that dune by the fence.”

Dieter glanced around, half expecting Lurline to appear. “Not very practical. But my group is developing explosives of our own.” He hoped Paul was making progress. “Come on.”

He led them through the scrub until they reached the line of bungalows, the Griswolds' standing at the far end. From the road a few hundred yards ahead of them, they could hear several passing trucks. A signal flare burst in the sky behind them, and beams of searchlights appeared from the beach.

"We're surrounded," Kircher said with a growl.

Dröge turned on him. "Don't be a nervous Nellie."

Closer to the road, Dieter could see the trucks, filled with sailors. "Quiet. We'll stay here until they pass, then cross."

***

It was dawn when Dieter led them across Montauk Highway to a railroad track, then along the track to the Amagansett railroad station. The four saboteurs were shivering in their wet clothes, but Dieter told them to wait out of sight.

At six, he entered the waiting room, where the station master was sipping coffee and reading the newspaper. "War news is good again, with the Japs losing those carriers at Midway. What can I do for you, young man?"

"Five tickets to Jamaica, please."

The station manager peeled off five tickets as Dieter paid him with money Dröge had provided. "Train arrives in less than an hour."

CHAPTER SEVENTY-FIVE

The ringing phone jolted Meg awake.

Danny answered on the second ring. “Yeah?”

She was in his bed. They’d left Roseland around one in the morning, having seen no more of Hal. He’d parked in front of his apartment because 45th Street was quiet and less traveled than Skillman Avenue and they’d started necking, growing more ardent than ever before. His invitation had been with his eyes, and her acceptance had been a kiss. He’d been so gentle.

Danny’s eyes grew wide. “What! When? Where?” He threw off the covers, still wearing nothing. She would have laughed if not for his agitation. “Yeah, okay, give me an hour. In the meantime, make sure your guys in Suffolk have Dieter Mueller’s photo.” He slammed down the receiver.

“Danny, what’s wrong?”

“It’s bad.” He dialed a number. “Lieutenant, it’s Danny, and I just got a call from Cogan. The coast guard reports a small group of suspected German saboteurs landed shortly after midnight near Montauk off a U-boat. The guardsman who saw them says he thinks there are four. I’m certain they’re headed for the city, and Dieter Mueller will hook up with them if he hasn’t already.” He listened, and his scowl grew deeper. "If I'm wrong, bust me back to patrolman. Cogan says he and his boss are meeting with the Coast Guard biggies at their Barge Office at the Battery at eleven. He wants one of us there. Please go… Can't be me, it needs someone with command authority… But that's not how the Coast Guard will see it. Besides, we don't have time to sit around while the Coast Guard gets into a pissing match with the G, which they'll lose, anyway. I need four radio cars, one for each of us—Frankie, Sean, Vinnie, and me. We need to be moving and we need to keep in contact." A longer pause. He relaxed a little. "Thanks, Lieutenant, we'll do our best. Whatever details you get, please radio them to me." He hung up, gently, this time.

Meg was already partly dressed. "Danny…"

"In a minute." He dialed another number. "Helen? Danny. I need to speak to him, pronto." A pause. "Frankie? Just got a call from Cogan." He repeated what he'd told Greco. "The four of us will each take a radio car. Meet me at the precinct as soon as possible."

Meg thought back on her conversation with Helen.

Danny dressed after calling McHugh and Rossi, not bothering to shave. He took her in his arms. "I'm sorry, honey, this is not how I wanted today to go."

She managed a brave smile. "I understand. A cop's wife's life. I'll be okay."

He dropped her at her apartment. "Better get inside before your neighbors get the wrong idea."

"You mean the right idea, don't you?"

He laughed. "I'll make an honest woman of you once this case is over."

***

By the time they had reached Jamaica Station, Dieter had been ready to jump on a train back to German Gardens to complain to Herr Schmidt. Dröge had no command ability, and Hoffstadt and

Kircher expressed their disapproval with open insubordination and obvious distrust of both Dröge and Bakhaus.

"Where do we get the train into New York City?" Dröge asked.

Dieter pointed across the platform. "A train will pull in shortly." But the police and FBI would be looking for them. "I suggest we split up, no more than two together."

"My thoughts, exactly," Dröge said. "Eugen and I will go directly into Manhattan."

Kircher's temper flared. "What are we supposed to do?"

Dieter took command. "You all need different clothes. Those look awful. There are several men's clothing stores down on the street, along Sutphin Boulevard and Jamaica Avenue, a block that way." He pointed north. "You and Hoffstadt can get another train later." He turned back to Dröge. "When you get off the train at Penn Station, Macy's department store will be a block away, Seventh Avenue and 34th Street. You can get what you need there."

Dröge nodded. "Check."

"You know where you're going?" Dieter asked.

"Check and recheck. I lived in New York in the thirties before returning to the Fatherland. Eugen and I will stay at the New Yorker. Hoffstadt and Kircher will stay at the Chesterfield." He drew himself up as if trying to look taller. "We'll meet at the automat in the basement of Macy's at five o'clock." He turned back to Dieter. "And where will you be while we shop for clothes?"

"Someplace else."

***

Greco was still at the precinct when Danny arrived. "The Coast Guard found two crates of explosives buried in the sand on the beach. And an FBI agent out east interviewed the station manager at Amagansett, who recognized Dieter Mueller's photo. He bought five tickets for Jamaica and got the 6:59 train. Cogan's got men scouring both Jamaica Station and Penn."

"Good, we can stick to the places Dieter is likely to go…"

"He's got four accomplices, now, so I want you in teams of two."

Danny had wondered when Greco was going to try this. "Dieter won't stick with them. He may not have even come into the city with them, since he only bought tickets to Jamaica, not Penn." Danny pulled out a BMT subway map. "He knows the subway system. They got off at Jamaica and he likely walked the one block to the Jamaica Avenue elevated line, the 15 train."

"So, he's headed for the Lower East Side?"

Danny pointed to the map. "If he stayed on the 15 train, possibly, but he could also have changed at East New York to the Canarsie Line, which he could take to Union Square. Or he could have walked up to Hillside Avenue and taken the new IND line to Lexington Avenue."

Greco groaned. "And from either, taken the Lexington Avenue line or the Third Avenue El up to Yorkville."

Danny was still studying the map. "I'm less concerned about what route he took, or is taking, and more concerned about where he's going."

"Sounds okay, but you guys are doubling up."

"That will make us half as effective."

"And half as vulnerable."

"Lieutenant…"

"That's an order, Detective. Besides, I could only get two radio cars."

CHAPTER SEVENTY-SIX

Danny briefed his team, who'd all arrived shortly after Greco left for the Battery. "We don't know where Dieter arrived in Manhattan, but we can be certain he's here. The saboteurs buried their explosives on the beach, so Dieter is likely more than just their guide. He'll make contact either with his uncle or Paul Gunther about explosives. We only have two radio cars, so Frankie, you take Vinnie with you and Sean comes with me."

"How do you want to handle this?" Larkin asked.

"You and Vinnie start with Gunther's place. If he doesn't answer, knock and be loud. Alert his neighbors we're looking for him, and talk to the woman across the hall, see if he's been cooking up any new recipes. Sean and I will start with Hermann Mueller. Dispatch has been instructed to keep us informed by radio of anything coming from the G, and we'll keep in contact that way."

***

"Mueller Plumbing."

The voice at the other end was a whisper. "A friend needs to meet with you in an hour. You know where." The line went dead.

Hermann laid the receiver in its cradle with care. Dieter was back.

A glance at the clock. It was twenty-five past eleven. He peered out the window, and the black Chevy he'd spotted the previous evening was still there. His back door led to a closed courtyard with no exit, which left only one way to do this.

He left his apartment and climbed into his truck. When he pulled away, the black Chevy followed. He turned left on Second Avenue, and the black Chevy followed, allowing a car to pull between them.

Good, he wouldn't want to shake them too soon.

***

"Where the hell is the FBI stakeout car?" McHugh asked as Danny parked on 86th Street.

"Good question. Mueller's truck is gone, too." He picked up the radio microphone and pressed the key on the side. "Dispatch, this is Special One checking in. Any contact from Lieutenant Greco? Over."

"Special One from Dispatch. Negative, will notify you when he calls in."

"Well, that's great," McHugh said with a humorless laugh. "What the hell are we supposed to do, now?"

Danny didn't quite stifle a yawn. "Let's head over a block and see if the bartender at the *Bier Garten* has seen our friend. Then, we can drop in on Leopold and Frieda."

***

Hermann parked the truck on 44th Street, just off Seventh Avenue. He walked slowly, as if checking building addresses, while an agent left the black Chevy and tailed him at a distance. When the traffic light changed, he darted across 44th Street just ahead of oncoming traffic, then hurried to the subway stop two blocks away through thickening crowds.

He didn't look back until he reached the platform of the Flushing Line. He watched for the agent until a Queens-bound train rolled in, but never saw him.

That was easy.

***

"Special Two to Special One."

Danny picked up the mic. "Special One, go ahead, Special Two."

"No luck, Danny." Larkin's voice. "Gunther ain't here. His neighbor says there's been no stench for a few days, but before that it was so bad that she considered checking into a hotel."

"See if he's at the magazine but leave Vinnie in the car for alerts." If Dieter contacted Gunther, it could only be to arrange for explosives. "On second thought, take him with you. If Gunther's there, take him into custody and back to the precinct. Otherwise, find out when he was there last. In either case, check in with me as soon as you're back in the car, over."

"Roger that, Danny, out."

McHugh stared at him. "What will that accomplish? We won't be able to hold him for long unless he confesses."

"That horrific stench was likely Gunther shifting to production mode. That it's stopped suggests he now has a stockpile. I want him out of circulation at least for a little while, keep him from hooking up with Dieter." He drove a short way in silence. "Unless he already has."

***

Hermann got off the Flushing train at Grand Central. The agent who'd trailed him to Times Square might very well return to his usual post to await further developments. So, he decided against the subway and walking through his neighborhood and hailed a cab.

***

"Special Two to Special One, Gunther's not at work and they haven't seen him since Thursday. What now?"

"Radio Dispatch and have someone contact Dennis Monroe to request a search warrant on his apartment based on the neighbor's reports of suspicious activity."

"Roger, Danny."

They left the car and entered the *Bier Garten.* No customers, just Emile. Good. "I'm going to ask you some questions, and I want straight answers. If I don't get them, I've been authorized to place you under arrest as a conspirator in sabotage and shut this place down."

Emile turned white. "I've done nothing. You can't do that. This isn't…"

Danny broke into a humorless grin. "Berlin? No, but isn't that the goal?" He didn't let the trembling bartender respond. "Yeah, yeah, you're loyal, true blue. So, now's your chance to prove it. Hermann Mueller's little cabal meets here, do they not?"

"No." When Danny glared at him, he added, "Not anymore."

"And when they met here, the regulars were Hans Brach, Christian Jenner, Paul Gunther, and Dieter Mueller, correct?"

Emile nodded but said nothing.

"Were there any others?" Danny asked. When Emile hesitated before shaking his head, Danny added, "You are walking a tightrope, here. You want to protect yourself, but you don't want to sell out your friends to do it. I appreciate your predicament, but sometimes the tightrope won't hold, and you must jump."

"That's where you are now," McHugh added.

"So," Danny continued, "were there any others, here or elsewhere?"

Emile swallowed hard. "They met here every Thursday evening for a few months but stopped several weeks ago. Hermann never said why. They would sit at a table in the back and talk in low voices. Several months ago, Hermann began receiving phone calls during their meetings, always at eight o'clock, from someone he addressed as Friedrich."

This was interesting. "Did you overhear any part of any conversation?"

"Just once. He told Friedrich to keep his group small but remain efficient. Please, for the love of God, don't tell him I told you."

Danny leaned on the bar, bringing his face closer. "You haven't told me anything. Who was this mysterious person? Where was he calling from? What group? You must have heard what he told his friends once he got off the phone."

McHugh scoffed. "Forget it, Danny, he ain't talking. He's stringing us along."

Emile cried out. "No, not at all."

"Then, convince us," Danny said.

"He mentioned one club here and one in German Gardens, and about Germany being interested. He also mentioned a Herr Schmidt. But I don't know who that might be. I swear, that's all."

"You believe him?" McHugh asked Danny.

Danny glared at the bartender for several moments. "He ain't lying, but he may not be telling us everything."

Emile's voice cracked. "I am, I swear, I've held nothing back. Nothing."

Danny grabbed the bartender's shirtfront and pulled him against the bar. "All right, I believe you. But if even one part of your story doesn't check out..." He released the shirt and stormed out with McHugh right behind. "Now, we bust in on that Coast Guard pissing match with the G and find out what the hell is going on."

***

Dieter, standing by the railing overlooking the river at the edge of Carl Schurz Park, checked his watch. Thirty-five minutes past noon. He dared not wait much longer.

But here came his uncle. "My apologies. I had to come by a circuitous route. The FBI has mirrored what American films portray the Gestapo to be. It can be very inconvenient."

Dieter turned to walk along the path away from the few passers-by in the park. "A team of four landed early this morning. They leave much to be desired, having left their explosives on the beach. I see no way to recover them. How is Paul getting on?"

"He's detonated a test charge and compiled a supply, but communication is becoming difficult. They've tapped my phone, your parents', Paul's, and probably the pay phone at the *Bier Garten*. They've had undercover men there as well." He described how he'd eluded his trackers.

"We'll communicate through predetermined meeting locations, as I did with Tommy McArdle. This will not be one of them. I'm to meet with the team later today. I will decide whether to use them and how."

"Surely, that's a decision for the Reich."

"You are a loyal German and Nazi, and I am proud to be your nephew, but leaders must prove their worth. The appointed leader of this operation, a Herr Dröge, is not fit to lead and his men realize it. I've seen how they distrust him, and so do I." He turned to the matter of when and where to meet. "I suggest we meet tomorrow in another borough. Return to your home this afternoon the same way you came and enter as if nothing has been amiss. Tomorrow, shake your pursuers the same way. From any point on Seventh Avenue, take the Flatbush Avenue line to Grand Army Plaza. Make certain you have not been followed and meet me on the path behind the memorials at noon. If you haven't shaken your pursuers, abort and double back. We will then meet at noon Monday at Bethesda Fountain in Central Park."

Uncle Hermann broke into a grin. "Very well, Dieter, anything else?"

"Where is Paul and where has he hidden his cache of explosives?"

His uncle extracted a piece of note paper. "He is staying at the Manhattanite Hotel on West 29th Street under the name of Peter Myers. This is the number of the pay phone on his floor. The explosives are in two valises he checked into the luggage room at Penn Station."

CHAPTER SEVENTY-SEVEN

While en route to the Battery, Danny received a call from Dispatch saying Greco wanted him at the FBI's shooting range in the basement of the federal courthouse at Foley Square. A judge had turned down ADA Monroe's request for a search warrant, so Danny had Larkin and Rossi continue to cruise Yorkville.

As he and McHugh entered the shooting range, Assistant Director Donegan, Bill Cogan, and Greco were standing amid an astounding amount of equipment in a meticulous array—explosives, detonators, fuse lighters, all presumably recovered from the beach at Amagansett.

"I've never seen anything like this," Donegan said. "There's enough explosive power here to inflict millions of dollars of damage. We've been incredibly lucky."

"I wouldn't cash in my chips just yet," Danny replied. "Hermann Mueller is nowhere to be seen, and neither is the unit that was shadowing him. Paul Gunther is neither home nor at work, and *his* shadow detail is sitting comfortably in front of his residence, oblivious. Dieter Mueller has been back in Manhattan for at least five hours, and no one knows where he is." He repeated what Emile had said. "Mueller's friends in German Gardens include one Herr Schmidt. That name mean anything to you guys?"

"Calm down, Danny," Greco said.

"Not in a month of Sundays. The saboteurs brought this, but Paul Gunther has been cooking up his own supply. ADA Monroe couldn't get a search warrant."

Donegan replied in a soothing voice. "The bureau is deploying a team to spend the night on Amagansett beach, ready to bag these guys when they return to dig up all this."

Danny was ready to explode. "No way Dieter Mueller will let them go back, knowing they were seen by the Coast Guard, especially when he's got explosives of his own."

"That's only your suspicion," Donegan replied. "We need to stick to facts."

***

Paul had been glad to hear from Dieter and assured him the explosives had been field tested. He'd also verified the location of the two valises. Dieter was in good spirits when he entered the automat.

It didn't last. He spotted Dröge and Bakhaus in an instant, surrounded by shopping bags.

"And here's our leader, now." Dröge's sarcasm was unmistakable.

Dieter stared at him as he sat. "Don't draw so much attention to yourself. Where are the others?" Before Dröge could answer, he spotted Hoffstadt and Kircher entering, both wearing garish striped jackets and carrying several bags of their own.

Dieter shook his head in disbelief.

"What's the beef?" Dröge asked as the newcomers pulled up chairs. "We got plenty of cash from the…"

"Shut up." Dieter glared at each of them in turn before continuing through clenched teeth. "You are all on a mission for the

Reich, not part of a Marx Brothers film. No flamboyance, nothing to draw attention. Be drab, blend in with the surroundings."

Dröge drew himself up but kept his voice down. "I'm the leader of this mission."

Dieter cut him off. "You were spotted by the Coast Guard minutes after landing. Who got you into the city undetected? Who knows the most likely targets, and who will supply the materials?"

"We'll recover our supplies as soon as we procure transportation," Dröge replied. "I assume you know how to steal a car."

Had the Abwehr found this man in an asylum? "I'm certain the Coast Guard has already dug everything up, and if you return, you will find a committee waiting to arrest you."

Hoffstadt turned to Kircher. "Just as I said."

Dieter glanced around. His group had drawn some curious glances. "We're conspicuous here. Finish your meals and return to your hotel rooms. Meet me tomorrow afternoon at three in front of Grant's Tomb, Riverside Drive and 122nd Street. Take the 7th Avenue Local to 125th Street and be prompt."

***

Danny and McHugh stood poised outside of the apartment of Paul Gunther, along with the building's landlord.

"Don't do it," McHugh said, "Greco will have your ass and I'll be screwed out of a shot at a gold badge.

"We need facts. This is the only way to get them." He gestured to the landlord, who unlocked the door with his key.

McHugh yanked out a handkerchief and covered his nose. "It's almost as bad as a dead body in here."

"I'll wait outside, if you fellas don't mind." The landlord withdrew.

A rubbish bin stood next to the kitchen table. There were empty bottles with labels that read, "Property of Bronx HS of Science."

Danny picked up the phone and dialed the number for Cogan, who was now back in his office. "What explosives can you cook up with nitric acid, mercury, and alcohol?"

"That's easy. Fulminate of mercury. Where are you?" Cogan asked.

"I'm in Paul Gunther's apartment. He ain't here. Looks like he left in a rush. He left traces of his supplies behind. I'd like to employ your detail downstairs—if they're not napping—to come up and pack up this stuff."

***

From the automat, Dieter made his way up Seventh Avenue, taking a room at the Foster Hotel. Hoffstadt's comment to Kircher came back to him. "Just as I said." Dieter would have to ask what he'd meant by that.

***

"You did what?" Greco was furious.

Danny repeated what he'd found at Gunther's place. Larkin and Rossi had also returned.

"Not only didn't you have a warrant," Greco said, "you'd asked and been refused."

"It's the landlord's building. He let us in. Gunther's been cooking up enough explosives to blow a few bridges to hell and gone."

"You're supposed to be working with the FBI, not trying to make them look bad. Jesus, Danny, go home and get some sleep."

CHAPTER SEVENTY-EIGHT

Sunday, June 14, 1942

Dieter's uncle was punctual, as always. "It's interesting. They follow me until I lose them, then wait for me to return."

"They know you won't abandon your truck. It might be interesting if you returned home today without it." Dieter pondered that for a moment. "They watch you because they expect I'll come to you. Once you leave the truck, they will need more resources to keep track of you, which could be useful."

"To what purpose?"

"Distracting them from finding me and the team the Reich sent."

"So, you will take command?"

"*Ja.* You will not see or hear from me again for a while."

***

Meg attended mass at St. Sebastian's with Danny. They left at communion.

"I've never done that before," she said once they were outside.

"Left mass early or declined to receive?"

"Both, I guess." She shrugged. "But fair's fair. In the church's eyes, I'm an adulteress."

Danny tried to protest.

She linked her arm through his. "No need to defend me. The church says I can't receive if I'm divorced and remarry. I could have confessed and continued to receive until we're married, but that would be hypocritical. I still have my faith. That won't change." She gave his arm a squeeze. "I hope it won't for you, either."

They stopped in a bakery for muffins before continuing to her apartment, where she put on a pot of coffee before sliding into his embrace. "So, what's next in the case?"

"You're just pumping me so you can tell Helen Larkin, aren't you?"

"Not just that, I need to know, too, Danny, and you promised you'd never hold back. I can take it."

He kissed her forehead. "Yes, you can."

***

Hoffstadt and Kircher were waiting for Dieter at Grant's Tomb.

"Where are the others?"

Hoffstadt snorted. "Who knows? After you left, Dröge suggested we all go to a whorehouse he knows. Bakhaus resisted because he's married, but when we both left in disgust, Dröge was wearing him down."

Dieter waited twenty minutes. Still nothing. "Who appointed him as leader?"

"Someone in the Abwehr," Kircher replied, "Reinhold Barth. Dröge got a job there when he returned to Germany several years ago. Bakhaus was a member of the S.A. but he lost favor after the purge in 1934. Dröge claims he begged to be included as a way of restoring his reputation."

Dieter caught the hedge. "But you don't believe that."

Kircher shrugged. "I'm not sure what to believe."

Dieter nodded toward Hoffstadt. "You two seem to get on well."

"We worked together for a few years."

"At Dornier," Kircher added.

"And you all lived in the United States for a time?"

"It was a requirement for this mission," Hoffstadt replied. "Here they come, now."

"Good afternoon," Dröge said, his voice hearty.

"You're late." No niceties.

"It's not like we don't have time." Dröge tapped his head. "The entire plan is here in my noodle." He pointed at Hoffstadt. "And you, my friend, should already be on your way to Chicago."

Dieter interrupted before Hoffstadt could reply. "What about Chicago?"

"He's got family, there, and his orders are to contact them to enlist their aid in seeking targets for sabotage," Dröge replied. "He should have already left."

"It would make more sense to contact my friends here on Long Island," Hoffstadt said.

Dieter turned to him. "What friends? Where?"

"The Obermanns, in a place called German Gardens."

"Friedrich Obermann?"

Hoffstadt brightened. "He's a friend of the family. You know him?"

Dieter turned serious. "Yes, he's been of assistance to me, but do not seek him out. That could be disastrous."

"Maybe it's dangerous for us to be associating with you," Dröge said.

Dieter flashed an icy grin. "It certainly is. Such is the nature of our mission, of which I am now taking command."

Dröge fumed. "You can't do that, Herr Barth appointed me."

"And you've blundered at every turn," Hoffstadt said. "You let that patrolman get away, left our supplies on the beach, and spent our funds on a whorehouse." He turned to Dieter. "Dröge doesn't want to complete the mission, he wants to disappear and stay here. I'd bet my last reichsmark on it."

Dieter stepped between them, glaring at Dröge. "If this is true, I will kill you." He turned to the others. "Tell me now whether you will continue the mission under my command." Hoffstadt and Kircher both agreed. Bakhaus nodded.

"Very well," Dröge said in a huff. "I turn command over to you."

"We will meet tomorrow evening at promptly six at the Horn and Hardart Automat in Times Square."

***

Danny and Larkin were waiting when Hermann Mueller returned home.

"Good afternoon, Mueller," Danny called as Mueller froze. "How was Brooklyn?"

"I don't know what you're…"

"Sure, you do," Larkin said. "Grand Army Plaza. Took your time coming back."

Mueller couldn't hide his shock.

"See," Danny continued in his calm manner, "the FBI had someone at the turnstiles, and he followed you down to the train. When you got off at Grand Army Plaza, so did he. You mean you didn't notice?"

"Must be the shell shock," Larkin said. "I hear it comes back later in life."

Mueller's stunned expression deepened.

Danny laughed. "Oh, you're surprised we know about that? You and your hospital-mates in 1918, along with Christian Jenner's older brother. As you might have already guessed, the G-man didn't follow you out of the station, although I would have, and Dieter would now be under arrest. But it's enough to confirm that he's here in the city. The FBI will keep a detail on you, and in your desperation to keep away from Dieter, you will eventually lead us to him."

***

"You don't think we should have squeezed him about Gunther?" Larkin asked as they got back in their car.

"Nope, he wouldn't have given us anything useful, and we upset him sufficiently so that he can't help him."

"Do you really think he'll do something rash to lead us to Dieter?"

"No, he'll stay put, and won't be able to help him, either." Danny parked in front of Gunther's building. "Let's see if we can manufacture a break."

He knocked on the door of the front apartment on the ground floor. A middle-aged woman answered in her Sunday best.

Danny flashed his badge and introduced himself and Larkin. "Are you acquainted with Paul Gunther?"

"Yes, he lives in the apartment right above me."

"When did you see him last?"

"Friday morning, he was getting into a cab. A Checker Cab."

"You sure about that?" Larkin asked.

"Oh, yes, can't miss that black and white checkerboard on the side."

"Did he have any luggage?"

She thought a moment. "Two large black suitcases. Probably going away on vacation."

"Yeah," Larkin muttered, "to have a blast."

"Did he talk to you before he left?" Danny asked. "Make arrangements for forwarding his mail?"

"No."

One last question. "When he's home, does he have many visitors?"

"No, and that's strange because he's such a nice-looking young man—tall, slim, blond hair, blue eyes, firm chin." She sighed. "Maybe he's gone off to find himself a wife."

Back in the car, Larkin asked, "So, now what?"

"We drop in on the Checker Cab Company and see if we can find the driver who picked him up, and then maybe where he dropped him off."

Larkin shook his head. "Two suitcases filled with fulminate of mercury. He's lucky that cab wasn't blown to Kingdom Come. I wonder how he sleeps in the same room with them."

"He doesn't, Frankie. He would have dropped them someplace before checking into a hotel. Dieter's in the city, so those suitcases must be, too."

CHAPTER SEVENTY-NINE

Monday, June 15, 1942

Danny awoke on the first ring and snatched the receiver from its cradle. “What?” For a moment, he feared it was Meg, but a glance at the clock—5:15 in the morning—ruled that out.

It was Cogan. “Sorry to wake you, Danny, but our office got a weird phone call yesterday, some guy saying he wanted a meeting with the Director. Said he had information the Director needed to hear directly from him, and he was planning on coming to Washington to deliver it.”

“Did he give his name?”

“Siegfried Wagner.”

Danny forced himself to full alert. “Is that a reference to Camp Siegfried?”

Cogan chuckled. “More likely the camp’s name was a reference to the same hero. Siegfried is the name of an ancient hero of Norse sagas, one that Wagner used in opera.” When Danny said nothing, he added, “Richard Wagner, Hitler’s favorite composer.”

“So, you think…”

“I’m not sure what to think. Donegan called Hoover before he called me. Hoover’s already busting a gut over how the Coast Guard handled this thing, and he wants to be sure we don’t blow this. If the caller is a saboteur now looking to save his skin, it changes things."

"Where did he call from?" When Cogan didn't answer, Danny added, "Your guys traced it, didn't they?"

"No, the guy taking the call assumed it was a crank. I overheard a casual conversation about it."

"Hoover might want to ease up on the Coast Guard." Danny told him the latest on Gunther.

"Since they never went back for their supplies," Cogan said, "you're probably right. Whatever Gunther cooked up in his apartment is what they'll use, and soon. Any idea where Gunther is staying?"

"We tracked down the cab driver last night who'd picked him up at his apartment, and he said he dropped him off at Penn Station. Gunther told him he was taking the Twentieth Century Limited to Chicago."

"Okay, I'll get on the horn to our Chicago office," Cogan said with a groan.

"He's not in Chicago, because the Twentieth Century Limited runs out of Grand Central, not Penn Station. Gunther is staying somewhere within walking distance of Penn Station. How many agents can you deploy?"

"At least a dozen. We'll start with every hotel within a five-block radius. If we don't find him, we'll expand it. Where will you be?"

"Exploring his other options."

***

Hoffstadt and Kircher were already at the automat when Dieter arrived at six that evening. They chatted easily. Dröge would be peevish and late, so Dieter encouraged the others to purchase something to eat while he did the same.

But, by 6:40, there was still no sign of them.

"They're not coming," Kircher said.

"As I expected," Hoffstadt added. When Dieter gave him a questioning look, he answered. "They left our meeting place yesterday, whispering between themselves as they walked away. I don't think Dröge ever had any intention of completing this mission."

"Why?" Dieter was studying both men, now.

Hoffstadt dropped his voice to a little above a whisper. "We went through weeks of training. Dröge never took it seriously, especially the operational aspects. We all had to build explosive devices. His never worked, and he always made jokes about it."

Kircher chimed in, his voice equally low. "He and Bakhaus were friends from the start, even though they'd never met before. And Bakhaus is married to an American woman. She lives in Berlin."

"And he left her to come here? That was putting her at quite a risk if he meant to stay here."

"I don't know what he's thinking," Hoffstadt replied, "but he's backed up Dröge ever since we boarded the U-boat."

Dieter glanced at the clock. 6:50.

Hoffstadt caught it. "If Dröge hasn't already turned himself in, he'll do it soon."

Dieter said nothing else until they'd finished their meals. "If you're right, we haven't much time. Check out of your hotel and find another close by. Once you've checked in, stay in." He scribbled the number of the Foster hotel's pay phone on a napkin. "Call me at seven tomorrow morning. If we've heard nothing further from Dröge or Bakhaus, we'll set a meeting place, then. By tomorrow night, we'll have accomplished our mission."

***

Dieter stopped at a pay phone and dialed the number Uncle Hermann had given him.

Paul answered after several rings. "Sorry, I wasn't expecting you to call so late."

"Couldn't be helped. There have been some problems. I'll need your supply."

"What's mine is yours. You know that. Should we meet?"

"Yes, sometime tomorrow. I'm still formulating my plan. I'll call you tomorrow morning at this same number."

CHAPTER EIGHTY

Tuesday, June 16, 1942

Danny received another pre-dawn call from Cogan. “He walked into our DC office yesterday. One of our agents has been taking a statement from him ever since. His name is Gerhard Dröge. He’s the leader of the Long Island team.”

“You mean there’s a second team?” An additional worry. “Where did they land? New Jersey?”

“No, Florida, near Jacksonville.”

***

“Very well, meet me at eight at the Times Square Automat.” Dieter replaced the receiver of the pay phone. Hoffstadt had called twenty minutes late, but if what he’d said was true, tardiness was the least of Dieter’s worries. He’d just set the automat as their meeting place. He’d never used the same meeting place twice.

The pressure was mounting.

He deposited a nickel and dialed the number at the Manhattanite. Paul answered on the fourth ring.

“Penn Station, main entrance, eleven o’clock this morning, and bring the luggage ticket.”

***

A half hour later, Dieter was sitting in the automat. Hoffstadt and Kircher sat with their arms folded, while Bakhaus poured out his story in hushed tones.

"So," Dieter said, "are you saying Dröge has already left for Washington?"

"Yes, he was in an all-night poker game. When he woke me yesterday morning, he said he was going to secure a better life for himself and me, and that he'd paid my hotel bill through today. He also left an envelope with three thousand dollars to cover expenses until he returned."

"And you let him go." Such treachery left Dieter shaking.

Bakhaus blinked. "I don't see what I could have done."

Dieter lowered his voice to a growl. "It's treason. I would have killed him. At the very least, you should have alerted me." He watched with satisfaction as Bakhaus drew back.

"I'll do whatever you ask, anything to allow me to regain your trust."

He addressed all of them. "Dröge has put our mission in peril. We have no choice but to strike today. Be at the stairway to the Long Island Railroad trains in Penn Station at precisely ten minutes after eleven. I will have two large valises, each packed with fulminate of mercury." He studied each of them in turn, deciding who should perform each task. "We no longer have the luxury of time to choose a military target. We will attack a transportation target, instead. Bakhaus, you and Kircher will each take a valise down to the platform for tracks 13 and 14 while Hoffstadt follows at a discreet distance. If anyone stops any of you, act as if you are lost."

Nods of agreement all around.

He continued. "Bakhaus and Kircher will follow the platform to the western end, the opposite direction of Long Island Railroad trains leaving the station, and, after assuring no one is watching, use the ladder at the far end of the platform to descend to track level. Proceed westward to where all the tracks narrow to just two. Place the valises with care inside the first two switches. When a train hits either, they will explode, blocking all entry to and exit from the west end. Hoffstadt will remain on the platform as lookout."

Hoffstadt agreed. "And if I see someone before the valises are placed, I'll collapse on the platform and cry out as if in pain."

He, at least, would be reliable. "Excellent." Dieter turned to the others. "If you hear him, lay the valises resting on whatever track is closest and hide until you can get out."

"Where?" It was Bakhaus.

"It's a poorly lit underground station, and with all the attention on Hoffstadt, you will find something."

"How much time will we have?" Kircher asked.

"The morning rush will be well past. Here is the schedule of the late morning trains. Make certain your watches are set with precision." He nodded toward Bakhaus. "He's already been derelict in his duty. If he so much as hesitates down there, kill him."

CHAPTER EIGHTY-ONE

Meg had just finished dressing for work when the phone rang. She tried to keep her voice steady when she answered. "Danny?"

"No, it's Helen. Frankie charged out of here at 6:00 this morning after a call from Danny. Did he tell you what's going on?"

"He didn't call me this morning. The big case they're on must have taken a sudden turn." She couldn't keep her voice from cracking.

"Easy, hon, just tell me what you know. Frankie hasn't said a word."

Meg had already told her about Dieter Mueller. She now filled in the parts about the saboteurs. "Danny's convinced this Dieter guy is their guide. They must have gotten some new lead. God, I hope they're okay." After a deep breath, she added, "The FBI is working with them, so at least they're not going it alone."

"Danny's too smart for that. Frankie, I'm not so sure, but Danny is."

"Thanks, Helen. You're a good friend."

"So are you, Meg, and thanks for the info. It's better to know."

"It also helps to talk about it when you do."

She hung up. Part of her lunch break would be spent at St. Sebastian's saying the Rosary. Just because she was at odds with certain church teachings didn't mean she was abandoning her faith.

***

Greco had authorized Danny to check out a radio car and head into Manhattan. The dispatcher would relay any news that came in from Cogan.

"I gotta hand it to you, Danny boy. I never thought it would amount to anything."

"What's that, Frankie?"

"That torch you carried for over a year."

"Not the first time you've been wrong."

"She's a terrific kid. Helen loves her. I just wish you wouldn't tell her so much because she turns around and tells Helen everything. Makes it tough on me."

"Meg has convinced me that not telling her makes it tough on her."

The radio speaker crackled. "Dispatch to Car 28."

"That's us," Larkin said, grabbing the mic, "Car 28 to Dispatch, go ahead."

"Message from Agent Cogan. The desk clerk at the Manhattanite hotel reports a male fitting suspect Gunther's description checked in Friday afternoon. No luggage, hasn't checked out. Agents on scene report suspect Gunther not currently on premises. Over."

Danny took the mic. "Dispatch from Car 28. Advise Lieutenant Greco we are en route to Penn Station. Request backup. Repeat, request backup for Penn Station."

"Dispatch to Car 28. Acknowledge backup request Penn Station. Dispatch out."

Larkin looked stunned.

"He checked in without luggage after being dropped at Penn," Danny said. "The explosives are checked at Penn. I'll bet Gunther's on his way there to meet Dieter."

"What if he just went out for breakfast?"

Danny glanced at his watch. "At ten-thirty-five? Not a chance. I hope to Christ we're not too late."

CHAPTER EIGHTY-TWO

Dieter hurried because Paul would be punctual and wouldn't want to loiter. He arrived ten minutes early and took up a position behind one of the massive columns facing Seventh Avenue. Traffic in and out of the station was heavy, with many men in uniform.

Excellent. Their attack would affect the war effort, after all.

***

Danny left the car parked near a fire hydrant on 32nd Street. No sign of any police activity. So much for backup. "Come on, Frankie, we'll have to take him ourselves."

Larkin blinked. "All of them?"

CHAPTER EIGHTY-THREE

Danny glanced up at the giant clock hanging over the center of the waiting room. Five minutes to eleven. He showed Dieter's photo to the clerks at the two open baggage windows, but neither had seen anyone looking like that.

"Has anyone checked in two black suitcases in the past few days?" Danny asked.

"Are you nuts? You know how many bags we see in a day? Sorry, Detective, can't help you."

"Can you at least check to see if you have two black suitcases on the same tag?"

A traveler in business attire stepped up waving a ticket. "Hey, Mac, can you get my bag? I'm in a hurry."

The clerk gave Danny an apologetic look. "Like I said, can't help you."

"What now?" Larkin asked. "Sit and wait?"

"Can't. We don't know if he's picked 'em up, yet." Danny glanced around. "Let's keep moving around the place but monitoring the baggage window."

***

Paul looked thin and haggard. "My work has affected my appetite."

Dieter shook Paul's hand. "You push yourself too hard. You should take it easy." The Americanism felt awkward, but no one noticed. "Oh, I've still got to pick up my luggage."

"I'll come with you to give you a hand."

They entered the station and followed the path to the massive waiting room. As they approached the baggage window, a loud group of sailors came through.

***

"Come on, the bar's right over here."

"You don't need another drink. You still haven't slept off last night."

"He knows he ain't gonna get another drop once we get back to Norfolk."

"If he ain't careful, he'll end up in the brig."

Their loudness didn't bother Danny, but they were blocking his view of the baggage window.

The still-drunk sailor turned belligerent, pushing another. "Don't preach at me. If I want a drink, I'll get one."

The other sailor pushed back and now the rest of the group struggled to prevent a fight from starting.

Danny and Larkin were walking toward the other side of the waiting room.

"Nice to see they provide live entertainment here," Larkin said.

***

Paul presented the claim ticket at the window. Dieter waited by his side, grateful for the melee developing behind them.

Over the loudspeaker, a voice announced a train was boarding. "... Richmond, Williamsburg, Newport News, Norfolk..."

"Come on, fellas," one sailor yelled. "Break it up. That's our train."

"Careful," Paul warned the clerk. "Fragile goods in there."

The clerk shrugged. "Hope you wrapped 'em good."

Dieter left a dime at the window. "Thanks."

Now to go meet the others.

***

As the knot of sailors untangled and they made their way to the stairway leading to the trains, Danny glanced back toward the baggage window. He turned away but froze. "Hold it, Frankie."

***

Dieter took one valise while Paul took the other. "Next, we meet our associates at the stairway to the Long Island Railroad trains."

He had only taken a step when Paul grabbed his arm. "*Scheiße.* Those two men are detectives."

"Go, use the crowds to shield you and make your way to the staircase." Dieter didn't wait for an answer.

***

"I saw Gunther, Frankie, I'm sure of it. He was holding one suitcase. The other guy had to be Dieter." But with the swirling midday crowd, he'd lost them both. "If they saw us, they probably split up."

"Mueller doesn't know who we are."

"No, but Gunther does. You cut across, away from the baggage window. See if you can spot him, and I'll do the same. Do whatever you have to do to stop him, but for the love of Mary, don't shoot the suitcase."

He'll be trying to get to track level and away from the crowds.

Nice trick if he can manage it.

CHAPTER EIGHTY-FOUR

Dieter hadn't gotten a good look at either detective, which put him at a disadvantage. His mission now hung in the balance.

He thought of Dröge, the traitor in whom the Reich had entrusted the mission. Then again, Dieter's orders had made clear who was the actual leader. Maybe Reinhold Barth had suspected all along.

I will not fail the Reich.

Even if it becomes a suicide mission.

***

Danny glanced at the clock. Five after eleven.

Forget the time. Black suitcase.

Everyone had one.

No, this woman's was brown, and that man's was a garish green.

Just ahead was the stairwell he was seeking. "Long Island Railroad Trains."

Three men were loitering nearby.

They appeared to be fidgeting and scanning the crowd.

Looking for someone.

Danny needed to find the black suitcase.

***

As Dieter approached the stairwell, he veered off to the side. Hoffstadt and the others were waiting. From the other side of the hall, he glimpsed Paul approaching in the same cautious manner.

And then Bakhaus spotted him. "Dieter!"

Gott im Himmel.

No choice but to double back.

***

Danny heard the shout. It had come from one of the three men near the stairwell.

He stared in the direction the three men were peering.

Black suitcase.

It was Dieter Mueller.

Walking briskly the other way.

He had to head him off.

But stay between Dieter and the stairwell.

***

The crowd in front of him thinned, and Dieter picked up his pace. No surprise Bakhaus had endangered the mission one last time.

He glanced back. A man in a fedora was hurrying in his direction. Looked Irish, like Tommy McArdle.

He'd make a wide circle and make it back to the stairwell. What happened to the others no longer mattered.

CHAPTER EIGHTY-FIVE

Go ahead, Dieter, try doubling back. I'll just keep myself between you and them.

But where the hell was Larkin?

Where the hell was the backup?

Dieter had spotted him. So, no one had the advantage of disguised moves, which made it easier for Dieter to avoid capture, but impossible to plant the explosives.

Then he heard Larkin.

***

"Freeze, Gunther. Police."

Dieter kept moving. If Paul did the smart thing and slammed his valise against the floor, that would be enough. If the blast didn't set off Dieter's charges, he would slam his down, too.

Moments crawled by as Dieter kept moving. The Irish detective was circling with him, trying to close the distance.

Dieter reversed direction.

***

Nice try, kraut boy, but it won't work. Larkin calling out Gunther changed the game. Dieter had to know it.

Which made him less predictable and more dangerous.

Dieter wasn't circling toward the stairwell any longer.

He must be headed toward Gunther.

Danny pulled his revolver.

CHAPTER EIGHTY-SIX

There was Paul, being handcuffed by the other detective, the black valise at his feet.

The Irish detective was now chasing Dieter, closing fast.

Dieter made a direct dash for Paul.

Hoffstadt and the others stood, frozen, watching. Useless.

Ten meters to go.

Dieter raised his valise over his head.

CHAPTER EIGHTY-SEVEN

A commotion erupted from the main entrance.

Dieter was running with the suitcase above his head, right toward Larkin.

"Frankie! Grab Mueller's bag! Grab the…"

CHAPTER EIGHTY-EIGHT

Gunther turned to run as Dieter lunged at Larkin.

Dieter swung the bag down with force.

Danny was now too close to avoid getting killed if it hit.

Several women screamed.

Larkin grabbed hold of Dieter's suitcase.

CHAPTER EIGHTY-NINE

Dieter lost his grip on the bag.

"Frankie! Hold the bag!" The Irish detective.

As the detective clutched the valise and fell backward, Dieter turned to grab the one that had been Paul's.

Valhalla.

CHAPTER NINETY

Dieter was reaching for the second bag. No mystery what he was going to do.

Too far away to reach.

Danny fired twice.

CHAPTER NINETY-ONE

Pandemonium.

People screamed and ran in all different directions as a steady stream of blue-coated police swarmed into the waiting area.

Larkin lay on the floor, clutching the black bag he'd ripped from Dieter's grasp.

Dieter lay several feet from him, inert, his head and shoulder wounds bleeding out.

Paul Gunther stood nearby, handcuffed and frozen, staring at Dieter.

"Officer," Danny called out to the crowd of police. "Detain those three gawkers by the stairwell. And someone please guard this guy." He nodded toward Gunther.

Larkin was shaking.

"You okay, Frankie?"

Larkin clung to the bag and gave a tight nod.

"What about you, Danny?" It was Cogan. "You all right?"

"I'll be a lot better when those suitcases are out of here."

Cogan laughed. "My guys will take care of that. Let's get Hermann Mueller in for some serious questioning."

"Let us question Gunther, first," Danny said.

"Be quicker if we do it at our place."

Danny turned to Larkin, who was pale as a ghost, as Cogan's men secured the two valises. "Why don't you head back to the precinct to update Greco?"

"I'll be okay."

CHAPTER NINETY-TWO

Cogan started it off once they were all at the FBI office. "You're in a pretty bad fix, Mr. Gunther. A naturalized American citizen, you abetted a group of enemy agents and engaged in an attempted act of sabotage. We've already gotten a full confession from your friend, Mr. Bakhaus."

"I don't know a Mr. Bakhaus," Gunther replied.

Danny stepped in. "No, you don't, but he was working with your pal, Dieter Mueller, who provided the materials for you to manufacture your own fulminate of mercury, which we caught you with today. We know all about Hermann Mueller's little ring—you, Dieter Mueller, Hans Brach and Christian Jenner."

"We'll be arresting Hermann Mueller shortly," Larkin added.

"You probably weren't aware of the enemy agents who landed on Eastern Long Island Friday night," Danny went on. "But you knew Dieter Mueller needed a supply of high explosives, because he provided you with the materials and specific instructions through his notebook."

"Which we confiscated from your apartment an hour ago," Cogan said.

Danny resumed. "Also, one of your group killed Hans Brach. It wasn't Dieter, because he was out of the city at the time, so it had to be you or Hermann, and one of you killed Christian. You can save us time and tell us which one, or we can try both of you for the conspiracy."

"You haven't done much right in this thing," Larkin added. "Now would be a good time to start."

"As of now," Danny said, "you're facing the chair as Dieter's right-hand man. We're at war, you're a traitor, and anyone on your jury will want to pull the switch."

Gunther sat with his head in his hands.

"So," Danny said, "who strangled Hans Brach and threw him down that hill? It wasn't Hermann Mueller."

"No," Gunther replied, "I did it on Hermann Mueller's orders."

One more count. "And Christian Jenner?"

Gunther only nodded.

CHAPTER NINETY-THREE

Hermann Mueller's truck was parked in the usual spot. Danny and Larkin climbed to his second-floor apartment with Rossi and McHugh close behind.

Mueller answered on the second knock. "I haven't seen him."

"And you won't," Danny replied. "Your nephew was killed this morning while trying to commit sabotage against the United States with your friend, Paul Gunther, who was arrested."

Mueller's stony façade crumbled. "Dieter is dead?"

"He was about to slam a suitcase filled with explosives onto the floor of Penn Station. I had no choice but to shoot him. I am placing you, as leader of the group, under arrest for treason, attempted sabotage, and the murder of Hans Brach."

All Mueller's fight was gone. "Dieter. Dead."

"A waste of a sharp mind," Danny said. "I'm sorry."

Mueller looked up. "Are you really, Detective?"

"That such a bright mind was twisted to treason and murder, yes, I am. And if I ever have a son, I will raise him to be a decent man." He signaled McHugh to handcuff him.

"May I use the lavatory, first?"

Danny nodded. McHugh followed Mueller back to his bathroom and waited outside the door.

A moment later, a shot.

CHAPTER NINETY-FOUR

Friday, August 28, 1942

It was a small wedding at City Hall.

Meg's 19-year-old sister, Emily, was her witness, while Frankie Larkin stood up for Danny.

Meg's parents and Emily, Frank and Helen Larkin, Sean McHugh and Rebecca Stoneman were there. So were Vinnie Rossi, Lieutenant Greco, Jimmy Fitzgibbon and Agent Cogan, all with their wives. After the brief ceremony, they all traveled uptown to Gallagher's for dinner.

At Meg's insistence, Danny had worn his dress blue uniform which now sported two medals—Meritorious Service for his role in tracking down Joseph Babić, and Meritorious Service Honorable Mention for his role in bringing Dieter Mueller and the saboteurs to justice.

After the dinner plates had been cleared away, the men fell to discussing the case of the German saboteurs. The four who'd landed in Florida had been apprehended the day after the Penn Station incident. All eight had been tried by a military tribunal, and six of them had been executed in early August and buried in unmarked graves. The sentences for Dröge and Bakhaus had both been commuted to long prison terms. Paul Gunther had pled guilty to treason and the murders of Christian Jenner and Hans Brach. He'd been sentenced to death. A man named Fred Obermann out in German Gardens would be tried for treason and 'trading with the enemy', and a woman named Lurline Griswold in Amagansett, where Dieter Mueller had stayed before the saboteurs arrived, would be tried for trading with the enemy.

"Her husband escaped prosecution by testifying against Obermann and his own wife," Cogan said. "Seems she and Dieter were canoodling."

"There's a juicy piece of gossip for you girls," Frank said to Helen.

Helen rolled her eyes and turned to Meg. "Don't you worry about a thing. Make yourselves at home."

Meg caught her mom's confused expression. "The Larkins have a summer bungalow at Breezy Point. They're letting us use it for our honeymoon."

"Is the water fit for swimming?" Meg's father asked. "I mean, with all the ships being sunk?"

"You'll need to be careful," Helen said. "If you see black splotches on the sand, there's oil in the water. If you do swim and get oil on you, there's kerosene in the bungalow to get it off."

Meg gave her dad a reassuring smile. "I think we'll save the swimming for after the war. Danny and I are going to buy a bungalow there because it's such a lovely spot."

"Which reminds me," Helen said, "the bungalow three doors down Pelham Walk from ours is for sale. Like ours, there's no heating, and it gets chilly at night this time of year."

Danny raised a glass of Jameson's. "Just like the old sod."

Larkin raised his. "Here's to interesting ways to keep warm." The other men raised theirs amid raucous laughter.

Meg's parents were shocked, while Rebecca and Emily stifled nervous giggles.

But Meg chuckled and shook her head. "Cops."

AFTERWORD

The two major criminal events depicted in *Enemies of All*—the murder committed by a serial rapist solved by the NYPD in cooperation with the FBI and police departments across the Eastern United States, and the landing of four German saboteurs on Eastern Long Island and four in Florida—are based on historical events. But the names of all the characters are fictional except for Fr. Flanagan, Thomas Donegan, and Reinhold Barth.

The timeline of the murder case is compressed and set several months later than it occurred to serve the needs of the story. The timeline of the saboteurs' landing is presented as it occurred, adjusted only for the impact of the fictional Dieter Mueller on their story.

ACKNOWLEDGEMENTS

I was finalizing *Proving a Villain* when I began work on *Enemies of All*. Creating the references to Kim Brady's grandfather required researching the Bronx in the 1940s, and once I got started on that, I split my time between the two projects. I had always wanted to give Dan Brady his own series.

In the acknowledgements at the end of *Proving a Villain*, I mentioned how I had created a character named for an old friend of mine simply because he'd asked, and I offered to give any of my readers the option of asking the same if they wanted to be considered for inclusion in a future Kim Brady mystery. I'd like to offer the same deal for anyone who'd like to be included in a future Dan Brady Mystery. E-mail me at ejl.author@gmail.com and let me know what kind of character you'd like to be, and I'll pick some to be included in a future book in the series.

I am blessed to have support from Kim Howe and Elena Hartwell at International Thriller Writers, and from great writers like Debbie Babitt, Jim L'Etoile, Sandy Manning, and fellow Black Rose Writing author, AJ McCarthy.

I'm grateful for the support I continue to receive from Black Rose Writing and Reagan Rothe's team of David King, Chris Martin, Minna Rothe, and Justin Weeks.

As always, I am blessed with sharp-eyed, honest beta readers in Jan Foley and Ray Lodato (who knew what lay ahead when we first became friends six decades ago?). But most of all, I thank my wife, Cindy, alpha-reader extraordinaire and traveling companion on this highway we call life.

ABOUT THE AUTHOR

Edward J. Leahy is the author of the *Kim Brady Mysteries* and was a finalist for the 2018 Freddie Award for Excellence. He is a member of the Mystery Writers of America and the International Thriller Writers and has been published by New York Teacher Magazine. He's a retired International Issue Specialist for the IRS with investigative experience and holds a B.A. and M.A. from St. John's University in Government & Politics. He serves on the Board of Directors of AHRC-NYC.

NOTE FROM THE AUTHOR

Word-of-mouth is crucial for any author to succeed. If you enjoyed *Enemies of All*, please leave a review online—anywhere you are able. Even if it's just a sentence or two. It would make all the difference and would be very much appreciated.

Thanks!
Edward J. Leahy

We hope you enjoyed reading this title from:

BLACK ROSE writing™

www.blackrosewriting.com

Subscribe to our mailing list – *The Rosevine* – and receive **FREE** books, daily deals, and stay current with news about upcoming releases and our hottest authors.
Scan the QR code below to sign up.

Already a subscriber? Please accept a sincere thank you for being a fan of Black Rose Writing authors.

View other Black Rose Writing titles at www.blackrosewriting.com/books and use promo code **PRINT** to receive a **20% discount** when purchasing.

Made in United States
North Haven, CT
17 November 2023

44163755R00233